THE WEDDING TREE

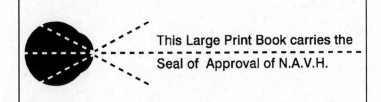

This Large Print Book carries the
Seal of Approval of N.A.V.H.

THE WEDDING TREE

ROBIN WELLS

THORNDIKE PRESS
A part of Gale, Cengage Learning

GALE
CENGAGE Learning·

Farmington Hills, Mich • San Francisco • New York • Waterville, Maine
Mason, Ohio • Chicago

GALE
CENGAGE Learning·

LIBRARY OF CONGRESS CATALOGING-IN-PUBLICATION DATA

Names: Wells, Robin (Robin Rouse) author.
Title: The wedding tree / by Robin Wells.
Description: Large print edition. | Waterville, Maine : Thorndike Press, 2016. | ©
    2015 | Series: Thorndike Press large print women's fiction
Identifiers: LCCN 2015048972| ISBN 9781410489104 (hardcover) | ISBN 1410489108
    (hardcover)
Subjects: LCSH: Divorced women—Fiction. | Grandparent and child—Fiction. |
    Family secrets—Fiction. | Louisiana—Fiction. | Large type books. | GSAFD: Love
    stories.
Classification: LCC PS3623.E4768 W43 2016 | DDC 813/.6—dc23
LC record available at http://lccn.loc.gov/2015048972

Published in 2016 by arrangement with The Berkley Publishing Group,
an imprint of Penguin Publishing Group, a division of Penguin Random
House LLC

Printed in Mexico
1 2 3 4 5 6 7 20 19 18 17 16

*To my brother, Charles Richard Rouse,
for the hard, heartbreaking work
of clearing out our parents' home.*

ACKNOWLEDGMENTS

With deep gratitude to the Greatest Generation, especially my parents, Charlie Lou and Roscoe Rouse, Jr.

Thanks to Annette Doskey for providing insights into New Orleans in the 1940s, and to fellow writer Nancy Wagner, aka Hailey North, for reading rough drafts, offering encouragement, and being an all-around dear friend.

I also want to thank my editor, Cindy Hwang, and my agent, Steve Axelrod.

And finally, this book wouldn't have been possible without the love and support of my two inspiring daughters, Taylor and Arden, and my dream-come-true husband, Ken.

1
ADELAIDE

Funny, how you keep telling yourself, *someday.* Someday I'll get organized. Someday I'll get everything sorted out. Someday I'll tackle the tasks I've been dreading all these years.

I kept waiting until I had a big block of time. A few free days, I thought. And, of course, they never came. No day is ever really free. And the truth is, if I'm entirely honest — and I haven't been on this topic, I admit it now — I didn't *want* to sort through my belongings. Sorting through meant looking back, and looking back meant confronting things I'd spent most of my life trying to avoid.

So I put it off and put it off, and then, just when I worked up my resolve and finally got started, *this* happened.

I'm foggy on what exactly it was *this* is — I can't remember how I ended up here — but here I am all the same, hovering over my own body in a hospital room. I'm pretty sure it's the hospital in my hometown of Wedding Tree, Louisiana, because I've visited lots of friends over the years and I recognize that awful gray linoleum flooring. When you're visiting someone who's really bad off, you spend a lot of time gazing down so you don't have to look at their pain.

Anyway, here I am, floating against the ugly acoustical tile ceiling, looking down at an old woman with tubes snaking out of her nose and her arm veins. Apparently I'm not dead yet, because the old woman's chest is falling and rising, and a machine wired up to her is steadily beeping — so hard to believe that ghastly-looking old gal is me! But if I'm up here watching the goings-on, I must be on the way out.

Which means it's too late to make good on my intentions to sort everything out and do what I should have done sixty-something years ago.

"Never put off till tomorrow what you should do today."

I turn my head at the familiar voice. "Mother?"

She's floating beside me. At least, her head is — and her shoulders, too. The rest of her seems to trail off into vapor, but maybe my soul has poor eyesight. Mother's hair is pinned up prim and proper, with neat waves on the sides, just the way she always kept it, and she's wearing the dress with the starched lace collar that she was buried in forty-something years ago.

"Did I — did I just die?" I ask.

"Not yet, although if I were you, I'd die of shame, looking like that in a public place." She looks down at the woman on the bed and clucks her tongue. Mother always had the highest standards for appearance and comportment, and clearly the woman on the bed was violating all of them. Her — no, *my* — hair is an unruly tangle of gray, far too long to be age appropriate. My skin is a blotchy testament to the fact I hadn't stayed out of the sun as Mother had warned, and my mouth gapes open in a most undignified fashion.

Still, a hospital room isn't exactly a public place, and —

"Don't you sass me, young lady."

I was hardly young — on what planet was ninety-one young? Besides, I didn't think I'd spoken aloud.

"Thoughts, words — they're all the same," Mother says. "It's all energy. There are no barriers on this side."

Oh my.

"Oh my, indeed."

11

"What happened?"

"You fell and hit your head. You're unconscious, and you're having an out-of-body experience."

"So I can't possibly help how I look."

"A lady always manages to look her best for visitors."

Oh — I had visitors! My view widens, like a zoom lens being reversed, to see three people gathered around my bed. I can only view the tops of their heads, but I'm sure the stocky man with the bald patch standing at the foot of the bed is my son, Eddie, and I think the tall, auburn-haired man beside him is his partner, Ralph.

I've always known Eddie is the way he is — they call it gay now, although in my day, that meant happy, and Eddie was always a sad, tentative, nervous boy. The word for Eddie's kind, a word I only heard whispered when I was young, was *queer.* I never thought badly of him for it. The way I figured it, Eddie liked men, just like I did, and he can't help it any more than I could. If someone told me to start liking women that way, I don't reckon I could, so it stands to reason that Eddie couldn't, either.

I tried to explain that to Eddie's father, but he wasn't having any of it. Charlie thought it was a character flaw and a choice.

He took it personally, as if it were something Eddie was doing to annoy him — which couldn't be further from the truth, because all poor Eddie ever wanted was to please his daddy.

But he couldn't, and he couldn't change the narrow minds of other townsfolk, and in a town as small as Wedding Tree, where everybody knew everybody else's business, well, it was no wonder Eddie went to college in California and never moved back. How old is he now? Fifty- or sixty-something? So odd to think that my baby is that old. The top of his head, all bald like that, looks a lot like it did the day he was born. The sight makes me want to cry. Oh, how I wish I could see Eddie's face!

Click.

All of a sudden, Eddie is framed in a portrait lens.

Oh, my — my soul is a camera! Well, that makes sense. It's been an extension of my body throughout my life. I've been taking pictures for so long that I tend to frame things, to look at them and move my right finger, as if I'm pressing the shutter. This moment — freeze it, capture it, make it live forever. And this moment. And this one. And this one here.

"She pressed my hand," a young woman says.

My view twirls as if my head were on a swivel mount. *Click.* Oh, there's my granddaughter, Hope, sitting on my right, holding my hand. Such a lovely girl . . . So beautiful, with her wavy light brown hair and eyes the color of iced tea — so much like my late daughter, Rebecca.

The thought sends a stab of pain through me. "Is Becky with you?" I ask Mother.

"She's on this side, but they wouldn't let her come with me. Said you don't get to see her until you clean up the mess you've made down there."

"You mean . . . I'm going to get well?"

"Well, now, Adelaide, that's like everything else in life. It's entirely up to you."

Was it? Was it really? I wasn't sure that anything in my life had really been my doing — except for the mistakes, of course.

Mother levels me with a steely frown. "If you know what's good for you, missy, you'll get back down there and unleash the truth."

Unleash — as if it were a dangerous animal. Well, that is about right. "I was trying to when I ended up here."

"You were going about it all wrong. You need Hope's help."

I look back at my granddaughter. She

14

looks so sad — sadder than she should look at the prospect of an old woman passing. She'd been sad when I'd last seen her, too — which was when? I was fuzzy about the recent past. All I knew was that when that cad of her ex-husband cheated on her, he'd stolen something from her — something more than her inheritance and her art gallery and her home, all of which he'd purloined right out from under her. That lowlife had robbed her of her view of herself as lovely and lovable.

We females are so vulnerable to that. Most of the women I'd photographed over the years didn't have a clue how lovely they really were. They'd look in the mirror and just see flaws — then, years later, when they looked back through their old pictures, they always exclaimed, "I was so thin back then!" or "I had such nice skin!" In the present moment, so many beautiful things go unseen, eclipsed by some over-imagined imperfection.

Men don't have that problem with their physical appearance — at least, not the straight ones. They all think they're irresistible just the way they are. Most of them, of course, are completely deluded. But other men, like Joe . . .

Oh, why was I thinking of Joe now? I did

not — *not* — want him to be my dying thought, not after spending so much of my life trying to forget about him.

"You get back down there and tell Hope everything," Mother says.

Everything?

"Yes, *everything.*"

My soul flushes scarlet. Oh Lord — was this a foretaste of hell, having my mother read my thoughts? Mother shot me her most reproving look.

"I — I don't see how that will make a difference," I mentally stammer.

"Yours is not to wonder why; yours is but to do or die. Now get to it, and no dillydallying." Mother turns her neat bun toward me, as if she were about to leave, then whips back around. "And be sure to dig up what Charlie buried."

The beeping machine attached to the old woman in the bed stops for a moment, then rat-a-tat-tats like a high-speed shutter. "What? What did he bury?"

She lifts her eyebrows in that I'll-brook-no-nonsense way of hers. "That's what you need to find out, isn't it?"

My soul flutters. "Do you know? My memory isn't very . . ."

"You didn't forget." Mother's voice is cold steel. "You never had the nerve to find out, and this is your last chance to rectify the situation."

"But . . ."

But Mother is gone. Not so much as a vapor trail remains.

Click.

A feeling of suction, as if I were being vacuumed downward from the ceiling, followed by heaviness, and then . . . Oh, my head! Oh, how it hurt. And my chest! Heavens to Betsy! Mother hadn't said anything about my chest.

"She's awake!" my granddaughter says. "Gran's eyes are open."

I stare at her. She looks a little like Becky, but she isn't. Becky is gone. Hope is alive.

And apparently, so am I. Although I have to say, it doesn't seem to have much to recommend it.

2
HOPE

"Do you know what day it is, Mrs. McCauley?" Dr. Warren leaned over Gran and shined a penlight in her eyes.

Gran scowled. "Of course I do."

I wasn't so sure. Gran had seemed to recognize me when she first opened her eyes, but then she'd closed them again, and when she reopened them a moment later, she called me by my mother's name. I'd hated to correct her, because her eyes had held such a blue sky full of happy that I didn't want to disappoint her.

Eddie had done it for me. "It's Hope, Mom. Becky is gone, remember?"

"Gone where?"

Uh-oh. Uncle Eddie and I had exchanged a glance. Fortunately, that was the moment Dr. Warren — an angular, hawk-nosed man in a heavily starched white coat — had stepped into the room. I'd relinquished my bedside seat and stood with Eddie and

Ralph as the doctor had asked Gran to move her arms and legs, to turn her head, to stick out her tongue, and to perform half a dozen other motor tasks. She'd passed each test with flying colors. Dr. Warren moved the light to Gran's left eye. "So what day is it?"

"Friday," Gran said.

The doctor moved the light to her right eye, then switched it off. "Actually, it's Sunday, Mrs. McCauley."

"Oops!" Gran gave a sheepish grin. "Guess I had one of those lost weekends I've always heard about."

I laughed along with everyone else, but I was worried. Gran's memory had always been encyclopedic. Facts, dates, numbers — she was more reliable than Wikipedia.

"Glad to see you still have your sense of humor," Eddie said.

Gran squinted up at him. "Charlie?"

Eddie's face fell. "No, Mom. It's Eddie."

"Oh, yes, yes, of course. Eddie, dear. And . . ." She frowned at Ralph.

"Ralph," the lanky man supplied, putting his hand on Eddie's shoulder. "Eddie's partner."

"Yes, yes, so nice to see you. When did you two get in from Chicago?"

"We live in San Francisco, Mom. Becky

19

and Hope lived in Chicago."

"Oh right." Her blue-veined hand went to her forehead. "Is Becky here?"

Eddie and I exchanged another look. "She died, Mom. Three years ago. Her car crashed, remember?"

"Oh no." Gran's hand drifted down her mouth. Tears formed in the corners of her eyes. "Oh, dear. I . . . I'd forgotten."

My fingers tightened on the steel railing. In the first few weeks after Mom's death, sometimes I'd awaken and have a pain-free moment. Then the memory would hit, and my heart would squeeze like a wrung-out dishrag, and I'd feel all tight and twisted and knotted up. I hoped Gran wasn't going through that hard, searing, brand-new pain all over again.

"Loss of memory is typical of a head injury," Dr. Warren said, adjusting his wire-rim glasses on his hooked nose. He was looking at Gran, but I'm pretty sure he was really speaking to Eddie and me. "So is emotional lability and confusion."

Gran's gaze landed on me. The lack of recognition in her eyes alarmed me.

"I'm Hope," I volunteered. "Your grand-daughter."

"Oh, yes, yes, of course. Hope, honey! It's so good to see you. My mind is all clouded up right now — you'll have to excuse me. How long have you been here?"

"Since early this morning." The clock on the wall said it was nearly four o'clock in the afternoon, which meant I'd been there for about twelve hours. "I came as soon as I heard."

I'd gotten the call from Gran's next-door neighbor, Mrs. Ivy, at eight thirty Saturday night. I'd been in my sublet apartment in Chicago, pulling on my pajama bottoms — the ones optimistically printed with sheep jumping over fences — and surfing the on-demand cable TV menu for a movie I could stand to watch.

Which isn't as easy as it sounds, now that I've grown bored with revenge movies. I've been bloodthirsty for nearly twelve months, and I consider it a sign of progress that I've moved beyond wishing the horrible, painful, humiliating things portrayed on the screen would happen to my ex-husband.

Still, I can't stomach romances. All those happily-ever-afters make me want to hurl. I can't stand movies about friends, either, because the woman I'd caught in *my* bed with *my* husband had been my very best friend — my high school BFF, my college roommate, the maid of honor at my wedding, who'd helped me pick out the very

21

linens she was lying under my husband on.

So anyway, I was surfing for a quirky independent film, or maybe an action/adventure movie, while tugging on my pajama bottoms at a ridiculously early hour in the evening — which I know is a pathetic thing for a thirty-one-year-old single woman to do alone on a Saturday night, but then, I'm apparently no better at being single than I was at being married — when the phone rang. I hopped over to the bedside table, one leg in my pj's, one leg out. The area code was southern Louisiana, but I didn't recognize the number.

"Hope?" said a wavering falsetto. "It's Eunice Ivy — your grandmother's neighbor."

A cement block of alarm hit my chest, sinking me to the edge of the bed.

"I've already talked to your uncle Eddie, and he asked me to give you a call," she said.

Heaviness pressed on my clavicle, constricting my airflow. I immediately feared the worst. "What happened?"

"Your grandmother fell."

My free hand covered my mouth. "Oh no."

"Yes, I'm afraid she did. Her new neighbor on the other side — he's Griff and Peggy Armand's widowed son-in-law; he moved to

Wedding Tree a few months ago with his two children. He bought the old Henry place. He's a very nice man, and —"

"My grandmother," I interrupted. "What's happened to my grandmother?"

"That's what I'm trying to tell you," she said, her southern accent maddeningly slow. "Matt Lyons — that's his name, the name of the new neighbor — saw Adelaide's shed door open, which was unusual — it wasn't even the day that Mr. Pickens comes to mow her lawn, and anyway, he's very conscientious and wouldn't just leave the door ajar — so he went over to check. He knocked at the front door first — he's very polite, this Matt Lyons — but Adelaide didn't answer. So he went around back to the shed, and that's when he found her."

My palm was so sweaty the phone started to slip. I tightened my fingers around it. "How is she?"

"Well, she fell. That's what I'm trying to tell you."

"Yes, but what . . . Was she . . ." I couldn't bring myself to think, much less actually say, the words. It was a telephone call a lot like this one that had brought me the news about my mother. *I shouldn't have answered the phone,* I thought wildly. *If I hang up, maybe it won't have happened.* I wanted to hit the "End Call" button; I wanted it so badly I could practically hear the dial tone. But I didn't. I couldn't. "What happened?"

"That's what I'm trying to tell you," Mrs. Ivy repeated.

So tell me already. For God's sake, just tell me! But another part of me wanted her to continue her conversational meandering, to put off the facts as long as possible.

"He found her lying on the floor of the shed," she continued. "Apparently she hit her head and fractured some ribs."

A flashlight beam of hope gleamed through my fear. People don't talk about fractured ribs if someone is dead — do they? "How — how is she?"

"Well, pretty bad."

"But she's alive?"

"Yes."

I lay back on the bed, relief melting my bones.

"The ambulance came and took her to the hospital," Mrs. Ivy continued. "I have the key to her house, so I went in and got her insurance card, then took it to the hospital. You know how hospitals are about getting the paperwork right. They don't want to do anything unless they have the insurance information, so I found her purse — it was in the kitchen, by the —"

24

"Mrs. Ivy, I really appreciate all your help on this," I broke in, "but please, just tell me . . . How bad is Gran? Can she talk?"

"Oh, no, dear. She hasn't regained consciousness yet, which has the docs pretty worried. They fear she had a stroke. They're running all kinds of tests, and Eddie is catching the first flight out. He asked me to call you so he could hurry up and make his travel arrangements. He said he'll call you as soon as he's en route to the airport."

Gran and Uncle Eddie were the only close family I had left. My father had died when I was seven, and Mom was killed in a car crash three years ago — which was one of the reasons I think I married Kurt as quickly as I did; I wanted to feel like I belonged to someone.

"I'm coming, too. Can you . . ." I hated to ask, but I hated the idea of Gran being all alone at the hospital far more. "Can you or someone else in town stay with her at the hospital until Eddie or I get to Wedding Tree?"

"Oh, it's already arranged, dear. Your grandmother's women's circle from church and her poker club and her Yahtzee group are taking shifts until Eddie or you arrive. And I'm pet-sitting Snowball — she's right beside me, wagging her tail — so you don't have to worry about her."

Thank God for close-knit small towns. The very thing my mom had always hated about Wedding Tree — the way everyone was always up in everyone else's business — was a blessing at a time like this.

As soon as I hung up, I flew into frantic action. I booked the first flight out, threw God-only-knew-what into a suitcase, and called my boss's voice mail to explain I wouldn't be at work on Monday — which wasn't really a problem, because I didn't really have a boss.

For that matter, I didn't really have a job. I was working as a temp at a graphic design firm, where I mostly updated websites. I used to run the ridiculously upscale art gallery Kurt and I had bought with my mother's inheritance, but we sold that — for a huge loss, I might add — as part of the divorce settlement. We also sold the extravagantly expensive home Kurt had insisted we buy — a house with a mortgage far greater than its value, thanks to the real estate market crash — and I currently would be homeless if a friend of a friend hadn't sublet me her apartment while she spent a year in New Zealand. As a result of the divorce, I had no home, no job, and next to nothing left of the considerable amount of money

I'd inherited.

Money that, in hindsight, was the real reason Kurt was so keen on marrying me in the first place. He'd burned through it at a rate that would have horrified me if I'd know the full extent of it — but I hadn't, because I hadn't wanted to see it. Like an ostrich, I'd kept my head in the sand. I still try very hard not to think about that, because it makes me feel like even more of an idiot than I already do.

Anyway, I landed at the New Orleans airport around three in the morning, then rented a car and made the hour-long drive to the Wedding Tree Parish General Hospital to find Eddie and Ralph already there. The three of us had been keeping a bedside vigil, taking turns dozing in the room's two recliner chairs and talking with a constant stream of visitors, ever since.

"What's the last thing you remember?" Dr. Warren asked Gran.

"Talking to Mother."

Eddie pressed his lips together as if he were trying not to cry. I awkwardly patted his back. Even though he was my mother's brother and a generation older than me, there was something boyish about him that brought out my maternal instincts. Maybe it was his babyish cheeks or his teddy bear

27

build — but most likely, it was the way he wore his tender heart on his sleeve.

He squeezed Gran's hand. "Mom, Grandmother's been dead for more than forty years."

"Oh, I wasn't talking to her down *here*," she said in a don't-be-silly tone. "I was talking to her up on the ceiling."

Eddie blinked, his eyes overbright and moist. "Do you remember falling?"

"No."

"Do you remember going to the shed? That's where your neighbor found you."

"What on earth was I doing out in the shed?"

Eddie shrugged. "Beats me, but it looked like you'd taken a shovel off the hook on the wall."

I saw a glimmer in Gran's eyes. *She remembers,* I thought — but instead of explaining, she turned to Dr. Warren. "When am I getting out of here?"

"That depends on where you think you're going." His craggy face creased in a friendly smile.

"Home, of course."

"Well, we'll talk about that later. You're here for a while, Mrs. McCauley. You sustained a serious head injury, and we need to keep an eye on you and make sure you don't have any bleeding or swelling in your brain. You've also fractured some ribs. We'll have to see how you do when we get you up and around."

"But I'll get to go home, won't I?"

Dr. Warren patted her leg through the blanket. "We'll talk about all your options later. Are you in any pain?"

"My head feels like it's cracked open, and it hurts to breathe."

"I'll order something to make you more comfortable. Just relax and get some rest, and I'll be back to check on you later." He said something to the nurse. As she fiddled with the IV drip, he scribbled on the chart, then signaled for us to follow him into the hall.

"How is she?" Eddie asked as soon as the door closed behind us.

"I'd say she's doing very well, considering her age. There are no signs of a stroke. But she's had a severe brain injury."

"She's awfully confused." Eddie folded his arms across his chest as if he were trying to hug himself.

Dr. Warren nodded. "That's to be expected."

"How long will it last?"

"She's likely to improve, but at her age, and with this level of trauma . . ." He paused. His face got that apologetic-sympathetic-uncomfortable look people get when they have to deliver bad news. "I'm afraid this was a life-changing event."

A life-changing event. A chill went down my arms. Such simple, everyday words, yet put together in that order, in this situation, they were catastrophic.

The doctor flipped through the chart. "She was living alone?"

Eddie and I both nodded.

"I'm afraid that's no longer going to be possible. You'll need to make other arrangements."

"She's very independent," I said. "Can't we wait and see how her recovery goes?"

The doctor shook his head. "The fact she fell indicates that living alone is no longer a safe option. When you add in the effects of severe brain trauma, well, it's just not advisable."

"What if she won't agree?" Eddie asked.

"You'll need to convince her."

"What if we can't?" I asked.

A tense pause stretched in the air. "If a person is deemed to be a danger to herself or others, Social Services will step in. It's preferable, of course, for the family to reach a resolution." He looked at Eddie, then at me, his eyes full of that apologetic-sympathetic-uncomfortableness again. "Does she have any family in town?"

Eddie shook his head.

"Well, then, I suggest you contact Pine Manor."

"Gran hates Pine Manor," I protested. I'd gone with her to visit some of her friends who lived there last Christmas.

On the way out the door, she'd grabbed my hand. "Promise you'll give me cyanide before you let Eddie put me in this place," she'd begged.

I can't say that I blamed her; the place smelled like old carpet, canned peas, and pissed Depends.

"Well, it's the only elder care facility in Wedding Tree," Dr. Warren said. "But there are some fine nursing homes and assisted living facilities in Hammond and Covington."

Eddie shook his head. "There's no point in moving her someplace where she doesn't know anybody. If she has to move, she'll come with me to San Francisco."

"That's your call, of course." He closed the chart and pushed his wire-rim glasses up on his nose. "In any event, she'll be here for several more days, so you'll have a little time to reach a decision. If need be, we can temporarily put her in Pine Manor or a similar facility until you complete your arrangements." He slid the chart into the plastic holder on the back of the hospital room door. "I'll check back on her in the morning."

Eddie rubbed his jaw as the doctor's loafers thudded down the hall. "Ralph and I have tried to talk her into moving to California for years. She can live with us, or move into an assisted living center."

I'd sat in on many of those conversations — the last one being during the past holiday season. "As I recall, she wasn't really opposed to moving."

"No. The problem is, she insists on sorting through everything in her house here first. She keeps saying she'll do it, but the truth is, I don't think she even knows where to start."

Ralph's lips curved in a wry smile. "Well, it *is* a daunting task."

"Beyond daunting," Eddie sighed.

They weren't kidding. Gran had grown up during the Depression, and her mantra seemed to be "Never know when this will come in handy." She'd mended socks and underwear, saved bread bags and twist ties, and reused sheets of aluminum foil long before recycling was trendy. Her home was clean and orderly — she was by no means a candidate for *Hoarders* — but every drawer, every closet, every shelf was stuffed.

"We should hire one of those estate liquidation companies," Ralph suggested.

"I tried to talk her into that a couple of years ago," Eddie said.

I remembered it all too clearly. "It was the Thanksgiving you were in London, Ralph."

Eddie nodded. "She threw a fit. I've never seen her like that."

I'd never seen Gran so agitated, either. She'd thrown her napkin on the table, her face flushed, the cords standing out on her neck. "I won't have some stranger pawing through my things!" she'd hissed. "I'll do it myself, and that's all there is to it." She'd left the table in the middle of Thanksgiving dinner and refused to sit back down until we promised to drop the topic.

"Well, she doesn't have a choice now," Ralph said.

"Maybe she does." I was thinking aloud, and was a little surprised to find the words coming out of my mouth. "Maybe I can stay in Wedding Tree and help her."

Eddie put his arm around me. "Hope, honey, that's a sweet thought, but it's just not practical."

"Why not?" The idea felt like a beacon in my brain, clear and bright, shining through

33

the fog of depression and lassitude and indecision that had immobilized me since my divorce. My pulse rate kicked up.

"Hope, it would take months," Ralph said gently.

"I've got the time." The light in my brain gained additional wattage. Heat flowed through my veins.

Eddie's arm tightened into a squeeze. "I know you want to help, but you haven't thought this through, honey."

What he really meant was, *Here Hope goes again, making another rash decision.* It hurts to admit it, but I have a bit of a track record of acting first and thinking second.

There was that time on my college study abroad program when I didn't make the plane home from Athens because I'd decided to run by the Acropolis one last time, and the professor in charge called Mom, who insisted he file a missing person report — but something got lost in translation and the police thought I was a fugitive wanted by American authorities, and I ended up spending two terrifying nights in jail.

And the time I lost the rarer-than-hen's-teeth entry-level job at the Art Institute of Chicago that my mother had pulled all kinds of strings to get me, because I changed around an exhibit to showcase Renoir's little-known *Vase of Flowers* instead of his more famous *Two Sisters,* which, in my opinion, is overexposed.

And, of course, there was my disastrous decision to marry Kurt four months after my mother's death.

My mother used to say I am overly optimistic and too impulsive, even on my ADHD meds, but I didn't believe her. Her death and my rebound-from-grief marriage had changed all that. I no longer had boundless faith in the goodness of the universe, the intentions of others, or my own abilities.

"You'd have to put your whole life on hold," Eddie said gently.

"What life?" I turned my hands palm up. "I don't really have one."

Ralph patted my back. "All the more reason you need to stay in Chicago and build one."

"Maybe this is just the way to do that." Conviction swelled in me like a religious experience, infusing me with a sense of energy and purpose that had been lacking for months. Maybe years. "A few months in Wedding Tree would give me a chance to figure out my options and decide what I want to do next."

"A few months in Wedding Tree will make

anything look like a better option," Ralph said.

"And maybe that's exactly what I need."

Ralph and Eddie exchanged dubious looks. But then, they didn't know what my life was really like — how isolated and shut off and rudderless I'd become. You couldn't even say my life was adrift, because drifting implied movement. My life was stuck on a sandbar and completely fogged in.

"Look — I'm working as a temp. My sublet is up in two months, and I don't have a clue where I'm going to move. My friends are all married and busy with their families or else they've moved away, and jobs in the art world are harder than ever to come by in this economy." I was voicing things I hadn't even allowed myself to think. Depression had kept me catatonic, but apparently I'd subconsciously been fretting about my future, because relief flooded through me as I talked. The prospect of getting out of Chicago and helping Gran sort through her belongings gave me a sense of direction, of meaning, of usefulness. "This is perfect timing. Helping Gran would help me."

Eddie sighed. "Hope, honey, do you remember what Mom's house looks like?"

"Yes."

"When was the last time you looked in

36

her attic and storage shed and garage and closets?"

"It's been a few years." Maybe even a decade. Come to think of it, I might have been twelve the last time I was in the attic.

"She's only continued to add things to them. Every square inch is crammed and bulging."

"Well, it has to be tackled by someone. Might as well be me."

"You can't simultaneously sort out the house and take care of Mom. We don't even know what level of care she'll need."

Ralph thoughtfully rubbed the auburn stubble on his jaw. "We can hire home health care workers."

Eddie and Ralph exchanged another long look, the kind of look that's a whole conversation. I felt a burst of longing; I'd never been that closely attuned to anyone. Certainly not to my husband, not even in the early days, back when I'd thought things were good.

Eddie ran a hand down his face. "Hope, honey — you're tired. This is a huge commitment, and it doesn't need to be decided right now. Go to the house, take a good look around, and sleep on it." He reached in his jacket pocket, pulled out a key, and handed it to me.

"You need sleep, too," I said, noticing the shadows under his eyes. "Why don't we take turns staying here with Gran tonight?"

"Nah. I'll be fine. I can sleep like a log anywhere."

"That's true," Ralph said, kneading the back of Eddie's neck. "He fell asleep at a Warriors game last week and nearly slid off the seat."

"You can't blame me." Eddie tilted his head down to give Ralph better access to his neck. "Our team was twenty points ahead."

"My point is, he can nod off in a chair just as well as on a bed. Maybe better. He'll be sawing logs as soon as his butt hits a cushion."

Eddie nodded. "It's one of my many mad skills."

Ralph ended the neck massage and swatted Eddie's butt. "And you have very many, very mad skills."

Eddie playfully elbowed him in the ribs. "Not in front of the children."

I laughed, but felt more wistful than amused. Eddie and Ralph had been together for more than a dozen years and shared the kind of warm, easy affection I'd hoped for in my own marriage.

"I, on the other hand, require a prone

position," Ralph said, "so I'm off to the Mosey On Inn." Ralph was allergic to dogs, and Gran had a shaggy mixed breed named Snowball, so Ralph and Eddie always stayed at the town's only inn whenever they visited Wedding Tree.

Eddie hugged him good-bye, then kissed my cheek and turned toward the door to Gran's room.

"Sure you'll be okay here alone?" I asked.

"I won't be alone. I'll have Mom for company."

"Not to mention his grandmother on the ceiling," Ralph said dryly.

Eddie rolled his eyes. "I'll chalk your insensitivity up to sleep deprivation this time, but it better not happen again." He turned the "Visitors Welcome" sign on Gran's door around to read "Patient Sleeping — No Visitors Allowed" and made a shooing motion with his hand. "Now get on out of here, you two. I need my beauty sleep."

I peeked in as Eddie entered the room. Gran was sleeping peacefully, her chest rising and falling. Eddie plopped into the bedside recliner, kicked back the footrest, and closed his eyes. Satisfied, I backed out. Before the door even closed behind me, the soft snuffle of Eddie's snore rose from the chair.

3
Hope

I always wax nostalgic when I first see Gran's house after a long absence, but this time, I steeled myself against it. I'd watched quite a bit of HGTV over the last few months, and I'd learned about the importance of curb appeal. I would try, I decided, to view the house through the objective eyes of a potential buyer.

My heart sank as I pulled my rented Sonata onto the familiar herringbone-patterned brick driveway and gazed at the gabled two-story house. I'd been here at Christmas, but my eagerness to see Gran and my sentimental attachment to the place apparently had obscured the fact the house was in need of an extreme makeover. Well, maybe not extreme, but at least substantial; the gingerbread trim needed painting, the gray wooden siding was dingy with mildew, and the railing on the wraparound porch looked like a gap-toothed fighter who'd lost a few rounds.

The landscaping wasn't any better. The gardenia bush on the west side hulked over the living room window, the azaleas in the front bed gasped for fertilizer and a trim, and the centipede grass had been hijacked by dollarweed and dandelions. The only spot of color was a large patch of tulips blooming in the front flower garden.

I climbed out of the car, grabbed my bag from the backseat, and headed toward the house, noting additional needed repairs with every step. A board on the third porch stair shifted under my foot, the paint curled and flaked off the porch railing, and the screen door sported several tears and dents. The hinges squeaked as I opened it and inserted the key into the faded red front door.

The lock tumbled, and I pushed the door open. The scent of Gran's house — of a million home-cooked meals mingled with floor polish and old furniture and the lavender potpourri she always kept by the door — flew out to greet me, sweeping me up in a whirlwind of olfactory-borne memories. All attempts at objectivity abandoned, I stepped through the door and into my past.

Funny, how almost all of my childhood memories were based here. I'd only visited Gran at Christmas and during summer vacations, yet my recollections of this place were sharp and clear, while memories of most of my childhood in Chicago were blurry or nonexistent.

Maybe it was because this was where I'd felt most alive, I thought, dropping my keys on the bureau in the foyer. Gran's house had always buzzed with possibilities, with wonderful things just about to happen — Christmas presents waiting to be opened, cake icing needing to be licked from beaters, long summer days stretching out like magic carpets, as full of promised delight as the stack of canvasses Gran always bought me.

Mom used to fly me down to Louisiana when school let out in early June, then pick me up again in August. While she managed portfolios and brokered big deals in Chicago, I ran barefoot, frolicked through schedule-free days, and indulged my passion for painting.

Gran has always been my biggest fan and supporter. She'd noticed my love of art when I was about four years old and she caught me sitting cross-legged on her white chenille bedspread, staring at the print of Van Gogh's *Starry Night* that hung over her high oak headboard. I told her that if I looked at it long enough, the stars seemed to spin.

"Would you like to paint a picture like that?" Gran had asked.

I'd nodded, and that very afternoon, Gran had taken me to the store, bought me paint supplies, and set me up with a little easel on the back patio. I worked out there until nearly bedtime, when I'd declared my painting finished.

"That's beautiful, sweetheart," Gran had said.

"It's very nice," my mother had remarked when I'd proudly shown her the piece a couple of months later. "But shouldn't the big star be on the other side?"

"Oh, I wasn't copying," I'd said. "I looked at the sky myself."

"That's my girl." Gran's laugh had vibrated against me as she enfolded me in a big hug. "Don't ever stop viewing the world through your own eyes, sweetie."

"Who else's eyes would I use?" I'd asked.

Gran had laughed again. "You'd be surprised, honey. You'd be surprised."

To my delight, Gran had hung my painting right over the Van Gogh print in her bedroom — and she'd taken to framing and hanging each summer's crop of paintings in the "art gallery" between two of the three

44

bedrooms upstairs.

"You shouldn't encourage her," I'd over-heard my mother say one evening years later, between my sophomore and junior years in high school. She and my grand-mother had been sitting in the kitchen, and I'd been in the dining room, sketching a mural on the wall. I was listening to my CD Walkman, but I'd pulled the headset off for a moment, and the solemn tone of my mother's voice had made me put my ear to the door. "She needs to start thinking about colleges and majors, and art isn't a serious career."

The words had knifed me in the heart. My mother was an investment advisor, all about P&Ls, track records, and potential.

"She seems pretty serious about it to me," Gran had said.

"Come on, Mom. There's a reason the word 'artist' is usually paired with the word 'starving.'"

"She could always teach."

"Then she'd be starving for sure. Tradi-tional female roles don't allow a woman to make a decent living."

"Well, dear," Gran had said, "making a living isn't the same as making a life."

I'd failed at both, I thought now. My shoulders slumping, I left the main door

45

open so air could circulate through the screen, shuffled into the living room, and flipped the switch for the overhead light. The old chandelier cast a soft glow over the cypress floor, the floral chintz curtains, and the hodgepodge of furniture that ranged from inherited Victorian antiques to 1980s-era "modern." My eye went to the crowded collection of photos that covered the walls — a rogue's gallery of my family, with a special emphasis on my mother and Uncle Eddie as children.

Centered over the sofa hung an old sepia-tone photo of my great-grandmother and great-grandfather. In the manner of old photos, they were formal and unsmiling. Next to it was a photo of them sitting on the back porch, playing cards and laughing. If Gran hadn't told me who they were, I never would have recognized them as the same people.

Gran had taken the porch picture with a Kodak Brownie when she was seventeen. She'd told me she'd hidden in the bushes and caught them unawares so that they wouldn't stiffen up like a couple of corpses.

As long as I could remember, Gran always had a camera handy. In the back of the house, she'd had a darkroom, where she used to let me help develop close-ups of

46

flowers and bugs and leaves. I inhaled deeply as I stepped further into the house, hoping to detect a hint of darkroom chemicals. No such luck.

I'd once told my mother how I loved the smell of Gran's darkroom.

"Oh, I don't," Mom had replied. "I think it smells like thwarted dreams and female repression."

My mother had been big on female empowerment. Gran said she was a women's libber, although Mom preferred to think of herself as a feminist. She was certainly a glass-ceiling breaker, a role model for women who wanted more out of life than a home, a husband, and children. She'd told me that Gran had worked as a photographer for the New Orleans newspaper during World War II and had dreamed of being a travel photographer, but she'd been the victim of a "misogynic era" and a "chauvinistic husband."

My mother had been talking, of course, about her father.

According to Mom, he'd been withdrawn and silent, always hiding behind a newspaper or a TV program. When he did talk, it was usually to offer some kind of "helpful" criticism, usually about her appearance or demeanor. She needed to smile more and study less. Her hair always needed combing, or her clothes needed pressing. He was dismissive of her deeply held political convictions or even her stellar grades. "No man wants to marry a know-it-all," he used to say.

Mom said he lacked respect for women. Gran said he was just old-fashioned and stubborn and sincerely believed that he knew best. He'd been raised to always please his parents, and he couldn't understand children wanting a life beyond their family and hometown. Gran said the fact he was paralyzed in his late twenties had left him out of touch with the changing world. My mother said there was no excuse.

He'd died before I was born, so I don't have any memories of him. I do have a memory of Gran and my mom visiting his grave when I was about five. They'd taken some roses, and I recall Mom crying as if she were trying to squeeze her soul out of her tear ducts as Gran laid the bouquet on the headstone.

The savagery of my mother's grief had scared me. Mom was always in control, always logical, always practical. I thought she was above sentiment. Where had this storm of emotion come from? What could I do to make it stop? Was it somehow my fault?

Years later, when I was a teenager — I must have been fifteen, because I was driving my mother's Mercedes and she was in the passenger seat, and the only time she willingly relinquished control of the wheel was when I'd been a student driver — she said something disparaging about her father.

"If he was such a jerk," I'd asked, "why did you cry so hard that time we visited his grave?"

"Because I never had a chance to impress him." She'd smoothed her already-smooth hair, which was an unusual thing for Mom to do.

"You wanted to impress him?"

She'd lifted her shoulders. " 'Impress' might be the wrong word. I wanted to — oh, I don't know. He just always made me feel . . ." My mother, who was always so sure of herself and never at a loss for words, had an uncertain wobble in her voice. ". . . inadequate." She'd clamped her lips together and turned her head to the passenger window. I'd kept my eyes on the road. I was afraid she was crying again, and the thought of my always-together mother crying scared me to death.

Mom never said that her father was the

reason she disliked spending time in Wedding Tree; she said Gran loved to visit us in Chicago and that there was a lot more to see and do there, which was true enough. Besides, she'd always add — Wedding Tree was too rural, the people too nosy, and the pace of life too slow.

Which were the very things I'd always loved about Wedding Tree. The community was like a fuzzy blanket — it made me feel safe and relaxed and cozy. In Chicago, I always felt hurried and pressured. Maybe it was because Mom packed my after-school life with activities and appointments and play dates. When we were at our apartment, she was always working on something, and I felt like I had to be constantly productive, too. "It's important to make something of yourself, to become someone," Mom used to say.

"Isn't everyone already someone?" I once asked.

"You know what I mean," she'd said. "Successful."

Yeah, I knew what she meant. Success to my mother meant academic achievements, professional accomplishments, and important titles. A type-A overachiever, Mom went from high school valedictorian to summa cum laude MBA graduate at Northwestern to vice president at a publicly traded investment firm at a time when female executives were unheard of. She'd wanted her only daughter — the daughter she'd had at the age of forty-two — to follow in her footsteps and benefit from all the inroads she and her fellow female type As had made in the seventies and eighties.

The problem was, my idea of success didn't jive with hers. I didn't want to become an attorney or doctor or high-powered executive. I didn't want to wear designer clothes or go to power lunches or board meetings. I just wanted to paint — to lose myself in a flow of creativity, to produce art that captured my thoughts and feelings.

Mother never said I was a disappointment, and I know she didn't want to make me feel like one, because her father had done that to her. But deep inside, I'm pretty sure I disappointed her all the same.

Pushing aside my thoughts, I opened the front windows to let in a breeze — it was a cool day in late March, not warm enough to warrant air-conditioning — then went upstairs to my mother's old bedroom, the room where I always stayed. I dropped my bag on the floor, peeled off my clothes, and took a long shower in the vintage black-and-white-tiled bathroom. When I came out, I rummaged in my bag and threw on a pair of sweatpants and an old T-shirt. I thought about taking a nap, but it was getting late and I felt kind of wired. I decided to look around the house and see just what I was getting myself into. I wandered downstairs into Gran's bedroom.

It looked the same as it always had. Gran's big oak bed with a curved footboard sat against the wall opposite the door, the large, elaborately framed print of *Starry Night* hanging over the high oak headboard, my smaller painting, in a simpler frame, hanging above it.

I smiled and focused my gaze on the Van Gogh print. I still love it, but now I appreciate it for different reasons. Now I love the way Van Gogh lets you see his brushstrokes, how he didn't try to hide the effort, how he lets you see where he dabbed and dawdled and meticulously layered color on color, where he reworked the parts that weren't right until they matched the picture in his head.

Even in a print, you can tell that his paintings are uneven and textured and layered with paint, and you just know that there are probably different colors under the colors you see, and maybe even a whole other picture under the picture you're looking at.

The underneath picture is probably just as beautiful as this one, but he needed it as a base to build this one on, so it's okay that you don't get to see it. It's enough to know it's there.

I'm sure God can see it. I wonder if people in heaven can see it, and if maybe one day I'll get to see it, too. I wonder if cats can see it. They look at things with those funny slanted eyes, and I've always thought they must see things we don't.

But there I go, off on a mental tangent. My mother used to scold me for getting distracted, saying I needed to stay on task.

When I'd told Gran one summer that I sometimes got in trouble at home and school for daydreaming, she'd given me a big hug. "That's the sign of a creative mind." She told me that when she was a girl, her mother had called her a flibbertigibbet. The word had made me laugh and had become something of a secret code between us.

I pulled my gaze away from the print and looked around the room. The furniture — a matching oak highboy with an attached mirror, a blanket chest, and two night tables with lamps on either side — was covered with a fine film of dust, but Gran's bed was as neatly made as ever, so neat you could bounce a quarter off the old white chenille bedspread. Her terrycloth slippers peeked out from under the bed, and I was certain I'd find her pajamas folded and tucked under her pillow.

I hadn't been in her closet since I was a child. I used to love to play in there, to try on her shoes, to put on her dresses. Her closet was large and cedar lined, and it smelled like an old forest. Remembering what Eddie had said about it, I walked across the room and opened the door.

"Holy Moses," I muttered. The cedar scent was still there — but instead of space under the clothes where I used to play, every square inch was taken up with boxes — boxes stacked on the floor and on the shelves above the hanging clothes, boxes reaching up to the ceiling.

The hanging rods were jam-packed with clothes that would probably bring a fortune at a vintage store. I personally loved vintage clothing — I was a regular at several vintage stores in Chicago — so I rifled through the hangers. They were so crammed together that I could barely move them. A filmy swatch of fabric way at the back caught my eye. Curious, I wrangled the hanger free and pulled it out.

"Oh wow," I murmured. It was a pale blue

54

peignoir set — a sheer float of a robe that went over an equally sheer nightgown. The floor-length gown was embroidered with strategically placed clusters of rhinestone-encrusted white flowers. I held it up in front of me. I had never seen anything so lovely, so ethereal. What a shame that people didn't wear things like this anymore! I wondered what year it was from. My guess was the forties or early fifties.

Before I stopped to think about it, I pulled off my sweats and slipped the nightgown over my head, then, carrying the robe, headed for the cheval mirror in the bedroom.

Holy cow — I looked like Lana Turner, minus the styled hair and makeup. The gown fit as if it had been custom made for me, with embroidery strategically placed to cover my naughty bits. I twirled around, admiring the back. Embroidered flowers formed an optical thong, then gracefully trailed down my leg. I had to hand it to the designer — he was a master of peekaboo.

It was gorgeous. It was sexy as sin. It was the kind of thing a woman would wear on her honeymoon, back in the days when wedding preparations involved sultry French words like *trousseau, peignoir, negligee.* I let out a sigh. Such magical words from another era.

I wondered what occasion Gran had bought this for. Or had it been a gift? I'd seen pictures of Gran as a young woman, and she'd looked a lot like Katharine Hepburn. She'd had the same tousled, shoulder-length hair, the same air of confidence, the same dazzling smile. Maybe she —

"Are you the tooth fairy?"

A child's voice abruptly startled me out of my thoughts. I whipped around to see a little girl wearing shorts and a Disney princess T-shirt, staring at me from the bedroom doorway. She had long blond hair with bangs and the kind of poreless skin you usually only see on dolls. I wasn't very good at estimating kids' ages, but I guessed she was about four. "Wh-who are you?" I stammered. "How'd you get in here?"

"I'm Sophie. I came in through the doggie door." She looked up at me, her brown eyes solemn. "Are you the tooth fairy? 'Cause my sister has a loose tooth."

"Umm, no. No, I'm not." I grabbed the robe and hurriedly pulled it on. "What are you doing in here?"

"I came to see Snowball and Mizz McCauley. Sometimes she gives me cookies."

That sounded like Gran. Grinning, I

struggled to fasten the sheer robe, which was fitted on top and held together by a rhinestone clasp at the waist. "She's not here right now. Do you drop in through the doggie door very often?"

"Sometimes." She tilted her head up and looked at me hopefully. "I know where the cookie jar is."

I laughed. "Well, then, why don't you show me?" I followed her into the kitchen, the floaty circle skirt of the robe billowing around me. She dragged a chair from the breakfast table to the counter, the leg screeching on the wooden floor. She climbed up, stood on the seat, and reached for the cat-shaped jar on the counter. Lifting the lid, she pulled out an oatmeal cookie. "Would you like one?" she asked politely.

I smiled at her hostessing skills. "Yes, thank you."

"You're welcome." She handed it to me, then extracted another cookie. Replacing the lid with great care, she set the cookie on the counter, climbed down, moved the chair back to the breakfast table, then retraced her steps to retrieve her treat. She carried it to the red stool in the corner — the stool where I'd spent hours as a child watching Gran bake — climbed up, and regarded me.

"Are you a princess?"

I looked down at the floaty negligee and smiled. "No. I'm Mrs. McCauley's grand-daughter."

"Nuh-uh." She shook her head. "You're too old to be a granddaughter."

An irrational sense of dismay swept through me. Ever since I'd turned thirty, I'd become sensitive about my age, and as the numbers crept higher — next fall I'd be thirty-two — so did my awareness of my biological clock.

"You look more like a mommy," Sophie said, biting off an edge of cookie and considering me as she chewed. "But you're dressed like a princess or the tooth fairy."

It took some effort, but I didn't laugh. "I promise I'm neither. But, Sophie — does your mom know where you are?"

She nodded solemnly. "My mommy knows everything."

Her mother must have told her the old "mothers have eyes in the back of their heads" line that had made me search through my mother's hair while she was asleep.

"She's in heaven," Sophie continued. "She lives there with God."

"Oh." The geoplates of my heart shifted. Losing my mother at the age of twenty-eight had been horrible. I couldn't imagine losing a mother as a preschooler. "Well, your dad must be worried about you."

"Nah. He's busy."

"So who's watching you?"

"Gramma was, but she left and Aunt Jillian took over."

"So . . . what's Aunt Jillian doing?"

"She's busy with Daddy." She took another bite and chewed. "My sister hopes she's gonna be our new mother."

Ooo-kay. I wondered just how busy they were. "Where do you live, Sophie?"

"Next door." She pointed to the left.

"Well, as soon as you finish your cookie, I think you should go ba—"

"Sophie!" A deep male voice drifted through the front screen door. "Sophie!"

"In here!" the girl yelled, so loudly I jumped.

Steps sounded on the porch. "Hello?" called a male voice.

"I'm in the kitchen with a lady who looks like the tooth fairy," Sophie shouted. "Come meet her!"

The screen door squealed open, and a moment later, a tall man filled the doorway. He had dark hair and blue eyes, and he was wearing a starched white shirt unbuttoned at the neck, with a loosened blue-and-gray-striped tie. He was good-looking, if you're shallow enough to notice such things — which, unfortunately, I am.

I'd like to think it was the element of surprise that turned me into a tree and made me just stand there, rooted to the floor, but the truth is, he looked like a cross between Jake Gyllenhaal, Hugh Jackman, Bradley Cooper, and a young George Clooney, with a nose that looked like it might have once been broken, because it was just a little bit skewed to the left, and something about that slight imperfection made my stomach speed-bump. It took several beats of silence for me to realize he was staring back in a way that made me highly aware of my state of deshabille.

Deshabille — another of those old-fashioned, peignoir-related French words. Once something enters my head, my thoughts keep circling back to it at the most inappropriate moments. A friend who majored in psychology said it sounded like OCD, but I never talked to a doctor about it, because having ADHD was bad enough and if I was more screwed up than that, I really didn't want to know about it.

Anyway. Here was this smoking-hot man in my kitchen, and I'm dressed like a 1940s screen siren, and it felt all kinds of weird. I shifted the cookie to my left hand.

"Want a cookie, Daddy?" Sophie asked.

"Uh, no thanks." He pulled his eyes from me and knelt down by his daughter.

I couldn't help but notice the way his thigh muscles bulged under the summer-weight wool of his gray pants. The guy was ripped.

"Sophie," he was saying to his daughter, "you know you're not supposed to wander off."

"I came to see Mizz McCauley, but the tooth fairy princess lady was here instead."

The man turned Gyllenhaal-blue eyes on me. "I apologize for my daughter barging in on you."

"Oh, she didn't barge in . . ." I hesitated. I didn't want to get her in trouble, but on the other hand, I didn't want him to think I'd been standing out in the yard dressed like Mata Hari, luring stray children inside. ". . . exactly. I mean, apparently she regularly visits my grandmother."

"So you're Mrs. McCauley's granddaughter," the man said, straightening.

Sophie scrunched up her brow. "You're really a granddaughter?"

I smiled down at her. "We come in all ages."

"Really?" Sophie asked.

"Sophie!" called a woman's voice from outside. "Sophie!"

"In here!" Sophie bellowed. "Come on in."

Great, just great. At this rate, the whole town would soon be in the kitchen, wondering why I was dressed like Lana Turner. The porch door squeaked again, and a moment later, an attractive blonde about my age walked in. Her eyes widened as she took me in. She glanced at the man, then back at me, then rushed to Sophie. "Honey, we were so worried! You know you're not supposed to leave the yard without an adult."

"I didn't. I came over to see Mizz McCauley."

The woman smoothed Sophie's hair.

"I'm Hope Stevens," I explained, extending my cookie-free hand. "I'm Mrs. McCauley's granddaughter."

"I'm Jillian Armand." She gave my hand a tentative squeeze.

The man held out his hand. "And I'm Matt Lyons." His palm was solid, his fingers strong. A rush of adrenaline zinged through my veins. The name sounded familiar, but I couldn't remember where I'd heard it. Touching him made it hard to remember much of anything.

"How's your grandmother?" asked Jillian.

"Better. She's regained consciousness."

"Glad to hear it," said Matt. "I was really worried when I found her in the shed."

Pieces of information clicked together in my head. That's why I recognized his name — Mrs. Ivy had mentioned it on the phone. Come to think of it, Gran had mentioned it last winter when she told me about new neighbors moving in next door. "I owe you a huge thanks."

Matt lifted his shoulders. "It was unusual for her shed door to be open, so I thought I'd better check."

"People in Wedding Tree try to look out for each other." Jillian's gaze flicked over my gown, then darted away, as if she were embarrassed. "But we can talk about all that later; it looks like we caught you at an inconvenient time." She nudged Sophie toward the foyer. "We need to get out of here and give you some privacy."

"Oh, um, that's all right," I stammered.

"Are you here with your husband?" Jillian asked.

"My husband? Oh, no. He's not — I mean, I'm, uh, divorced." Oh, God — did she think I'd been in the middle of an afternoon delight? The attire certainly suggested it. Holy furburgers — did Matt think the same? My face burned. "I was just, uh, trying on some of my grandmother's clothes. I was looking in her closet . . . I'm a vintage clothing freak, and . . ." My voice trailed off weakly.

"Well." Jillian glanced at Matt as she herded Sophie toward the door. "We should leave you in peace."

"Oh, no, it's okay," I babbled. *Way to go, Hope. Beg them to stay so you can humiliate yourself some more.*

Jillian opened the screen door and ushered Sophie onto the porch. "Nice to meet you. I'm sure we'll see you later."

"Bye!" called Sophie. "Thanks for the cookie."

"You're welcome."

"Sorry for the intrusion," Matt said. I could tell he was trying to keep his gaze above my neck, but it slipped downward as he exited the house. A wave of heat flushed over me.

Terrific, I thought, closing the heavy door behind them and sinking against it. Nothing like making a good first impression on the neighbors.

4
MATT

"I can't believe she was trying on her grandmother's clothes," Jillian said as soon as we'd stepped through the front door of my house.

"I can't believe those clothes belong to anyone's grandmother," I remarked. My head was still reeling with the image of the fresh-faced brunette in that sheer gown and robe, standing in the kitchen, eating cookies with my daughter. The juxtaposition of the domestic scene with the erotic attire was jarring, to say the least — not to mention sexy as hell. I have to admit, the sight had aroused me as nothing had in the two years since my wife's death. My reaction to the tousle-haired woman left me feeling edgy and oddly guilty.

"What's wrong with playin' dress-up?" Sophie asked.

"Nothing, honey." Jillian smiled down at

her, then gave me a pointed look. "If you're four."

"I thought she looked bootiful," Sophie said.

I didn't get a back view, but I imagined Sophie was right.

"I can't believe she opened the door wearing nothing but a nightie," Jillian sniffed.

"She didn't," Sophie said. "I crawled in through the doggie door."

I laughed, then realized laughter was an inappropriate parental response to the situation. I forced my mouth into a more somber line. "It's wrong to sneak into people's homes that way, sweetie."

Sophie gazed up earnestly. "Mizz McCauley doesn't mind."

"You've crawled into her house before?" Jillian asked, her voice alarmed.

"Yeah. Mizz McCauley said I can come in for a cookie anytime I want."

Jillian frowned. "Sophie, it's very rude to go into someone's home uninvited."

I was a lot less concerned with manners than with the fact that my just-turned-four-year-old had been unsupervised — repeatedly, apparently — long enough to visit a neighbor. "What's Gramma doing while you're roaming the neighborhood?"

66

"I dunno. I only go over when *you're* home."

My daughter was making these unauthorized visits on my watch? Oh, terrific. I knew I wasn't in the running for Father of the Year, but this was veering into intervention-from-the-authorities territory. "Sophie, you know you're not supposed to leave the backyard without someone with you."

"I don't go through the gate or out the front door. I just go through a hole in the fence."

"That's leaving all the same."

My voice must have sounded firmer than I'd realized, because her bottom lip trembled. She looked up at me in a way that made me feel like a monster.

Oh hell. I was hopeless at disciplining the girls, because I hated to make them unhappy. Christine used to tease me about how they had me wrapped around their little fingers. As usual, she'd been right.

God, she'd been right about so many things. The thought made the Christine-shaped hole in my heart ache. Up until a few months ago, grief would strike like an unexpected karate chop, sudden and fierce. Now it was just a flat, dull emptiness that expanded and contracted. I sort of missed that ragged edge of grief, so sharp it was almost tangible. It had felt like a physical link to my late wife.

"Am I in trouble?" Sophie's voice wavered.

I crouched down beside her and pulled her into my arms. "No, sweetie. But now that you know it's wrong, don't do it again."

"Okay." She hugged me back, then pulled away and flashed me a smile, her sunny mood instantly restored. "Can I go play with Zoey?"

"Sure." I blew out a sigh as she scampered off to the den.

Jillian put a hand on my arm. "I'll help you keep a closer eye on her."

Her palm felt heavy and hot. I shoved my hands in my pockets as an excuse to move away. "I was home. It's my responsibility." Although technically, Jillian was partially to blame for this lapse, because she'd cornered me to tell me how she'd taken the girls to the park, preventing me from actively watching them.

"I'm happy to help. I love Sophie and Zoey as if they were my own."

Yeah, but they're not. The uncharitable thought gave me another twinge of guilt.

Jillian gave me a smile that seemed a little too intense and lasted a little too long. "Well, all's well that ends well. I'd better get

68

dinner started."

"You don't need to do that." The truth was, I was ready for her to leave.

But she was already moving toward the kitchen. "I promised the girls I'd make spaghetti and meat sauce. Mom bought all the ingredients this afternoon."

I swallowed as I followed her. When I first moved to Wedding Tree, Jillian occasionally cooked dinner for the girls when I was held up at work, but lately, she was doing it even when I was home. I wanted to break the pattern, but tonight didn't seem like the time to do it, what with promises made and ingredients bought and all. "What can I do to help?" I asked.

"You can chop the onions."

I'd hoped she'd say "nothing," so I could leave the room. Working beside her in the kitchen seemed too couple-ish, too . . . intimate. Jillian was my sister-in-law, but lately, she was acting more and more like a wife.

I hadn't foreseen this complication when I'd moved from New Orleans to Wedding Tree in January. Christine's mother and father had offered to help with the kids, and it had seemed like the ideal solution — especially after the third nanny quit.

The girls didn't do anything in particular

to drive the nannies away, although heaven knows they can be a handful. The first nanny, Miranda, had been a gem. A grandmotherly woman with a gold front tooth and a nurturing nature, she stayed with us for a year and a half. The girls were at their worst then — it was right after their mother's death and all of us were raw. She'd been a lifesaver. But then Miranda's daughter had triplets, and she'd moved to Houston to help her — which was understandable, but it left us in the lurch, and the girls grieved Miranda almost as much as they'd grieved their mother.

I put the girls in daycare, but one or the other was always sick, and as the attorney heading up the Public Protection Division of the Louisiana Justice Department, I had court dates and other hard-to-miss job obligations, plus I had to frequently travel.

So I hired Ashleigh. I should have known better — she was a nineteen-year-old anorexic brunette who reported for nanny duty in high heels — but I was desperate. She was inattentive and constantly texting her friends, interested only in planning her nights out, sulking if I needed her to stay late. As soon as she found a job that left all her evenings free, she was gone.

The woman after her was Gretchen, and

well . . . the girls just never warmed to her. She was fortyish and hyper-efficient, but her personality was as frosty as her streaked hair. The girls started throwing tantrums and clinging to me and acting out in ways that the pediatrician said were normal for kids who've experienced a loss, but I couldn't help but think it was partially due to Gretchen's aura of detachment. When she told me another family had offered her more money, I wished her luck and said good-bye.

My in-laws, Peggy and Griff Armand, had suggested that we move to Wedding Tree before, but I hadn't wanted to uproot the girls. Maybe I hadn't wanted to uproot myself, either; the thought of leaving the home I'd shared with Christine had seemed like more than I could bear.

Two years after Christine's death, though, continuation of location seemed a lot less important than continuation of caretakers. Wedding Tree was halfway between New Orleans and Baton Rouge, and since I split most of my time between the two cities, it made sense logistically.

The move made sense emotionally, as well. "Why hire a stranger to help with the girls, when we would love to watch them?" Peggy had said. "Zoey starts kindergarten

71

next year, so this is a good time to move and get settled. And there's a fabulous half-day preschool run by our church that both girls would just love."

"And I can help," Jillian had added. She was a middle school teacher and her late afternoons were free, although that wasn't really a consideration when I made the decision to move to Wedding Tree. If Jillian crossed my mind at all, it was only as a backup for Peggy.

I certainly hadn't anticipated the way Jillian would insinuate herself into our lives. Every evening when I went to Peggy's to pick up the girls, there she was. She trailed us home and made dinner. She stayed and washed clothes and cleaned the house. It was almost as if she lived here.

As if she *wanted* to live here. I was getting the uncomfortable feeling that she harbored romantic aspirations I didn't share.

Her hand brushed against my leg as she reached into the bottom cabinet for a pan. Was the touch deliberate? It seemed like her body was grazing mine with increasing frequency, but maybe I was just more aware of it. I shifted away.

"How was your day?" she asked.

"Okay."

"Any interesting cases?"

72

"I really can't talk about them." More to the point, I didn't want to.

"You used to talk about them with Christine."

"Christine was my wife." The words came out a little too bluntly.

The pans rattled as she extracted one. "Well, I know how to keep a confidence, too, if that's what you're worried about." She carried the pan — or was it a pot? I didn't really know the difference — to the sink and filled it with water. "Christine told me lots of things I never told anyone."

What kind of things? Things about my cases, or more personal things about the two of us together? What kind of mind game was Jillian playing here?

Irritation flashed through me, rapidly followed by a chaser of guilt. My thoughts drifted back to the woman next door. I wished I were standing in her kitchen right now. No history, no baggage, no awkward sense of subtle coercion — nothing but a slinky, Hollywood-style nightie standing between us.

"It's been a long day, and I'm kind of fried," I said. "I don't much feel like talking."

She nodded sympathetically. "I'm sure your work exhausts you."

73

What exhausts me is dealing with you. It was an unkind thought, but it was the truth.

Somewhere along the way, it had become awkward, always having her around. And there were other things, things that weren't her fault.

Sometimes, when I caught a glimpse of her from the corner of my eye, she looked so much like Christine that my heart would skip a beat. She was far from a dead ringer, but there were odd little physical similarities — the curve of her back when she knelt to talk to the girls, the shape of her calves, the way her toes perfectly slanted downward in her sandals. A year ago, these things were daggers to my heart. Now, they were just irrational annoyances.

And lately, it had gotten worse. She'd grown out her hair, and two weeks ago, she'd turned up blond. And she'd lost weight, as if she were trying for Christine's willowy frame. I wondered if she thought that by making herself look more like Christine, I'd find her more attractive.

But then, maybe I was just imagining it all — which means I'm a total ass. It's possible I'm looking for reasons to resent her just because she's similar to Christine, but not Christine. Close, but no cigar.

I finished chopping the onion. I slid the

cutting board toward her and put the knife in the sink, then washed my hands. "If you've got things covered here, I'll go hang out with the girls."

"Oh. Okay, sure." Was I looking for it because I felt kind of guilty, or did her voice carry an undertone of disappointment?

All I knew for sure was that the air seemed lighter in the foyer. I inhaled a deep lungful and headed toward the sound of my daughters' laughter, the tightness in my chest melting with every step.

There they were, the two halves of my heart — sprawled on the floral rug in the middle of the den, their blond heads close together, shoving stuffed animals into their Barbie Dreamhouse. I stood in the doorway and drank in the scene. Winnie the Pooh hung upside down out the third-floor window, a naked Barbie rode astride Eeyore through the dollhouse living room, and a teddy bear's pink fur overflowed the kitchen's door and windows.

Zoey looked up at me with her big brown eyes, too serious for a five-year-old. "Hi, Daddy! We're playin' zoo."

"Looks more like *Animal House*," I remarked.

If Christine were here, she would have said something like, "Let's make little teddy bear togas." She'd always been willing to laugh at my lame attempts at humor, always been ready with a quick comeback, always been able to crack me up with a witty observation. Playful banter, I think it's called — that's another thing I miss about her. How long would I keep discovering new things I missed?

Or rediscovering old ones. My thoughts flicked to the woman next door.

"Let's go to the real zoo this weekend," Zoey said, cramming a toy zebra onto the dollhouse potty.

I sat down cross-legged on the floor beside them. "Okay." We had a family membership to the Audubon Zoo, the Aquarium of the Americas, and the Insectarium in New Orleans, and when we'd lived there, the girls and I were frequent visitors.

"Aunt Jillian said she hasn't been to the zoo since she was a teenager," Zoey said. "She can't wait to see the monkeys."

Wait — the "we" included Jillian? My enthusiasm tanked. "How about just the three of us go?"

Zoey's jaw jutted out. "I want Aunt Jillian to come, too. She said she could."

Once again, plans had been set in motion without my knowledge or consent. I stifled a sigh, reminding myself that I'd moved here so that the girls would have a sense of family. Looking at them now, I had to say it was a good decision. They were both thriving; they slept through the night now, their appetites were good, and neither one had thrown a tantrum in months.

It was only natural that they'd grow attached to Jillian; she was their aunt, and she loved them. It was wrong of me to deprive them of her company just because I was a little paranoid. "Okay," I said. "The more, the merrier. Let's see if Grandpop and Gramma can come, too." Having the in-laws along would defuse the Jillian factor.

"Wahoo!" exclaimed Zoey. She jumped to her feet and headed for the kitchen. "Aunt Jillian!" she called. "We're all gonna go to the zoo!"

Sophie looked up at me. "Can the tooth fairy granddaughter lady come, too?"

The image of the brunette next door flashed in my brain like neon. "I, uh, think she'll need to stay and take care of her grandmother."

"We could ask her."

"We don't know her well enough to invite her out like that." Although it would certainly make things a lot more interesting from my perspective.

"If she went with us, we'd get to know her better."

I ruffled Sophie's hair. "She's just visiting. I don't think she'll be in town very long."

I wondered just how long she planned to stay in Wedding Tree. I wondered what she did for a living and where she lived.

I wondered why I was wondering all these things about a woman I'd barely met.

I thought about the way she'd filled out that sparkly sheer gown, and I immediately knew the answer. I unwound my legs and rose. "Come on, sport. We'd better wash up for dinner."

And while I was at it, I'd better clean up my thoughts, as well.

5
ADELAIDE

THE FOLLOWING MONDAY
"Watch your head, Mom." Eddie cushioned the top of my noggin with his hand as if I'd never gotten into an automobile before — when the fact is, I'd ridden in enough cars to fill an antique road show, starting with my granddaddy's Model T.

Of course, that's what I was now. An antique.

One thing those old cars had going for them — you didn't have to fuss with that ridiculous strap contraption Eddie was easing over my head and clicking across my lap. What the heck was that annoying thing called? I can't remember. I can remember the license plate of our family car back in 1939 — 122-147 — but I can't remember the name of this silly restraint device. It's sad to remember just enough to know how much you're forgetting.

"Ralph and I will meet you at the house,"

Eddie said.

"Fine," I said, although I didn't really register what he'd said. I was too caught up in noticing that there seemed to be two Eddies. Something was wrong with my vision, because sometimes I saw double and even triple.

Becky — no, it was Hope; I'd seen her face fall too many times when I'd called her the wrong name over the last few days, and I sure didn't want to do that again — smiled at me. "Does the seat belt hurt your ribs?"

Seat belt — that's what it was called. And why on earth was she asking about my ribs? Something must be wrong with them. That must be why my lower chest throbbed. "I'm fine, dear."

But I wasn't. I was confused and disoriented, and my hands were clammy. Thoughts flitted in and out of my head like hummingbirds, pausing for just a few seconds before winging on their way. I couldn't seem to hold on to any of them.

I knew I was in a car, but where the heck were we? I looked around, searching for clues. A woman in a blue medical outfit — what do they call it? Scraps? — was pushing a wheelchair away from the curb. "Take care now, Mrs. McCauley," she said.

The hospital — that's right. I'd fallen, hit

my head, and cracked my ribs. Relief washed through me — first relief that I could remember where I was, and then relief that I was leaving. The next time I came here, I was pretty sure I wouldn't be so lucky.

My days in the hospital all blended together in my memory like that cottage cheese and Jell-O recipe I used to make, opaque and filled with chunks of crunchy stuff that tasted the same — only instead of apples and celery, these chunks were made up of having my blood pressure checked, being helped to bathroom, and feeling a stranger's hands bathe me in the shower.

It was humbling, being on the receiving end of bathing and bathroom care. I'd performed the tasks for Charlie when he was first injured, but getting the help myself . . . well, I knew it had been hard on Charlie, but I had a new appreciation of just how hard. I think it must have been worse to get help from a spouse than from a stranger — especially knowing that the spouse had been about to leave you.

One thing I do remember clearly about my stay in the hospital — it stands out, as sure as nuts in Jell-O — was that visit with Mother. If I didn't want to spend eternity getting tongue-lashed, I had to tell Hope everything and take care of that piece of business I'd put off for decades. The thought made my breakfast turn sour in my stomach.

I must have closed my eyes and dozed for a moment, because the next thing I knew, Hope was pulling up in front of the house. Time has become uneven. It slides by unnoticed, as if nothing is changing, and then all of a sudden, I look around and everything's different.

"Sit tight, and I'll get your walker out of the trunk," Hope said.

My walker? I didn't need a walker, like an old lady! Or did I? Maybe so. I couldn't risk falling again until I finished following Mother's instructions.

The sun was shining, and the tulips in the yard were in full bloom — bright bursts of brilliant yellow and white, blinding as a flashbulb. A handsome officer's face floated into my memory, and my mind started to go down a rabbit hole, but then my eye caught the hot pink flash of azaleas, just starting to bud, and my thoughts zoomed even further backward, back to childhood.

I was five years old, crouched beside the azalea bed with my mother. She wore her brown-checked housedress, flowered cotton gloves, and her floppy straw gardening hat.

I had a gardening hat and a pair of gloves, too, but I'd taken them off after about two minutes. I'd never liked the feel of things on my hands or head.

"Your skin is going to turn as brown and rough as leather," Mother had fussed. She'd always been after me for unladylike behavior, but I didn't think that ladies seemed to have much fun. Gardening was the one ladylike activity I loved, because it involved digging in the dirt. On this particular day, Mother and I were mixing old coffee grounds into the soil under the azaleas. She said it made them bloom longer. I remember dipping the grounds out of a big Crisco can, and inhaling deeply. I'd loved the mingled scent of coffee and dirt and growing things.

So odd, how I could remember long-ago things like they happened yesterday, yet yesterday's events seemed covered with moss.

Eddie and Ralph pulled their car into the drive behind us, and I used that infernal walker to get to the porch. Eddie helped me up the steps — the steps were a nice, clean gray, as if they'd been newly painted — and then I was in the house, and Snowball was bouncing around my feet, dancing as if it were Christmas, New Year's, and every other holiday all rolled into one big, fat, joyful, beefy bone.

Hope picked him up so I didn't trip over him, while Eddie led me into the living room and got me settled in a chair. Hope set Snowball in my lap, where he licked my face and wagged his tail as I talked to him and petted him, and it was only after he calmed down and curled into a soft, strokable ball that I realized I was sitting in the floral chair where my mother used do her hand sewing when she listened to the radio. Of course, that was back when the chair was in her house, and the radio was a piece of furniture.

I closed my eyes and it was like I was transported back to my childhood home. I could practically feel the itchy wool sofa. Daddy's leather chair was angled beside it, the armrest worn and cracked, and . . .

"Okay, Mom?"

Eddie's question made me jerk my eyes open. He was sitting on the sofa in my living room and I believe he'd been talking for quite a while, but I hadn't been paying attention. Oh dear. How rude of me!

"Okay?" he asked again.

I was ashamed to admit that I hadn't been following his conversation. "Fine," I said. *Fine* was a word that seemed suitable for most responses.

He rose, and the red-haired man seated beside him — Rufus? Rupert? I couldn't recall his name, dadburn it — rose with him. "Well, then, we'd better get going. Our plane leaves at noon." Eddie came over and kissed my cheek. "We'll be back to get you at the beginning of June."

Alarm shot through me. "Get me?" I echoed blankly.

"Yes, Mom. To move you to San Francisco." He spoke in a patient tone, as if he were talking to someone who didn't understand English well or was slow-witted — or nuts.

I hadn't lost my mind. I had the feeling he thought I was crazy.

"We've talked about it a lot, remember?"

"Yes," I said, although I didn't remember, not entirely. I remembered talking with Eddie and Hope and some lady at the hospital about how I couldn't live in my house anymore, and I knew I'd agreed to something, but what that something was, I couldn't quite fix in my mind. The one thing that really mattered was the one thing I knew for sure: Hope was going to stay here and help me pack up the house, bless her heart, and I'd have the chance to set things right.

But Eddie was talking about what would

85

happen afterward. Maybe I'd better speak up before Eddie's plans got too far along to change. "I don't know if we've discussed it, dear, but as much as I love you, I want to live on my own."

The redhead's muffled snort let me know we'd discussed it plenty.

Bless his heart — Eddie's eyes remained warm and patient. "I know, Mom. We're going to find a nice assisted living center for you and Snowball."

"And I insist on paying my own way."

"You will, Mom. You have your savings and you'll have the proceeds from selling the house." He bent down and squeezed my hand. "The important thing, Mom, is that you'll be near me. I'll get to drop by your apartment all the time."

Apartment? "An apartment won't have much space. Where will I . . ."

I'd been about to say "develop my photos," but then I remembered that I quit doing that a few years ago. Everything was digital now.

Digital. Used to mean you did it by hand — with your fingers, to be exact. Now digital just meant a machine did it for you. Which was easier and maybe even more precise, but something was lost in the process. I'd quit taking photos when that became the thing everyone wanted.

Eddie's brow wrinkled. "Where will you what?"

I patted the back of his hand. "Never mind, dear — just having a senior moment. I seem to be living one long senior moment these days."

Eddie turned his hand to take my palm. "You had a hard blow to the head, Mom, but it's all going to be okay, and you don't have to worry. While you're here, you're going to have round-the-clock home health care. And when you get to California, we'll take good care of you." The way he looked at me made my finger press down, wanting to capture the moment. His eyes glowed with that caring, worried, earnest, eager-to-please puppy dog look that was quintessential Eddie. He'd had that expression when he was four, and he still had it fifty years later. He used to look at Charlie like that, wanting, so badly, his approval.

Charlie thought that praising a child too much made him weak, that Eddie needed toughening up, that I'd spoiled him into sissy-hood. His parents had done that to him, I knew, but still, a surge of anger shot through me. He'd been wrong — so very, very wrong.

"Mom? Are you all right?"

I realized I'd closed my eyes. I opened them to see Eddie squatting beside my chair. I blinked. I saw three of him, and then two.

"Yes, yes, I'm fine."

"And you're okay with me leaving now and coming back in June to help you move?"

I don't have much choice, do I? I didn't say it, of course; he was doing the best he could. He was a dentist with an established practice. He couldn't just up and leave it and move out here. Even if he could, I wouldn't ask that of him.

And, truth be told, I was ready for a change. The thought of a move, a whole new life, was exciting. I was ready. I'd always wanted to live on the coast. And yet . . .

I flashed him a smile. "I'm fine with it, honey."

"I'll call every day, and with Hope here, we can Skype each other."

I had no idea what that meant, but I nodded all the same.

His brow furrowed. "Are you sure you don't want to come now? We could catch a later flight. I could pack up a few of your things, and you can just let Hope deal with the house on her own."

"Oh, no, Eddie." A memory formed in my mind, a long-ago memory from when I was a girl. I'd wanted to play outside, but Mother had insisted that I resew a button I'd just sewn in the wrong place on my sweater. "Finish what you start," she'd said. I could see her clearly, so clearly, as if she were standing beside me right now. "Always clean up your messes before moving on to the next thing."

I blew out a long sigh. Maybe Mother had arranged all this.

"What?"

I opened my eyes at Eddie's voice to see him peering at me, his brow still knitted. I hadn't realized I'd closed my eyes or spoken aloud. "Oh, nothing," I said, feeling sheepish. "I was just remembering something Mother told me about seeing things through."

Robert — or was it Richard? I knew his name started with an *R*— leaned in. "Is she on the ceiling here?"

"I — I don't think so." I started to explain that she could read my thoughts, then realized how cuckoo that sounded. They already thought I was crazy enough.

"So . . . where do you and Hope plan to begin?" Eddie asked.

"Oh, my — I don't think it matters. Usually if you just dive in, you'll end up where you need to be sooner or later. Thinking too much can paralyze you."

"Interesting philosophy," the redhead said. "You'll have plenty of options."

I followed his gaze into the dining room. For the first time, I realized it was stacked with trunks and boxes from the attic. He and Eddie must have moved them down while I was in the hospital.

I patted Eddie's hand, then turned it loose. "You'd better get going or you'll miss your train."

"Plane," Eddie said softly.

"Yes, of course." How could I have forgotten how the world had speeded up?

After a flurry of good-bye hugs and kisses, the screen door banged shut, and a car engine growled to life in the driveway.

As the sound receded into the distance, Hope handed me a tissue and sat down in the chair beside me. "You okay?"

I hadn't even realized a tear was snaking down my cheek. I quickly wiped it away. "Just fine, dear. Looking forward to spending time with you."

"Me, too."

"I have so much I want to tell you. I . . ." A sound from the kitchen made me jump. "Who's that?"

"The home health aide."

Oh bother! I didn't want a third party

90

hanging around while I spilled the secrets of my soul.

"I don't need a nursemaid," I grumbled. "Can you get rid of her?"

"Not entirely," Hope said. "Eddie absolutely insisted you have help here around the clock."

"But I want to talk to you privately."

"Well, then, I can send her on an errand."

The suggestion brightened my mood. "Why don't you do that, dear, then put on some tea. You and I are due for a nice long chat."

6
HOPE

I was a little nervous about being alone with Gran. It was kind of like the time I'd babysat my friend's toddler — the child had no knowledge of her own limitations, I had no confidence she would heed my warnings, and I worried she was going to fall and hurt herself. What if I didn't watch her closely enough and something happened? I reached for Gran's arm to help her stand up, then realized my efforts were only thwarting her own.

"I can do it, child," Gran muttered, pushing out of her chair. "Stop hovering over me."

"I promise to quit hovering if you promise to use your walker."

"Fiddlesticks. That thing's more likely to trip me than help me." To my relief, though, she reached for the walker all the same and shuffled through the dining room into the kitchen.

She stopped in the doorway and eyed the array of cakes, pies, and cookies lined up on the counter. "Good Lord! Looks like we're having a bake sale."

"You should see the refrigerator," I said. "Half the town sent over a casserole."

A grin spread across her face. "That's the way things work around here. Someone has a hard time, and everyone tries to feed them better." Scooting her walker in front of her, she shambled to the kitchen table and sat down.

"Do you want iced tea or hot tea?" I asked.

"Hot, please. And are those Mabel Tharp's brownies?"

A parade of people had brought food over the past few days. I scanned my memory for the brownie bearer. "Is she a thin, elderly lady with rosy cheeks?"

"Yep, she always looks like she fell into the rouge pot. But she's not elderly. Why, she's only seventy-eight."

Practically a spring chicken. "I stand corrected." I carried the plate of brownies to the table, then filled the teakettle and put it on the stove. I had just gathered up a couple of napkins and dessert plates when the doorbell rang.

"Sit tight," I told Gran. "I'll get it."

A couple who looked to be their early sixties stood on the porch. The man was tall and broad-shouldered, and reminded me of Ronald Reagan. His arm was looped around the waist of a round-faced blonde with lively blue eyes and pale, dewy skin that looked like it had never seen the sun. She held a large covered bowl. "I'm Peggy Armand, and this is my husband, Griff. We live across the street." She shifted the bowl to her left arm and held out her other hand. "We brought over a salad. Figured you'd need something green to balance out all the casseroles."

"How nice!" I introduced myself and shook their hands. The screen door creaked as I opened it wider. "Come on in. Gran's in the kitchen."

Peggy stepped inside. "How is she?"

"Better, thanks."

"We visited her in the hospital, but I don't think she knew us."

"She still has those moments," I warned them. I didn't want to say too much, for fear of Gran overhearing.

"Well, that's perfectly understandable." Peggy peered into the dining room. "So you're the artist who painted that beautiful mural."

I nodded. Gran had been repainting the interior of her home the summer before my junior year in high school. She'd intended to wallpaper the dining room, but she couldn't find any paper she liked. "I know!" Gran had exclaimed. "You can paint a mural!"

"Of what?" I'd asked.

"What about the backyard?"

So I had. I'd covered the wall with an acrylic painting of the lawn and garden, complete with the shed and a couple of trees that had since blown down in Hurricane Katrina. Using one of Gran's photos, I'd created an early springtime scene much like the view out the kitchen window now, complete with azaleas and a bed of tulips.

Working on that mural had been one of my all-time favorite projects. Every time I'd lifted my paintbrush, I'd gone into a state of flow — instinctively mixing colors and riffing on my sketch, losing myself in the joy of creating.

"I've always admired that so much," Peggy said, stepping into the dining room and gazing at it. "Do you still do murals?"

"That's the only one I've ever attempted."

"Look at this, Griff." Peggy edged around a stack of boxes to step closer to the wall. "It's almost like looking out a window."

"Fine work." He nodded. "Mighty fine."

Peggy touched the trunk of a painted tree.

95

"It's absolutely exquisite." She turned and followed me into the kitchen, where she spotted Gran trying to push out of her chair. "No, no, Miss Addie — don't you dare get up on our account!" Setting the salad on the counter, she hurried over to the table, leaned down, and kissed Gran's cheek.

"So nice to see you," Gran said. I wondered if she had a clue who these people were.

Griff went over and kissed her cheek, too.

"Oh, my, you smell so good," Gran said. "I love a man who wears shaving lotion!"

"So does Peggy," he said. "She keeps me around as air freshener."

"Peggy." From the way Gran repeated the name, I could tell she'd just placed the woman. "I take it you've met my grand-daughter, Hope?"

"We just met. But I'm afraid Sophie made her acquaintance a few days ago."

Gran looked puzzled.

"The little girl next door," I explained. "She crawled through Snowball's doggie door."

Gran's face lit up. "Oh yes! I just love that child to death."

"I was horrified to learn she'd been sneaking into your house," Peggy said.

"She's welcome anytime. Her visits always brighten my day."

"Well, she's not supposed to leave the backyard. It caused quite a stir when Matt and Jillian discovered she was gone. Jillian said they were frantic."

The pieces fell into place. So these were Jillian's parents — and Sophie's grandparents. The parents of Matt's late wife.

"Jillian said she and Matt found her here in the kitchen with Hope," Peggy said.

My face flushed. If Jillian had mentioned that we'd met, it was a sure bet that she'd mentioned what I was wearing. I didn't think Gran would be offended I'd been trying on her clothes, but the fact I was doing it while she was lying in the hospital seemed, well . . . inappropriate. Insensitive, even.

The teakettle whistled. I hurried over to deal with it, relieved at the opportunity to change the topic. "Can I get you some tea?" I looked at Peggy, then Griff. "Or a beer? Eddie left some Abita in the fridge."

"I'll take one of those," Griff said.

"I'll have tea, dear, if you're sure it isn't any trouble."

They settled at the table. I set out plates, napkins, and spoons, along with a selection of baked goods. "Oh, are those Mabel's brownies?" Peggy asked.

"Yes, indeed," Gran said. "Help yourself."

I poured tea and brought Griff a beer, then sat down with them, a cup of Earl Grey in my hand.

"I was telling Hope how much I admired the mural in your dining room," Peggy said.

Gran beamed. "Hope has a lot of artistic talent."

I smiled self-consciously and bit into a brownie. Rich chocolate flavor flooded my mouth. Mabel's reputation was well deserved.

"My granddaughters want their room painted like a castle," Peggy said. "I've been looking for someone to do it."

"Hope could paint it," Gran volunteered.

I froze in mid-chocolate ecstasy.

"It'll give her something to do in the evenings," Gran continued. "After a day of helping me sort and pack, she's going to need to get out of the house."

I tried to swallow my mouthful of brownie, but it stuck in my throat. I hadn't picked up a brush since my divorce. Actually, since well before it.

"I'll pay you, of course," Peggy continued. "It's my gift to the girls. I'd arranged to hire an artist from New Orleans and pay him six thousand dollars plus travel expenses, but he decided he didn't want to make the drive."

Six thousand dollars? I have to say, the prospect of earning some money during my time in Wedding Tree had a certain appeal. So did the idea of painting a mural. My ex would have scoffed at the idea, calling it lowbrow and common.

Which, come to think of it, was a great reason for me to go ahead and do it. "Sounds interesting," I said. "But I haven't painted in a long time."

"Oh, it'll come right back to you." Peggy looked at Gran. "Miss Addie, are you sure you can spare her?"

Gran flapped a wrist dismissively. "Eddie's hired round-the-clock aides to stay with me. I'll be just fine."

"Wonderful!" Peggy clapped her hands together. "I'll talk to Matt and see when would be a good time for you to meet with him and the girls and discuss it."

The conversation drifted to other topics. The aide, a wide-hipped, pleasant-faced woman named Nadine, came back from the store and announced it was time for Gran to take some medicine.

Griff and Peggy rose to take their leave. "I'll be calling you," Peggy said as I saw them out the door.

When I returned to the kitchen, Gran's

face looked drawn and pale, and Nadine was helping Gran out of her chair.

"Are you okay?" I asked, alarmed.

"My head hurts. And I'm afraid my get-up-and-go got up and went." Gran leaned hard on the walker. "Let's have our chat tomorrow."

"Sure thing, Gran."

Between chats, visitors, naps, tea, nursing aides, and lining up a potential painting project next door for me, I'd begun to wonder if sorting through her belongings was even on Gran's radar.

While she'd been in the hospital, Eddie had arranged for a contractor to repair and paint the exterior of the house, and I'd gone through her refrigerator and pantry, throwing out everything past its expiration date. That had been easy enough, so I'd thought I'd tackle her linen closet. I quickly found myself in over my head. What did she want to take to California? What did she want to give to Eddie?

Shifting gears, I'd started researching the worth of Gran's furnishings, but dollars seemed a totally inadequate way to value a chair Gran's great-great-grandmother had sat on before the Civil War. It was a dilemma, because I had no place to put it, and Eddie's aesthetic was modern minimalism.

The prospect of dismantling a household filled with family treasures and lifelong memories was going to be at least as tough emotionally as it was physically, I realized — and if I found it daunting, I could only imagine how hard it was going to be for Gran.

7
ADELAIDE

I woke to find the sun shining through the sheer curtains of my east window, which meant it was at least nine o'clock. Three kind-faced women wearing blue shrubs — no, that wasn't the word; what the heck was it? — loomed in the doorway. They morphed into two.

"Good morning, Miss Addie," one said.

Wait. There was only one woman — my eyes were playing tricks on me — and I didn't know who she was. My expression must have told her as much, because she smiled. "I'm Nadine, your daytime health aide. You had a fall and you're recovering in your own home, and your granddaughter is here, too."

I was grateful for the information, even though the fact she was providing it told me she thought I was a nitwit. She helped me to my walker and to the bathroom, where something tall with handles had been added to my toilet. When I came out, Becky — no, Hope; I had to keep that straight! — was standing by my bedroom door.

"Ready for breakfast?" she asked. "I just scrambled some eggs and made a fresh pot of coffee."

"Sounds wonderful."

I let the aide help me dress, then used that confounded walker contraption to get to the kitchen. Hope brought me coffee, scrambled eggs, and oatmeal topped with blueberries and walnuts. The aide — Nay-nay? Narnia? Naysayer? Her name started with an *N*, I was sure of it — gave me a handful of pills to take. The coffee and food — or maybe the pills — perked me up and helped my addled thoughts coalesce into something of a memory: Hope was here to help me go through my things. I needed to tell her about Joe.

I looked at the aide as she cleared the table. "Would you be so kind as to go the store for me?"

"I just went yesterday afternoon."

"Well, I'm sure we need some groceries."

Her heavy eyebrows knitted together. "The house is practically bursting with food."

"I have a hankering for some fresh peppermint. Do we have any of that?"

The aide's forehead creased. "I — I don't think so."

"Then I'd like for you to go find me some. Hope, let's get started in the dining room."

The aide helped me get settled at the head of the dining room table, then left, muttering under her breath.

Hope laughed. "She knows you were trying to get rid of her."

"That's okay. Eddie's paying her the same whether she's meddling in my business here or running off on a fool's errand."

Hope brought me a glass of water and set it down on a felt-backed silver coaster. A wave of nostalgia swept over me. How many times had I sat here with family? Too many to count. It had been my mother's formal dining table — and my grandmother's before that. Christmas, Thanksgiving, Easter, dinner parties. My goodness. The table held a lot of memories.

But then, so did the boxes and trunks from the attic. I pointed to a slender black trunk. "Let's begin with that one."

Hope lifted it and set it on the table in front of me. She — or maybe it was Eddie; bless his heart, he was the tidiest man I'd ever known — had dusted it off, but it still smelled stale.

Hope fiddled with the latch. "It's locked."

"The key is in the top drawer of the cupboard."

Hope located the big skeleton key and put it in my hand. My fingers trembled as I fitted the key in the hole. It was funny — I felt like I was looking at my grandmother's hands on the ends of my arms. I don't think I'll ever get used to having these veiny, spotted hands with such big knuckles — just like I don't think I'll ever get used to seeing that old woman's face staring back at me in the mirror. It's not how I see myself at all, although Lord knows I should.

I heard a little click, and felt the give on the lock. "I bought this trunk when I was in high school. Saved up all my money from babysitting and working at the drugstore and bought this my junior year. I had a yen to travel." I'd collected photos of places I wanted to go — Paris, London, Rome, Athens. I hoarded travel magazines under my bed like men hid girlie mags. "Now, turn it up tall."

Hope picked up the trunk and set it down vertically, then undid the latch. Her eyes widened. "Oh wow! It's like a little closet."

"Yep." On the left side was a clothes rod, with several hanging garments. The right side held four drawers.

Hope ran her hand over it. "This is too

cool! Did you take this lots of places?"

I shook my head. "Only to New Orleans."

"But you took all those photos of France and Greece and Egypt!"

"Oh, I traveled the world — but not until the kids were grown and Charlie had died. I never went further than Alabama until I was fifty-six. Then I made up for lost time."

The funny thing was, by then I'd realized that the big deals in life weren't necessarily big at all. A newborn's finger, a drop of dew on a blade of grass, an ant carrying a grain of sugar . . . enormously powerful wonders were all around, enough wonders to fill a lifetime, right in your own backyard, maybe under your very feet. It's not where you are; it's how you see it.

"By the time I started traveling, this trunk was obsolete. It was too large for air travel."

Hope ran her hand over it. "It's in beautiful condition."

"Unlike the green dress in it. Take it out, would you, honey?" The silk rustled as Hope carefully lifted the padded hanger. Originally the dress had been pale jade, but age had yellowed it to a soft moss green. The fabric-covered belt was slightly stained where the buckle had rusted. "I fell in love in this dress."

"Oh, I can see why." Hope held it up

against herself, then carefully placed it on the table. "It's absolutely gorgeous."

She was missing my meaning. I fingered the hem. "I don't mean I fell in love *with* the dress, honey. I mean I was wearing this dress *when* I fell in love."

Hope's eyebrows pulled together. "With Granddad? I thought you two were childhood sweethearts."

"Oh, we knew each other all our lives. We lived just down the street, two houses away, and our parents were best friends. My mother and his mother were tight as sisters. Charlie's older brother had died when he was two, so Charlie was an only child, and I might as well have been — my brother was twelve years older than me and away at college by the time I started school. But the sweetheart part . . ."

"That came later?"

I hesitated. Here was where I had to turn off the road paved with illusions and steer onto the bumpy dirt path of truth. "The fact of the matter is, the sweetheart part was always pretty much one-sided."

Hope's eyebrows rose in surprise.

"Charlie always liked me a lot more than I liked him. In a romantic way, I mean."

Funny, the way you remember things. Memories don't lie down flat like stripes on

107

a road or photos in an album. They pop up and flap around, like those Mexican jumping beans Uncle Ronnie brought me that time he went to Tijuana.

I wanted to tell Hope about meeting Joe, but instead, all of a sudden — *poof!* I'm viewing a mental film of the night of my first high school dance.

My mother is at the front door, wearing a ruby shirtwaist dress with her grandmother's pearls, and she's opening it for Charlie. Charlie is dressed in his father's best suit, his hair slicked back, and he's holding a white orchid corsage. I'm excited about the dance for lots of reasons. For one, I'm wearing a new dress — it's baby blue chiffon, with a full skirt, cap sleeves, and a lace sweetheart neckline that I'd had the dickens of a time sewing just right — and I can't wait to show it off. Secondly, I'm eager to see everyone's reaction to the "heavenly night" decorations I'd helped hang in the gym; and thirdly, I've never danced to a live band before, and Billy Bob and the Crooners are supposed to play.

But then I see Charlie in the living room, and he's looking at me in a way I'd never noticed before, and it hits me: he's thinking about the dance in entirely different terms than I am. He doesn't think I'm going with him just because he has his daddy's car and my mother doesn't like me out at night by myself and he always gives me a lift to group events and we're lifelong buddies; in his mind, this is a date — a real, honest-to-goodness, boy-and-girl date. My stomach does a cold, funny flip, like a fish trying to get free from a hook. The thought of being romantic with Charlie just, well . . . it makes me kind of squirm inside my skin. I don't think of him that way. Maybe I'm not ready for it. Maybe I just don't want to change the easygoing way we get along.

And then — *poof!* again.

I'm seven or eight years old, and Charlie and I are playing tag with a group of other kids on the school playground. When Charlie is "it," he always, always chases me. It annoys the dickens out of me, because I don't like being caught.

"You never chase me back," he complains.

"I used to, but you just turn around and make me 'it' again. And the other kids get mad because we're leaving them out and it's like only the two of us are playing."

"I like it that way," Charlie says.

And then — another *poof!*

We're four or five, and playing doctor. Charlie wants to listen to my heart. I unbutton my shirt, and he puts his ear on my chest. Even back then, when our chests look just the same, he's fascinated with mine. He wants to see under my skirt, and I might have let him, but my mother walks in, and . . . oh mercy, does she get into a dither!

I have to confess, I never felt any curiosity at all about Charlie's private parts. Junk, they call it now. Junk — what a hilariously terrible name for something they're all so proud of.

"Are you okay, Gran?"

I realized I'd closed my eyes. I opened them and saw a lovely, worried, young face. It took me a moment to remember: I was in the dining room with my granddaughter. "Yes, dear. I just got caught up in some memories." I smiled at her. "Where were we?"

"You were telling me about you and Granddad. I thought you two dated all through high school."

"Oh, we did. Although at first, I didn't

110

even realize we were dating. By the time it dawned on me that everyone thought we were a couple, well, we'd been together so long that no other boy even thought I was available."

"Did you like someone else?"

"No. This was a very small town, honey, and as the saying went, the pickin's were slim and none, and Slim had left town. The senior class at our school had only thirty-five students, and Charlie was the best of the bunch." I toyed with a silk-covered button on my old dress. "I tried to break up with him after graduation, but he wouldn't take no for an answer."

"What do you mean?"

"Well, the war was on. Like most boys in my class, Charlie enlisted right after graduation. Before he went off to basic training, I told him we should see other people."

"And?"

And nothing. "He didn't want to hear it." He'd cried, in fact. I'd never felt so bad about anything in my life.

The whole thing flickered in my mind's eye like a Technicolor movie, but I kept talking as the mental movie played.

We'd been sitting in his father's car — a 1939 Ford, red as a firecracker, with a gray interior — parked out at the lake. We ended every date that way, talking and necking at a place called Lover's Point.

Charlie's breath had been hot on my neck. His fingers moved from my back to my breast, but I shooed his hand away.

"It's okay, Addie," he'd murmured against my skin. "When I come back from the war, we'll get married." He reached for my breast again.

I pushed him away and pulled myself against the door. "I've told you over and over, Charlie. I don't want to get married." What I really meant was, I don't want to marry you. I don't know why he couldn't take the hint.

"You want to be an old maid?" he'd demanded.

How many times had we covered this same ground? "I want to be a photographer. I want to travel the world and make my mark on it."

"So work as a photographer while I'm gone. Then when I get back, we'll get married."

"No, Charlie. I've got other plans."

"Plans that don't include me?"

I didn't want to hurt him, but sometimes he was thick as a brick. I pulled at a loose thread on my sweater. "I just don't feel

112

about you the way you deserve to have a girl feel."

"That's only because you're such a good Christian. Once we're married and you know that everything is blessed by God, your conscience won't bother you, and you'll enjoy the kissing and touching and all."

I was pretty sure that a church ceremony and a ring on my finger wouldn't suddenly make me feel all quivery and excited to kiss him, the way other girls talked about kissing their boyfriends — or make me want to grope him the way he wanted to grope me. "Neither of us has ever dated anyone else. I think it's a good idea for us both to see other people."

His face had gotten all mottled. He'd been a pale boy, pale and slight. His lips looked kind of mushy when he pressed them hard together. His eyes had teared up, but behind the wateriness I glimpsed a flintlike hardness I'd never seen. "Who is it?" he asked.

I was too surprised to take him seriously. I laughed.

"This isn't funny." His voice was tight and low. "Is it Ted Riley? I've seen the way he looks at you."

Ted was a tall, thin, painfully shy boy with

glasses and an Adam's apple like a goiter. I couldn't remember him ever saying a word to me — or to any girl, for that matter. "Don't be ridiculous. You know there's no one else. But if I were to meet someone — and if you were to meet someone — well, I just think we should be free to date other people if the occasion arises." I tried to smile, but Charlie was blinking fast, trying so hard not to cry that it cut me to the quick. I tried to lighten the mood. "I hear those French girls are really something."

"Jesus!" Charlie never cursed or took the Lord's name in vain, so the word jolted me. So did the way his hand banged down on the steering wheel. "I don't want to see anyone else, Addie, and I don't want you to, either." He looked away, wiped his face with his knuckle, then turned back to me. "Say you'll wait for me. Promise me you'll wait."

I couldn't. But I had to promise him something. This was Charlie — my lifelong friend, my companion since we were both in diapers. I couldn't send him off to war crying with a broken heart. "I'll write. I promise I'll write."

"Every day?"

"You know I'm not that good about writing. I'll send a letter every week or two, though."

"Every week."

"Okay. Every week. Or at least every ten days."

"Every week. Promise?"

I blew out a sigh. "I promise."

"That's better." He put his arm around me. "And when I get back — well, by then, you'll be ready to settle down."

It did no good to argue with him. I looked down at my hands.

"You will," he insisted. His hand tightened on my upper arm. "You will. You'll see."

Jiminy! I just wanted him to give it a rest. "Maybe," I'd muttered.

"That's more like it." He tried to pull me in for a kiss, but I drew away.

"Come on, Addie. It's my last night. Let's seal it with a kiss," he said.

"I need to get home," I said. "You can kiss me good night in the driveway."

"So you wrote to him?"

Hope's voice made me open my eyes. I'd forgotten she was there. "Oh, yes. Just as I said I would." I also wrote to four other servicemen. It was part of the war effort, keeping up the morale of the boys. I used to write the same letter five times, copying it onto scented stationery. "They weren't really personal letters — just chitchat about the weather, the latest movie, the war effort at home, what was happening at my job . . . just general stuff."

"He was hurt in the war, wasn't he?" Hope said.

"Yes." My mood darkened. We were jumping ahead, getting to a part of the story I dreaded talking about. "Right after the holidays, he took shrapnel in the foot and lower leg."

"In England, right?"

"Well, it happened in France, but he was sent to a hospital in England, and they weren't sure he was going to make it."

"How awful!"

"Yes, it was. He had a fever. And back in those days, fever often meant gangrene. Penicillin wasn't available until later in the war. While he was in England, they thought they'd have to amputate his leg."

"Oh, Gran!"

"I felt so sorry for him, and for his family. His parents were terribly upset. But . . ." I sucked in a breath. It felt callous saying it, but I was on a mission to tell the truth. "It didn't jar me into a sudden realization that I couldn't live without him."

I fell silent for a moment. I was surprised to hear rain pattering on the roof. "I kept him in my prayers, of course. And I wrote him more frequently, trying to cheer him up, telling him I was praying for him, just generally trying to make him feel like he had someone rooting for him. I even knitted him a scarf. This happened just before I met Joe."

"Joe was the man you fell in love with?"

"Yes." Joe's face floated into my memory, his smile calling up one of my own.

"What was he like?"

"Oh my. He was . . ." The years were falling back now, peeling back like bedcovers, inviting me to climb right in. "He was really something."

Poof!

All of a sudden, it's 1943, and I'm in New Orleans. And this time I'm not just watching a film in my mind; this time I'm reliving it. I'm pretty sure I'm telling Hope about it, but I can't hear the words, because the memories are so crisp and clear, it feels like it's happening all over again.

8
ADELAIDE

APRIL 1943
NEW ORLEANS
It was cold that Friday night, a damp cold
that went right through you — which was a
little unusual, because it had been un-
naturally warm that April, although early
spring can be a fickle season in New Orleans. I'd worked all day in the darkroom at
the *Times-Picayune* — I'd gotten a job at
the newspaper three months after high
school graduation; thanks to the shortage of
men, they'd taken me on as a photographer's assistant — then dashed back to the
little house in the Irish Channel, where I
was staying with my friend Marge and her
aunt Lucille. Fridays were dance nights at
the USO.

I wore that green silk dress for the first
time. First-time wearings were special.
Heck, store-bought dresses were special! I'd
bought this one on sale at D. H. Holmes. I

talked the sales manager into marking it down even more than the sale price because it had a little rip under the arm right by the seam, so I got it for a song. I was handy with a needle, and all I had to do was take it in, which it needed anyway.

The dress rustled as I stepped into it. Marge zipped me up. "That dress fits you like a dream."

She was wearing a new dress, too — a red one that complemented her permed black hair and clung to her curvy figure like wax. The dress was so low cut as to be a little immodest. She wore a buttoned-up white sweater to make it past the USO door chaperone. We were running late because she'd wanted to style her hair like Barbara Stanwyck and had trouble getting the bangs just right.

"Tonight's our lucky night, I just know it," Marge said as we rode the streetcar down St. Charles. I knew what Marge meant by "lucky": we were both hoping to meet the love of our lives.

Marge was looking to marry and settle down, and I . . . well, I was looking for love like the movies portrayed — dramatic, exciting, adventurous. I wasn't against marriage — no girl wanted to be a spinster; that was a fate worse than death — but marriage was somewhere off in the distant future. I had a hazy, Hollywood-fueled vision of passionate kisses and a deep soul connection — something far more glamorous and thrilling than anything I'd shared with Charlie.

Romance aside, I was pretty much living my dream, residing in a city and working as a photographer. True, I spent most of my time in the darkroom, but the assignment editor had sent me out on a few stories when they were shorthanded, and I had high hopes that given just a little more time, I'd be out on the street every day. With a little luck, I'd build a portfolio that would lead to a job as a travel photographer, and when this darned war ended, I'd be off to see the world.

If there were still any world left to see, that is. It was a fearful time, I have to tell you — but I was young, and like all youth, I had an irrepressible streak of optimism. I was more afraid of having to go back to Wedding Tree than I was of the world ending.

It hadn't been easy, getting my parents to agree to let me come to New Orleans. They were both strict, tight-laced conservatives, and they thought a young woman should live with her parents until she married.

I'd worked on them in stages.

Stage One: I'd swanned around the house, looking bored and heartbroken, complaining bitterly about how there were no decent jobs in Wedding Tree.

Stage Two: I'd convinced them to let me take the train to New Orleans to visit my friend Marge from high school and her war widow aunt — both of whom worked at the Zatarain's cannery — for a long weekend.

Stage Three: While in New Orleans, I'd applied for a job at the *Times-Picayune.*

Stage Four: I'd come back talking about the fantastic job opportunities in the city, but complaining about how strict Marge's Aunt Lucille was (which was a total fabrication; Marge and I seemed invisible to Lucille).

Stage Five: When I was offered the job in New Orleans, I said I wanted to live at a boardinghouse — which prompted my parents to insist that I live with Marge at Lucille's.

Stage Six: Voilà — exactly what I wanted!

I'd been living there since August, paying a few bucks a week to share a room with Marge. We worked pretty long hours, and most evenings were spent on chores — washing and ironing clothes, cleaning house, grocery shopping, cooking, and tending our victory garden — not to mention shampoo-

121

ing, rolling, and drying our hair. Everything took longer then.

Like most folks at the time, Marge and I volunteered for the war effort. On Mondays we rolled bandages for the Red Cross, and on Fridays we worked at the local USO club, which was held at the recreation room of the Catholic church on Prytania Street. We were junior hostesses, which meant we helped serve refreshments and clean up afterward (or at least I did; more often than not, Marge was still flirting with one or more servicemen when the lights came up at midnight), but our main job was to entertain servicemen on leave or waiting to be shipped out. We were there to dance and talk and generally boost morale. Not exactly a hardship for two single young women.

We entered the church rec hall a few minutes before seven thirty.

"Marge, Addie. There you are." Mrs. Brunswick frowned as she bustled forward. A tall, stout matron with tight gray curls and a high-pitched voice that seemed incongruent with her size, she was both a senior hostess and in charge of the church's women's auxiliary, so she ran the show on all fronts. "You're late."

"The streetcar was running behind," Marge lied effortlessly.

"I was getting worried about you. Three of the other girls are out with colds."

"Well, we're here now. And there's nary a sniffle between the two of us," Marge said.

Mrs. Brunswick eyed her uncertainly. She was never sure if Marge was making fun of her or just being personable, as junior hostesses were encouraged to be. I was relieved when she turned away and waved her arms as if she were gathering butterflies in front of the refreshment table. "Girls, attention, please! Circle up. Is everyone wearing their name tags?"

The twenty or so other young women milling around the room wandered up.

"Who wants to work the refreshment table tonight?" Marge and I raised our hands, along with several other girls. "Margie, you and Tina can serve cake, please. And Addie, sweetheart, would you pour the punch? And please make sure no one spikes it."

"Of course," I said, although I had no idea how I was supposed to keep that from happening.

"Last time, some spirits found their way into the punch, and three of our girls got sick," Mrs. Brunswick said.

Marge's eyes widened in disingenuous shock. "How awful!"

I knew for a fact that Marge had let a

soldier from Georgia pour a bottle of hooch into the punch about an hour before the dance ended. A redhead also privy to this misdeed giggled and poked Marge, causing Mrs. Brunswick to give them a suspicious frown.

I tried to create a distraction. "Oh, what beautiful flowers!" I exclaimed, bending down to examine a vase of yellow tulips on the table between the punch and cake.

"Aren't they lovely?" Mrs. Brunswick smiled appreciatively. "Schmidt Florists donated them."

"They're just trying to cover up the fact they're Huns," sniffed a girl named Eloise.

The crease in Mrs. Brunswick's forehead deepened. It occurred to me that the name Brunswick sounded somewhat Germanic, as well. "They can't very well help their name, now, can they? They're a good American family, and I won't tolerate talk like that." She glanced at her wristwatch and clapped her hands. "All right, now — places, everyone."

Flora, a pale, nervous girl from an upper-crust New Orleans family, whom Marge had nicknamed Florid because she blushed so easily, took her place at the registration book. The other girls scattered around the room.

Mrs. Brunswick nodded to the two women at the front door. They opened it, and a stream of servicemen poured in.

The refreshment table was quickly swamped. During a lull in the action, Marge elbowed me.

"My, oh my, look what just walked in!"

There was no mistaking whom she meant. He was tall, probably six two or six three, with brown wavy hair, a movie-star handsome face, and an army officer's uniform. His most attractive attribute, though, wasn't physical; it was his bearing. There was something about the way he carried himself, something deliberate and steady and so self-assured that other men stepped out of his way. He wore the mantle of a leader, of someone accustomed to the respect of others, as surely as he wore a four-button army uniform. When he turned to the side, I could see the Army Air Force insignia on the upper sleeve.

Marge saw it, too. "Oooh, he's a flyboy!" she cooed. In Marge's mind — and mine, too, I admit — airmen were a special brand of wonderful. "I call dibs."

He looked around the room, and for a second, our eyes met. My skin felt hot.

"Seriously," Marge murmured. "He's mine."

I had always acquiesced to Marge's preferences, turning down offers to dance with men she liked. After all, I reasoned, she was my roommate, and chances were, we'd never see any of these men again. But this time was different. "I'm making no promises," I replied.

"But I saw him first!"

"Doesn't matter."

I watched him bend to sign the registration book. Marge and I weren't the only girls attracted to him. Flora's face turned hot pink as she handed him the pen. Two other girls quickly appeared at the registration table as if to help him. One of them — a big-chested brunette from the Seventh Ward, named Betty — leaned over the book directly in front of him, deliberately displaying her generous décolletage. He straightened and handed the pen to Betty, his gaze sweeping up to her face with admirable smoothness. He smiled at her, inclining his head to listen as she said something. I saw him respond, smile, then say something to Flora. Her blush spread to her neck. Her face was the color of a rooster's crown.

"He's coming this way!" Marge whispered, unbuttoning her sweater. She whipped it off in record time.

But he looked at me. His glance was a

physical thing; it warmed my skin like a lingering caress. My mouth went as dry as the inside of a Q-tip box. I tried to smile, but my lips pulled into the kind of unnatural curl that makes for bad photographs.

"Hello, Flyboy," Marge said as he approached. She had a breezy way of talking with the soldiers, which I envied. "New to the air base?"

"Actually, I'm just passing through. I'm here for a couple of weeks to learn the ins and outs of a new plane."

She fluttered her eyelashes. "Well, then, you'd better make the most of your time in New Orleans."

"I intend to." He looked at me again. I started to attempt another smile, then gave up and glanced down at the punch.

"Would you like some cake?" Marge pressed.

"Maybe later." His voice was deep. There was a throb in it — or maybe that was my own pulse, pounding in my ears. I risked a glance up, and found him still gazing at me. I nearly melted under the blaze of his smile. "What I'd really like is some of that punch."

I picked up the punch ladle. My brain was so fizzed by his smile that it couldn't send the proper signals to my hands. The ladle slipped through my fingers and crashed to the table, knocking over the vase of tulips.

His hand zoomed out and caught the vase before it tumbled to the floor — but the good deed came at a cost. Water splattered all over his uniform.

"Oh no!" I gasped. "Oh, dear. Oh, I'm so sorry!"

I was beyond sorry; I was mortified.

"No harm done." He set the vase upright. One of the tulips had fallen out and the others listed forward.

"Your uniform is soaking wet," I murmured.

"Here." Marge handed him a stack of napkins.

Mrs. Brunswick bustled over. "Good heavens, Addie," she scolded. "You must be more careful!"

"It was entirely my fault," the man said. "I was reaching for a napkin and I knocked the ladle out of her hand."

He'd done no such thing. It didn't seem right to let him take the blame, but then, I couldn't very well call him a liar — especially in front of Mrs. Brunswick. My face burned.

"I should have had a better grip on it," I stammered. Not to mention on my nerves.

He bent and quickly wiped the floor with the napkins. "There. Good as new." Picking up the fallen flower, he straightened and held out the tulip to me. "Please accept this, along with my apologies."

The flower wasn't his to give, but Mrs. Brunswick gave me a nod, indicating I should accept it. I smiled. "Thank you."

He tossed the napkins in the trash can against the wall. Satisfied that the situation was handled, Mrs. Brunswick moved away.

I twirled the tulip in my hand. "That was very chivalrous, taking the blame for me."

"Yeah," Marge chimed in.

It was as if Marge hadn't spoken — as if she weren't even around. I know it sounds corny, but it really felt like we were the only two people in the room.

"I'm afraid you've gotten water on your dress, as well."

I glanced down. Sure enough, water spots splotched my skirt.

"Well, there's only one solution for this," he said. "We'll have to dance together until we dry."

"Oh — I can't! I have to stay here and man the punch bowl for the first hour."

"I'll get you a replacement."

"What?"

He held up a finger. "Be right back."

A crowd of servicemen converged on the refreshment table, relieving me of the need to talk to Marge. As I ladled punch and handed it out, I caught glimpses of the airman heading to the registration table. Flora's face turned the color of an inflamed tonsil, and Betty put her hand on his arm. He said something to her and she laughed.

I lost sight of him for a few moments as I served three sailors. When I looked up again, the airman was talking to a chaperone at the door, Betty clinging to his arm.

A serviceman from Wyoming tried to start a conversation with me. When he finally left the table, a line had gathered behind him. Marge leaned over to me. "Looks like Buxom Betty stole the prize."

I followed her gaze. The tall airman was crossing the room, the curvy brunette clasping his arm. To my chagrin, they stopped in the punch line.

I handed out glasses to the sailors and soldiers ahead of them, my heart racing harder and harder, until they stood right in front of me. "Betty here has generously agreed to do me a favor," the airman said.

"Anything to help a serviceman," she said in a breathy voice.

"Anything?" Marge asked pointedly.

Betty didn't have the grace to blush or the wit to respond. She batted her eyes at the airman.

"Well, that's wonderful," he said, "because I'd like you to take Addie's spot serving punch."

Betty's face fell. "But . . . I . . ."

He put his hand in the small of her back and guided her around the table, then took the ladle from my hand and placed it in Betty's. "This is what I love about you southern girls," he said. "You're so polite and helpful and genteel. Not to mention lovely." He flashed Betty a smile that left her dazed and glassy-eyed.

He took my elbow and inclined his head toward the dance floor. "Shall we?"

Feeling dazed myself, I let him lead me through the crowd. His fingers were warm on my bare skin. My elbow had never felt so alive.

"That was shameful," I said.

"I think you mean shameless."

"It's shameful to be so shameless," I said.

He laughed as we reached the dance floor. The band was playing "I Remember You." He took my right hand, put his other hand on my back, and pulled me into a foxtrot. "Well, a man's got to do what a man's got to do."

The heat of him, the brightness of that smile, the scent of soap and faint aftershave and virile male made me slightly dizzy. "And what, exactly, do you have to do?"

"Get to know you." He spun me around. "I knew it from the moment I saw you."

I felt like I was still spinning even though the twirl had ended. "I'm disappointed," I said. "I thought you'd have more original material."

"That's not a line." He pulled me closer, smoothly moving me across the dance floor. "I mean it. And here's something that's going to sound even cornier: I feel like I already know you. As if I've seen you in my dreams."

"You're right. That *did* sound even cornier." But the funny thing was, I felt the same way. It was as if my soul had recognized him, as if a puzzle piece had just slipped into the right slot.

He guided me backward. "Seriously. Have you ever been in California?"

"No."

"Texas?"

"No."

"Is your picture on a billboard or a soup can or something?"

"No." I laughed at the outrageous question as he spun me around. "I tend to stay behind the camera, not in front of it."

"You're a photographer?"

"Yes. For the *Times-Picayune*." I felt so

132

proud, saying it.

"A newspaper woman? Like Katharine Hepburn in *Woman of the Year?*"

"Oh, exactly like that." I gave a dry smile. "Minus the wardrobe, the salary, the hairstylists, and the ability to dance in and out of the newsroom at will."

"Still, that's really something."

I was pleased that he thought so. "I love it, although right now I spend most of my time in the darkroom developing photos shot by more experienced photographers."

"You're far too pretty to be kept in a darkroom."

"No," I said, tilting my head up at him. "I'm far too good a photographer to be kept in a darkroom."

He laughed. "Maybe so, but you're also awfully pretty."

I felt my face heat.

"So what makes a good photographer?" he asked.

The music swelled around us. "Timing. Getting the moment right. Framing things. Lighting. Trying to see just what the camera will capture — although you never entirely do. It always surprises me how the lens can see things differently."

"It's like people." The music swelled. He guided me around the edge of the dance floor. "You can never be really sure that what you mean is what someone else understands. Everyone frames things in the context of their experience and according to their mood."

I looked up at him. It was not the kind of conversation I expected. I'd just met this man, and yet we'd jumped from getting-acquainted chitchat to really talking.

"It's interesting how we all move around in the same space, yet live in our own interior worlds," he said.

My interior universe seemed to have just collided with his. Our exterior universes were connecting pretty well, too. I was keenly aware of the warmth of his hand on my waist, the warmth of his fingers gripping my hand.

I tried to put the conversation back on familiar ground. "So what about you? What do you do?"

"I'm a pilot."

There must be a thousand different jobs in the Army Air Force, and most of them were on the ground — but somehow I'd known from the moment I first saw him that he was a pilot. "I've always wanted to fly. Is it as marvelous as I imagine?"

"What do you imagine?"

"Well — a sense of boundlessness, I suppose. Not freedom, exactly, because, after all, you're in the military and you're not able to steer wherever you want — but a sense of not being fettered by gravity."

I was afraid I'd gone too far — that I'd waxed too eloquent and that he'd laugh at me. But he didn't. He swung me about. "That's pretty much exactly it."

"The perspective of everything from the air — well, it must be amazing to look down and see the world so far below."

He nodded. "I never lose my sense of awe about it. You can see patterns in things — the farm fields, the roads, the forests cut by streams and rivers. It's beautiful. Even a junkyard is beautiful if you're high enough above it."

"It's like the plane is your camera lens."

"Never thought of it that way, but yeah." His thigh pushed against mine, causing a wave of heat to radiate up my leg. "Problem is, my camera drops bombs and gets shot at."

I was immediately chagrined. "I'm sorry. I didn't mean to imply that you're up there joyriding."

"You didn't. I just can't wait to fly under other circumstances."

"You plan to be a pilot after the war is over?"

"Oh, yeah. Absolutely. Commercial aviation will grow by leaps and bounds after the war."

"Oh, I can't wait! I'm dying to fly."

"I'd love to take you up."

The song ended. Before the last note had cleared the air, a sailor tapped him on the back. "Can I have this dance?" he asked.

"Afraid not." My partner kept his arm around me. "She's my fiancée."

Over his wide shoulder, I saw the sailor walk away.

"I'll get in trouble," I said, dropping my hand from his shoulder and stepping back. "I'm supposed to dance with everyone who asks."

He gave me a slow grin. "For all the chaperones know, he was just asking the time."

I put my hands on my hip. "What makes you so sure I *want* to keep dancing with you?"

"Don't you?"

Of course I did, but I cocked my head and pretended to consider it. "Well . . ."

The band started playing "Blues in the Night." He gave a low chortle and pulled me back into his arms.

"You're awfully smug, aren't you?" I said as we swayed to the music.

"No. I'm just awfully determined to keep

136

what I want once I find it."

I don't know if it was the words, or the feeling of his body against mine, but all of a sudden, I was covered in hot chill bumps. "You ought to at least feel a little remorse for lying to that sailor like that."

"Who says it was a lie?" He pulled me close as the music started. "Maybe it was just a premature truth."

I should have been put off by his brashness. I mean, who talks like that? But there was something about him. Something that made my insides melt like ice cream in July. "I don't even know your name," I said.

"Joe." He pulled me closer. "Joe Madison. Pleased to meet you, ma'am."

"Madison," I repeated. "Like the town in Wisconsin and the avenue in New York City?"

"That's right. Ever been either place?"

"No, but I'd love to. I'd love to see the whole world."

He smiled down at me. "Sounds like you've got a vagabond spirit."

"Absolutely."

"So where do you want to go first?"

"Well, I have a list, but I'm not particular about the order."

"Let's hear it."

"It's too long to remember in its entirety,

but let's see . . . San Francisco. New York. The Grand Canyon. And if the war ever stops, Europe. I'd especially love to see the Eiffel Tower, if it's still standing. And Egypt: I'd love to photograph the Sphinx and the pyramids. And India. I want to see the Taj Mahal. Oh, and a tropical island — I'd love to go to a tropical island." He spun me around the floor. "I want to be a travel photographer."

"Isn't that a man's job?"

"Who says it has to be? A woman can take photos just as well as a man."

"Don't you want to marry and settle down?"

"Why does everyone act like they have to be one and the same?"

His left eyebrow rose. His lips curved, but his smile lacked condescension. "You, apparently, have a different opinion?"

"Well, I think it would be grand to marry, to have a life partner and travel companion. But as for the settle-down part, I'd like to put that off awhile."

"You're a freethinker, Adelaide."

"Yes, I suppose I am."

"Very unconventional."

"Well, a lot of conventional things that women are supposed to do strike me as kind of silly."

"Such as?"

"Wearing white gloves, and acting like a weakling so men will feel big and strong and protective. Don't get me wrong — I don't mind being protected, when I need it. But I love being strong myself, and I don't think a real man would be intimidated by that." He whirled me around again, and I feared I'd said too much. "I suppose you think me unfeminine."

"Quite the opposite." His eyes were warm blue pools. "I think you're amazing. And I think it would be amazing to see the world with a woman like you."

I tamped down the thrill running through me. "You're laying it on a little thick there, Joe. Better save some of those suave lines for the next girl."

"What if there isn't a next girl?" He spun me in a turn.

"With a guy like you, there's always a next girl."

His hand tightened on my back, pulling me intoxicatingly close, so close that my chest touched his, and his thigh once again pressed against mine. "Not if I've found *the* girl."

9
ADELAIDE

Joe didn't leave my side the rest of the evening. Mrs. Brunswick shot me increasingly disapproving looks, and strode up when we finally took a break from the dance floor. "I'm sorry, Adelaide, but you need to mingle with the other servicemen."

Joe turned his considerable charm on the older woman, explaining that this was his first visit to the USO and the only dance he'd get to attend before he shipped overseas, and could she possibly find it in her heart to let him consolidate the time the other servicemen would get to spend with me over the course of a normal leave into just tonight?

"I can't believe the old bag made an exception to her own rules," Marge said hours later as we rode home in the nearly empty streetcar after the dance. We were seated across from each other on the hard wooden seats, and she'd been quizzing me about Joe ever since we'd escaped the chaperone who escorted us to the streetcar stop.

I told her some of the things he'd said, and she feigned a swoon. "Ooh, what a charmer!"

"Maybe a little too much of one," I replied.

"Well, I guess I'll have to forgive you for not honoring my dibs." She dug in her purse for a peppermint. "I think this is a case of love at first sight."

"You can't love someone you just met," I scoffed.

"Sure you can!"

"No. That's a myth."

"Well, myth or not, you have to admit you like him."

"Maybe." For some reason, I was hesitant to talk too much about him. Part of me longed to gush, but another part of me wanted to hold the memories close and just think about him in private. Everything that had transpired between us felt intensely intimate and oddly momentous.

"No 'maybe' about it. You've got a glow about you."

"I'm sure he's got girls glowing all over the place."

"He's a charmer, all right, but he really zeroed right in on you." She huffed out a sigh. "Maybe I should try pouring water all over someone."

The streetcar jangled to a stop. Marge's brown eyes widened. "Oh my goodness. Speak of the devil!"

I was facing away from the door, so I twisted around, and lo and behold, there was Joe, dropping coins in the box. My heart pattered hard as he strode down the aisle, smiling widely, and took off his hat.

I tried to act unruffled as he sat beside me. "Are you following me?"

He grinned. "I prefer to think of it as seeing two ladies safely home."

"How did you get to this stop so quickly?"

He hadn't left the church rec room more than five minutes before I did. I'd explained that the rules prohibited the junior hostesses from leaving with a man, and that he couldn't just wait for me on the street corner, because the chaperones kept a careful eye out for that sort of behavior. He'd hung around until the servicemen were asked to leave, and then managed to stay inside longer by charming Mrs. Brunswick into allowing him to help fold and stack chairs. Then he'd gotten my phone number and said good-bye, and I thought I'd seen the last of him for the evening.

"I grabbed a cab and asked to be dropped

off a couple of streetcar stops after the church."

"Who does a thing like that?" Marge said.

"A guy who really wants to see a girl again." He grinned. "Would you two like to go somewhere for a drink?"

"Sure!" Marge said.

I shot her a look. "It's late, and we really should be getting home."

"Well, then, I'll see you two ladies to your door."

And he did. He included Marge in the conversation. She flirted with him — I guess it's just in her nature; I don't think she can help herself — but he didn't flirt back. He told us that he was from Sacramento, that he'd lived with his sister and an aunt, and that he'd been studying engineering at Berkeley before he'd signed up.

Marge had the grace to duck into the house once we arrived, leaving me alone with Joe on the porch. "I only have a few more days in town, but I'd like to see you as much as I can before I leave."

All I could do was nod.

"Are you serious about wanting to fly?"

"Yes. Why?"

"I'm going to take you up."

"What?"

"I'm going to figure out a way to take you

143

for a flight. Are you game?"

"I —" I looked at him. He was proposing the biggest adventure of my life. "Yes. Absolutely!"

"You have to promise not to tell anyone."

"Not even Marge?"

"Only if you're one hundred percent sure she won't tell a soul until I've left town. Once I'm overseas, it won't matter. They need pilots so badly they won't care if I set the commissary on fire." He grinned. "Which, now that I think of it, might improve the food."

I laughed. "I'll keep it on the QT."

"All right, then. I'll be in touch."

He seemed to be serious! As thrilled as I was, I needed to get one thing straight. "I can keep my mouth shut, Joe, but I can't tell an outright lie."

"Very ethical of you."

"When I say 'can't,' I mean it literally. I'm a terrible liar."

"There'll be no need." He put his hands on either side of my face, and my heart felt as if it were going to burst through my dress. His thumbs caressed my cheeks. "You're really something, Addie."

I couldn't breathe. I thought he was going to kiss me, and I would have let him, even though we'd just met, and only loose girls

144

kissed on a first date back then — and this wasn't even a date.

But he just looked at me, looked straight into my eyes, in a way no one had ever looked at me before, as if he were really seeing me, seeing inside me, seeing my thoughts and feelings, seeing my very soul.

And then he dropped his hands. "Good night."

My voice wouldn't come out above a whisper. "Good night." I opened the door, my legs all weak and shaky.

"Addie?" he called softly.

I turned. His eyes were warm and luminous. His lips tipped up in a smile. "I'm really glad I met you."

10
HOPE

While she'd been talking, Gran had leaned back in her chair and gazed at the far wall. I'd sat there completely spellbound, feeling almost as if I were a watching a movie, more than a little stunned by this glimpse into my grandmother's youth.

Gran paused and closed her eyes. I wasn't sure if she was falling asleep or just gathering her thoughts.

"Wow, Gran — did he take you flying?" I asked softly.

She opened her eyes, her mouth curved in a small smile. "Yes. Oh yes."

"In what?"

"An air force bomber. A B-something."

This was so unlikely that for the first time since she'd started talking, I wondered if this had really happened. She was, after all, a very elderly woman who'd just had a serious brain injury. I decided to dig for more details. "A B-17?"

"I think it had a higher number. I — I don't really remember." She ran a hand across her forehead and closed her eyes again.

I leaned forward. "Are you feeling okay?"

"I'm afraid I'm getting a headache," she said.

"I'll check and see if it's time for your medicine."

I went into the kitchen and picked up the hospital discharge instructions from the counter. As I was reading them, the back door opened and Nadine bustled in, carrying an entire mint plant. "I had to go all the way to the plant nursery in Covington to find this," she grumbled, setting the plant on the windowsill.

I explained that Gran had a headache, and Nadine made a tsking sound. "It's no wonder. She's overdue for her medication, and she probably needs to lie down besides." She gave me an I'm-onto-you look. "If you'd let me take care of her instead of sending me off on ridiculous errands, I could keep her a lot more comfortable."

"She has some things she wants to tell me in private."

"I figured." Nadine went to the sink and washed her hands. "All you have to do, dear, is tell me you need some privacy. I can listen to an audio book — I have earphones and an iPod — and I can be in another part of the house doing laundry or cleaning the bathroom or otherwise making myself useful without hearing a word. The same goes for the aides on the other shifts."

"I'll tell her. Thank you."

"No problem." Nadine lifted one of Gran's medicine bottles. "She needs two of these."

I took the pills and a glass of water back into the dining room, gave them to Gran, and relayed the message.

"Hmph." Gran swallowed the meds. "Can't trust folks not to eavesdrop. Everything anyone says in Wedding Tree gets repeated all over town."

"Nadine's not from here. She lives in the country about twenty minutes away."

Gran closed her eyes for a moment, then opened them to look at the pile of boxes. "We haven't made much progress, have we?"

"Not a lot."

She lifted her hand and pointed to a large box in the corner marked "bed linens." "Well, I think everything in that can go. It's full of old tablecloths and towels and such."

"What do you want me to do with them?"

"Oh, honey — whatever you think is best."

She placed her hand on her forehead. "I think I need to lie down until this medicine kicks in."

I called for Nadine. She helped me get Gran settled in bed and brought an ice pack for her head.

I went back into the living room, opened the bed linens box and pulled out the contents. It was filled with yellowed sheets and tablecloths worn to near translucence and neatly patched. I ran my fingers over the hand-sewn stitches, probably the work of my great-grandmother. No wonder Gran had saved them; the care and frugality that had been lavished on these linens made my chest tighten. My job was to dispose of them, though; I was here to do what Gran hadn't been able to bring herself to do.

I'd contacted a couple of vintage stores back in Chicago, and they'd agreed to look at photos of anything I thought might be valuable. I'd also set up accounts on Craigslist and eBay, and I knew the addresses of local charities that took donations.

I decided to take the linens to the local animal shelter. As I emptied the box, I wondered what had happened to Joe and how Gran had ended up marrying my grandfather. I wondered if she'd really been up in a bomber, or if her mind was playing tricks on her.

All I knew for sure was that I couldn't wait for her to tell me more.

After lunch, Gran took another short nap, then a physical therapist showed up to work with her. Gran needed another rest after that. I sorted through some of my mother's old clothes in the guest room, then Nadine prepared a too-early-for-anyone-under-the-age-of-eighty dinner. The night-shift worker, a middle-aged woman named Hazel, arrived at six. I'd no sooner gone through Gran's schedule and shown her around the house than three ladies from Gran's Sunday school class dropped by for a visit. After greeting them, pouring iced tea, and chatting for a few moments, I excused myself and headed out for a run. Gran had been right; after a day being cooped up, I needed to get out of the house.

I saw Peggy heading out of Matt's house as I trotted down the porch steps. We both waved, then met halfway across the lawn.

"How are things going?" she asked.

I smiled. "We're off to a slow start sorting through Gran's belongings, but I'm hearing all kinds of fascinating stories."

"You ought to write them down."

I'd been thinking the same thing. I nodded.

Peggy hooked her thumb toward Matt's house. "I was just putting the girls' laundry away. They're at our house playing Wii with Griff. Matt was held up at work."

"What does he do?" I asked.

"He heads up the Public Protection Division of the Louisiana Justice Department. He investigates and prosecutes charges of pollution, consumer fraud, equal opportunity violations, and other things that affect the public welfare."

"Wow. Sounds like a big job."

"It is. Which makes being a single parent especially tough. I'm so glad he moved to Wedding Tree so we can help out."

"I'm sure the girls enjoy being near you."

"Yes, but a move is still a big adjustment. That's why I'm so excited about you doing a mural in their room. I'm afraid I sweetened the idea of moving here by promising that their room could look like a princesses' chamber. Do you have time to take a look at it now?"

"Sure." I was curious to see the inside of the house. It was a Georgian-style home, much larger than Gran's, with big white columns. An elderly woman had lived there when I was a kid, and Gran and I used to take her cookies and flowers. I remembered an overgrown lawn, faded floral wallpaper, and drape-dimmed windows. The place had struck me as dark and spooky.

Now it was anything but. Peggy opened the new beveled-glass door and led me into a wide, hardwood foyer. A large chandelier hung over the entryway. Sunlight poured in through the transom windows around the door and from the large windows in the dining room and living room. "Wow!" I looked around, taking in the fawn-colored walls. "This is gorgeous! I remember it as being kind of dark and run-down."

She nodded. "After Katrina, it was bought by a furniture store owner from New Orleans. He completely renovated it, then kept it in spotless condition. It was move-in ready when Matt bought it." She gestured toward the staircase. "The girls' room is on the second floor."

I moved toward the stairs, then Peggy's phone beeped. "Excuse me," she said, pulling it out of the pocket of her denim jacket. I admired the carving on the newel post while she had a brief conversation.

She clicked off and gave me a chagrined smile. "I'm sorry, but I have to go pick up Griff's heart medicine before the pharmacy closes."

"No problem. We can do this another time."

"No, no, dear — you go right ahead. Take a right at the top of the stairs. It's the first bedroom on the left — the one with the twin beds." She dropped the phone back in her pocket. "Take your time. And thank you so much!" She hurried out and pulled the door closed behind her.

It was weird, being in someone's home with no one there. This would never have happened in Chicago. But then, small-town life in southern Louisiana was completely different. With a shrug, I headed upstairs.

I found the girls' room easily enough. It was painted pink, and there were two twin beds with Disney princess comforters, two gold-trimmed white dressers with mirrors, a child-sized bookcase, and a tall antique bureau. The room had a large window with built-in plantation shutters that looked out to the front yard.

The walls were bare of artwork, but I noticed several framed photos on the bureau. I stepped closer. Every picture featured a beautiful blond woman — holding an infant, reading to a baby, sitting in front of a Christmas tree with Matt and two towheaded toddlers. My heart swelled with the magnitude of their loss. They'd been a picture-perfect family — the kind you'd see in a packaged picture frame. The girls were adorable, their mother as gorgeous as any model, and Matt . . . My stomach gave a funny little dip. Well, he wasn't hard on the eyes, either.

But I wasn't here to think about Matt. I was here to think about painting this room as if it were part of a castle. I forced my attention to the layout, took some snapshots with my phone, and started imagining what and where I could paint. Maybe I could put the girls' mother somewhere in the painting. The idea sparked a rush of creative excitement unlike anything I'd felt since college.

Inspired, I studied the photos on the bureau again. I needed to see more pictures of her, shot from different angles. Maybe there were more photos in other rooms. I headed out into the hall and toward the master bedroom. Through the open door, I could see a collection of frames on the long, mirrored bureau. Curious, I flipped on the light and walked inside.

The room was as plain as a vanilla wafer. The walls were bare and beige, and the tailored drapes exactly matched the walls. I guessed they'd come with the house and Matt had simply moved in. The furniture was simple yet elegant, a tasteful mix of new things and antiques — most likely the furniture he'd shared with his wife. The king bed was covered with a plain brown comforter, unbrightened by throw pillows or a colorful blanket. A lone lump against the headboard indicated the comforter covered a single pillow.

I walked over and picked up a silver frame on the bureau. It held a wedding picture, showing a glowing bride and a beaming Matt. My heart fluttered. Once again, I was struck by the stunning beauty of the couple. They looked like the figurines on top of a cake. Perfect. Just perfect. The kind of perfection that makes your chest ache.

It wasn't the bridal gown — which was fitted and strapless, breathtaking in its simplicity — or the woman's hair or flowers or even her flawless face and figure that made my throat thicken. It was the way Matt was looking at her. His gaze were so tender, so full of love . . . It was exactly the way every woman longed to have a man look at her.

"What are you doing in here?"

I jumped at the gruff male voice, nearly dropping the photo, and whipped around to see Matt standing in the doorway. He regarded me in exactly the way every woman does *not* want a man to look at her. Angry. Outraged. Suspicious.

"I, uh . . . Peggy, uh . . ."

He stood there, glaring.

". . . Peggy let me in," I managed.

"To go through my bedroom?"

"No." My face burned. I could feel it turning the color of a boiled beet. "I, uh, was looking at the girls' room to see about painting a mural."

"This isn't the girls' room."

"I — I know." Sweat broke out on my upper lip. "I saw it, and I looked at the pictures, and I thought your ex-wife looked so beautiful . . ." I ran out of words.

His scowl deepened. "First of all, she's not my *ex*-wife. We didn't divorce."

"I — I know. I meant your dead wife." I immediately realized how harsh that sounded. "No — late! Your *late* wife. Or — or your wife who's passed. Or . . ."

He slashed his hand through the air, cutting me off. His scowl was so dark it reminded me of those scary trees in *Snow White.* "Secondly, being let in the house doesn't give you the right to snoop through my belongings."

"I wasn't snooping!" But I was, and my shame knew no bounds. "I mean, I didn't open drawers or anything. I just wanted to see your pictures."

"So you just invited yourself in for a look around?" His glower deepened. "You just thought that would be okay?"

I slinked backward. "I, uh . . . didn't really think."

"You didn't think."

Oh fudpuckers. Hearing my own words come out of his mouth made me feel like a total moron.

"Do you usually have impulse control issues?"

"No. Not . . . not usually." He was being a jerk, but he had every right. I wanted to melt right through the floor in a puddle of mortification. "Look — I'm so, so sorry. I shouldn't have come in here. But the photos in the girls' room were so beautiful, and I was thinking I might be able to incorporate your . . . your . . ." Oh, God. Here I was again, faced with the same problem. "I mean, their *mother* in the painting, and I wanted to find a photo that showed her from different angles, and your bedroom door was open, and I saw the . . ."

The front door opened, then slammed. Excited girls' voices sounded below.

"I don't want the girls to find you here," Matt said in a dark, low voice.

"Okay." I stood stock-still, not knowing

157

exactly what he wanted me to do. Was there another staircase? Did he want me to hide in a closet? Bail out a second-story window? "Where . . . ?"

"Daddy!" called a child's voice from downstairs.

"Get out of here." His voice was a whispered growl.

"But they'll see me if I go downstairs."

"So don't." He looked at me as if I were a halfwit. "Just get the hell out of my *bedroom.*"

"Oh!" I set the photo down, accidentally tipping it over. I tried to right it and fumbled.

He snatched it from me. "For God's sake — go back to the girls' room. *Now!*"

I scampered out the door, nearly tripping over my own feet in the process, and flew down the hallway.

"Daddy, where are you?"

"Up here, girls!" His tone was completely different. He sounded easygoing, friendly — *nice.*

Multiple feet charged up the stairs like a tiny herd of rhinos. "I got news!" called a girl's voice.

"I can't wait to hear it." His voice held no trace of the snarl I'd received a moment earlier.

I stood in the pink bedroom, my heart pounding, and listened to the scamper of feet. I drew several deep breaths, trying to calm myself, feeling guilty as a burglar.

11
MATT

My reaction to finding Hope in my bedroom was all out of proportion. I knew it even as I was chewing her out, but I couldn't seem to dial it down. Seeing her standing there holding my wedding picture had hit some kind of primal button.

I don't need a shrink to tell me why: I'd fantasized about Hope while I was showering last night, and I felt guilty as hell about it. When I'd sought release since my wife's death, I used to conjure up memories of Christine, or think about some anonymous female body part. I hadn't fantasized about a specific, living person. Finding the woman I'd jacked off to the night before standing in my bedroom, holding a picture of Christine and me at our wedding . . . well, it just set me off. And I didn't want my daughters to come home and find us in my bedroom together, and to think . . .

I balled my fingers into fists so hard that

my fingernails dug into my palms. What the hell was I worried they would think? They were four and five years old, for Christ's sake! My own dirty mind was creating problems that didn't exist.

The girls clambered to the top of the stairs, wearing tutus over their leotards, their hair pulled back in ballerina buns. I pulled them both into a tight hug.

"What's your news?" I asked.

"I've got a new loose tooth!" Zoey stepped out of my embrace, opened her mouth, and wiggled an incisor.

I grinned. "Well, the tooth fairy needs to be put on notice."

"Hey — she's already here!" Sophie pointed down the hall.

I looked up to see Hope standing in the girls' bedroom doorway, her face a flaming shade of fuchsia.

She lifted her hand in a little wave. "Sorry to disappoint, but I'm really not the tooth fairy."

"So why are you here?" Zoey asked.

Damn good question. I decided to let Hope answer it herself.

"Your, um, grandmother asked me to come take a look at your bedroom and see about painting a mural."

Zoey cocked her head at a quizzical angle.

"What's a mural?"

"A painting on a wall. I understand you want your room to look like a castle."

"Yay!" Both girls jumped up and down and squealed.

"What's the cause for celebration?"

I turned to see Jillian standing at the top of the stairs, with Peggy behind her.

"Hope's gonna paint our bedroom like a castle!" Sophie announced.

Jillian's lips pulled tight. It was an expression Christine used to make — a mix of displeasure and worry. It was gone so fast I wondered if I'd imagined it, but it tapped into a reflexive, vestigial husband part of me that immediately dumped an I-need-to-fix-this rush of adrenaline into my bloodstream. The additional adrenaline only served to exacerbate my irritation, but now it focused on Jillian.

Damn it. Why did she always have to be around, with those ghostly little micro-expressions and Christine-like body parts and other creepy similarities to my wife?

"How lovely." Jillian was smiling at Hope, but the curve of her mouth looked forced. "But how will you find the time while caring for your grandmother?" Her tone was innocuous, but the implied judgment was hard to miss.

It wasn't lost on Hope, judging from the way she wrapped her arms around herself and stiffened. "Gran, uh, has home health aides around the clock."

"Adelaide volunteered her, and I talked Hope into accepting the job," Peggy said, coming up the final stair and joining us at the top of the landing. "Hope can't spend all of her time cooped up in that house or she'll go crazy."

"No one told me anything about it," Jillian said.

Because it's none of your business. The thought made me feel unkind and petty.

"Did you bring your paints?" Sophie asked.

Hope shook her head. "First I need to talk to you and find out exactly what you want. Then I'll draw a sketch, then I'll make any changes you want, and when everyone agrees, then we'll get started on the actual walls."

This induced another round of girlish jumping and squealing.

"Well." Jillian gave a tight smile. "I'll go start dinner."

"Thanks, but no need," I said. "I'm going to fire up the grill."

"Hamburgs?" Sophie asked eagerly.

"Yeah."

"Yay!" From Sophie's standpoint, it was shaping up to be a perfect evening.

"I can make a salad," Jillian said.

"Thanks, but I've got it covered."

Silence hung heavy in the air.

"Maybe Jillian can join us," Zoey said.

I swallowed. "I thought we'd have a quiet night with just the three of us."

"It can be quiet with Jillian, too," Zoey said.

Peggy turned to Jillian. "Dad and I were hoping you'd have dinner with us. We're going to Covington to Del Porto. You said you wanted to try the place."

Relief flooded through me. I sent her a silent thanks for the bailout.

"Sure," Jillian said. "Sounds lovely."

"Well, then, let's leave these folks in peace and let Hope talk to the girls about what they want."

Peggy hugged the girls, then kissed me on the cheek. Jillian followed suit. I tensed as she approached me. Had Jillian always kissed me hello and good-bye, or was this a new development? I wasn't sure. I only knew that lately I'd become uneasy with it, but I didn't know how to stop it.

I caught the scent of her perfume as she moved in. A band squeezed around my chest. Good God — she was wearing Clinique's "Happy," the same scent Christine used to wear.

I wasn't the only one who noticed, either. "You smell like Mommy," Zoey said.

Jillian patted her cheek. "Well, I'm the next best thing."

The answer made me irrationally angry. There was no next best thing. No one was like Christine — not even close. And the fact Jillian was trying just made me crazy.

I drew a deep breath and held it until she and Peggy had made their way down the stairs and out the door. I blew it out in a heavy sigh.

"You okay, Daddy?" Zoey asked.

"Sure." Zoey could be way too perceptive. I forced a smile and ruffled her hair. "I'm going to start the burgers. Why don't you and Sophie tell Hope what you want your room to look like?"

With that, I headed downstairs, drawing my first easy breath since arriving home.

12
HOPE

Zoey was the spitting image of Sophie, but taller, thinner, and much more solemn. She regarded me skeptically as she sank down on her bed. "Are you really an artist?"

It was a question I sometimes asked myself. "Well, I have a college degree in painting and design."

"I like to paint, too," she said.

"Really? That's great! You can help with the mural."

Her face lit up with a gap-toothed smile. "Cool!"

"Me, too!" Sophie said.

Zoey shook her head. "You're too small."

I tried to play peacemaker. "I'm sure we can find parts for both of you to paint."

Zoey looked doubtful. "She's really messy. We want it to look good."

"Oh, it will." I sat down beside her. "So tell me what you want."

Sophie climbed up on the bed with us. "A

castle with a moat and a drawbridge and a tower!"

"That's the outside," Zoey said. "Our room will be inside."

I was impressed with her understanding of perspective. "Maybe we can paint a big window, and it will look like we see the moat and drawbridge through it," I suggested.

"Yeah!" Sophie said.

Zoey's eyes brightened. "And a tower that's on the other side of the castle."

"Great idea. Do you have some paper so I can write this all down?"

Sophie brought me a pink piece of construction paper. I jotted down some notes. "What color should it be?"

"Pink!" they both exclaimed.

I grinned. "The inside or the outside?"

"Both," Sophie said.

Zoey looked thoughtful. "Yeah, but castles are made of stone, and stone isn't pink. It's white or gray or brown."

"I don't want brown." Sophie made an ick face.

"What if the outside is white, but a sunset is making it glow pink?" I suggested. "And what if a beautiful vine with pink flowers is growing up the side?"

"Yeah!" Sophie bounced on the bed.

Zoey nodded.

167

"Okay." I made another note. "We have a plan. Do you have any pictures that might help me?"

"I've got some castles in my coloring books," Sophie said.

"And we've got some real books with pictures, too." The girls dragged out a half dozen or more books from their bookcase, along with a couple of DVD covers. We sprawled together on the floor, a girl on either side of me, and they took turns pointing out what they liked most.

Their enthusiasm was contagious. Ideas bubbled in my mind, and I rapidly scribbled them on the construction paper.

"How's it going?" asked a masculine voice about thirty minutes later.

I looked up to see Matt standing in the doorway. To my relief, he'd lost his angry face.

Sophie jumped up. "Daddy, this is going to be so cool! She's gonna paint a tower and a window and a moat and a drawbridge!"

"Sounds like a lot. We'd better let Hope tell us how much she can do in the limited time she has."

I scrambled to my feet. "Don't worry. I won't start anything I can't finish."

"I didn't mean to suggest you would."

168

That was pretty much exactly what he was suggesting, but I decided to let it go. "I'll sketch out a few ideas, and bring them over tomorrow. Then the girls can tell me what they like and what they want to change, and we'll go from there."

"Hey — want to see my princess dress?" Sophie asked.

"Sure."

She ran across the hall to another bedroom and returned with a yellow Belle ball gown.

"I have one, too," Zoey said. "Plus I have a princess gown dress my mom made, but I'm too big to wear it now."

"I'd love to see it," I said.

Matt cleared his throat. "Peggy has it. She's getting it professionally preserved."

"How nice." And how sad, I thought. Were memories ever just one or the other?

"Here's a picture of our mom." Sophie pointed to one of the framed photos on the dresser.

"She's very beautiful." I sheepishly glanced up at Matt. "I was admiring photos of her before you got home."

"We're gonna look just like her when we grow up, because she looked just like us when she was our age," Sophie said authoritatively.

"Yeah," Zoey confirmed. "My gramma has a photo of Mommy that was taken when she was my age."

"Actually, Hope's grandmother took that photo," Matt said.

I turned to him. "Really? I didn't know Peggy and Griff had lived in Wedding Tree that long."

"They had a home on the other side of town when Christine and Jillian were growing up, then they moved to Houston for Griff's job. They moved to their current house when he retired a few years ago."

"And Jillian?"

He shifted his stance, as if the question made him uncomfortable. I wondered what the situation was between them. "She got a job at the local middle school when they moved here. She has her own place about a mile away."

"I can understand why they'd all want to move here. I spent every summer in Wedding Tree when I was a kid, and it's a great town."

"Did you know the people who used to lived in this house?" Sophie asked.

"When I was your age, it was an elderly lady."

"Did she give you cookies like Mizz Mc-Cauley?"

"No, but Gran and I used to take cookies to her. The house was much different back then. It's far lighter and brighter and more beautiful now. I always wondered what the upstairs looked like."

"I'll show you the rest of it!" Sophie pointed down the hall. "Daddy's room is that way, an' next to it is a sittin' room."

"I, uh, saw those when I came upstairs." I was keenly aware of Matt watching the proceedings from the hallway. "Let's not intrude on his private space."

"Okay." She grabbed my hand and pulled me into a Jack-and-Jill bathroom. "This is our bathroom. The first sink is mine." She opened a door and led me into another pink room. "This is supposed to be my room, but Zoey and I decided to share."

"We've shared a room ever since Mommy died," Zoey said. "I didn't want to be alone, and Daddy said I couldn't share his bed."

Matt ran a hand across his jaw, looking uneasy.

Sophie pulled me across the hall into a room with a sofa, a desk with a computer, and toys scattered on the thick rug. Zoey followed. "This is our playroom. And next to that is another bathroom, and then there's Jillian's room," Zoey announced.

Matt cleared his throat again. "It's actually the guest room."

"Yeah, but Jillian's the only guest."

"That's only happened a couple of times when I had to be away overnight and your grandparents were busy," Matt said.

Was he trying to clarify the nature of Jillian's sleepovers for the girls' sake, or for mine? What was the real nature of their relationship? I'd picked up a territorial vibe from Jillian earlier. "It's got to be convenient, having family so close by."

He nodded. "That's why we moved here." He suddenly looked ill at ease, as if he'd said too much. He thumped on the doorframe. "Well, I'd better go check the burgers."

"Do you want to stay for dinner?" Sophie asked.

"She's not invited," Zoey said flatly.

Matt raised his eyebrows and opened his mouth, but Zoey continued before he could get a word in edgewise. "You wouldn't let Jillian stay. You said you wanted a night with just the three of us. So she can't stay, either."

I quickly lifted both of my hands. "Actually, I've already eaten. Gran's on the senior dining plan, which means dinner is served at five o'clock sharp. And speaking of time . . ." I made a show of looking at my watch. I wasn't wearing one, so I had to pull my phone out of the pocket of my running shorts to look at the time. "I'd better get going so I can get started on the sketches."

I said good-bye to the girls and headed down the stairs. Matt followed me into the foyer. I was about to open the door, but Matt reached around and opened it for me. He wasn't touching me, but I could feel the heat of his body as I turned toward him. Or maybe not; maybe the heat was coming from me. All I knew was that the air between us suddenly felt a whole lot warmer.

I paused. "Look — I'm really sorry about earlier. I had no business looking at your pictures."

He raised his shoulders. "No harm, no foul. I overreacted."

Up close, he was more attractive than ever — and I was close enough to see the lighter blue facets around his pupils. He smelled of starch and soap and testosterone. My stomach fluttered. I gave a nervous grin. "Well, from now on, I promise to stay out of your bedroom."

The minute the words left my mouth, I realized how they sounded. My cheeks flamed.

The corners of his eyes tensed. For a long, hot moment, I couldn't breathe, I couldn't think, I couldn't move. I just looked at him, trapped in a bubble of thought-erasing heat.

His gaze shifted to my mouth, then back to my eyes. He smiled. "I've got about a dozen clever rejoinders swirling around in my head, but I'd better not say any of them."

I couldn't think of a single response to save my life. My face on fire, I muttered a fast "good night" and ducked out the door.

13
ADELAIDE

I must have dozed off in my favorite living room chair — a green wingback with birds embroidered on the fabric — because I awakened to the sound of the kitchen door closing. The hearing loss I'd acquired over the last few decades made it difficult for me to tell what direction noises were coming from, but I recognized it by its sound; the kitchen door made an alto thud, as opposed to the softer soprano clunk of the front one. How many times had I heard those doors close?

Must be a million. The first time was as a new bride, when Charlie had brought me to see the home he'd found for us, so proud that the buttons had practically burst off his vest. They'd swung open and closed about a thousand times a day when Becky was a child; she was always coming and going, and she closed doors hard — the way she did everything. Eddie always shut doors softly, as if he didn't want to call any attention to himself. My parents had sashayed in and out of them without knocking, as long as they were alive and mobile.

And then there was Charlie. At first I never heard the door close, because he would call my name the moment he walked in. In later years, his arrivals and departures were marked by angry slams that resonated in the pit of my stomach.

Funny thing about doors, you don't really notice them when you're the one doing the opening and closing. It's only when they herald someone else's comings and goings that you give them any thought. You can cross over major thresholds in your life and not even realize it until years later.

"Don't go getting all maudlin, Adelaide," said my mother, her voice as clear as any closing door.

I looked at the ceiling, but I didn't see her. I wasn't sure if I'd heard the words with my ears or only in my mind.

"Time's a-wasting. Hope is home, and you need to get on with it." Her voice held that imperative tone that used to mean "step lively, child, or I'll get the switch." I wasn't sure if I were being haunted or going crazy, but I knew better than to go against my mother when she got that tone. I reached

176

for my walker and hobbled to the kitchen.

Sure enough, there was Hope, putting on the teakettle. A sturdy-looking woman sat at the kitchen table, wearing one of those loose-fitting medical outfits — struts? spuds? — I never could remember the name of those clothes. I couldn't remember the name of the woman, either, although I knew I'd seen her before.

"Mrs. McCauley!" She jumped to her feet. "Are you ready to go to bed?"

Why on earth would she ask such a ridiculous question? "No, of course not. I want to talk to my granddaughter. In private, if you don't mind."

"Oh." The woman looked nonplussed. "Well, then . . . What . . . Where should I . . ."

"You can watch television in the living room, if you like," Hope suggested. "Gran and I can talk in here."

Hope helped me into a chair as the woman left the room. I heard the television blare. Hope closed the door between the two rooms. "Would you like some tea?"

"Please." I watched her move to the stove.

"Chamomile or Sleepytime?"

It must be evening. I looked out the window and was surprised to see it was dark. Belatedly, I understood why that woman wanted to put me to bed. Time was a muddle in my mind. I glanced at Hope's feet and saw she was wearing sneakers instead of running around barefoot as she usually did in the house. "You've been out," I said.

Hope nodded as she filled the kettle at the sink. "I planned to go for a run, but I ended up next door talking to the neighbors about the mural you volunteered me to paint."

"Oh. Good." I remembered nothing about a neighbor or a painting project, but I hated appearing stupid almost as much as I hated not being able to hold a thought in my head. "How did it go?"

"Fine. I think I'm actually going to enjoy it."

I wasn't sure what neighbor she was talking about. Actually, at the moment I couldn't remember who any of my neighbors were. "Well, wonderful."

She sat down across from me. "When we last talked, you were about to tell me about going up in an airplane with an air force pilot."

"Oh yes." I closed my eyes. The next thing I knew, images were flickering on the inside of my eyelids, slowly at first, then faster, as if they were happening all over again. I heard myself telling Hope about it, but the

178

words seemed to be coming from somewhere else, like a news reporter explaining
the newsreels they used to show at the movies.

1943

It was a Monday night. I remember because
I'd taken photos for the society column
about a group called the Monday Mavens,
so I came home late.

Marge was already asleep in her twin bed
in the room we shared, which was unusual.
The hot water bottle on her pillow told me
she'd probably had one of her migraine
headaches, which meant she'd taken some
of Aunt Lucille's medicine that knocked her
out. I quietly put up my hair — I always
pinned it in a bun on top of my head at
night, which would leave it curly for the next
day — and crawled into my narrow bed,
under a fraying blue quilt. I was adjusting
the pillow under my head when I heard
something softly hit the bedroom window.

At first I thought it was a bug, but it happened again — and yet again. Whatever it
was made a definite pinging sound —
harder than a bug, and strangely rhythmic.
A bird, perhaps? My grandmother had once
told me about a cardinal that kept flying
into her window, thinking that its own

reflection was another bird that he needed to fight off. It was dark, though, and most birds didn't fly at night — except maybe owls, and an owl would have made a bigger ruckus.

I headed to the window, pulled aside the cherry-printed curtain, and peered outside.

There, standing in a pool of light from the lamppost on the corner, was Joe — wearing what looked like a flight suit. My heart drummed hard and fast. I'd thought of him often in the two days since the dance. He hadn't called, and I'd begun to think that he'd just been blowing smoke about seeing me again.

I pulled up the window sash. "What on earth are you doing?" I softly called.

"I came to take you flying. Dress warm and come down."

I hesitated. I wasn't the kind of girl who sneaked out at night to meet men. I knew about those girls — fast girls, loose girls, girls who got in trouble and shamed their families. I could only imagine my mother and father's reaction to such behavior.

But to go flying! It was the adventure of a lifetime — beyond the scope of my family's imagination. It was exactly the sort of adventure I longed for. How could I say no?

I couldn't. I wouldn't!

"I'll be right down." I threw on a sweater, a wool skirt, and my thickest socks and oxfords. I grabbed a cardigan, then pulled the bobby pins out of my hair, leaving them scattered on the dressing table. I ran my fingers through my hair and started to reach for my lipstick.

No. I wasn't going on an assignation. I was going flying. I grabbed a scarf and my Kodak 35, then sneaked out the back door.

"Hello, there." He kissed my cheek — just a quick peck, nothing sexual, but it was an uncommon thing for a man to do back then. The nearness filled my senses with him — his height as he bent down, the scruff of his five-o'clock shadow, the softness of his lips, the scent of leather and wind and faint shaving cream. A thrill chased through me.

"What have you got there?" he asked, looking at my hand.

"My camera."

"Sorry, Addie girl. No photos allowed."

"But . . ."

"No photos. No evidence this ever happened. Can't put my cohorts in danger."

I wasn't the only one with something to lose if I were caught, I realized. Sneaking a civilian — especially a woman — aboard a B-24 was probably grounds for a court martial. "Okay."

He took it from me, then put his hand in the small of my back. "We need to hurry."

He hustled me to a panel truck parked on the street near a streetlamp and tapped on the passenger-side window. A man wearing a gray jacket embroidered with the words *Benson's Produce* rolled it down. "This is Carl," Joe said. "He's my bombardier. And Kevin is driving."

The two men nodded at me. The driver tipped his hat. He was wearing a Benson's Produce jacket, as well.

Joe handed the camera to Carl. "Stash this and give it back to her at the end of the evening, okay?"

He nodded. "Sure thing."

Joe tugged my arm and led me to the back of the truck, where he opened the double doors. Inside I could dimly make out crates of tomatoes, cartons of fruit, and barrels of potatoes. "I've got a space carved out for you." He made a stirrup with his hands and boosted me into the dark interior.

My throat tightened with second thoughts as he hoisted himself up behind me. What was I doing, crawling into the back of a dark truck with a man I didn't really know? What if this was some kind of ominous setup? I hoped he didn't think . . .

Joe turned on a flashlight. "You can sit

right here." He indicated an overturned wooden carton hidden between a high stack of crated tomatoes and squash. "I'll be on the other side."

Relieved, I sat down where he indicated.

"When we get close, you'll have to get on the floor, and I'll arrange the crates around and over you to hide you." He sat on the truck bed behind barrels of potatoes. "This truck delivers to the commissary just about every night, so hopefully they won't check the back, but we have to be ready just in case."

"What'll happen if we're caught?"

"We won't be."

"But if we are?"

"We won't be, so don't worry about it."

Easier said than done. My heart thudded hard.

Maybe he heard it from across the truck. "Having second thoughts?"

I was, of course — I was terrified. But I was tired of waiting for my life to begin — tired of waiting for a big break at work, for a chance to travel, for the war to be over. I wanted a big life, a life full of adventure, the kind of life I'd seen in the movies. Having a big life meant taking big risks. "No," I said with more confidence than I felt.

"All right, then." He knocked on the front

wall of the truck cab. The engine roared to life, so loud that further conversation was impossible.

The truck swayed. The crates shifted. The ride probably only lasted thirty or forty minutes, but it felt like it went on all night. I don't usually get carsick, but the fried chicken I'd had for dinner churned queasily in my stomach.

At last a rap sounded from the cab wall. Joe turned on his flashlight and lurched across the truck. "We're nearing the base." He motioned for me to lie on the floor and arranged the crates around me, stacking two long crates over me, about three inches over my head. My face was close to a bag of onions, and the pungent, earthy scent heightened the sense of being buried alive.

Joe quickly returned to his hiding spot, adjusted a barrel of potatoes, and pulled a crate of celery over his head. Through the cracks between the boards, I saw him put his finger against his lips. I nodded, my mouth dry. He turned off the flashlight, plunging us again into blackness.

The truck slowed, then stopped. I guessed we were at the check-point to the base.

"Howdy, Tex," I heard Kevin say.

"Howdy, yourself," came the twang-tinged reply. "What y'all got tonight?"

"Same old turnips and shit. Hey, you ever get to that jazz club I told you about?"

"Not yet. Is it the kinda place you take a girl or meet one?"

"Both."

"Maybe I'll check it out this weekend."

"You won't be sorry," Kevin said.

"Is the back unlocked?"

"Yeah. But there's no need to look in there."

"Rules are rules, man."

I heard footsteps, then the back door opened. Light poured in. I shut my eyes and held my breath, certain the guard could hear my pulse pound.

The floor of the truck dipped and groaned. Oh God! He was climbing in. Every fiber of my body tightened like overstretched bridge cable, ready to snap. The truck shifted as the footsteps drew closer. Even with my eyes clenched, I could tell a flashlight was shining on me — I saw red inside my eyelids. The crate on top of me moved, pulling my hair. I thought I was going to pee myself.

"Hey, you were holding out on me!" yelled the guard.

My mother's face flashed before my closed eyes. Oh, my Lord — she would die of shame. And then, miraculously, the foot-

185

steps receded and the van door slammed shut.

I heard the soldier walk back around to the front of the truck. "What's the big idea?"

"What do you mean?" asked Kevin. His voice was thick, as if he'd just swallowed pudding.

"Didn't tell me there were apples." I heard a loud crunch.

"Yeah, well, I didn't need to. Figured you'd just help yourself."

"A man needs sustenance to stay up all night, keeping Nazis off the base." A thump sounded, as if he'd slapped the side of the truck. "Y'all have a good evening!"

The truck jerked forward. I took a breath — the first one I'd drawn in a while. As we rattled down the road, Joe turned on his flashlight. Through the cracks, he gave me a thumbs-up sign. I grinned, almost giddy with relief. He put his finger to his mouth, signaling the need to remain quiet.

At length, the truck stopped and Joe turned his flashlight off. I tensed once again as the back door opened. "All clear," Kevin said.

Joe sprang from his hiding spot and rapidly crossed the truck, lifting the crates off my head.

"You okay?"

"Yeah." I took his hand and let him pull me to my feet. My legs were like rubber. Through the open truck door, I could see that we were inside a large, barrel-roofed hangar. "Addie had a bad scare," Joe announced. "I shouldn't have put those apples on top of her head."

"Oh, man." Carl grinned at me.

"What you really shouldn't have done was put the onions so close to my nose," I said, making a face.

The men laughed.

"See why I'm crazy about her?" Joe grinned down at me in a way that made the scare completely worth it, then turned as a short man wearing army green mechanic's overalls approached the truck door. "Hi there, Ace. Got her gear?"

"Right here." The man stepped forward and handed Joe a large duffel bag.

Joe pulled out a thick blue jumpsuit and passed it to me.

"What's this?" I asked.

"A blue bunny. It's heated, and you'll be glad you're wearing it once we get airborne."

Joe reached back in the bag and extracted some thickly lined boots and a thing that looked like a swim cap. "Put these on, too. And tuck your hair under the cap."

Joe hopped out of the truck and left me to

change, closing the door enough to give me privacy, but not so much that was I completely in the dark. It was difficult pulling on the jumpsuit over my skirt, but I was determined not to take it off, so I ended up wadding it around my waist, which made it look as if I were wearing an inner tube. I left both sweaters on under the jumpsuit, and did my best with the rubber cap.

I pulled on the boots, but I could barely walk in them, they were so big.

Joe grinned when I waddled to the doorway at the back of the truck and pushed it open. "You look like Humpty-Dumpty wearing clown shoes. Sit here in the doorway and I'll fix your boots."

I did as he asked. He knelt before me and tightened the laces, winding them around my ankle. His large hands were surprisingly agile and gentle. His light brown hair was thick and sun-streaked, with a counterclockwise swirl at the crown. When he finished, he rested his hand around my ankle for a second — a little ankle hug, as tender as any mother with a child, then smiled up at me.

When my eyes met his, I felt a silent little click — probably like a safecracker feels when he gets the combination just right. It was like an invisible door unexpectedly swung open, and without even thinking about it, I walked right through. Something about the sight of that big man messing with my shoes, going to all of this trouble to make a dream of mine come true — well, I fell for him. Fell hard. And he hadn't even properly kissed me yet.

"Give them a try now."

I jumped down from the truck and lifted first one foot, then the other. "Good as gold."

"Great." He held out a leather flight jacket. "Now put this on." I slipped my arms into the too-large jacket. He put a hat with earflaps on my head, on top of the head-hugging cap I was already wearing, then turned me around. There were five men with us in the hangar — Kevin, who was still in the driver's seat of the produce truck; the mechanic who'd brought my clothes; a ruddy, auburn-haired man dressed like Joe; a private in uniform; and Carl, who was standing there wearing a jumpsuit just like mine.

"What do you think?" Joe asked. "Will she pass for Rodeo?"

The mechanic gave a doubtful frown. "She's awful short, even for him."

"Yeah." Joe eyed me appraisingly. "Better take her out on a supply truck."

189

"I've got a driver right here." The red-headed man clapped the thin shoulder of the private. "If we're stopped, what's our story?"

"You're replacing a broken gun mount," Joe said.

"Good thinking." He gave me a gap-toothed grin and hooked a thumb at Joe. "Better watch this guy. He's too clever by half."

"So I'm learning." I held out my hand. "I'm Adelaide."

"I know. Joe's told us all about you."

What could Joe have said? We barely knew each other.

"I'm Ted, his radio operator."

"Nice to meet you," I said.

"Likewise. Come on, I'll drive you out to the plane."

"Put her in the tailgunner's seat," Joe called.

I turned around. "I can't sit with you?"

"Sorry. Only room for the pilot and copilot in the cockpit." He paused and looked at me. "Are you okay with this? I don't want to force you into anything you're too scared to do."

The words were like a gauntlet. Having them thrown out there only solidified my decision — which, I realized later, was exactly what Joe meant to do.

I tilted up my chin. "If I don't do things that scare me a little, I won't have much of a life, will I?"

"I love the way you think, Addie girl." Joe's gaze warmed me from the inside out. He turned to Ted. "Better put her under the tarp. There's not a chance in hell she'd pass as a guy."

Ted and the private helped me into the back of a Jeep truck. For the second time that night, I sprawled on my belly — this time next to a spare tire. They fastened a tarp over me and I lay there, inhaling the scent of rubber, moldy canvas, and exhaust, as the Jeep jerked forward. After a few moments, the truck abruptly stopped.

Figuring we were at the plane, I was debating whether to try to unfasten the canvas tarp on my own or wait for assistance, when I heard two doors slam on another vehicle.

"Where are you two going?" said a deep voice.

I froze, my muscles quiver-tight.

"To the Queen of New Orleans, sir," the private said.

"We need to remove a loose gun mount," I heard Ted add.

"Oh, that's right. The Queen is taking a

rookie crew on a night spin," another man said.

"All right," said the first voice. "Carry on, soldiers."

"Yes, sir. Good evening, sirs."

The truck lurched forward again. The next time it stopped, I lay still even after the engine died and I heard both doors slam shut.

Ted lifted the tarp. "All clear," he said. "We're on the side of the plane away from the tower, but we still better hurry."

I scurried out of the truck bed and followed him to a small hatch at the front of the plane. He boosted me in, swung in himself, then led me down a long, narrow aluminum catwalk over a cavernous opening in the middle of the plane.

"What's this?" I asked.

"The bomb bay. You're going to sit in the very back."

I followed him down the precariously skinny walkway. At the back of the plane, he motioned to a seat surrounded by Plexiglas windows, facing backward. "Here's your seat."

I hesitated. "Do I need to put on a parachute?"

"Do you know how to use one?"

"No."

He gave me a crooked grin. "Well, then, it won't do you any good."

I swallowed as I sank into the seat. My mouth felt as if it had been swabbed out with cotton, then packed with sand.

"Here's something you will need, though — the plug-in for your flight suit." He pointed to an electric socket and handed me the cord of my flight suit. "Plug it in when you start to get cold. You'll need your oxygen mask, too, if we get above much above ten thousand feet." He handed it to me and showed me how to put it on and how to turn on the tank.

"How will I know when to use it?"

"I'll come tell you. But once we're airborne, you can go ahead and put it on if you start feeling light-headed."

I wondered if I could just put it on now. When I'd agreed to this adventure, I'd known I was in danger of being arrested and killed by my mother if I were caught. I also knew there was a possibility of dying in a plane crash, but I hadn't realized I would also be at risk of freezing to death or being starved of oxygen.

I must have looked as scared as I felt, because Ted grinned at me. "Hey — don't worry. Joe's the best pilot around, and he won't let this young pup get too far out of

193

line before he brings him to heel."

My anxiety ratcheted up a notch. "Joe won't be piloting?"

"He's training someone. But relax — Joe will be in complete control. He always is."

In the next twenty minutes or so, my apprehension grew to stark terror. I was sweating in the flight suit and wasn't sure if it was because of the heavy clothing or fear.

I heard other men board the plane, and I thought Joe would come back and reassure me before we took off, but he didn't. I guess he couldn't. As far as I know, the kid he was training wasn't even aware I was aboard.

Someone handed me an ear set, and when the engine started, I was glad my ears were covered. The roar was like standing by the tracks when a train raced by, only twenty times louder. My stomach dipped as the plane began to move. I stared out the window as we lumbered down the runway, gaining momentum. We were going fast, then faster still — fast as a train. I saw the lights of buildings rush by as we raced on and on. I was beginning to think we were too heavy to lift off — how could something so large and heavy ever get off the ground? Oh dear God — we were going to plunge into Lake Pontchartrain! I closed my eyes and prayed, and then my stomach seemed to hit the back of my spine.

When I opened my eyes, I realized the floor was no longer level. We were going up! I peered out the window. Sure enough, the land was falling away, the view looking more and more like it did on the D. H. Holmes escalator — slanting away below me. The lights on the land were getting further and further away.

"We're flying!" I yelled. There was no one around to hear me — the radio operator, navigator, engineer, pilot, and copilot were all at the front, and the engine was so loud that words would have been impossible to understand — but I was airborne, and Joe was the reason.

The next hour passed in an adrenaline high. We flew over the city, and then over a black void that I guessed was either swamp or Lake Pontchartrain. The full moon and the stars above were the only way I could tell we weren't just sitting in an airplane hangar — that, and the bumping, rocking, and vibrating.

I felt a tap on my shoulder and turned around. Ted motioned for me to put on the oxygen mask. I nodded and complied, my stomach a knot of nerves, but after the first few pulls of air, I realized all was well. Ted returned to his seat somewhere in the front of the plane.

We flew over some lights again. I lost all track of time, but at length I saw a streak of light in the distance. My fingers itched for a camera. Dawn was breaking. As night faded, the view grew more miraculous. We were floating over clouds! They were beneath us, and above us was sky. A second later, the clouds thinned, and I could see water. We were over Lake Pontchartrain. We flew back over land again — I think it was New Orleans, but it might have been Slidell — and then, after a while, I saw the river. The mighty Mississippi curved through the land just like on a map. The houses and buildings all looked like toys.

It was jarring, how clearly everything was laid out — how the streets and blocks and crops were all so clearly divided and platted. This must be how God sees the world, I thought. I couldn't begin to imagine how he could know everything that was happening in every house, in every car, in every person's mind — and this was just one city in one state in one country on one planet! All those other stars and planets out there — and he knew what was happening there, too.

As the sky lightened, the plane slanted

downward. Everything grew larger. My ears popped as the engines roared louder. The ground rushed up at me, and as it got nearer, I closed my eyes, my stomach tight with terror. I felt a bump and a bounce, then another, and then . . .

We were on the ground. The plane raced like a locomotive, causing me to fear, once again, that we would run into the lake. Just when I was certain something was terribly wrong with the brakes, the plane slowed, and then slowed some more. At length it turned and headed back to the buildings. It stopped on the tarmac, about a hundred yards from a hangar. A moment later, the engines quit. The silence was nearly as deafening as the engine's roar had been a second before.

I twisted in my seat to face forward but I stayed seated, figuring someone would tell me when it was time to leave. After a few minutes, I saw Joe walking toward me over that narrow bridge in the middle.

"What did you think?" he asked.

"Oh, it was wonderful! Beyond wonderful."

He looked at me and grinned, as if whatever he read on my face pleased him immensely. He reached down and unbuckled my seat belt, then helped me to my feet.

My knees wobbled. His arm circled around me. "Are you okay?"

"Yeah." I leaned against him, feeling the hardness of his body. I couldn't tell if it was the adrenaline from flying, or the nearness of him, but I was trembling.

He rubbed his hands up and down my arms, as if to warm me, then pulled away. "I have to do a debriefing. Carl and Ted will take you home."

He headed to the front of the plane. A few moments later, Ted came back and guided me down the bridge over the bomb bay, then helped me out of the hatch. Carl was waiting outside in a Jeep. They once again tucked me under the tarp in the back for the short ride to the hangar. Carl left, and Ted politely turned his back while I peeled off my jumpsuit. A few minutes later, Carl returned to the hangar, this time driving a beige sedan. Ted opened the back door for me.

I hesitated. "Don't I need to hide?"

"Nah. The guards don't care who leaves the base, just who gets in."

I closed my eyes as we passed the guard station, pretending to be asleep. Lord only knew what kind of girl the guards must think I was, being taken home at dawn! On the ride home, I learned that Carl was Joe's best friend, and that his esteem for Joe bordered on hero worship. Carl had some kind of health condition that made him occasionally pass out. He'd hidden it from the authorities so he could join the service, but he'd been discovered. He'd been pulled from active duty and was now a bombardier instructor at the New Orleans lakefront flight facility.

I was polite, but I didn't really want to talk. I just wanted to replay the evening in my mind, to burn it all into my memory.

As we neared Lucille's house, I asked the men to let me off a block away. It was nearly six o'clock in the morning, and there was a real risk someone would see me. I made up my mind to say I'd awakened early and gone for a walk if I ran into anyone, but I made it back to the house without incident. I let myself in with my key. To my almost unimaginable good luck, both Marge and Lucille were still asleep.

I crept into bed, and although an hour remained before I had to be up for work, I couldn't doze off. The thought that I'd been a mile or more up in the sky chased through my veins. It was a toss-up which thrilled me more: the hour's ride in the B-24, or the fact I'd been with Joe.

14
HOPE

Eddie had arranged for both occupational and physical therapists to work with Gran a few times a week, and the next morning, one of them arrived as Gran and I were finishing breakfast. Gran shooed me out of the house, so I grabbed the sketch of the girls' room I'd stayed up half the night drawing and headed to a coffee shop I'd spotted downtown.

It was located in what had once been the newspaper office on the town square, and it had a green-and-white-striped awning with *The Daily Grind* emblazoned in black script. The rich scent of coffee enveloped me as I opened the door. The interior was rustic and funky, with high ceilings, exposed beams, and a redbrick back wall.

Most of the tables were full, and several people were in line ahead of me. A pretty redhead about my age worked behind the counter. She was petite and slender, dressed in jeans and a T-shirt, over which she wore a green restaurant bib apron emblazoned with the cafe's logo. She chatted with the customers as she filled their orders, apparently well acquainted with them all.

She handed a large paper cup in a cardboard sleeve to the man in front of me. "There you go, Mike. Say hello to Joan for me."

He nodded. "Sure will. Do the same to Sam."

She turned her attention to me, then broke into a big smile. "Hey, you're Adelaide McCauley's granddaughter, aren't you?"

I nodded, trying to place her. So many people had come by the hospital and the house to visit Gran that it was hard to keep track of them, but surely I'd remember meeting such a striking redhead.

My consternation must have shown on my face, because she gave me a reassuring smile. "We haven't met. I recognized you from all the descriptions. This is a small town, so any new person is a hot topic." She leaned over the counter and held out her hand. "I'm Kirsten Deval."

I shook her hand. "Hope Stevens. Nice to meet you."

"What can I get you?"

I ordered a skinny cappuccino.

"Your grandmother practically saved my life when I was in fourth grade," she said, pulling a bottle of skim milk from an under-counter fridge.

"Oh?"

Her auburn ponytail bobbed as she nodded. "She took all the class pictures when I was in elementary school. I had the wildest, frizziest red hair you've ever seen, and even though I always wore it in a ponytail or pigtails, it still looked like a hot mess." She poured a little milk into a metal pitcher. "I lost my mother when I was six, and my father — well, he didn't know much about girls' hair, and after he fell and hurt his back, we didn't have money for extras for beauty salon visits. Your grandmother heard one of the kids call me Cheeto Head — which, believe me, was one of the nicer names I was called."

She put the milk back in the refrigerator. "Well, Miss Addie made a big deal out of complimenting me in front of everyone, saying how my hair was just like some famous actress's, and she could see that I was going to look just like her when I grew up. It immediately made me feel better. Then that night, she dropped by our house."

Kirsten scooped espresso grounds out of

a can into the metal cappuccino basket, then fitted it onto the machine. "She talked to my dad — said she'd been struck by my similarity to her daughter who'd moved away, and how much she missed her, and that her daughter had left her blow-dryer and brush behind, and would he mind if she gave it to me and showed me how to use it.

"My dad was proud — oh, he wouldn't take any charity from anyone! — but your grandmother made him feel as if he was doing *her* a favor. So she gave me a round brush and a blow-dryer and showed me how to use them — and a few weeks later, she somehow arranged for me to 'win' a free haircut at the local salon every two months for the next five years through a PTA drawing. I've never forgotten her kindness."

I'd always known Gran was thoughtful and generous, but the tale touched my heart. Especially considering that my mother's hair was fine, straight, and light brown — not at all like Kirsten's. "Gran's pretty amazing, all right."

"She sure is. I was so sorry to hear about her fall. I visited her while she was in the hospital, but I don't think she knew who I was." She frothed the milk, raising her voice to be heard over the noise of the espresso

203

machine. "How's she doing? Is she still planning to move to California?"

I filled her in on Gran's progress as she poured the espresso into a cup, then scooped milk foam on top. "At the rate we're going through her things, though, it'll take a year or more."

She handed me the steaming mug. "Maybe that's her plan. I'm sure she enjoys your company."

"And I enjoy hers — but she's actually eager to move. She talks to Eddie every night, and she's excited about living by the ocean." I took a sip of foam. "That's one of the wonderful things about Gran. She's always so enthusiastic about whatever's happening next."

Kirsten nodded. "Her enthusiasm's motivated a lot of good in this community." She lifted up a pamphlet from a stack on the counter. "She was one of the founders of this."

I read the title. " 'Friends of the Forest?' "

She nodded. "It's a reforestation program to help save the wetlands. It started with Miss Addie getting the city to collect used Christmas trees and use them to stop coastal erosion along Lake Pontchartrain. She'd read about the state doing that along the Gulf, and saw no reason why it couldn't work along the lake, as well."

I knew Gran had started the Christmas tree project, but I didn't know her efforts had spawned a whole year-round organization. I glanced over the brochure. "You plant trees in the wetlands?"

She nodded. "Once a month during the spring and fall. We're going out this Saturday. You should join us."

"Where is it?"

"The nature preserve just outside of town. We'll meet here at seven and drive out together. We'll be done by nine or nine thirty. Your grandmother always used to go. I'm sure she'd love for you to participate."

She was right — and I loved the idea of supporting a cause Gran had originated. I nodded. "I'll try to make it."

"Great!" Leaning her hip against the counter, she cocked her head and looked at me quizzically. "So what's happening with the mural at Matt's place?"

"You know about that?"

She nodded.

Once again, I'd underestimated the power of the Wedding Tree grapevine. "I just looked at the room last night." I held up my sketchbook. "I'm working up some ideas."

Her eyes lit up. "Can I see what you've got so far?"

"Well, it's still rough, but . . ." I opened the sketchbook and showed her.

She drew in an admiring breath. "Oh, that's wonderful!"

"Everything the girls showed me was Disney, and this is a completely different style," I said. "I hope they'll like it."

"They'll love it! You did all this last night?"

I nodded. "I work fast." Embarrassingly fast, my ex used to say. Real art, he'd repeatedly told me, took time.

"This is fabulous!" She looked up from the sketch. "Do you have any interest in painting a mural in here? I'm opening the back room, and I'd love to have a historical drawing of the town square on one of the walls. It would be so great to have the faces of local people in it, maybe wearing old-timey clothing like their ancestors wore. I'm sure the stores that you'd draw would sponsor it."

Potential angles and images immediately popped into my head. A wave of excitement surged through me. I tamped it down. "I don't know how long the one at Matt's house will take, and I've barely gotten started on going through my grandmother's things."

"Well, think about it. If you have time and you're interested, I would love it. I'm sure the merchants on the square would, too. I'd make sure you were very well compensated."

The bells over the door jangled. I turned to see Jillian walk in. I lifted my hand in a wave, and she froze just inside the doorway.

"Hey there, Jill," called Kirsten.

She smiled and moved stiffly toward the counter. "Hi, Kirsten." She nodded at me. "Hope."

"Want your usual?" Kirsten asked.

"No, thanks. Just black coffee today."

"Wow, you're really sticking to your diet," Kirsten observed.

"Yes, well . . ." She nodded, her hands smoothing her skirt. "I'm trying."

"Whatever you're doing sure is working." Kirsten poured a large paper cup, put on a lid, and handed it to Jillian. "You look wonderful."

"Thanks."

"Hope was just showing me a sketch of the mural for Sophie and Zoey's room."

"Is that a fact." I expected Jillian to ask to see it, but she just dug in her purse and paid for her coffee. "I've got to run or I'll be late for school. Nice seeing you both." She gathered up her drink and turned to leave.

"Will I see you at Matt's later?" I called after her.

"I — I'm not sure. I have a parent meeting after school." She tossed out a quick "good-bye" over her shoulder and scurried out of the coffee shop.

"I don't think she much likes me," I said as the door closed behind her.

"Oh, that's just Jillian. She's a little socially awkward — the exact opposite of her sister that way."

"Oh yeah?" I was curious about Matt's late wife.

Kirsten nodded and wiped down the counter. "Christine never met a stranger. She was one of those people that others just gravitate to, you know? And Jillian — well, she just doesn't have the gift of gab."

"What's the story with her and Matt?"

"She's his sister-in-law."

"I got the impression there was something more."

"Really?" She considered it for a moment. "Nah. I just don't see it. Although I'm pretty sure Jillian would be open to the idea. What single girl wouldn't be, right?"

I lifted my shoulders and took a sip of cappuccino.

"What about you?" she asked. "Are you single?"

"Divorced." It still felt like a failure, saying it. "You?"

"I'm married, though you wouldn't know

it from the amount of time my husband and I are together." She grabbed a white bar towel and wiped down the counter. "Right now he's in the North Sea. Before that, he was off the coast of Africa."

"Is he in the service?"

"He was, but not anymore. Now he's the captain of a supply ship that largely works on military contracts. Did you see that movie *Captain Phillips*? Well, that's him — except his boat has guns."

"Wow. Do you ever go with him?"

"No passengers allowed." Her face grew tight. "He keeps saying he's going to quit, but then he always signs up for another voyage."

Uh-oh. Sounded like trouble in paradise.

The door jangled and three chattering middle-aged women came in, followed by two men in ball caps advertising the local feedstore. I picked up my coffee and sketchbook. "I'd better let you get to work — and I'd better do that myself."

Kirsten smiled. "So nice to meet you. And please try to join us on Saturday! It'll be a good time. The carpool group is a bunch of women about our age."

"I'll try to make it," I said. I carried my cappuccino to a table in the corner, got out

my pencils, and started detailing stones on
an ivory tower.

15
ADELAIDE

I hated the idea of someone bathing me. I needed help stepping over the side of the tub and getting seated in that shower chair from the medical equipment store, though, and I could no longer reach my back or my feet. Thank heavens the aide lets me wash my personal parts myself so I can cling to a shred of dignity.

By the time she'd helped me dry off and dress, Hope was back. Through the window, I watched her lug a trash can full of flattened empty boxes and garbage bags to the curb. At my request, the aide settled me in my bedroom rocker, then left the room.

"Let's go through my closet," I said when Hope came back inside and stuck her head in my room.

"Oh boy!" She pulled out her little portable phone — they call them cell phones, though I don't know why. I think they should call them camera phones because they can take pictures. "I've been looking forward to this. If it's okay with you, I'll take pictures of your clothes as we bring them out. Then I can send an e-mail to a vintage store in Chicago or upload them on eBay."

I had no idea what she was talking about, but I loved the idea of taking photos of my clothes. I should have done that years ago myself.

"Whatever you want to do is fine, dear. I thought that going through my closet would help me remember the things I need to tell you, because I can recall what I was wearing when special things happened." I gave her a sheepish grin. "Although I'm afraid I can't remember what we were talking about when we left off."

"You'd just told me about the night Joe took you up in the bomber."

"Oh yes. Yes, indeed! Oh, that was quite an experience. Pull out that green plaid skirt at the back."

She dug around in my closet. "This one?"

"Yes. That's what I was wearing that night."

She took a picture of it with her phone camera, then did something with her thumbs.

"There's a blue-and-white polka-dot dress

in there, with a fabric-covered belt. Do you see it?"

She rooted around and pulled it out. It had a V-neck, short sleeves, and navy buttons down the front. She hung it on the door and took a photo.

"Did you ever get your camera back?" Hope asked.

"What?"

She pulled the dress off the door and handed it to me. "You said you gave your camera to Kevin or Carl that night."

"Oh!" A scrap of the past floated by like flotsam. "Yes. Yes, I did. He gave it back to me when he let me out of the car that morning."

"Do you have any pictures of Joe?"

I nodded. "Not taken that night, but yes, I have a few."

"I'd love to see them. Where are they?"

I drew a blank. I frowned and tried to think. Nope. Nothing came. "I can't seem to recall at the moment. I'm sure it will come to me later." At least, I hoped it would. I knew I'd put them somewhere Charlie couldn't find them, but since my fall, I can't recollect exactly where.

I leaned back and closed my eyes, letting the past swirl and thicken around me like smoke, until it was something I seemed to breathe. Once again, I heard myself talking.

1943

I had the hardest time keeping quiet about that plane ride the next day — especially around Marge. I didn't think I could keep my mouth shut — and I was totally exhausted anyway, so I pretended to be sick on Tuesday and spent the day in bed.

By Wednesday, it all seemed like a dream. I was beginning to doubt my sanity. Had it really happened, or had I made it all up? Why hadn't I heard from Joe?

I dressed in that polka-dot dress and went to work, and that made it seem more unreal — going on as before, as though nothing as life changing as flying through the sky had occurred. I was assigned to the darkroom that morning, and it only added to my gloom. I was gathering up the police beat photographer's film from the night before when the senior editor, a roly-poly man named Thomas Coppler, called my name.

I turned and looked at him, startled, as he waddled toward me. He was three layers of management above my supervisor; I didn't think he even knew who I was. He had wavy gray hair, a coarse salt-and-pepper mustache, and a big belly. He liked to wear knitted sweater-vests, and the one he wore on that particular day was brown and covered with what looked like cake crumbs. "You've got a phone call," he said.

I must have looked surprised. I'd never received a call at work.

"From your cousin." His eyes were soft and sympathetic, in a way that conveyed bad news. "You can take it at my desk."

I followed him across the newsroom, my heart racing, my mind scanning through my cousins. I had five of them, but I wasn't particularly close to any of them. If something had happened to a member of my family, my parents would call — unless something happened to my parents. In that case, though, my grandmother or Aunt Beula would have called. Unless something had happened to them, as well, and then . . .

The phone was lying on his desk, off the hook. He handed it to me. My hand shook as I lifted it to my ear. "Hello?"

"Pretend I'm giving you bad news," said a deep, smooth baritone. *Joe.* My heart stopped for a second, then beat double time.

"What?"

"Look shocked. Pretend I'm telling you that dear old Uncle Leo bit the dust. That's what I just told your boss."

"But . . ."

"Just listen to me. I know you don't want

215

to lie, so I did it for you. All you need to do is gather up your stuff and leave. He'll let you off for the rest of the week."

"But . . ."

"He's standing there listening, isn't he? So don't say a word. I already told him your uncle in Mississippi died and we need you here to help with arrangements. I've got leave until Sunday. If you're asked specifics, say you're going to Coldwater, just outside of Jackson. It won't be a lie. I'll take you to Mississippi."

"I — I don't . . ."

"Just look shocked. From the way you sound, I imagine that's how you look anyway, so you won't even have to do any acting. Just grab your purse and leave. If anyone asks for an explanation, just say you have a family situation — which, of course, you do. Having a family is a situation in and of itself. Then take the trolley . . ."

"Streetcar," I automatically corrected.

". . . streetcar to Jackson Avenue. I'll meet you there in half an hour."

"I — I don't know."

"Let me talk to Thomas again."

I was acutely aware that Mr. Coppler was watching me. I numbly I held out the phone. "He — he wants to talk to you."

Mr. Coppler gave me a sympathetic smile

and took the receiver. He listened for a moment. "Of course. I understand completely. I'll take care of it."

He cast me a kindly look — his eyes were big and brown and expressive like Charlie Chaplin's — and set the phone in its cradle. "I'm so sorry."

I nodded. I had the strongest urge to laugh, but fear kept me from it.

"Now, don't you worry about a thing. Take the rest of the week off. And don't concern yourself about money. I'll see to it that you get hardship pay."

"Oh! I couldn't. I mean, that — that's not necessary."

He patted my shoulder, then pulled his hand back, as if he was unsure if he should touch me. He was endearingly awkward. "That's all right. We take care of our own around here."

Guilt stabbed me. "Really, you don't need . . ."

"It's our policy." He made a shooing motion with his hands. "Now go. And don't worry about a thing here."

I nodded, gathered up my coat and purse, and left the building in a numb daze. As I climbed on the streetcar, the numbness gave way to a bizarre combination of delight and outrage. I'd never known a man like Joe —

217

so take-charge, so willful, so forceful. How masculine, how movie-star-ish, how thrilling!

Yet, on the other hand, how *dare* he? He was playing fast and loose with my career, making decisions that weren't his to make.

It was as if he'd staked a claim on me. As if I belonged to him.

A shiver of excitement spun up my spine. The idea of belonging to Joe, of Joe belonging to me . . . well, it positively bewitched me. At the same time, it scared me to death.

Which took me back full circle to outrage. How *dare* he? Just who did he think he was?

Joe was leaning on the lamppost at the intersection of St. Charles Avenue and Jackson when the streetcar clanged to a stop. I climbed down the wooden stairs behind a matron with a cane, my heart pounding so hard I could feel it in my throat, attraction buzzing through me like a hive of bees. He stepped toward me as if he was going to hug me, but his smile punched my anger button. I pushed him hard on the chest with both hands. "That was awfully presumptuous of you."

He gave me a crooked grin. "I wanted to see you."

"So you concocted a cockamamie story and lied to my boss?"

He lifted his shoulders. "You could have told him I wasn't your cousin — that I was just a cheeky soldier trying to get you to play hooky with him."

Oh Lordy — he was right. I stared at him, mentally smacking my palm to my forehead, feeling like the worst kind of fool. I had to turn away from him to collect myself.

The thought of not playing along hadn't even occurred to me. I'd been over my head before I even knew I was in hot water. I whipped back around. "I can't believe I let you put me in this situation! I've not only misled my boss and skipped work, but there will be unending repercussions to this. I'm going to have to tell all kinds of lies and answer all kinds of questions when I go back, and —"

"No, you won't," he cut in. "I told Thomas you're a very private person and you won't want to talk about it, and that no one should send sympathy cards or flowers."

"Still, I'll have to say something. People will ask about me about the funeral."

"So we'll attend one." He pulled a news-paper clipping out of his pocket. It was the obituary of an elderly man in Mississippi who would be buried this afternoon.

"Who's this?"

"Uncle Leo, of course."

"Your uncle?"

"No, but you can bet he's somebody's." He grinned. "We'll go to his funeral — it's on the way to my friend's fishing camp — and then you'll be absolutely honest in talking about it."

I put my hands on my hips and glared at him. This was beyond presumptuous. It was flat-out insane. "Are you out of your *mind*?"

"No. I'm completely in it. I happen to be one of the few people in this world who is."

"Now you're not even making sense."

"Most folks don't have a clue what they really want. I do."

And, apparently, he wanted me. The thought sent chill bumps coursing down my arm.

"I can't just go away to a fishing camp in Mississippi with you."

"Sure you can."

I pulled myself to my tallest posture, but I still only came up to his shoulder. "Look, I don't know what impression you have of me, but I'm not that kind of girl."

"I didn't think you were. But I also didn't think you were the kind to let a bunch of archaic social conventions keep you from having an adventure, either."

"An adventure is one thing; ruining my reputation is quite another."

"It won't be ruined if nobody knows about it." He put his hands on my shoulders. "Here's the plan: You'll pack a bag while your friend and your landlady are at work. Leave a note just stating the facts: that you got a phone call at work telling you that Uncle Leo had passed away, and you've gone to Mississippi to his funeral. You'll be back Saturday."

"Saturday! That's three nights from now."

"Yeah."

"I'm *not* sharing a room with you."

"I don't expect you to. You'll have your own bedroom. And I promise to treat you with the greatest dignity and respect."

"Will there be a chaperone?"

He looked me straight in the eye. "No."

"So it'll be just you and me out in the woods?"

"That's right. But I give you my word I will be a total gentleman. Your virtue will remain intact."

I knew better. I knew it wasn't prudent. I knew my parents would have a stroke if they ever found out. But I wanted to go so badly that I convinced myself it would be all right. I told myself that he was an honorable man — after all, he was an Army Air Force officer, wasn't he? Surely I could trust the word of a man that the government entrusted with an enormous bomber, thousands of pounds of explosives, and the lives of other crewmen.

In retrospect, I was overlooking one important fact: the person I couldn't trust was myself.

Looking back on it now, it's hard to explain exactly what it was about Joe that affected me like catnip affects a cat. It wasn't just his appearance, although — Lordy, oh Lordy! — he was one good-looking man. Joe just had something extra. He was more alive than most people, as if God had packed an extra dose of vitality into him, or maybe a double soul. He radiated something — heat or light or magnetism or some such. He sparkled and shone and shot off electric sparks.

And when he turned his attention on me full throttle, it was like standing in front of a fire hose. It knocked me plumb flat.

Joe was impervious to the rules that everyone else lived by. And when I was with him, I felt impervious, too.

That was my big mistake. I forgot who I was — a small-town girl, bound by small-town rules.

16
HOPE

I wasn't sure if the rumbling of the garbage truck outside her house broke Gran's storytelling trance or if her memory just suddenly shifted gears, but one moment she was weaving a spell with her words, and the next she was leaning forward, gripping the arms of her chair. "The photos of Joe — I know where they are! They're in the attic, in a box marked 'bed linens.' "

Eddie and Ralph had brought down all the attic boxes — and I'd gone through most of them. "Is there more than one box marked 'bed linens?' "

"No, just the one."

"I went through it yesterday," I said. "There weren't any photos."

"It's hidden under an extra piece of cardboard at the bottom."

Oh, no. My stomach knotted. "I — I threw that box out." Remorse welled up like nausea. "And the garbage truck just came."

"Well, child, go and get it!"

I raced outside. Gran's old metal garbage can stood empty on the curb, but the truck was stopped in front of Matt's house. "Wait!" I yelled.

Two trash workers froze, each holding one of Matt's thirty-gallon plastic bins.

"I need to get back a box I accidentally threw out."

The shorter man shook his dreadlocks. "If we've already emptied your can, it's too late, lady."

"Please — you just picked it up." I pointed to Gran's empty can. "Can I look in your truck? I'm sure it's on top of the pile."

The larger man — he was the size of a mountain, wearing a dirty black T-shirt that read *If you don't like bacon, you're wrong* and a colorful do-rag — cocked his gloved thumb toward the cab of the truck. "Ask the driver."

I ran to the window and looked up at the weather-beaten man behind the wheel. He chomped on a piece of gum, his expression bored. "Please," I begged. "I accidentally threw out some of my grandmother's photos."

He cast me a disinterested glance. "Sorry. Too late."

"Please — if I can just look. You just

picked up her trash — it was the last house — and I'm sure . . ."

He really looked at me for the first time. "You talkin' 'bout Mizz Addie?"

"Yes."

"She took my sister's wedding photos and didn' charge no fee."

I'm not named Hope for nothing. I gave him my best smile. "Well, then, you know how sweet she is. It would mean a lot to her to get her pictures back."

With a sigh, he looked at his watch. "I'm not supposed to do this, and I'm runnin' behind schedule. But seein' as it's Mizz Addie . . . you got three minutes."

"Oh, thank you!"

"Three minutes, hear? That's it, then we gotta roll."

I raced back around the truck, grabbed the railing, and hoisted myself up the tall step. When I stuck my head inside the garbage bay, I was hit by a stench so strong and foul that I gagged. I pulled out my head and took a deep gulp of air. My eyes watered, making it nearly impossible to see.

The large garbageman took pity on me. He climbed up beside me, his weight making the truck dip. "What's it look like?" he asked.

"It's an old box."

225

The shorter worker spit on the pavement and let out a coarse laugh. "Oh, that really narrows it down."

"It says 'bed linens' on the side," I added. "You just picked it up."

"Should be on top. Let's just pull out all the boxes we can reach," said the larger worker.

He heaved out two boxes. I held my breath, reached for one, and threw it out. Packing peanuts sprayed all over Matt's lawn. The worker hurled three more boxes. I tossed one, spewing what looked like rotten lettuce. The man grabbed another box.

"Hey, this is supposed to trash pickup, not delivery," said an angry male voice from below. "What the hell are you doing?"

The trash worker blocked my view, but I immediately recognized Matt's voice. My stomach, already tight and queasy, seized into a fist. Why, oh why did he always show up when I was doing something weird?

"Sorry, man," said the trash worker on the ground. "Your neighbor threw away something by accident, and . . ."

I spotted Gran's scrawl on a box in the large trash worker's hand. "That's it!" I yelled. "The box you're holding — that's it!"

"Yeah? Well, then, here you go." He

handed me the box. The top half was dripping with something that smelled like decaying shrimp.

I held it upside down, not wanting to get the bottom wet, and turned around to climb down, only to realize the step was too high for me to manage without hanging on to something. If I just threw the box on the ground, I might get the pictures wet. If I jumped holding it, I was likely to crush the photos by landing on them.

Matt stepped into my line of vision, a dark scowl on his face. I hesitated. "I, uh . . ."

"Oh, for God's sake." Matt reached up, grabbed me around the waist, and swung me down as if I were a doll. When he set me on the ground, I realized I'd coated his suit jacket, tie, and dress shirt with wet, fish-scented goo.

"Th-thank you," I said to Matt.

He looked down at his clothes, grimaced, then looked back at me. "You're welcome."

The burly driver leaned out the window. "All set?"

"Yes," I called. "Thank you!"

"Tell Mizz Addie that George Myers says hello." He waved back as the truck rumbled away, leaving me alone with Matt and my remorse.

I shifted the upside-down box to my other

227

hand. "I'm so sorry. If you wait here, I'll get some paper towels, and . . ."

He held up his palm and looked down at his clothes. "I think this'll take more than a couple of sheets of Brawny."

"Oh!" Nervous motormouth-itis kicked in. "Yes, yes, you're right. I'll get your clothes cleaned. Just take them off and give them to me, and . . ."

He arched an eyebrow.

Oh, dear — it sounded like I wanted him to drop trou in the middle of the street. "I mean later. When you're in private, probably inside your house." I was sounding weirder and weirder, and I just couldn't stop myself. "You can take them off and give them to me. Not that I'll be right there to take them. I mean, I won't be watching you undress." I was just digging a bigger and deeper hole. "You can bring them to me, or I'll come and get them, and . . . and I'll take them to the cleaners. To get cleaned." I wished one of those sinkholes I'd seen on the news would form right under my feet.

He looked at me. I wasn't sure because the sun was shining behind him, but I thought there might be a glint of amusement in his eyes. "Thanks, but I can manage." He gestured to the box. "Just tell me one thing: why did we go to all this trouble

228

for an empty box?"

"Gran says she hid pictures in it."

"It's empty."

"It has a false bottom."

"A false bottom." He looked at me as if I were ready for a rubber room and a straight-jacket.

I felt as if I were. I desperately tried for humor. "I know, I know — it sounds like something from a bad movie. Or the title of a bad country-western song title." I gave him a hopeful grin. " 'Her bottom was false and so was her heart.' "

Oh, thank God — Matt laughed! The sound was deep and throaty, and it did something funny to my chest.

"The way you look right now reminds me of an actual song," he said. "It goes something like, "I Like My Women a Little on the Trashy Side.' "

I looked down and realized the front of my shirt and shorts were smeared with gunk. I gave a sheepish grin. "If that's the case, I must be pretty irresistible just now."

Wait. Had I just made *another* suggestive remark? What was my *problem*? My face heated.

It didn't seem to bother him much. "Stay here. I'll be right back."

He jogged into his open garage. I carefully

set my prize box upside down in his driveway, then picked up the boxes I'd helped throw on his yard and put them in his now-empty trash can.

Matt returned a minute later, minus his jacket, with a roll of paper towels and bottle of hand sanitizer under his arm. He dabbed at his shirt and tie as he walked toward me. By this time I was collecting packing peanuts.

"Here." He handed me the towels and sanitizer and took the box from me. I cleaned my clothes as best I could as he reached into his pocket and pulled out something shiny.

"A pocketknife?"

"Yeah."

"Well, aren't you the Boy Scout."

"Actually, I was."

"Eagle Scout?"

"As a matter of fact, yes."

"I'm impressed."

"You should be." He knelt down and inserted the knife in the corner of the box. "That knitting badge was a bitch."

Kneeling beside him, I furrowed my brow. "Knitting?"

He shot me a get-real look. "I'm kidding."

Of course. How could I think otherwise? I felt that old familiar embarrassment creep over me, that sense of being a screwup that I'd often felt with Kurt. I immediately fought to squelch it. "I didn't know you knew how."

He looked at me, his brows raised questioningly.

"To kid," I explained. "Not to knit."

He laughed again. My chest felt strangely warm as I watched him work the knife along the seam of the box, cutting off the soiled top flaps, then slicing off the sides. His hands were sure and steady, tanned and square and masculine. Watching them made my mouth go dry.

"Son of a gun," he said. "There *is* something here." He pried up an extraneous piece of cardboard, then handed it to me. "Here — you do the honors."

I lifted the cardboard and glanced at the top photo. It was the profile of a man in the driver's seat of a shiny car, a car like you might see in an old Bogart movie. My heart tripped.

"Who is it?" Matt asked.

"Gran's first love." It was taken at a distance, but he was handsome, all right. Light hair, a dazzling smile, a muscled arm resting on the rolled-down window of an old sedan. He wore a buttoned short-sleeved shirt, and even though it was a black-and-white photo, I could tell he was tan.

"Why'd she hide his pictures?"

"She said she didn't want my grandfather to see them, but I think she was mostly hiding them from herself. I don't think she ever got over him." I swallowed. "And . . . I don't know. From the way the story's going, I think a family skeleton is about to be revealed."

I looked at the next picture. It was the same man in another short-sleeved shirt, at a closer viewpoint. This time he was lying in the grass, his hands behind his head, grinning at the photographer, his eyes warm and lively. Something about him made the hair on my arm stand up.

"Hey — are you okay?"

I glanced up and met Matt's concerned gaze. "Yeah. I just . . ."

. . . *think I might be looking at my grandfather.*

Matt leaned over my shoulder and looked at the picture. "He looks familiar."

Yeah. Real familiar — as in like my mother. Like me.

I swallowed and mustered a smile. "I think I might pass out from the fumes of my own funk." I straightened and stood. "I'd better get inside and let Gran know I saved her photos. And you'd better change clothes and get to wherever you're going. Thanks so much for your help."

"Glad to assist."

The fact he was being so nice about this when he'd been such a dick about me just being in his bedroom was disconcerting — so I did what I usually do when I'm disconcerted. I rambled. "I meant what I said — I'd like to pay your cleaning bill. And I promise to come back and pick up all the packing peanuts on your lawn, and . . ."

He held up his hand. "Don't worry about it. The lawn service is due to come this morning. They'll get all that."

"But . . ."

"Seriously. It's not a problem." He peered at me. "You sure you're okay? You look like you've seen a ghost."

"I'm fine."

It wasn't a ghost I'd seen, I thought as I scurried across the lawn and up Gran's porch.

It was my own eyes staring back at me.

17
ADELAIDE

I lay my head back in my rocking chair and closed my eyes. I could hear Hope outside, talking to a man. I couldn't make out the words, just the low rumble of his voice, along with the sound of his laugh. Wasn't there a handsome widower in the neighborhood? There used to be. Seemed like there was another one now. I wondered if he was attracted to Hope, and vice versa. Wouldn't that be something, if sparks flew between them?

Those man-woman sparks. Oh my, how powerful they could be! Astonishing, really, how much energy those sparks consumed, considering how little time, in the big scheme of things, people spent actually making love. But oh, how it colors everything — and how strong that pull can be!

Stronger than the need for food or sleep, back in the day. Stronger, even, than my need to sleep now, which seems to constantly pull at me like a deadweight.

Best not to think about dead, I tell myself.

Although, now that I know the dead are floating, the concept of a deadweight doesn't really apply. I opened my eyes and looked up at the ceiling. I'd heard Mother, but I hadn't seen her since I'd been home. I wondered if dead people watch us.

"Not all the time," Mother's voice promptly answered. "Only when you call us with your thoughts, or when you have a shining moment."

"Oh." I made a mental note to get better control of my thoughts.

"Course, we don't see as you do," Mother continued. "We see through all the external stuff, straight to the beautiful you."

"There's a . . . beautiful me?" Mother had never been much on praise. She'd thought it might give me a big head and make me vain.

"It's not ladylike to fish for compliments," Mother sniffed now. "And there's certainly no excuse for ever letting yourself go, but I'll tell you this, young lady: all those times you fretted about a little blemish or a couple of pounds or a wrinkle — well, that was just plain nonsense. Up here we only see your beauty, because that's the truth of you, and God's truth is always lovelier than an

235

earthly mind can imagine."

"Oh, how wonderful!"

"What's wonderful?"

Hope's voice made me open my eyes. I saw three of her standing in the doorway. The three Hopes settled into two. I stared, confused, and then I remembered — I see multiples of everything lately.

I hadn't seen even one Mother. Had I been dreaming, or had she really talked to me again?

I decided to go with the less-crazy-sounding explanation. "I must have dozed off." I straightened in my chair, crinkling my nose against a fetid smell, and squinted until the two Hopes merged into one. Her shirt was smeared with something wet and green, and her shorts were covered with grime and something that looked like coffee grounds. "Good heavens, child — did you fall into a trash bin?"

"Pretty much." She looked down at her clothes, her mouth turned down with chagrin. "I had to do a little garbage-truck diving, but I managed to save your pictures of Joe." She handed me a stack of photos.

My heart quickened as my fingers closed around them. "Did you look at them?"

She nodded. "He was movie-star handsome."

"Yes. Yes, he was."

"I want to hear all about him, but I need to get cleaned up first." She pulled her wet T-shirt away from her skin and looked down at it with disgust.

I wasn't about to argue. She reeked like a shrimp trawler's net. "Go right ahead, dear."

I sat back and slowly sifted through the photos, my heart rat-a-tat-tatting in my chest. There was Joe, holding a fish. Me holding a fish. Joe building a fire. Joe in a canoe. Joe shirtless and dripping wet. A photo of us together, taken at arm's length — what I'd heard Hope call a "selfie."

I grinned as I gazed at those photos, a sweet ache growing inside me. You'd think I'd be past sexual desire, and for years now, I haven't had too much interest. In fact, I've sometimes wondered what all the fuss was about, even though I remembered the strength of the urge. Seeing these photos of Joe, though . . . well, I know it's hard for young people to hear this about old people, but you never move totally beyond desire. It's like chocolate — once you've had really good chocolate, the very thought of chocolate, when you dwell on it, makes your mouth water. And lovemaking with Joe had been chocolate heaven.

I was staring at a photo of a shirtless Joe

lying in the grass, when Hope reentered the room. I looked up from the photo and felt my face heat, as if I'd been caught looking at pornography.

She settled into the chair beside me. She smelled like soap and shampoo, and her hair was damp. "You were telling me about Joe getting you out of work and trying to convince you to go to Mississippi."

I nodded.

"Did you go?"

"Yes."

"Did you have a good time?"

Oh my! I've lived seventy-plus years since then, yet no period of time stood out as clearly as those three days. They were wrapped in sunshine, so bright it almost hurt to look at them. Maybe that's why I'd so seldom fully reflected on them. I settled back and closed my eyes, letting the brilliance heat me from the inside out, and lapsed back into storytelling mode.

1943

There I was, sitting in a bright blue Ford De Luxe sedan — a car with three windows on each side, rounded fenders, and a funny, snubbed trunk — flying along Highway 11, the wind blowing the tail of the blue and green chiffon scarf wrapped around my hair like a kite. Joe had borrowed the car from his tailgunner's father. "You've been flyin' my son two miles up in the air over enemy territory," Joe said the middle-aged man had told him. "Reckon I can trust you to drive my Ford to Mississippi and back."

It was a beautiful April day, clear and bright and unseasonably warm, and I felt like springtime personified — young, alive, full of rising sap. We joked and laughed and sang out-of-tune accompaniments to the radio, our spirits in perfect harmony. I felt like Katharine Hepburn — free and daring and larger than life, too wild to be confined by anything as stuffy as convention.

My next clear memory is of pulling into the parking lot of the Mt. Zion Baptist Church in Coldwater, Mississippi. We were late — the parking lot was full, and everyone was already inside — but Joe took my hand and led me into the squat cinderblock building all the same.

One thing the obituary hadn't mentioned was that "Uncle Leo" was black. We walked through the door and stood out like two flour-covered thumbs — so out of place that the soloist, a large woman wearing a wide veiled hat decorated with black cloth roses, stopped in mid-lyric.

It was odd enough for white folks to at-

tend a Negro's funeral back then, but it was
even more unusual for a young white couple
from out of state to attend the funeral of an
elderly Negro man — a man who'd lived in
this town of less than five hundred souls all
his life and, as we later learned, never
ventured further than two counties over.

The room rustled as the entire congregation turned and stared. Joe smiled, nodded,
and lifted his palm in a little wave, as if it
were perfectly normal for everything to
grind to a halt just because he'd entered a
room. The soloist nodded and smiled back,
then resumed singing with renewed vigor.
The mourners took a little longer to finish
staring at us, but they turned back around
in time to dutifully sing, "Ain't that grand!"
to the call-and-response line of a hymn
about laying down swords and shields.

One song followed another for a good half
hour. The music was alternately heartbreaking and rollicking, accompanied by an out-
of-tune piano. The mourners swayed in time
to the beat, occasionally breaking into riffs
and adding extra "Amens" to the endings.

At last we were allowed to sit. I could see
a plain pine box at the front of the church,
with a single wreath of carnations atop it.

A minister in a sharply tailored black suit
took the pulpit behind the coffin and point-

edly welcomed us, then launched into a hellfire and brimstone sermon without a single word about the deceased. "Uh-huh," "Praise God," "You tell 'em, Brother" and other bursts of encouragement from the congregation punctuated his relentlessly fiery diatribe.

After the service — which went on for two full hours, and included a mandatory "viewing" of the gray-looking, emaciated old man in the coffin — a middle-aged woman dressed head to toe in black made a beeline toward us. "Thank y'all for coming." She clasped both my hands, then Joe's. "How'd y'all know Daddy?"

"We, uh, didn't." Joe squeezed her hands. "But your father helped my granddaddy out of some kind of scrape when he was young. Never would give us the details, but he said your father was a hero. He saw the obituary in the paper, and he insisted we come and pay our respects."

"Oh my." The woman released her grip on Joe to clasp her hands to her chest. "You don' say. Ain' that won'erful! Why didn' he come hisself?"

"He couldn't."

"Whyever not?"

Joe looked her straight in the eye, his expression somber. "He's in an iron lung."

I nearly laughed out loud. Joe stepped on my toes as a warning.

"Oh mercy! So sorry to hear that."

"It's okay. He's over a hundred years old and he's ready to meet his maker."

"Well, it's so nice he sent y'all to pay his respects." She turned to a large woman beside her, similarly clad for mourning, and grinned like a kid who'd just gotten a new bicycle for Christmas. "Roberta, these here people say Daddy done somethin' good!"

As it turned out, apparently Uncle Leo had been a meanspirited old goat and his family had been concerned about his afterlife destination. They were thrilled to learn he'd had a generous moment, no matter how long ago or vague, and they insisted we join them for lunch at the home of one of his daughters. They fed us pulled pork, black-eyed peas, smothered greens, and cream pies until I thought the buttons on my dress would pop.

"We did those folks a world of good," Joe said after we'd finally taken our leave.

"We lied to them."

"We made them feel better about Leo." He headed back onto the highway.

"It was still a lie."

"The world isn't like your newspaper photos, Addie girl. Not everything is black

242

and white."

"Black-and-white photos happen to have lots of shades of gray," I pointed out, meaning that gray things were made up of black and white, negating his argument.

"Exactly," Joe said, as if I'd just agreed with him.

The conversation drifted to lighter topics, but I filed his remarks in the back of my mind to discuss later. We talked about family — I learned his father had left his mother shortly after he was born, that his mother had died when he was fourteen, and that he and his older sister had been raised by an aunt in California. He deflected most of my questions by asking about me. I chattered away like a magpie. I told him my father was a parish judge, and my brother, Andy, worked as an analyst for the War Department in Washington, D.C., and he was more like a distant uncle than a brother because he was so much older and I hardly ever saw him. I told him about the rest of my family and Wedding Tree and even Charlie.

We drove all afternoon, stopped around dusk at a diner for sandwiches, then drove another hour before turning off the highway onto a dirt road. It was black as pitch, and the tree frogs sang a loud, nighttime chorus. The road grew narrower and narrower, the tree branches scraping the sides of the car. I thought for sure we were lost, when the headlights finally lit up a little cabin. It was unpainted clapboard, and it had a ramshackle, untended look to it.

Joe kept the headlights on while he rummaged around a rocking chair on the porch and pulled a key from under the left back rocker. He opened the screen door, then unlocked the oak one behind it.

A musty smell fluttered out. "The place could do with an airing," he said, stepping inside and flipping on the light. "But it's clean. Hank's father hires a local lady to come in, change the sheets, and dust every month."

"Even when no one comes here?"

"Yeah."

What a luxury to be so rich, I thought, following him in. The inside was neat as a pin, but just as worn as the outside — two cracked, worn leather chairs and a plaid, saggy sofa sat against unfinished wood walls. The kitchen opened directly off the living room. Corkboard covered one wall and was covered with clippings of faded, yellowed newspaper. I leaned in and looked at the date on one. "This is from 1902!"

Joe nodded. "Hank said this place belonged to his great-granddad, and he used to come here as a kid. They added an indoor bathroom a few years ago." He gestured toward the back. "It's in the back, by the bedroom."

I froze. "*The* bedroom?"

"Yeah."

"I — I thought you said there were two bedrooms."

"I said you'd have your own bedroom," he replied. "I'll sleep on the sofa out here." He carried my bag into the room, which featured a rustic metal bed meticulously made up with an old, faded quilt.

He set down my suitcases and grinned at me as I stood frozen in the doorway. Tension stretched between us. He patted the mattress. "Come try it out."

"I wonder if I can trust you," I said, only half jesting.

"Are you really worried?"

"A little, now that I know how easily lies roll off your tongue." I tentatively sat on the edge of the bed.

"At the funeral?" He plopped down beside me and leaned back against the wall, his arms behind his head. "Those weren't lies. That was fiction."

I shot him an arch look. "What's the difference?"

"The reason behind it. A lie is when

245

you're telling an untruth for your own benefit. When you're doing it for the good of someone else, it's just a story."

"That's a very questionable line of reasoning, because any untruth — even about terrible things, like murder — can help someone."

"How do you figure that?"

"Well, a murderer is protecting his parents when he says he didn't do it, because they're bound to grieve having reared such an awful son."

"It's always wrong to cover up a crime."

"Every crime? Because it's probably a crime to take a civilian up in a government plane."

He grinned. "As I recall, I didn't tell any untruths about that. Besides, no one was hurt. I like to think I helped make a dream come true." He looked at me, and our gazes locked. His voice lowered to a goose-bump-making rumble. "I'd like to make all your dreams come true, Addie."

From another man, it would have seemed like nothing but a line — a prelude to seduction. The way he looked at me, though — that all-the-way-through-to-my-soul, I-really-see-you-and-I-think-you're-wonderful look he gave me — lifted it to a different level. So did what he did next.

He rose to his feet and headed to the door. "It's late. You should go to bed. Fishing is a crack-of-dawn activity."

"We're really going to fish?"

"Sure. We want to eat, don't we?"

He pulled the door closed.

I raced across the room and yanked it open. "Aren't you going to kiss me good night?"

"No." His eyes seemed somehow backlit, deep and multifaceted.

"Why not?"

"Because I don't know that I could stop, and I promised you I'd be respectful." He pulled the door closed, and I didn't dare open it again.

I remember bits and pieces of the next two days — the rest of that night, lying in bed awake, knowing he was in the other room, tossing and turning and burning, wondering if he were doing the same. I didn't drop off until dawn, then awoke with the sun in my face.

Other memories are random, framed in my mind like snapshots. The unexpected blue of the lake behind the cabin. The scent of sweet olives in the air. The rocking of the rowboat. His chest behind me as he taught me how to cast a rod. Making sandwiches together in the kitchen. Fishing from shore — and then wading in as the afternoon sun grew warmer and warmer. The feel of my skirt clinging to my legs, the way the bottom of my white blouse turned transparent.

That second night was long and hot, despite the fact it was April and my screen windows were open. The awareness of Joe made me feel fevered and chilled all at the same time. I remember falling into an exhausted sleep, and awakening to the pure joy of another day with Joe.

The unseasonably warm weather continued. That afternoon, I pushed him out of the rowboat. He pulled me overboard, and we frolicked like two kids in the water — splashing and chasing each other, and then . . . oh, the pleasure of being caught in his arms! I turned and looked into his eyes. I swear my heart kept time with the crickets, it was going so fast. And then his mouth claimed mine, his lips warm and hard, and I was drowning in emotion, not wanting to let go.

He was the one who pulled back. "Damn it, Addie," he murmured. "You're enough to make a man lose his mind."

I had already lost mine. All I could think of was getting close again, feeling his mouth on mine. I raised my leg and wrapped it around him, half floating in the water. He put his hands on my shoulders and put me away from him. "This was a mistake."

"What was?"

"All of it. Bringing you here, kissing you . . . Hell, this damned whole trip." He wiped the water from his face. "A man shouldn't put the girl he wants to marry in a dangerous situation."

Two words hit my brain simultaneously: *marry* and *dangerous*. The first word overrode everything I knew about the second.

"You . . . you mean, you want . . . ?"

"I want to marry you, Addie. I love you." The words came out in a rush, in a tone that sounded almost angry.

"Is that a proposal?"

"Yeah, I guess it is." He looked at me, his eyes clear and serious in the tree-dappled light. "So what do you say?"

Joy filled me, making my heart rise and float like a helium balloon. "Yes!" I threw my arms around his neck, splashing both of us. "Yes, oh yes!"

The kiss left us both breathless. At length he pulled back. "Okay, then. Let's do it." Taking my hand, he started pulling me toward the shore.

Do it? Do what?

He seemed to read my mind. "Let's go

find a justice of the peace."

"Now? Today?"

"Right this minute."

"Oh, but I can't!" I stopped, up to my waist in water. "My family . . . why, they'd die if I eloped!"

"Addie, I have to be back on base tomorrow night. I ship out the day after."

"But I'm the only daughter, and my mother has always dreamed of planning my wedding. And my dad — he needs to give you permission, and he has to walk me down the aisle!"

Joe blew out a hard sigh.

"You don't understand about small southern towns," I said. "My parents would be disgraced. Lisa Sue Adams ran off and married a man no one knew three years ago, and it's still a big scandal."

Silence welled between us.

"I want to, Joe, but I just can't do that to my parents."

"No, I don't suppose you can." The sun was in my eyes, making it hard for me to read his expression. He tightened his grip on my hand. "Well, go get your things together. We can't stay here."

He intended for us to leave? To abandon paradise? The thought was unacceptable. "Of course we can."

"Damn it, Addie, I'm crazed with wanting you. If this were a mission, I'd have to turn the controls over to my copilot, because I'm not in my right mind."

"Well, me, neither."

"Which is exactly why you need to go back to the cabin, put on some dry clothes, and pack up your things." He took my shoulders and pointed me toward shore. I turned around to face him, but he was plowing through the water, swimming for the opposite shore at a speed I couldn't possibly match. I wasn't a strong enough swimmer to even attempt to follow him.

I reluctantly headed to the cabin, my body burning with need. I don't know what came over me or where I found the courage; I only knew I couldn't bear the thought of leaving here, of sending Joe off to war, of going back to my everyday life without getting as close to this man as I could possibly get. Like Eve with the apple, I needed to know what I didn't know. I dried off, but I didn't dress. I dabbed on perfume, wrapped in a dry towel, then sat on the sofa and waited.

My already-pounding heart thundered as I heard his step on the porch. The screen door creaked open, and then he filled the doorway. His eyes moved over me. "Why

251

aren't you dressed?" His voice was harsh.

"I was waiting for you."

"No."

"Yes." I stood up and dropped the towel. I heard his breath catch. I stepped toward him before I lost my nerve. "Joe — I want to be with you. This is our last chance. And Marge told me you couldn't get pregnant the first time."

"You can't bank on that."

"Well, aren't there . . . devices?"

"Condoms?"

I nodded. "Do you have any?"

"Some military-issued ones in my shaving kit, but that's not the question here. I gave you my word, Addie, and . . ."

"I don't want your word. I want you." I don't know where my boldness came from. It was like I was somebody else. I picked up his hand and put it on my breast. "You're not the only one who has a say in this, you know."

His breath hitched. "You're playing with fire here."

"I'm counting on it." I pulled his head down and kissed him.

Once again I was swimming, swimming in emotion and a depth of desire I hadn't known existed. I became a creature I didn't recognize, a creature desperate and intense, straining for something I couldn't name. He touched and kissed me in places that shocked me, yet made me crave more. He whispered words of love and caressed me until I was aching with need. I couldn't get close enough, yet we were so close I couldn't breathe without inhaling the air he'd just exhaled. I couldn't imagine ever breathing on my own again. Every stroke took me higher and higher, until I cried out and shuddered and thought I was flying and dying all at the same time.

"You're mine," he whispered afterward.

"Likewise," I said.

"We'll marry as soon as I get back."

"Yes."

"I'll write your father and ask for your hand. Make all the fancy wedding plans you want."

We stayed in bed the rest of the day and night, making love over and over, sleeping and talking, talking, talking. We made plans for the future, plans about where we'd live and travel, about what we'd do, about how wonderful life would be. I was walking on air, flying higher than a B-24, soaring above rainbows and moonbeams toward all my wildest dreams.

18
MATT

My whole day was thrown off by Hope and that trash collection incident. I'd worked at home that morning, preparing for a huge meeting at the state capitol with the attorney general and the EPA. We're prosecuting a chemical plant that illegally dumped waste near Shreveport, and it involves a lot of mind-numbing scientific information. I managed to change clothes and arrive on time for a lunch pre-con before the afternoon meeting, but instead of being sharp and focused on toxic chemicals, my mind kept drifting to a toxic woman.

As I drove back from Baton Rouge that evening, I found myself looking forward to seeing Hope again, and I'll be damned if I quite understood why. She was a disaster waiting for a place to happen. She was the last thing I needed — a flighty, accident-prone distraction who seemed to bring out the worst in me. She was only in town for the summer, so even if I could overlook those traits, she wasn't a good candidate for a relationship. Yet every time I was around her, I had some strong, inappropriate, unwanted emotional reaction.

I don't like emotions; I prefer logic, reason, and coolheaded thoughtfulness over stomach-churning highs and gut-wrenching lows. Fatherhood was inevitably an emotional minefield, but it's one I willingly inhabit because I love my girls more than life itself and they're the very best part of me. Christine had been, too, of course, and her death — well, that's a bottomless pit of pain I don't want to ever fall down again.

So why do I keep thinking about a woman who yanks my chain so thoroughly that I do things without thinking, like pick her up off a garbage truck when I'm freshly dressed in a suit and tie? This morning's behavior had been irrational and ridiculous. I just as easily could have taken the box from her, being careful to handle only the clean side — or I could have asked the garbage collector who was so enthusiastically helping her litter my lawn to give her a hand down — but did I do that? No. I'd waded right in like a knight in a shining business suit and picked her up, muck and all, as if she were a fairy-tale princess descending from a magic carriage in one of my daughters' Disney flicks.

She sure hadn't felt like a fairy tale in my arms, though. She'd felt like a completely real, completely carnal, sexy-as-sin woman. What was it about her that gave me this reaction? I hadn't felt attraction like that since Christine — certainly not for any of the appropriate women my various friends had tried to fix me up with since her death. If I was going to be drawn to a woman — and even Peggy and Griff had been encouraging me to start dating — why did it have to be this one?

Maybe because she *was* so completely inappropriate, I thought. Maybe my subconscious was trying to keep me from starting anything serious. Everyone thinks I should be ready for a relationship, but the truth is, I'm probably not.

I'm more than a little afraid that I may never be — and the thought is depressing as hell. I wonder if a part of my brain will keep me from ever getting that close again because it will always be thinking, *at any second, something can happen to her.*

Nothing about that last night with Christine had seemed out of the ordinary. We'd had dinner and put the girls to bed, and I'd turned on the TV. When Christine said she was going upstairs to take a bath, I'd just nodded and kept on watching the basketball game. It wasn't until the game was over — LSU had been playing Texas A&M — that I realized she'd been gone a long time. I went upstairs and found her stretched on the bed, still fully clothed — her eyes open and vacant.

I've never felt fear like that — cold, sickening, desperate, crushing. My heart had stopped, then damn near jumped out of my chest. I immediately lifted her to the floor and started mouth-to-mouth resuscitation. Christine and I had both taken CPR classes before the girls were born. I paused for a nanosecond to find the phone and call 911, then I kept at it, rhythmically compressing her chest and breathing into her mouth.

This couldn't be happening, I remember thinking. This was a mistake. She was a young, healthy woman with two small children who needed her. *I* needed her.

The worst part was her eyes. If she'd close her eyes or blink, I just knew it would be okay. But that vacant, unseeing stare — was anything colder, anything more hopeless than the unseeing eyes of the already gone?

I hated turning her over to the medics when the ambulance arrived, but I figured they would know what to do. They used a defibrillator. She jerked off the floor, her eyes still open and vacant. Again. And again.

A neighbor had come over when the ambulance arrived and offered to stay and watch the kids. I agreed. I followed the ambulance to the hospital — I don't know how I drove, but my car was there later, so I must have. At the hospital, she was whisked into the ER. They made me wait outside. I called her parents. And then the doctor came out and told me she was gone.

Gone where? From what? How?

The medical staff asked *me* questions. The police came and asked me questions. So many questions, and I had no answers — no answers at all. The next day, I learned she'd died of a brain aneurysm, but I still couldn't answer the biggest question of all: *Why?*

I still can't answer it. I hate it when the girls ask, as they sometimes do.

In the two years since, I've learned to live with uncertainty. We all live with it, whether we're aware of it or not. We're all just a piece of bad news away from having our hearts broken.

The only defense is to not care that deeply. I can't help it with my daughters, but I've wondered if I'll ever let another woman close enough to cause that kind of pain again.

I pulled into my drive, noting with relief that Jillian's car wasn't parked there — nor was it across the street at her parents' home. Good. I wouldn't have to deal with her wife-like concerns. I was looking forward to seeing Hope without Jillian's hovering, stifling presence.

"Daddy's home!" yelled Sophie as I walked through the door.

As always, my chest filled with warmth. Both girls came barreling toward me. I dropped my computer case on the credenza, then bent and scooped them both up in my arms, whirling them around in a way that made them squeal. They're growing so fast I won't be able to hold them both at the same time for much longer. The thought gave me a pang.

Griff toddled in behind them, his face creased with a wistful smile. The sight of the girls hanging on to my neck seemed to give him a pang of his own. "I remember when my girls greeted me like that."

Sophie tugged at my arm the moment I set them down. "Daddy — come see the drawing I did at school!"

"Me, too. And I've got some papers to show you — and they all have stars!" Zoey said.

"Okay, okay — just let me get my coat off."

I looped my jacket over a dining room chair and grinned at Griff. "You're on babysitting patrol all by yourself?"

"Briefly. Peggy stepped next door a few minutes ago to say hello to Miss Addie. Think she wanted to check on Hope's sketch of the girls' room, as well. She left a pot of gumbo for you and the girls on the stove."

"That was mighty kind of her," I said, loosening my tie and unfastening the top button of my shirt. "Peggy's gumbo is the best."

The only problem was it reminded me of Christine, because she'd used her mother's recipe. Every time I tasted it, I got a lump in my throat that made it hard to swallow.

Griff waved good-bye and let himself out the front door.

I headed into the kitchen, sat down with the girls, and admired their papers. Peggy had also left a salad in the refrigerator, so as the girls set the table, I dished up salad and bowls of gumbo, and we sat down to dinner.

I hadn't realized how much I'd been listening for the sound of the doorbell until it rang as we were cleaning up.

"That must be Hope!" said Sophie.

"I'll get it," I said, drying my hands on a dish towel. My pulse irrationally picked up speed.

She wore a white T-shirt and shorts. Her hair was loose and floaty, and a large sketchbook was tucked under her arm. "Did you make it to your meeting on time this morning?"

"Yeah. It was fine."

"I'm so sorry about getting your clothes messed up." Her eyes were big tea-colored saucers of sincerity.

"Forget about it."

Sophie and Zoey appeared beside me, bouncing up and down with excitement. "Are you here to paint our room?" Sophie asked.

"I'm here to start the process. The first step is showing you the sketches, and then you can tell me what you like and what you want changed."

The girls shrieked with delight.

"Why don't we go to your room," Hope suggested. "That way I can point out what goes where."

The girls scampered up the stairs. I motioned for Hope to precede me, thinking I was being polite. My chivalrous intentions

261

morphed into lascivious thoughts as I gazed at her backside in those shorts. Good grief, but the woman was hot.

It was something of a relief when we reached the landing and headed down the hall to the girls' room. Hope stopped between the headboards of the twin beds and opened her sketchbook. "This is what I drew for this wall."

We all gazed at it.

"Oh wow!" Sophie gasped.

"It's perfect," Zoey pronounced, eyes big and solemn.

I'm not a big fan of princess art, but even I thought it was pretty cool. Two enormous arched windows covered much of the wall. Out of one window, you could see a drawbridge and people on horses crossing it, with mountains and a village in the distance. The other window revealed a tower covered with a pink-blooming vine. "I thought these windows would be on either side of the beds," Hope said.

"Awesome," Sophie murmured. Zoey, usually the critic, nodded in agreement.

"And I thought we might make little canopies for each bed coming out from the wall."

Hope flipped the page in her sketchbook and showed a drawing of the same windows, this time with the twin beds, each topped with little partial canopies.

The girls gasped.

"What would the canopies be made of?" I asked.

"Fabric, plant hangers, and curtain rods," she said. "I made one for my first apartment."

"Would you make them, or would we need to find someone to sew?" I asked.

"Oh, I can do it. Gran taught me how." She grinned at the girls. "So what do you think?"

Zoey clasped her hands. "It's splendid-did."

I looked at Hope and saw her stifling a laugh. It felt good, enjoying a silent, isn't-she-adorable moment with her.

"What about the other walls?" Sophie asked.

"Good question." Hope motioned to the dormer window with the built-in window seat. "This wall really just needs drapes and a cushion to match the canopies. We'd paint the wall to look like stone, so it would feel like we're inside a castle room. We'd do the same on this wall over here . . ." She motioned to their bureaus. "And I thought we might also paint a tapestry on it." She flipped her sketchbook to another page.

"Like this."

"Oooh," Sophie breathed.

Hope motioned to the wall with the closet. "Over here, all we need to do is the stone treatment over, between, and around the doors." She showed another sketch.

The girls oohed, aahed, and jumped up and down.

"This is really nice, but I thought we were just doing a mural on one wall." Last thing I needed was for her to get halfway finished, then leave town. "I'm sure you have your hands full with your grandmother, and this seems like a lot of work."

She waved her hand. "The whole thing will probably take me about three weeks."

Sounded like a Pollyanna-ish time estimate to me. "That's all? Are you sure?"

"I work fast." She looked down, her expression almost embarrassed. "Too fast to be a serious artist, I've been told."

I wondered who'd told her that. "Sounds like an asset to me."

"I can't wait!" Sophie said.

Zoey nodded.

"Has Peggy seen this?" I asked.

Hope's curls bobbed on her shoulders. "She came over to Gran's and I showed her. She approved the sketch as well as the estimate. She said she's paying."

"Peggy is *not* paying." Peggy had promised the girls a real princess room when we moved to Wedding Tree, but I had no intention of letting her pick up the tab.

"Well, that's something the two of you will have to work out. Here's the estimate." Hope handed me a professional-looking bid form.

I looked it over. It was less than what I'd been willing to pay the artist from New Orleans, minus the travel expenses.

"Looks good. When do we start?"

"As soon as you'd like. If we use the current color as the base, I can just start sketching directly onto the walls."

"Yes!" yelled Sophie, throwing up her arms.

"Let's start now!" said Zoey.

"Do we need to do anything to prep the room?" I asked.

"Not just yet. Having the furniture in place will be a help while I'm sketching. Once I start actually painting, though, we'll need to pull the furniture out of the way, cover the floor, and move the girls to another bedroom until the project's finished."

"No problem."

"Can I help? I can paint!" Zoey said. "I painted some pictures at school today."

"Me, too," chimed in Sophie. "Wanna see?"

Hope grinned at them. "I'd love to see your artwork. And, yes — once I get it all sketched out, you can both help."

They jumped up and down and shrieked so loudly I was tempted to cover my ears. Then they thundered downstairs to gather up their art collection.

Silence hung between us for a moment, the kind of charged silence that comes from being alone with someone you find attractive. "They're excited."

"I can tell." Hope's smile transformed her from pretty to dazzling. "They're adorable."

Another charged silence electrified the air. "So . . . did your grandmother tell you anything about the man in the photos?"

She nodded, tucking a stray strand of hair behind her ear. "It's a wildly romantic tale, but . . . well, I'm afraid of where it's all leading."

"Now you have me intrigued."

"What's intriguing?"

I started at the sound of Jillian's voice in the hallway. I hadn't heard her come in; she must have let herself in the back door with her key. I felt oddly guilty, as if I'd been caught doing something I wasn't supposed to do, and the feeling rankled.

"What's intriguing?" Jillian repeated.

None of your business. I squelched down my irritation and forced a tone of nonchalance. "Oh — just some things Miss Addie is telling Hope about the past."

"How interesting." Jillian looked from my face to Hope's. Now Hope felt on the spot. My irritation mounted.

"I wasn't expecting you tonight, Jillian."

"I finished with the school meeting early and thought I'd drop in to see if you and the girls were all right."

"We're fine." The words came out curter than I'd intended. I knew she meant well, but damn it, it was just too invasive, her walking right into my home without ringing the bell, just assuming she was welcome. I mean, I'm grateful for the way she watches out for the girls and all that she does around the house, but there needed to be some limits. I felt my jaw tighten into what Christine used to call my Mount Rushmore face — the one she said was stony and cold. "It was nice of you to stop by."

The color drained from Jillian's cheeks. She visibly swallowed. "I — I didn't mean to intrude."

The thunder of feet rumbled again on the back stairs, and the girls burst into the room. "Aunt Jillian!" Zoey made a beeline

267

to hug Jillian. Sophie followed suit. "Come
see what Hope's gonna do to our walls! An'
look at the pictures we drew today!"

"I — I'm sorry, girls, but I think I need to
go," Jillian said, stepping back.

"Why? You just got here!"

"Yeah. Don' you want to see my pictures?"
Sophie echoed.

Jillian put her hand on Sophie's hair. "Of
course I do, sweetheart, but I don't want to
intrude."

Zoey looked at him quizzically. "You're
not 'truding. Right, Dad?"

Oh, for God's sake. I ran a hand down my
face and blew out a hot breath. "Of course
not. I wasn't expecting you, Jillian, that's
all."

Sophie tugged at Hope's hand. "Show
Jillian the sketches, Hope!"

Hope complied. I stood there in the
doorway, all too aware of the way Jillian's
presence had completely changed the dy-
namics, disliking both the interruption and
my reaction to it.

Hell. I wasn't all that happy about my reaction to Hope, either. She was a distraction I probably didn't need right now —
especially since she was going to be here
every evening for the next few weeks. If I
knew what was good for me and the girls,

I'd keep my distance.

My phone rang. It was an assistant working on an important brief. Excusing myself, I went downstairs to my office, glad of the excuse to escape.

19
HOPE

The next day Gran was scheduled for a bath by an aide, then a doctor's appointment, then a physical therapy session. We barely had a moment alone, and all of the activity exhausted her. She didn't bring up the topic of Joe again the following day, or the one after, and I decided not to push it. I worked on packing up the china, crystal, and sterling serving pieces in her dining room. Sending photos to Eddie and Ralph and following up on their requests to save certain items, to sell others on eBay, or to request appraisals from antiques dealers kept me plenty busy.

On Saturday, Gran was scheduled for her quarterly perm at the beauty parlor. It would take all morning, so at her urging, I decided to let her aide drive her to the appointment so I could go to the Friends of the Forest planting.

"It's a good cause, it's always fun, and it's

a great group of women," Gran said. "I've known most of them since they were small-fry. Knew most of their mothers, grand-mothers, and great-grandmothers, too."

I felt a moment of trepidation when I walked into the coffee shop and saw a group of women chatting and laughing together. They all were obviously good friends, and I felt like the new kid at school.

Kirsten quickly put me at ease. "Hope, I'm so glad you made it!" She gestured toward the other women. "Everyone, this is Miss Addie's granddaughter."

"Oh, the artist!" exclaimed a pixie-faced woman in a green quilted vest. She reminded me of an elf, or maybe Peter Pan. Her strawberry blond hair was cut very short. Freckles danced across her nose, and her green eyes were bright and lively. "I'm Aimee." She pronounced her name the French way — *Em-may*.

I shook her hand.

"Aimee is a high school English teacher," Kirsten explained.

"And I'm Clarabel." A middle-aged woman with platinum blond hair and rhinestone-studded eyeglasses grasped my hand. "I work at the Hair You Are beauty salon."

"Oh, my grandmother's going there this

morning!"

Clarabel nodded sagely. "She's Miss Bernice's client. I saw on the appointment sheet that she's down for a perm."

"This is Marie." Kirsten gestured toward a dark-haired young woman with a shy demeanor. "She's a stay-at-home mother with beautiful three-year-old twins."

"Oh my, that must keep you busy!"

"You have no idea," Marie said, shaking my hand.

"This is Freret." Kirsten gestured to a tall woman about my age with dark, chin-length hair, who looked chic in skinny jeans and a safari-style top. "She's the chief loan officer at the bank, which makes her a very handy person to know." Kirsten put her hand on the arm of another brunette, with a friendly smile, curly hair, and red lipstick. "And this is Jen. She's the librarian."

Jen gave a wide smile. "I've heard so much about you."

I could feel my face heat. "I can't imagine how."

"Well, this is a small town."

I was also introduced to a friendly-faced woman named Blythe who worked at the coffee shop part-time, as well as a high school student who helped out on weekends. Kirsten clapped her hands together.

"All right, ladies — let's get going!"

Everyone except Blythe and the teenager trooped out and piled into Marie's red minivan.

"I heard you're doing a mural for Matt's daughters' room," Aimee said, settling next to me in the center seat of the second row for the fifteen-minute drive to the nature preserve.

I nodded.

"Oh, my — that Matt is a dream cake." Clarabel fanned herself as if she were having a hot flash. "If I were ten years younger, I'd make a play for him in a New York minute."

"Just ten years younger?" teased Kirsten.

Clarabel rolled her eyes. "Well, ten years would put me in the game if he liked cougars."

Everyone laughed.

"I don't know how anyone could follow in Christine's shoes," said Marie.

"I've heard she was really something," I commented.

"Something and a half," Aimee said. "In high school, she was head cheerleader, valedictorian, and captain of the volleyball team."

"Not to mention popular and sweet," Freret sighed.

"You wanted to hate her, but you just couldn't," Kirsten added.

The women all laughed, their expressions wistful.

"You name it, and she not only did it, she did it beautifully and graciously and with magnificent style," Aimee said. "She was a successful attorney, a wonderful mom, and drop-dead gorgeous to boot. Matt and she were just the cutest couple."

The praise of the dead woman left me oddly jealous, which made me feel petty and small. "I've seen photos," I said. "She looked like Kate Bosworth."

The women nodded.

"Speaking of photos, your grandmother took my wedding pictures," Marie said. "She was wonderful. She took lots of care to make everyone look great."

"That's what's so special about her," Jen added. "She sees the best in everyone."

"I have three generations of Miss Addie pictures hanging on my wall," Clarabel said. "My christening, my daughter's christening, and my grandchildren's christenings."

My throat grew thick with emotion.

"How's she doing?" Aimee asked.

"Very well, all things considered, but that head injury really took a toll on her."

Clarabel looked at me sympathetically.

"On her mind?"

"Well, on her short-term memory, for sure. She'll forget something that was said five minutes ago, but she remembers a lot about the past. At least, I *think* she's remembering it."

"Dementia's so common in someone her age," Marie murmured.

"I don't think it's that," I said. "Some of her stories are pretty far out, but I think they really happened. What worries me is that sometimes I find her all alone, talking out loud."

"Oh, I do that," Clarabel said. "I talk to myself all the time. And sometimes I talk to Saint Anthony to help me find stuff. Why, just the other day, I lost my car at the grocery store, and . . ."

She told a funny tale about getting into the wrong car, which inspired Freret to tell about getting lost in the French Quarter, which led to other stories and confessions. My stomach hurt from laughing by the time we'd piled out of the van and joined a group of about a dozen more people.

To my surprise, Matt, Zoey, and Sophie were among them. I spotted the children first — then Matt turned around, and my stomach somersaulted.

Sophie gave a squeal and ran toward me.

"Hey, Hope! Look — Zoey lost her tooth!"

I bent and looked into her widely opened mouth. "That's wonderful, sweetie! I can see your big-girl tooth already coming in."

"Yeah! And the tooth fairy came and gave me a dollar!"

"That's wonderful."

"Are you going to come work on our room tonight?" Sophie asked.

"If it's okay with your father."

Matt had been friendly, but largely invisible for the last few evenings. The girls were in and out of the bedroom while I sketched on the walls, chattering about their day, the sleepover birthday they were both going to the following weekend, how caterpillars turn into butterflies, and a million other things, but Matt mostly stayed downstairs. He seemed to want to keep his distance — and who could blame him? I did something weird every time he saw me.

My exchange with Sophie was cut off when a man in a green uniform with a Louisiana Agriculture and Forestry Service badge motioned for everyone to gather around a white pickup with the department logo on the door. "Thanks for coming out today. As you know, we're planting trees to help stop erosion of the wetlands." He opened the bed of the pickup to reveal neat piles of what looked like twelve-inch twigs, along with a stack of shovels. "Our mission is pretty simple. We'll plant these trees beyond the orange ropes. Today we've got Leyland cypress, and they need to be planted about eight to ten feet apart. I've cut these strings the right distance, so you don't have to guess."

A woman wearing a big straw hat raised her hand. "My gardening guide says cypress should be planted about twenty feet apart."

"If you're planting them as ornamental trees at your home, that's right. But we're hoping to form a wind break, so we want them close enough together to support each other."

"Don't you worry about the roots growing together?"

"Yeah. Or the branches, like the Wedding Tree?" Clarabel pointed behind me. I turned and saw an arch joining two massive live oak trees. I looked closer, and saw that two branches had grown together, forming an arbor.

This was the town's namesake, I realized. Gran had brought me here to see it when I was a child, and I'd seen numerous photos she'd shot of it — at dawn and dusk, summer and winter, with and without couples under it — but seeing it in person as an

277

adult was something else.

"That's a pretty rare occurrence, called inosculation," the forestry officer said. "It sometimes happens that two branches of separate trees, usually of the same species, form a graft of the branches or roots. A tree like that is actually called a husband and wife tree, or a marriage tree. Local lore has it that anyone who kisses under that tree will be together for life."

Murmurs of "Oh, how sweet!" and "How romantic!" arose from some of the volunteers.

The forestry guide gave further instructions, answered a couple more questions, and handed out shovels. "You can work alone, or in groups of two or three."

"Hope — come with us!" Sophie said, grabbing my shovel-free hand.

"No, Sophie. That would make four," Zoey corrected.

Kirsten grinned at her. "The two of you make up less than one adult, so I'm pretty sure you'd still be within the guidelines." She looked at me. "We've got the perfect number for two groups, and I'm sure Matt can use the help. Right, Matt?"

From the way he'd been avoiding me when I worked on the mural, I was pretty sure he didn't want to be stuck with me.

"Oh, I don't want . . ."

"Great." Kirsten smiled as if it were all settled before I could finish my thought or Matt could utter a word. "We'll see you back here when we're finished." With that, she turned and marched off. Clarabel gave me a broad wink and followed Kirsten.

Once again, I wished the ground would open up and swallow me. Why did every encounter with Matt end up being awkward?

"Yay!" Sophie exclaimed, tugging on my hand. "Let's go see the tree!"

I shot Matt a questioning look.

"Sure," he said.

Sophie sprinted over to it, and the rest of us followed after her. "Did the trees have a real wedding?" She craned her head up and gazed at the arch joining the two live oaks.

"Trees can't get married, dummy," Zoey said disdainfully.

"I'm not a dummy!"

"No, she's not. And you know the rule about name-calling," Matt said. "Apologize, Zoey."

"Sorry."

"I forgive you." Sophie's face was sunny, as if the incident hadn't occurred. "I'd love to go to a wedding."

"Maybe Daddy and Jillian will have one,"

Zoey suggested.

Matt shifted the shovel to his other hand. "Jillian is your aunt."

"Yeah, but she could marry you, and then she'd be our mother," Zoey said. "I asked her."

Matt's lips flattened. "This isn't something you should be discussing with Jillian."

"Why not?"

"Well, because . . ." He shifted the shovel again. "Marriage is between a man and a woman."

"It's 'tween the kids, too," Zoey insisted.

"Well, it involves them, of course, but first, it's a man-woman thing," Matt looked as if he'd rather be discussing anything else. "You'll understand when you get older."

"It has to do with kissing and stuff," Sophie piped up.

"Jillian kisses Daddy," Zoey volunteered.

I saw Matt's ears redden. "Just as a greeting. It's not the same."

"Hey — maybe Dad and Hope will kiss!" Sophie looked at me, her eyes wide and optimistic. "The forest man said anyone who kisses under the tree stays together!"

My mouth felt incapable of moving, even if my mind could have formed words.

I didn't mean to look at Matt, but he caught my eye, and a bolt of heat shot between us. I felt my cheeks burn.

"Sounds like you two have been watching too many Disney princess movies," Matt said easily, stepping away from the arbor of the trees' intertwined branches.

"Well, I'll kiss Hope." Before I knew what was happening, Sophie grabbed my hand and kissed it. "There. Now you'll have to stay in Wedding Tree forever."

"It doesn't work that way," Zoey sniffed.

"You don't know everything." Sophie looked at me with such affection that my heart turned over.

"Hey — that looks like a good place to plant a tree over there." Matt gestured in the distance in an obvious bid to change the subject. "What do you think?"

"Yes!" Sophie exclaimed.

Matt led the way, and we all traipsed along. Zoey picked the exact site, and Matt drove his shovel into the dirt.

I started digging, too, but my shovel only got in the way of his. The girls argued over which tree should be planted first, then what the tree should be named. "Belle" was finally settled into the soil, and Matt and I — okay, mostly Matt — scooped dirt back around it. Matt placed a hand on top of the tree. "Belle, I hereby beseech thee to live long and prosper."

The ritual was repeated eight more times, with the girls taking over each tree's blessing. The words grew more and more mangled as we proceeded, like a game of telephone. The last tree's solemn injunction, muttered by Sophie, sounded something like, "Jasmine, I hear 'bout bee's itchy to live large and posture."

Matt and I grinned over their heads. Once again, I felt a zing of heat pass between us. The girls played tag on the way back, and Matt and I joined in. We were all laughing as we joined the other volunteers at the truck thirty minutes later.

The forestry officer gathered up the shovels. "Great job! Thanks a million."

I waved good-bye to Matt and the girls, and piled back into the van with the women. "Husband and wife tree," Jen said as we passed it. "That's so beautiful — the thought of those two trees grafted and growing together."

"After a while they're just holding each other up," Clarabel said.

"That's beautiful, too," said Jen.

Everyone laughed, but we all murmured sounds of agreement. I twisted in my seat to gaze at the tree until it was no longer in sight.

20
ADELAIDE

I sneaked out to the backyard while Nadine the aide was in the bathroom. I thought that if I went outside, it might trigger something. I didn't expect a memory, exactly — how could I remember something I hadn't known in the first place? — but I figured that I might get some kind of notion where to look.

The Meyer lemon tree against the far fence was in bloom. The scent was dizzyingly sweet. The tulips were still bursting with color, as dazzling and warm as new love. And the azaleas — oh, what colors! In the last few days they'd opened wide, their petals of fuchsia and pink blazing so brightly they practically burned my eyes. My fingers twitched, longing to connect with a camera button. It was one of my favorite times of the year, when God seemed to just burst through the leaves in a sudden, overflowing abundance of beauty. I felt sorry for people who rushed right by, never seeing the colors, never acknowledging the love the creator poured into making such an opulent display, just to gladden our hearts and assure us of his glory.

But I needed to think about how the yard had looked back then. Goodness, that would have been sixty-some-odd years ago! The yard had changed a lot over time. It still has the big oaks, some magnolias, and a couple of birch trees, but a giant elm, some pines, and a pecan tree have since died or been toppled in a hurricane. The vegetable garden is still on the right side, but it's much smaller than it was back then, and I didn't have the flower beds encircling the trees. The only place I'm pretty sure I can rule out was the center of the lawn. Charlie couldn't have buried anything there, or I would have seen it.

Or would I? It had been fall, and the ground was covered with leaves. Maybe right out in plain sight would have been the best hiding place of all.

I leaned heavily on my walker. The truth is, at the time, I hadn't wanted to see anything. I'd even asked Charlie if I should skip planting vegetables or flowers that spring, and he'd replied, "No reason not to." Still, I'd only planted a few tomatoes and peppers and squash plants, no root vegetables or anything deep, and I'd felt uneasy in the backyard all that summer, and most of the summer after. There's a possibility, I suppose, that he actually left our property that night to bury that suitcase somewhere else, but the gate squeaked, and opening it wide made it bang against the house, and I think I would have heard it.

Funny how you can fear something so much that you just can't bear to think about it, but the more you push it to the back of your thoughts, the stronger the dread of it grows. All these years, this fear had been festering in its dark corner. Waiting. Lurking. Spreading in the dark, like a fungus.

Now that I'm finally bringing it forward, it's shocking, how much it tortures me. Shame is so corrosive. How could I have left it unaddressed for all these years? How had I lived with it? How had Charlie?

Ah, well. What is done in secret will be brought into the light. That's what it says in the good book, and I guess that's the way it is.

"Gran?"

I turned to see Hope and the aide standing behind me.

"What are you doing out here?" Hope asked.

"Enjoying the azaleas." The lie felt bitter on my tongue. *Time for the truth, old girl.* "And . . . trying to remember something."

"You shouldn't be out of the house without someone," the aide scolded.

I smiled at her. "No offense, dearie, but now and then, I need some time alone. At my age, I think I've earned that right."

The aide put her hand on hip, as if she was about to give me a lecture, but Hope spoke first. "Of course you have. Be careful not to get too tired."

She motioned the aide back inside and followed her. I could feel Hope, though, watching me through the kitchen window.

She was worried. And it was no wonder; the fact was, I was frail and old and feeble. Standing out here wasn't helping anyway. I shuffled back to the kitchen, surprised and chagrined at how arduous a trek it was.

"Would you like some tea?" Hope asked.

"Yes, dear. Pour some for yourself as well, and then let's take it into my bedroom and tell the aide not to disturb us."

I slowly scuffled into my room and settled in the rocking chair. Hope brought in two steaming mugs, set them both on coasters on my side table, and looked at me expectantly.

"Look in the very back of the closet, on

the left. There's a black-and-white pin-striped dress."

She stepped into my closet and pulled it out. "This?"

"Yes."

She brought it to me. It was rayon, had long sleeves, a patent belt, and a flared skirt, and it used to fit me within an inch of my life. I'd always felt so polished and professional when I wore it. I fingered the fabric. "Lay it on the bed, dear, and have a seat."

She picked up her mug and settled on the bed beside the dress.

I leaned back in the rocker, closed my eyes, lapsed into storytelling mode. "Two days after I got back to New Orleans from my trip with Joe, I got a phone call from my mother. In those days, a long-distance phone call was a rare thing indeed."

1943

I'd been in my room, composing a letter to Joe, when Lucille called me to the phone. I'd raced downstairs, hoping it was Joe, but that dream was squashed as soon as I dashed into the living room and saw Lucille's cloth-curlered head pressed against the receiver, her forehead creased. "But I'm sure she said it was an uncle who died," she was saying.

Oh, dear Lord. As the kids say today, I was busted. I'd told Marge all about the trip and Joe's proposal, of course, but not Lucille. She'd no doubt offered my mother condolences on Uncle Leo's passing. My chest felt like a truck was parked on it as she extended the phone to me, her gaze reproachful. "It's your mother."

I hesitantly took the receiver. "Hello, Mother. Is everything all right?"

"Yes, yes. But what was Lucille saying about you going to an uncle's funeral last week?"

"Uncle Leo? He's a, uh, jazz musician. Everyone calls him that. He's the uncle of a, uh, close friend." For a person who never lied, I was spinning quite a spiel. I turned my back to Lucille, who was hovering nearby, obviously listening. I needed to change the topic, and fast. "I'll tell you all about it in a letter — I don't want you buying out the phone company. What are you calling about? Is everyone okay?"

Fortunately, the news that had spurred the call was more urgent than Mother's curiosity about my weekend. "We're great. Charlie's coming home on Friday!"

My heart rolled in my chest like a ship in high waves.

"You have to be here," Mother said. "He

specifically asked."

My heart lurched again. "But, Mother, I have to work."

"You can come afterward."

"But . . ."

"No buts, Adelaide. He specifically asked for you, and I'm not telling Virginia that you can't make it."

"But, Mother — I — I've met someone else. In fact, I'm writing you a letter telling you about him, and . . ."

"Stop right there, young lady. This isn't the time for that kind of thing. You put that aside for now, you hear me?" Mother's voice was as commanding as General Patton's. "Put that aside, and come home Friday. And I expect you to be the girl you've always been with Charlie. He's lost enough already."

My throat tightened. "What do you mean? Did he . . . did he lose his leg?"

"No, but they had to amputate some of his toes."

Relief poured through me. Toes were so much better than an entire leg! And yet, it was still a loss. "Poor Charlie."

"Yes. His leg is very weak, but he still has it. He's on crutches, but they expect him to be able to walk on his own eventually. Now I expect to see you Friday night. There's a bus that leaves New Orleans at six thirty in the evening and gets here at nine thirty. See that you're on it. The town is doing a big party in his honor Saturday, and you have to be here."

There was really no help for it. How could I not go to Charlie's welcome home celebration? He was my childhood friend, my high school sweetheart, the only child of my mother's dearest friend.

I hung up the phone, despondent. I had no choice.

Was life always going to be like this . . . a good thing happens, and then a bad one? At what point did everything start to be okay?

Back then, I thought there was some golden moment I would arrive at, a turning point after which everything would be fine and dandy. During most of my youth, "after the war" had looked like that moment.

It was naive and juvenile, I know now. It probably came from reading too many books and watching too many movies with happy endings. But when Joe left and Charlie came home, that was the first time I began to realize that maybe there was no such thing as a trouble-free ever after. Maybe life would always be a constant mingle of good and bad. Maybe no matter how perfectly I dreamed and planned, something would always be undone, missing, lacking, or askew. Maybe I would always think, "I'd be perfectly happy, if only . . ."

At the time, of course, I didn't know this. I spent most of the long bus ride thinking how I would let Charlie down gently. All my thoughts were focused on Joe and how marvelous our lives would be together.

I'd expected to see my mother at the bus station — and possibly my father. The person I hadn't expected to see was Charlie, standing right there where the bus unloaded, propped up on crutches. His parents stood on either side of him.

"Adelaide," he said, his voice thick with emotion.

He was pale and thin — so much thinner than I remembered. His eyes were sunken and ringed with shadows. My heart gave a sick little clutch, just like it had that time I'd found a bald baby bird with a broken neck under the oak tree. "Oh, Charlie." I stepped toward him, and the next thing I knew, he'd dropped his crutches and grabbed me. He kissed me full on the mouth, so hard it hurt my teeth, smashing my nose against his, making it impossible to breathe. I pulled back, but he clung to me, burying his face against my neck and sobbing into my hair.

All I could think was — God help me! — how much better Joe had felt; how much taller, sturdier, stronger, and manlier he'd been, how the press of his body against mine had unleashed a dizzying surge of desire, while Charlie's frail, childlike frame filled me with pity. I flushed with shame at my thoughts. A ripple of revulsion rolled through me — not at Charlie's touch, but at his naked devotion, at his beggarly need.

"Charlie," I murmured. "My parents. Your mother . . ."

That seemed to bring him to his senses. My father cleared his throat. Charlie's mother stooped and picked up his crutches, and his father steadied him as I drew back.

"When did you get here?" I asked, smoothing my skirt and trying to hide my embarrassment under a show of normalcy.

"At noon," Charlie said.

"The whole town turned out," his father added. "The high school band played, and the mayor gave a speech."

"How wonderful."

His mother grew teary-eyed. "Yes. It was."

"Well, I'm sure you're exhausted," I said. "I didn't travel nearly as far as you, and I'm about to drop."

"Yes, we'd better get you both home," my father said.

"You two young people can catch up tomorrow," my mother said.

"Yes, indeed," Charlie's father echoed.

I rode home with my parents. Mother talked the whole time, telling me how Charlie had taken shrapnel from a grenade, how brave he'd been, how they'd feared he would die, how his mother had been beside herself.

"It's just so wonderful to have you both back home! Didn't I tell you Charlie was anxious to see you? As poorly as he felt, nothing would do but that he come to the bus station to see you the moment you got here."

Words built inside me like steam in a kettle, until they fairly burst out of my mouth. "Mother — I tried to tell you on the phone. I met someone. A pilot. And . . . he's asked me to marry him. And I said yes."

"What?" My parents spoke simultaneously. Mother twisted around the front car seat and stared at me, her jaw slack. "No!"

"Yes. I'm engaged."

She looked at my hand, obviously noting the lack of a ring. "You are no such thing." She whipped back around to face my father. "Tell her, Robert. This man hasn't asked for her hand or even met us. She is *not* engaged."

My father glanced at my mother, then looked at me in the rearview mirror. "Adelaide, your mother's right. He hasn't done any of the things one does to make it official."

"There's a war on, for heaven's sake! He's on his way to the Pacific. The rules can't be followed to the letter during a war. He's writing you, Daddy. He told me he was going to write you and ask for my hand."

"We haven't received any such letter," Mother said. Before I could tell her that there hadn't been time, she demanded, "Where did you meet this man?"

"At the USO."

"How long have you known him?" Father asked.

I hated to say, because I knew how it would sound. "A while."

"How long a while?" Mother pressed.

"Long enough to know I love him."

"How long is that in calendar terms?" my father queried.

I drew in a steadying breath. "About two weeks."

"Two weeks! Did you hear that, Robert? Two weeks." My mother leaned back in her seat, as if it were all settled. "You can't possibly be telling us that you know this man well enough to want to marry him in that length of time."

"But I *am* telling you that. I love him."

"Love." She said the word as if I were either too big of an idiot to know anything about it, or as if the very concept itself were ludicrous. "I refuse to listen to this nonsense. And I forbid you to say anything about this to anyone while you're here."

"Mother!"

"You listen to me, young lady. You are *not* going to break the heart of a man who's known you his whole life and who loves you to pieces and who just returned from the war with a missing limb. Why, he nearly died, defending our freedom!"

I wanted to say that a few toes didn't qualify as a limb, but I didn't. "Mother, I don't want to hurt Charlie. But I don't want to get his hopes up, either."

"You don't have to do either, Adelaide. Just be nice to him. Just act like you used to when you were dating. I venture to say that after you're around him again, you'll realize you still have feelings for him."

"Mother, we broke up before he left."

"Nonsense. You've been writing to him."

"I've been writing to several soldiers. I send them all the same letter."

"Adelaide LeDoux." My mother's voice was shocked and disapproving. "I raised you better than that."

"Better than what? I haven't done anything wrong." A hot flare of anger shot through me. "There was nothing of a romantic nature in those letters. I've told you and told you. I don't love Charlie."

"Well, that doesn't matter right now. He loves you, and this is not the time to break his heart. You need to do everything you can to make him happy."

What about my heart? I wanted to say. *Don't I have a right to be happy, too?* But I bit my lip and kept my mouth shut. Arguing with my mother was futile.

When we arrived at the house, I went up to my childhood bedroom and crawled into the bed where I'd slept since I'd outgrown my crib, feeling just as helpless and under her thumb as I had back then.

By the time I got up for breakfast, Charlie had already called, and our mothers had made plans for our day.

"I'll pack a picnic lunch," my mother said. "You can drive his father's car, and you two can have a lovely day down by the river. Just be back by four. The town is throwing a potluck celebration at the Baptist church at

296

five thirty, and you want to have time to dress for it."

Which is how we ended up driving to the country, out to the Atchafalaya River. As we left town, Charlie put his hand on my neck, playing with my hair. I told him it interfered with my ability to concentrate on my driving, and he'd chuckled, as if it pleased him. He kept his hands to himself, though — and when we got out of the car, his crutches and the fact I was carrying the picnic basket and blanket kept him from trying to hold my hand.

I tried to deflect every romantic thing he uttered.

"I can't tell you how much I missed you," he said.

"I'm sure you missed everyone and everything about home."

"Oh, yeah. But you most of all."

"Tell me all about life in the army."

He did. I spread a blanket on the riverbank, and he talked and talked, telling me about maneuvers and battles and the personalities of his fellow soldiers. The tight guardedness in my chest eased. This was Charlie, my lifelong friend. He'd been through hell and back, and my heart ached as he talked about the cruel, ugly, unremitting horror of the war.

"How did you get injured?" I knew the general story, but I hadn't heard the specifics.

He lay back on the blanket and draped his arm over his eyes. "We were in a trench, under heavy fire. I was sick with dysentery. All of a sudden, a grenade landed at my feet. Like most of the others, I scrambled to get away. But there was one soldier . . ." Charlie's Adam's apple bobbed in his throat. "His name was Albert, and he was from upstate New York. He came from money, big money, and he'd enlisted against his family's wishes. He kept to himself all the time. He wouldn't drink cheap hooch or cut up or joke around with the rest of us. I figured him for a snob — you know the kind, the type who thought he was too good for us. But Albert . . . well, damned if he didn't throw himself on that grenade."

Charlie's face was still covered by his arm, but I saw a tear trickle down his cheek. My chest felt both floppy and tight at the same time.

"Truth is, he saved our lives. Mine, and three other guys who got hurt. My leg — well, it was covered with parts of Albert, as well as dirt and metal."

My hand flew to my mouth. "Oh, Charlie!"

He sat up and turned away, not wanting me to see him cry. For some reason this touched me more than the tears themselves. I watched him wipe his face with his fists, the same way he'd done when he fell off his bike in his front yard when he was seven, and my eyes grew wet, as well. I scooted toward him and put my hand on his arm.

"I relive it in my mind over and over," he said. "I hear the thud of the grenade landing. I can hear John Ansom scream, 'Live grenade!' I remember feeling kind of frozen for a second, not sure what to do." He wiped his face with the sleeve of his free arm and gazed at the river. "The whole time I was in the hospital, I wondered why Albert had done it. Why didn't he just run, too?"

His throat worked and he drew a ragged breath. "There's something else, I wonder, too. Something I can't stop thinking about." He closed his eyes for a long moment. "Why didn't *I* throw myself on it?"

"You can't think like that, Charlie."

"Why not? I was closer to it than Albert. He had to kind of shove me out of the way — out of harm's way." His throat moved again. "He had courage, and I didn't."

"You had plenty of courage, just being over there."

"That's not how it feels. And I've got to tell you, I've struggled with it. Still do. And I hate everyone treating me like a hero, when the truth is, I'm a damned coward."

His expression reminded me of how he'd looked in first grade, when one of the older boys had called him a sissy for not fighting when they tripped him on the school bus. I'd stood up for him then, and I felt the same tug to do it now. "Listen to me, Charlie McCauley. You are, too, a hero. You were over there in a trench, fighting for freedom, and you were wounded. And that makes you a hero, absolutely and positively."

He shook his head.

"I bet you were trained to run when a grenade is thrown, correct?"

He slowly nodded.

"Well, then, you did the right thing, the absolute right thing, the thing you were trained to do. And it must have been harder for you than for the others, because you were sick and weak with dysentery. So don't you waste one more moment of your life thinking you're anything less than the hero you are. Do you understand me, Charlie?"

A lone tear tracked down his cheek. He brushed it away and pressed his eyes tight together.

"Tell me you understand," I demanded.

He opened his eyes, gave a slight smile, and snapped a salute. "Yes, ma'am."

I grinned at him. "That's more like it."

"Boy, you're beautiful when you're bossy." He reached out and touched my hair. "You have such a way about you, a way of making everything better." He twisted my hair strand around his finger. His eyes glowed with a soft love light, so adoring and tender that it made me queasy to know I would hurt him. "You're the best thing that ever happened to me, Addie. Thinking about you was what pulled me through. And now — well, I can hardly believe you're here."

A torrent of love poured from his eyes. He was about to kiss me.

I couldn't let that happen. I abruptly lifted my fingers from his arm and shifted away. I tried to hide the awkwardness of the moment with a bright smile. "You mean *you're* here. You're home! And everyone is so happy and relieved."

"Everyone?" His gaze practically burned my face. "Are *you* happy and relieved?"

"Of course." I busied myself opening the picnic basket.

"Happy and relieved enough to marry me?"

My hands froze on the picnic lid. "Oh, Charlie . . . no."

"Because of my foot?"

"Of course not!"

"I'm getting special shoes. They say that after a while, I won't even have much of a limp."

"Oh, Charlie — that's wonderful. But that has nothing to do with this."

Silence pulsed between us. Blue jays chattered in the trees, and a car motor purred down the road behind us. I opened the picnic basket and pulled out a covered dish of fried chicken just to have something to do.

I could feel his gaze on me. "Is it because of what I just told you?"

"Of course not. Don't you dare try to turn that into an issue!"

"So why won't you say yes?"

"I told you before you left. I don't —" God, why was this so hard? "I don't feel about you the way you deserve for a woman to feel."

He leaned in and gripped my upper arms. It wasn't romantic; it was uncomfortable and desperate. I was still holding the fried chicken. "I can make you feel that way, Addie. When we're married, and you know everything is sacred and blessed, why, then you can relax and everything will be just the way it should be."

I didn't say anything. What could I say? I clutched the dish of chicken as if it were a shield.

"You think that life is like the movies, Addie — that love is like some kind of magic spell. It's not that way in real life."

I knew damned well that it could be, but I couldn't say it. "It's not just that, Charlie. I love being independent. I want to work and travel and see the world."

"Travel's not what it's cracked up to be. It's messy and inconvenient and believe me, there's no place as wonderful as home. Move back here, Addie. Move back, and let's get married."

I shook my head, tears welling up in my eyes.

The wounded look in his eyes made me feel like I'd just kicked a puppy.

"Is there someone else?"

I didn't answer. What could I say? I looked through the picnic basket as if I were ravenous. "I've had enough of this talk, Charlie. Let's eat."

He put his hands on my wrists, stopping me. "Answer me, Addie. Is there a man waiting for you in New Orleans?' "

Joe wasn't in New Orleans anymore, so I could answer truthfully. "No. And I'm seriously tired of talking about this. Let's just eat our lunch and have a good time, Charlie. I'll tell you all about my job and all the news about Margie and the USO, and you can tell me more about the funny things you wrote me about — about the pranks the guys pulled on each other on the ship over, and how you hid the sergeant's shoes. Let's just have a good time and not spoil everything by talking about the future."

"Talking about the future will spoil everything?" His voice had a bitter edge to it I'd never heard before.

"I'm just not ready, Charlie." *And I never will be.* But I couldn't tell him that. Not with his shoeless, sock-clad foot hanging out of his pants, and his collarbones sticking out of his shirt, and his eyes so haunted and forlorn that I couldn't bear to meet his gaze.

21
MATT

I came home late Thursday evening — I'd been to a three-day conference in D.C. — and was greeted at the door by both daughters and Jillian.

"Our room's all sketched up and Hope's ready to start painting!" Sophie said breathlessly as she hugged my neck.

"Come and see!" Zoey took me by the hand and pulled me toward the stairs. "We're all in the picture."

"Is Hope still here?"

"No," Jillian said. "She left about half an hour ago."

I followed a prancing Sophie up the stairs, feeling a little tug of disappointment. The thought of seeing Hope had added lead to my foot on the drive home from the airport.

In the bedroom, Sophie stood against the wall and flung out both arms. "Isn't it boo-tiful, Daddy?"

I had to step closer to see it. In very light

305

pencil, Hope had drawn stone walls and two large arched windows. The view out one of the windows showed a sprawling hill with a winding trail leading from a forest toward us. On the trail, two little princesses in flowing gowns rode ponies over a drawbridge.

"Look — that's us!"

I looked closer, and the faces of the princesses were, indeed, Zoey and Sophie.

"And there you are, Daddy!"

Zoey's finger pointed to a knight accompanying them over the bridge, sitting astride a tall steed, holding his helmet. The face bore an uncanny likeness to me.

"She put Mommy in, too!" Sophie said.

"Up in the clouds," Zoey pointed again. "See?"

Sure enough, right where the sun was breaking through the clouds, hovered an angel with Christine's face. My heart warmed. Without thinking, I reached up and ran my hand over it.

"An' look here," said Sophie, pointing to another part of the photo. "She put Gramma and Grandpop an' Aunt Jillian in there, too!" I looked closer. Sure enough, the three of them were climbing out of a carriage in the courtyard out the second painted window. The likenesses were disconcertingly accurate.

"We need to move the furniture so she can start painting," Zoey said.

"Yeah. An' we're gonna need to sleep in the other room."

"I'll move your furniture first thing in the morning," I said.

Jillian clapped her hands together. "All right, girls, it's past bedtime. I let you stay up to show your father the room, but now you need to go brush your teeth."

They reluctantly trudged off. Jillian smiled at me. An awkward silence grew between us. I wished she would just go. "Thanks for staying with them."

"My pleasure. Did you have a good trip?"

I nodded. "Always good to be home, though. And now that I am, I'm sure you've got things you need to do."

"Not really. Do you want some dinner?"

"No. I grabbed something at the airport."

Her face fell. "Well, I'll go clean up the kitchen, then."

"Leave it. I'll get it after I tuck the girls in bed."

"It's no problem." She left the room just as the girls came back in. The girls knelt and said their prayers, then climbed into their twin beds. I pulled up a chair and read two chapters of *Pippi Longstocking*. After kisses and tuck-ins, I went downstairs.

Jillian was in the kitchen, wiping an already immaculate countertop. She turned and smiled, her face expectant. "Would you like a glass of wine?"

"No, thanks."

"I thought maybe you could use someone to talk to."

Yeah, I could — but the person I wanted to talk to was Hope. I needed to tell her what a great job she'd done on the wall sketch. "What I could really use is about twenty minutes of fresh air. Would you mind staying with the girls while I run out for a bit?"

Her smile dimmed, but it didn't vanish. "Not at all. Go right ahead."

"Thanks." I walked out, closed the door, and drew in a deep breath. Sometimes the air was so heavy with expectation around Jillian I found it hard to draw a lungful.

I walked across the lawn — deliberately breaking my own rules about sticking to the sidewalk — and knocked on Miss Addie's door. A stocky, graying woman in scrubs opened it.

"I'm the next-door neighbor," I explained. "I was wondering if I could see Hope for a moment."

"She's out walking the dog," the woman said.

308

"Do you know which way she went?"

"She headed off that way." She pointed to her left.

I took off at a jog. A block later, I spotted her on the side street, underneath a street-lamp. She turned at the sound of my foot-steps.

"Hi!" I called, slowing as I approached.

"Hi, yourself. What are you running from?"

I fell into step beside her. "Maybe I'm running toward something. Or someone."

It sounded more profound than I'd meant it to be. I cleared my throat. "Actually, I just wanted to catch up with you and tell you the mural looks great. Although I'm not sure that I deserve to be depicted as a knight in shining armor."

"Your girls think so." She smiled. "And after saving my grandmother's photos, I think so, too."

The compliment left me disconcerted. "Well, the girls love all of it — the pictures of themselves and Jillian and Peggy and Griff." I paused. "And their mother."

"Are you okay with that?"

"Sure. Why wouldn't I be?"

"Well, you were pretty upset the other day when I was looking at the photos, so I didn't know if you'd approve."

Once more, I regretted how I'd over-reacted. "You caught me off balance, that's all. Sorry I was so harsh."

"No worries. I understand how some things can push buttons." Snowball tugged on the leash, and she started walking.

I fell into step beside her.

"What was your conference about?" she asked.

To my surprise, I told her. I described a bunch of new federal regulations, and she not only listened but also asked questions. I told her about the big case that was taking up most of my time. It felt great to talk to someone who wasn't working with me or against me, who seemed really interested and engaged — so great I lost all track of time. When my phone buzzed, I pulled it out, glanced at the screen, then grimaced. "It's Jillian. I told her I'd be back in twenty minutes, and it's been nearly forty-five."

Hope and I had circled around on our walk and were now only about a block from our homes. We stopped. "Are you and Jillian . . ."

I knew what she was asking, but I didn't help her out. I just stood there and waited for her to flat out ask. I didn't have to wait long.

". . . involved?"

I shook my head. "She's my sister-in-law, that's all."

"Seems like there's more to it than that."

"Why do you think that?"

"Because she's at your house all the time, and . . ." Her voice trailed off.

"And what?"

"Well, I've picked up a certain vibe. And there's no reason you couldn't date her."

"Yeah, there is." I waited until she looked up and met my gaze. "I don't want to."

"Oh."

Damn, I wished there were more light, because her expression changed and I couldn't get a good read on it before she looked down at Snowball. She watched him sniff the grass as if it were the most fascinating thing in the world. "Have you dated since your wife . . ."

Why did people shy away from the word? Did they think I'd forgotten what had happened to her? "Died?"

She nodded.

I lifted my shoulders. "A few times. Why do you ask?"

"Well, your wife was beautiful, and everyone talks about how wonderful she was."

"Yeah, she was. So?"

"So I'd imagine it would be hard to find anyone who can measure up."

"I don't expect anyone to measure up." I shoved my hands in my pockets and dug around for the words. "I mean, I'm not looking for an exact replacement, like a lightbulb."

"Still, I would think it would be hard not to compare someone new against her." Hope angled her face up at me, her eyes earnest and bright. "I've done a lot of reading about moving on after a marriage ends since my divorce. Not that my divorce was anything like losing your wife — your tragedy was much, much greater." Her eyebrows pulled together, and I could see she was worried she'd offended me again. Once more, I felt a stab of remorse for acting like such a jerk around her. "Anyway, from what I read, apparently the first few times you're with someone new, it's inevitable that you'll be thinking of the ways the person is physically like or unlike your ex — or in your case, deceased . . . or late . . . or missing . . . or . . . Oh, you know what I mean." She looked down. It was too dark to see her face, but I was pretty sure she was blushing. The fast, nonstop way she was talking was a dead giveaway that she was rattled. "The point is, when you kiss them, chances are you'll be thinking about your spouse."

I looked at her, amused. "Is that right."

"Well, I wouldn't know, personally. I mean, that's what I read. I still have to go through it."

I gave her a teasing smile. "Want me to help you out?"

I thought I'd embarrass her into silence, but when Hope was on a roll, apparently there was no stopping her mouth. "What a chivalrous offer! I mean, you're really living up to your picture on the mural. Not that a real knight would actually kiss a lady — not on the mouth, I mean. I don't think real knights touched a lady except maybe on the hand. We studied the Middle Ages pretty extensively in my art history classes, and . . ."

I'd made the offer in jest, but then I looked at her mouth, which had abruptly quit moving, and I realized she was looking at mine. And then . . . well, it just happened. I'm not sure of the specifics — if I stepped toward her, or she leaned toward me, or if we both moved simultaneously. I just know that the minute my mouth made contact with hers, an arrow of heat shot through my chest, down my belly, and kept on traveling south. My arms found their way around her, and hers wrapped around me, and then everything got all hot and smoky and urgent. I pulled her closer, and she stood on her tiptoes and pressed into my erection, and . . .

A car rounded the corner, the headlights glaring. Snowball barked. We simultaneously jumped away from each other.

We stood there, breathing hard, awkward and self-conscious as the car passed. Hope shifted Snowball's leash to her other hand.

"Well," I had the genius to say.

"Yeah. Well," she echoed.

I hooked my thumb in the direction of my house. "I, uh, better be getting back."

"Me, too." But she didn't move. We stood there, staring at each other, the awkwardness swelling to a crescendo.

"So, thanks for helping me past that hurdle," she said.

My brain was still swaddled in lust. It took me a moment to recall what we'd been talking about. "No problem. Glad to be of service."

I could think of another service I'd like to provide, but offering it would only make the situation worse.

She smiled at me — a quick, amused, embarrassed little half smile that made my temperature start rising all over again. "I'd better get Snowball home."

I nodded and trudged along beside her.

At the sidewalk to her grandmother's porch, she turned to me.

"I didn't think of him." She spoke so softly I wasn't sure I'd heard her correctly.

"What?"

"My ex. When you . . . when we . . ." She ducked her head. "I didn't think of him." She flew up the porch steps, opened the door, and slipped inside before I could muster a response.

I stood there for a long moment, staring at the closed door. Because the truth of the matter was, I hadn't thought of Christine, either.

22
ADELAIDE

A heavy blanket of fatigue, along with a clutter of daily activities — doctors' appointments, physical therapy sessions, and home nurses, aides, and friends running in and out of the house — made me lose a few days. It might even have been a week. Or more.

But one afternoon, I found myself awake and alone with Hope. "Where did we leave off talking about Joe?"

"You never told me if you saw him again after he left New Orleans."

The memories came crowding in like animals on Noah's ark, and then I was sailing into the past.

1943
I received a letter from Joe the Monday after I returned from Wedding Tree.

Lucille had placed it on my bed, where she regularly put my mail, and I found it after work. I stared at it for a while, thinking it must be some kind of a joke. It was too soon for me to have gotten a letter from anywhere out of state, much less from the Pacific.

"What are you waiting for? Open it," Marge insisted.

My hand shook a little as I pried up the flap, thinking, *His lips touched this to seal it.* *"Dear Addie,* I read in a big, masculine scrawl. *"Just wanted you to know I take my correspondence promises seriously. Love, Joe."*

"What an odd thing to write!" Marge said, peering over my shoulder.

"He means he's written to my father," I said. I turned it over and saw the base's postmark. He'd mailed the letter before he left.

"You think? Oh, that's so exciting!" Marge's smile faded into a pout. "But that means you'll be engaged before me!"

As far as I was concerned, I was engaged already — but no one, Marge included, considered it official. The next day, I had another note. *Dear Addie, To make sure you don't forget about me, I left some letters with Carl and asked him to mail one a day to you. Hopefully this will tide you over until you start getting my letters from overseas. Love, Joe.*

After that, I raced home every day at noon to see if the mail had come. Thanks to the efficiency of the U.S. Postal Service, some days there were no letters; other days there were two. They were all just a line. "Your kiss haunts my lips." "You are my everything." "Your face is like a flower — bright and open and beautiful."

Oh, be still, my heart! I slept with the letters under my pillow, as if they somehow kept him close to me.

I waited for my parents to mention a letter from Joe. Given the way they'd reacted to my news about him when I'd last gone home, I figured it was best to let the letter arrive and let them broach the topic with me. My mother's letters were full of news about Charlie, telling me how well he was doing, how he was gaining weight, how his color was better. I heard all about how he was learning to walk with just a cane now instead of crutches, and how he was religiously doing the exercises the army hospital had prescribed.

Charlie wrote me, as well. Long, gushy letters, telling me how much he adored me, how he couldn't wait for me to get the photography thing out of my system and come home, how he was working half days at his father's lumberyard. The store had fallen on lean times, but that was sure to end once the war was over. In every letter, he begged me to come home for at least a visit. I dutifully wrote him back, short letters about my job, how much I enjoyed it and how busy I was. We made plans to go to dinner together when he came to New Orleans in May to attend a lumberyard trade show.

After two weeks, Joe's stash of pre-written letters ran out. I continued mailing letters to him, but I didn't get a single letter in response.

And then I missed my period. At first I thought it was just late, but within a week, I started to feel sick. I stayed home from work because I threw up one morning, but later in the day, I was better. The next morning, I threw up again.

I opened the bathroom door to find Marge standing outside it in her robe, her face slathered in cold cream, her eyes round. "Oh my God. You're pregnant!"

The word squeezed me in a vise of panic. "No. I can't be."

"You can't?" Marge asked. "Or you can't bear to think about it?"

"But — but we used rubbers!"

"They're better than nothing, but they're not foolproof," Marge said.

I dropped my head and cried.

Marge insisted I see a doctor she knew.

I used an alias — Mrs. Patterson. After a humiliating exam, the doctor confirmed what I already, deep in my heart, knew. "Congratulations, Mrs. Patterson. You're just a few weeks along, but you're going to have a baby."

"What are you going to do?" Marge asked when she came home from work and found me sobbing on the bed.

"I'll write Joe," I said. "He'll know how to make it right."

Although how, I didn't know. I only knew that Joe was extraordinary, and he could accomplish extraordinary things. Maybe he could use his wiles and connections to get transferred back to New Orleans for another training mission so we could quickly marry. Maybe he'd arrange for me to sneak aboard a transport plane and fly to California so we could marry before he left. Maybe he'd wire me to take a train to the West Coast and he'd jury-rig a reason to fly back to a base there. I didn't know how, but I was sure that Joe would come up with a way to solve this problem. Why, oh why had I refused to elope? In hindsight, I could see so clearly that *getting* married wasn't nearly as important as *being* married.

Marge wanted me to see a special doctor she'd heard about, but I wouldn't hear of it. I refused to consider anything but somehow marrying Joe. I continued to write him every day, and every day, I rushed home from work and checked the mail. Nothing — except more letters from Charlie. One of them said he was coming to New Orleans on the twenty-sixth on business and he wanted to take me to dinner.

I'd known I was pregnant for exactly two weeks when I rushed home to find Joe's friend Carl in the parlor, his Army hat in hand, his expression grim. He wouldn't look me in the eye. My heart pounded so hard I thought I would pass out. I knew something was wrong, and I knew it was bad.

"What is it?" I asked.

"I, uh, got some news about Joe."

The breath left my lungs in a sudden whoosh, and I couldn't draw another one for the life of me.

His fingers tightened on the brim of his hat. "His plane was shot down over the Pacific."

The room seemed to spin. "Did he . . . did he bail out?"

Carl swallowed. His voice came out low and tight. "He was part of a formation, and no one saw any parachutes."

"But still . . . maybe . . . ?"

Carl pressed his lips together and blinked several times. "Addie — officially he's MIA, but his family's been told he's presumed dead."

"But if he's MIA, that means there's a chance . . ."

"What it means, Addie, is that they don't have a body." His voice broke on the last word. He glanced up for just a second, just long enough for me to see his eyes. What I saw there killed all hope. "Joe made me promise that if anything happened to him, I would come and tell you."

"How did you find out?"

"I was on a list he'd left with his aunt."

I don't remember much after that. I don't remember Carl leaving, or going to my room. I remember being sick to my stomach, and Marge trying to get me to eat soup, and being unable to get out of bed the next morning, or the morning after.

I remember Marge coming home from work that day, and holding me while I sobbed.

"Addie, honey — you've got to pull yourself together, or Lucille is going to call your parents to come get you."

That hit me like a pitcher of cold water. "Oh, Marge! What am I going to do?"

"You're going to get your situation taken care of. This girl at the cannery knows a doctor who took care of her friend who was in a similar situation, and . . ."

"I can't get rid of Joe's child!"

"Well, Addie, you can't have a baby."

"Yes, I can."

"Listen to me, sweetie. The paper will fire you when they learn you're pregnant. And your parents — well, you know your mother."

The thought rolled another wave of nausea over me. My upright, proper, virtuous mother would be devastated. And my father . . . The shame would likely kill him.

My mind sorted through various scenarios, the way it already had a thousand times. I could move away, claim to be a widow — war widows were becoming horribly common. But I wouldn't receive a widow's benefits. How would I explain that? Who would care for my child while I worked? The lack of money would create suspicions, and suspicions would create whispers. And oh, dear Lord — it would be so horrid for my child to have the taint of scandal attached to him!

I'd seen what it was like, how cruel life was to kids conceived out of wedlock. I'd gone to school with a boy whose mother had never married, and he'd been treated as if he had some kind of contagious venereal disease. Parents had forbidden their children to play with him, so he'd been shunned and taunted. "We don't associate with people like that" had been the mysterious explanation, and the dark tone of it had implied it would lower one's own social standing to befriend him.

The word *bastard* had clung to him as if it were pasted on his forehead. He'd been bullied and badgered, and even some of the teachers had treated him with barely disguised disdain. He'd dropped out in eighth grade, then left town when he was barely fifteen. Word had it he'd hopped a train and become a hobo.

I didn't want that kind of life inflicted on my child for my mistakes. I'd have to put my baby up for adoption — although that, too, was unthinkable. There were no options I could live with.

Unless . . . maybe Joe's family would take me under their protection, and treat me as his widow. Maybe they'd help me care for his child, at least until I could get on my feet and support us both. If they backed me for just a little while, I could emerge from this as a respectable woman. "I'll call his aunt," I decided.

I got the number from Carl. It took me two days to work up the courage, and another one to find the right time when Lucille was out of the house.

My hand shook as I picked up the phone and asked the operator to connect me. "Mrs. Madison, you don't know me, but I'm Adelaide LeDoux, and I was Joe's fiancée."

"Joe didn't have a fiancée."

"Yes, he did. You can check with his buddy Carl. We got engaged right before he left. And . . . and it turns out that I'm . . . well, I'm pregnant."

I heard a deep gasp on the other end of the line, then silence for such a long moment that I thought the connection had dropped.

"Hello?" I said.

"Young woman, I don't know who you are, but you are *not* going to work a scam on this family, do you hear me?" The voice was an angry, vitriolic, wavering hiss, scarier than anything I'd ever heard. "We are in the deepest grief, and if you think you can use this opportunity to further yourself by sullying Joe's name . . ."

"No! You don't understand. I don't want money! Not . . . not for myself anyway. I . . ."

"The hell, you say!" Her voice rose in both

325

pitch and volume. "So what *do* you want? To drop your bastard on our doorstep?"

"No! I loved Joe, and . . ."

"How dare you!" she spit. "You leave us alone. We're decent people. My brother-in-law is in law enforcement, and I'll have you arrested if I get another call from you or if you dare show your face here. Have I made myself clear?"

I hung up, my hand shaking, and turned to Marge. "She — she said . . ."

"I could hear her, the loud old witch."

"Oh, Marge." Tears brimmed in my eyes.

She hugged me, then pulled back and looked at me, her brow creased. "Are you okay? You look pale as a ghost."

I felt weak and nauseous. "I'm — I'm going upstairs to lie down."

I lay on the bed and sobbed, feeling more alone than I'd ever felt in my life. I was still in bed when the doorbell rang some time later. Marge went and answered. I heard a familiar voice — Charlie's voice. Oh, dear Lord. I pulled the pillow over my head. This was the night we were supposed to have dinner together! In all of the chaos, I'd completely forgotten. Oh, I couldn't, I absolutely *couldn't* deal with him now.

I thought that Marge was sending him away, because she stayed downstairs a long time, but then I heard footsteps on the stairs. I kept my face turned to the wall as the door creaked open. "I can't see him," I said. "Tell him to go away."

"I'm not going anywhere."

I rolled over to see Charlie standing by the bed, his lips pressed tight, his eyes red.

"Charlie — I, uh — I'm not feeling well. I'm sorry, but I can't . . ."

"Marge told me everything."

"Everything?" I echoed blankly.

He nodded, his mouth pinched. "About the . . . the pilot. And the baby."

Shame, fear, grief — it formed a cannonball in my gut. I buried my face in the pillow and sobbed.

He sat down beside me and put his hand on my back. The sympathy and forgiveness in that simple gesture unleashed all my emotional self-control. This was Charlie, my childhood friend, and I needed a friend in the worst way. I raised up, hugged him, and sobbed.

"Marry me, Addie," he murmured.

I stared at him through tear-blurred eyes, at first not comprehending. "I — I can't. I thought Marge told you . . ."

"She did, and yes, you can. You need to. I'll give you and the baby a home."

"But . . ."

"But, nothing. Everyone will think the baby is mine."

"But . . ."

"That's all I ask, Addie. Let everyone think the baby is mine. I'll raise it as my own and we'll be a family. We'll put this behind us and everything will be all right."

"But Charlie — that's not fair to you."

"Addie, all I've ever wanted is you. This way I get you. And the baby gets a home."

And I got to keep the baby, and raise it. I got to keep a piece of Joe alive.

"We need to do it as soon as possible," he said. "Tomorrow. We'll tell our folks afterward that we eloped."

It was too soon. How could I marry someone else when I was so deeply grieving Joe?

He sensed my hesitation and spoke before I could even voice it. "If we wait any longer, Addie, your pregnancy will start to show, and people will whisper. We don't have time to let our mothers plan a wedding."

He was right. If we were going to do this convincingly, we had to do it right away.

"It's a wonderful solution," Marge said.

I looked up to see her standing at the end of my bed. I hadn't even realized she'd come into the room.

It was the only solution, as far as I could

tell. The only solution that would let me keep my baby without subjecting it to a life of shame.

I took the tissue Marge handed me, wiped my eyes, and looked at Charlie. "You're so kind, Charlie. You're such a good man. You deserve someone who will love you better than I can."

"I'll love you enough for both of us."

Oh, God, I prayed he was right. I drew a ragged breath and said the words I'd been so sure I'd never say. "All right, then, Charlie. All right. If you're sure you want to, I'll marry you."

23
ADELAIDE

1943

The very next day, we went down to city hall, got a license, and said our vows before a justice of the peace, with his secretary and receptionist as witnesses.

I wore a white suit that Lucille loaned me. It was too large, but I borrowed Marge's white belt, and it gave it a stylish peplum effect. Marge and Lucille both wanted to come to the wedding, but I wouldn't allow it. Charlie's and my parents would be crushed that we were getting married without them present; to learn that we'd invited anyone else would just add insult to injury.

Charlie bought me a bouquet of orchids and baby's breath. I didn't think to get him a boutonniere, but Lucille cut a white rose from her garden, and I pinned it to his lapel.

"I now pronounce you man and wife," intoned the justice of the peace — a tall, lanky man in his mid-fifties, with thinning gray hair. Charlie kissed me. I fought back the feeling of being smothered by his mouth.

We took the train to Biloxi for our honeymoon, and called our parents from the hotel.

The reaction was an odd mixture of delight and outrage. "How could you elope?" my mother cried. "Virginia and I have been planning your wedding since you two were born!"

"That's exactly why we did it," I said.

"We didn't want a big fuss," Charlie added. "We figured we'd save a lot of money this way."

We checked into a beachside hotel and ate crab at a local restaurant. I didn't have much appetite. Morning sickness now seemed to hit at random times of the day.

I thought about pretending to be too sick to perform my marital duties, but Charlie seemed heartbreakingly eager. My mother's advice for handling things you'd rather not do ran quite unromantically through my mind: might as well get it over with.

I put on my nightgown in the bathroom — it was a gift from Marge, a sheer blue peignoir set with sparkles, an outfit better suited for an experienced seductress than a reluctant bride, but it was all I had. I could feel my face flaming as I walked into the bedroom wearing it. Charlie was waiting for me in bed.

He was nervous. His hands were clammy, and he had a sheen of perspiration on his upper lip that moistened my face when we kissed. The preliminaries were bumbling, and as for the actual consummation . . . well, it was over almost before it began. To make matters worse, I cried.

"Did I hurt you?" Charlie asked.

"No," I said.

"Then what's wrong?"

You're not Joe. I didn't say it, of course, but Charlie was no dummy. After all, I was pregnant by another man, a man I'd loved and planned to marry, a man whose death I was grieving.

Poor Charlie — he didn't know what to do. He looked like he was about to cry himself.

"It was a lot better with him, wasn't it?"

"Don't," I told him.

"Don't what?"

"Don't ask me about Joe."

"It's almost like he's here with us, since his baby is inside you."

I sat up and swung my legs to the side of the bed. "I was crazy to think this would work. We'll get a divorce or annulment in the morning."

"No. No McCauley has ever gotten a divorce. No one in your family has, either, and it's not going to start with us. Besides, what about the baby?"

The baby. My spine sagged. "Charlie, you knew the situation when you married me. If you can't accept it, we'd best end things now."

"I accept it. At least, I'm trying to." His voice broke. Tears streamed down his face. "Oh, Addie — I just love you so much. And it's killing me that you gave yourself to another man."

"Look, Charlie . . . I can't — I *won't* — put up with you throwing it in my face. You said as far as the world was concerned, this is your baby."

"Yes. Yes, it will be."

"No. It *is*."

"Okay. You're right. It *is*. It's our baby."

"And I'm your wife," I said, "and you're my husband."

He drew me into a kiss so desperate it seemed as if I were his source of oxygen. He didn't bring up Joe again that night, but he was right there with us, every time we tried to make love.

I say "tried" because instead of getting better, Charlie just got worse. The second and third times, he couldn't even wait until he was inside me.

I held him in my arms and stroked his hair, as if he were the doll we used to play house with. "It's okay," I told him. "It'll get better. We've got a lifetime to figure it out."

That calmed him down. I felt him relax in my arms. I eased his head down on the pillow and lay beside him. As my new husband's breathing grew deep and rhythmic, I spent the rest of my wedding night silently crying into my pillow.

24
HOPE

I have to say, ever since I'd seen the photo
of Joe, I'd been pretty sure how Gran's saga
would unfold. I knew unwed motherhood
was a shocking scandal back in the day, but
Gran had always struck me as more progressive — progressive enough that I was surprised she felt it was such a dark source of
shame.

All the same, this new piece of information went a long way toward explaining the
differences between Uncle Eddie and my
mother. For one thing, there was their appearance; Mom had been fair-headed, while
Uncle Eddie was dark-haired like my granddad. And then there was their temperament.
Mom had been almost frighteningly single-
minded, no-nonsense, and in charge, where
as Eddie . . . well, Eddie was a caregiver,
emotional and eager to please.

I patted Gran's hand. "This is a surprise,
Gran, but it's totally understandable. I don't

think any less of you, and I don't think Mom would have, either. And I'm sure Eddie will just feel bad for you, that you've felt so much shame about this all these years."

"Oh, phooey. I'm not worried about Eddie knowing about this."

"No?"

"No. Eddie'll be just fine learning I'm no saint. But he'll need your support for the rest of it."

"There's more?"

"Oh, child — this is just the background story." She blew out a sigh, and her face crumpled. Her eyes radiated a depth of despair that scared me. "I was part of something awful, and I need your help to make it right."

I tried to hide my alarm. "Gran, I'm sure there's nothing . . ."

"You just wait, child. You just wait." She rubbed her head.

"Are you in pain?"

"A little." She closed her eyes for a moment. When she opened them, she frowned. "Can you get those fireflies out of here?"

"There aren't any fireflies in here, Gran."

"Are you sure?" She flicked a hand over her head, as if to bat them away.

"I don't see anything, Gran."

She flapped her hand again, then looked

at me. My dismay must have shown on my face, because her brow softened. "You must think I'm losing it."

"I think you had a hard blow to the head, and you're tired. Let me help you to bed."

"Everything I've told you, dear — I plan to tell Eddie myself. But this next part — well, he'll be devastated about it. He needs to know the whole story, and I'm not sure what that is. I need your help to find out the truth."

"I'll help you in whatever way I can."

She gave me a soft smile. "I know you will, dear. Mother said I could count on you." Her hand dropped from her head. "The first thing I need help with is getting to bed."

I helped her to her feet, wondering — no, *hoping* — that her misdeed was like the fireflies, alive only in her imagination.

"Do you think she really has a horrible secret?" Kirsten sprinkled cocoa on top of my cappuccino the next afternoon and handed it to me across the counter. I'd wandered down to the Daily Grind and found the place nearly empty, so I'd perched on a barstool at the counter. Without revealing exactly what Gran had told me, I told Kirsten that my grandmother had been sharing some stories about her past and had hinted she was about to reveal an ominous skeleton in her closet.

"I don't know. I believe what she's told me so far."

"Well, I don't think you should worry." Kirsten put the milk pitcher in the sink. "It's probably something that was considered shocking back then that we don't bat an eye at today."

"That's what I'd think, too, except she's already told me a lot of shocking-back-then stuff."

"Really?" Kirsten's eyes twinkled. "Good for her!"

I laughed.

"Seriously, I can't imagine that that sweet little old lady ever did anything all that wrong." Kirsten rinsed the pitcher. "I mean, how bad can it be?"

"I don't know." I took another sip, thinking about the stricken look on Gran's face. "Have you ever done anything you'd be afraid to die without confessing?"

Kirsten looked thoughtful for a moment, then gave a wry smile. "I'm not sure about confessing, but there are a few things I'll probably take to the grave."

I laughed. "Oh, yeah? Such as?"

"Oh, I couldn't possibly say." Grinning, she wiped down the cappuccino machine.

338

"At least, not without a few mojitos in me."

"You're on."

Kirsten laughed. "Okay, but I'll only spill the juicy stuff if you talk, too. And one of the first things I want to know is, what's going on with you and Matt?"

Just the mention of his name made my heart rate kick up. "Nothing." I looked down at my drink. "I've been working on the mural early in the evening with the girls. When he comes home, I duck out as soon as possible."

"Why?"

Because I had no intention of going through another emotional wringer just as I was beginning to get over my ex. I was only in Wedding Tree for another six weeks or so, so there was no point in getting anything started. Besides, there were the girls to consider. I'd grown close to them as I painted their room — I gave them little tasks to do, and they loved helping — and it was obvious how much they yearned for a mother. Zoey harbored the hope that Jillian and Matt would marry, but Sophie had begun lobbying for me.

Instead of explaining all that to Kirsten, though, I just lifted my shoulders. "I don't want to be in the way."

"That man needs someone in his way."

The bell over the door jangled. "And speak of the devil . . ."

I turned around to see Matt striding through the coffee shop door. My heart jumped like a jackrabbit. It was the first time I'd seen him since that kiss without Sophie, Zoey, or Jillian present.

Seen him in person, that is. I'd seen him plenty in my imagination. I'd played and replayed the moment, expanding and embellishing it in my mind until it felt as though we'd done a lot more than lock lips. My face felt hot.

"Hey, Matt," Kirsten said. "Want your usual?"

Matt nodded and greeted us both.

Kirsten bent and pulled a pitcher of iced coffee out of the under-counter refrigerator. "How are the girls?"

"Great. They're loving the way their room is coming along." He turned his eyes on me in a way that made the heat spread down my chest. "Hope is doing a terrific job on the mural."

"I've been trying to talk her into doing one here," Kirsten said.

"Well, it's amazing how fast she works."

I know he meant it as a compliment, but Kurt's sarcastic comments over the years still made the words sting. I forced a smile.

"That's because I've got two helpers."

"That kind of help can only slow you down. But I appreciate the way you're including the girls in the project. They're loving it."

I felt tongue-tied and awkward. "Well, I'm enjoying them. They're adorable." I lifted my cup in a small salute to Kirsten. "See you later. I'd better get back to Gran."

"Hold on a moment, and I'll give you a lift," Matt said.

I had no choice unless I wanted to be rude. Ignoring Kirsten's knowing smirk, I stared at the wall as he paid for his drink, then walked beside him out of the shop.

The afternoon sun was nearly blinding. "How's the case going?" I asked.

"Slowly, but it's moving in our favor."

"That's good news."

"Yeah." He gestured to a blue Camry at the curb. "Here's my car."

He opened the passenger door, and I climbed in. The leather seat heated my thighs below my shorts. I busied myself with the seat belt as he climbed in and closed the door. He started the engine, then looked at me. "You've been avoiding me."

"I don't know how you can say that, when I'm at your house every evening."

"You scamper out like a scared squirrel

341

the moment I come in." He put the car into gear, then pulled out of the parking spot. "Is it because of that kiss?"

My face probably looked like I had a third-degree burn. "Maybe."

"I'll take that as a yes." He cast me a sidelong glance. "Care to explain?"

"Not really."

He grinned. "Explain anyway."

I contemplated just opening the door and jumping out, but since the girls' room was only half painted, that wouldn't serve as a long-term solution. "I guess I'm not sure where we are after that."

He drove two more blocks, then turned into his driveway, braked, and killed the engine. "I'll tell you where I am."

My mouth went dry. The air in the car suddenly seemed too thick to breathe.

"I'd like to kiss you again."

I took a nervous sip of my cappuccino, trying to form a thought, much less a response.

"You've got some foam on your lip."

I ran my tongue around my mouth. His eyes followed.

"You need some help." He leaned over and softly kissed the top of my lip — a gentle, slightly parted-lip kiss that left me weak and hot and flustered. "Got it." His voice was a husky rumble.

"Uh, thanks," I mumbled like a moron. It was as if he'd sucked the brains out of my head as well as the cappuccino foam off my mouth. That simple little kiss had turned me to mush.

"Let me take you to dinner tomorrow."

I sat there, zombified, unable to form a thought, much less a word.

"I'll pick you up at seven."

I started to nod, then I saw a curtain move in his bedroom. I looked up to see Jillian standing in the window, watching.

"No," I said. "It — it's a bad idea."

"Why?"

"It just is." I scampered out of the car and fled to the safety of my grandmother's house before he could kiss me again.

Later that afternoon, my phone rang as I was sorting through the dishes in Gran's dining room buffet. I fished it out of the pocket of my jeans and answered it.

"How's it going down in Dixie?"

It was my friend Kaitlin from New York. She and I had both been art majors in college, and I'd been a bridesmaid in her wedding. We'd somewhat drifted apart after she married, moved to New York, and had a child — we mainly stayed in touch through social media — but she knew about my job-less dilemma, and she'd promised to keep her ear to the ground. She had a part-time job with a prestigious art foundation and was well connected in the art world. I briefly filled her in on what was happening with Gran — and with Matt.

"Well, girlfriend, you need to speed up the housecleaning and forget the hunky neighbor, because I'm calling with great news," Kaitlin said. "Art Consulting Inc. is looking for a new associate, and they want to talk to *you*."

"What? Where did you hear this?" Art Consulting Inc. was a major player in the exclusive world of art advisors who helped large corporations, wealthy clients, and museums acquire investment art. Associates dealt with extremely wealthy, well-connected clients — the kind of clients my ex-husband had tried — unsuccessfully — to pander to.

"From the director of the Chicago office. She called me to get your number."

"How on earth did she get my name?"

"From Mrs. Harris Van Dever. Apparently you made a wonderful impression on her when she visited your and Kurt's gallery."

Technically, it had been "our" gallery, but since Kurt had disdained my input, I never felt any real ownership.

"By advising her not to buy the Rantlon piece?" I asked.

"Exactly."

That move had driven Kurt insane. One of the doyennes of Chicago society and a major benefactor to several museums, Mrs. Van Dever had come to an opening at our gallery. She'd been debating between purchasing a piece by another up-and-coming artist at another gallery and the Rantlon at ours. When she'd specifically asked me which piece I thought would appreciate the most, I'd given her my honest opinion. Kurt had been so angry I'd feared he'd become physically violent.

"AC's director is Ms. McAbbee, and she'll be calling you soon," Kaitlin said. "Hope, this is a dream job. Great salary, benefits, bonuses, travel — everything anyone would want. And you know how rare that is in the art world."

I did. It was like finding a Van Gogh at a garage sale.

"I immediately called my contacts," Kaitlin continued, "and they specifically want *you,* because Mrs. Van Dever is such a huge client."

I found it hard to wrap my mind around

the concept. "Any idea when this job would start?"

"I think that'll be negotiable, but, girl — you'd be crazy not to hop on this as fast as you can. I can think of a hundred people who would sell their mothers for this opportunity. It's amaze-balls."

"If it's true."

"Oh, it's true, all right. Call me back after you hear from them."

I hung up and stared at the wall.

It was next to impossible to find a job in the art world — especially a high-salaried job, a job with benefits and travel and security. By all rights, I should be thrilled.

So why didn't my heart dance and sing? This was what I'd been looking for ever since my divorce — better than anything I could reasonably expect to find.

It was good to be wanted. But was I wanted by someone I wanted to be wanted by?

For reasons that made no sense, Matt's face floated in my mind's eye.

Whoa, I told myself. *That's a whole other kind of wanting.*

My cell phone rang. It was a Chicago area code. This was it. I stood up and smiled at the wall — I'd been told by a college job placement counselor that if you stand up to take a call, your voice will have more energy, and if you smile, the pleasantness of your expression will shine through — and answered my future.

25
ADELAIDE

After my nap, I found Hope packing up a drawer of saucers in the dining room, her bottom lip caught in her teeth, her eyes dark.

I rested on my walker and studied her. "You look like something is weighing on you. Have I scandalized you with my tales?"

"Oh, no, Gran." She straightened and gave me a big smile, but her eyes still looked troubled. "Actually, I just got some good news. I just got off the phone with the biggest art consulting firm in Chicago. One of their major clients remembered me because I advised her not to buy a piece of art from Kurt, and she recommended me to be an associate."

"How wonderful, dear!"

Hope nodded and smiled, but the smile still didn't reach her eyes. "It's a terrific opportunity. I'll get a great salary and full benefits, and travel to art shows all over the world."

What I would have given for such an opportunity as a single, young woman! "Oh, how fabulous! Do you need to go back right now for an interview?"

"No. They said the job was mine if I wanted it. I said yes, of course. I'll start in June." There was that funny smile again. It was hard to tell because I still see two of everything, but it sure didn't seem to come from the inside. She seemed more anxious than joyful.

"But?"

"But, what?"

"Well, I have to say, you don't seem all that thrilled to have just landed the job of a lifetime."

"I am! Of course I am. It's wonderful. It's just so . . . unexpected. I think I need time to process it."

"Maybe you should take a walk or go down to the coffee shop." I'd been glad to hear that Hope was forming a friendship with Kirsten.

"Maybe later. Right now, I'd rather get back to your closet."

She wanted to postpone thinking about it. It was a sentiment I could relate to all too well. I thought about warning her about the

349

dangers of avoiding things. On the other hand, her news was recent, and sometimes a little time helps us see things more clearly.

"I can't wait to hear more of your story," she said.

And I needed to get on with it. I nodded and let her help me back to my bedroom, where I settled in my rocker. "Pull out that dark blue dress on the left."

"This one?" She lifted a navy wool, a dress I'd originally bought for my great-grandfather's funeral when I was seventeen.

I nodded. "That's the dress I was wearing when Charlie and I returned to Wedding Tree after our honeymoon."

"How long was your honeymoon?"

"Five days." I closed my eyes and shifted into storytelling mode.

1943

They were five of the longest days of my life. I'd been grieving Joe, fighting near-constant nausea, and dealing with Charlie's almost pathological lovesickness.

I felt — and God help me for this, because I loved Charlie on so many levels — like a hostage. Oh, I knew I wasn't; I'd entered into the marriage completely of my own volition — but still. He had the right to paw me, to kiss me, to touch me, to look at me anywhere and anytime, and I didn't have the right to tell him no. I'd signed up for this. It struck me that marrying Charlie was a lot like joining the service; I would do my duty, even if it killed me.

And there were times I felt like it might. Oh, he was very gentle and sweet and considerate, but he was overeager and inept and desperately anxious to please, and his anxiety . . . well, it kind of repelled me, which made me feel ungrateful and monstrous. Charlie was doing me and the baby a favor, I reminded myself. The constant lump in my throat that threatened to gag me was morning sickness and grief, but it was hard not to think it was revulsion at Charlie.

On the fifth day, we went back to New Orleans. We stopped by Lucille's house, gathered up my belongings, then swung by the newspaper so I could turn in my resignation. I had wanted to stay and work until Charlie found us a place to live in Wedding Tree, but he wouldn't hear of it.

"No." His voice had been adamant. "We'll go back and live with my parents."

He insisted on accompanying me to the paper to turn in my resignation. It was our first fight, and it was a doozy.

"This job is the only thing in my life that

was all mine," I told him. "The only thing that I made happen all on my own, the only thing that really, truly belonged to me, just me, and I want to leave it on those terms."

He thought I was ashamed of him, of his gimpy leg. I told him not to be ridiculous. He wanted to know if there were other men at the paper that I'd been involved with. I glared at him.

"What kind of girl do you think I am?"

"Frankly, I'm not so sure," he'd snapped. "I never would have thought that you were the kind of girl to find herself in this position."

That stung, but the truth was, I'd never thought so, either. And here I was.

"If it's so damned important to you, come on," I'd told him. "But understand this, Charlie: I will never get over resenting you for it."

To his credit, he acquiesced. I went in and met with Thomas while he paced the sidewalk outside. I hugged people good-bye. I cried. I gathered up my things. I went in the darkroom for the last time.

Thomas took me aside. "Is he treating you well?"

"Yes, of course. Why would you ask?"

"Well, it's none of my business, but you don't look like a bride should look." He looked down and busied himself flecking crumbs off that day's sweater vest.

I realized then that I needed to step up my game or I wouldn't be able to pull this off once we got back home. It was important for my baby's future that everyone think I was happy so they wouldn't suspect Charlie wasn't the father. "I'm fine. I've just got a little bug, that's all."

He patted my arm. "We wish you the best, Adelaide. You did a splendid job. Never expected a woman to take such good photos. You're just as good — actually, you're better — than most of the men working here."

Hope laughed, pulling me back to the moment. "He actually said that?"

I grinned. "It must sound silly to you, but back then, it was the highest compliment I could get. I walked out of there feeling ten feet tall."

Until I saw Charlie, waiting on a bench on the outside sidewalk.

"Go on with your story," Hope urged.

1943

It was evening when our bus pulled into Wedding Tree. Both sets of parents were waiting at the station, and they threw rice as we disembarked.

My mother's face was positively aglow. "I swear, Adelaide, I don't know whether to hug you or spank you! Don't you know I've been looking forward to your wedding since you and Charlie were both in diapers?"

"And, Charlie, my only child!" his mother cried.

"We didn't feel like making a big fuss," Charlie said. "We just wanted to be together."

I smiled throughout, but it was tough. We went to my parents' home, where my mother had prepared a small wedding cake, and half the town showed up to wish us well.

My father took me aside as the evening wore on.

"Are you all right?"

"Yes, Father."

"I have to say, this comes as a quite a surprise — especially considering the things you said last time you were home."

I swallowed hard. Part of me wanted to tell him the truth, but a bigger part knew it would just break his heart. Besides, apparently Joe hadn't gotten around to writing him a letter. Marge had flat out told me that Joe might have lost the matrimonial urge once he got a little time and distance. According to her, it was more common than not for a woman to think a relationship was more serious than it was, and for men to get cold feet.

In any event, I needed everyone to think the baby was Charlie's. "That . . . didn't work out. And I realized I've always loved Charlie."

"I see."

I didn't think he did, but neither of us wanted to get into it. Better to just let it fade away.

The party ended at midnight, and we went home with Charlie's parents. We all had to share a bathroom. Charlie's bedroom was directly across the hall from his parents.

As we settled into his childhood bed, he reached for me.

I pulled away. "I can't, Charlie," I whispered. "Not with them so close."

"But you're my wife. It's okay."

"No. Not here."

That was all the incentive he needed to find us a house. He located one the very next day. It was small, but it had everything we needed. His mother offered to buy us furniture.

Shopping with her was a nightmare. I wanted sleek and modern, and she was into reproduction Victorian. Charlie worked for his father, so his parents, in effect, held our purse strings. This was my first experience butting heads with Virginia.

She finally just sighed. "Well, pick out what you like, then, dear. I'm sure Charlie will get used to it."

To compromise, I let her pick out the bedroom furniture. It was a horror show in there, anyway; why not have furniture to match? I selected the living room furniture and the kitchen table. The rest of the house was furnished with hand-me-downs or heirlooms, depending on how you wanted to look at it.

We moved in three days later. I made a pot roast, and Charlie bought a bottle of wine. When we sat down at our new table, he raised his glass. "To wonderful beginnings with my new bride."

I was too nauseous to eat. But the wine seemed to give him courage, and the single glass I drank eased my queasiness.

"I love you so much, Addie," he said later as we climbed into our new bed. "Do you think you could find it in your heart to love me just a little?"

"I've always loved you," I said. "You know that."

"I mean like a wife loves a husband."

I couldn't find it in my heart to lie. "I want to be a good wife to you, Charlie. Sometimes it just takes a little while for a man and woman to get in sync."

"Apparently you didn't have that problem with Joe."

I pulled away. "You promised me you wouldn't bring that up."

"I'm sorry. I just . . ." He'd untied the bow on my nightgown. "Oh, Addie, I just love you so."

He tried to please me, but I just wasn't feeling it. As the weeks went on, I grew to dread the nightly encounters.

Virginia gave me a gift-wrapped book and told me to open it when I was alone. It was called *A Woman's Guide to Marriage*. It talked about how I should serve my husband and try to please him "in every possible way." I was mortified.

"What on earth did you say to your mother?" I demanded when Charlie got home that evening.

"Nothing."

"You must have. Why else would she give me this book?" I'd waved it in front of him.

He'd lifted his shoulders. "She probably just thought it would be helpful."

I didn't think he'd blatantly complained about me, but I suspected she'd asked some nosy questions, and Charlie, being the only child and doting son he was, had probably answered honestly.

Most of the time, I didn't mind being married to Charlie, I really didn't. I just didn't like the physical part — and he showered me with physical affection, both in public and in private. He was always reaching for my hand, touching my waist, putting his arm around me in church. I felt . . . well, *smothered* is the only word for it.

He wanted so desperately for me to love him back. And I wanted to, at least intellectually. But part of me — an irrational, emotional part, I guess — resented him for not being Joe. And I felt terrible about it. He couldn't help who he was.

And Charlie genuinely loved me, I knew he did. Any woman should be glad to be loved like that. But the more desperate he seemed for my affection, the more I withdrew and curled into myself.

We told our families I was pregnant five weeks after the wedding. I'm sure they'd already figured it out. I'd thrown up every morning while staying at Charlie's parents' house, and even though I'd tried to be discreet, it only had one bathroom. It helped, I suppose, that I didn't show early. I'd actually lost weight, but my body was shifting. My waist thickened, and I had to safety-pin my skirts.

Charlie told his biggest-mouthed pal that we'd "gotten close" the night of his return from the army hospital. He wanted people to think we'd made love then, obviously. And I couldn't really blame him — heaven only knew people would be counting the months before the baby's birth — but still, it embarrassed me.

The baby came February 12. If I had conceived on our honeymoon, it would have been born in March, but Rebecca was small — just barely seven pounds — so it was less of a stretch to say she came early.

I went into labor in the night. I'd felt achy all day, and in the middle of the night, I awoke with sharp cramps. My water broke when I got up to go to the bathroom.

Charlie drove me to the parish hospital. I was afraid I was going to have the baby right there in his car, but I needn't have worried. Rebecca wasn't born until nearly seven in the morning.

My memory of the hospital is fuzzy. I remember being wheeled down the hall and hearing a woman screaming and cussing her husband. I was very upset that she was carrying on so. They used an anesthetic back then called twilight sleep. I remember — vaguely — being strapped down, and then the next thing I knew, I was in a room with another new mother, and a white-uniformed nurse was bringing me a pink-blanketed bundle.

Charlie seemed delighted. He handed out cigars and smiled broadly, but he was more concerned about me than the baby. Maybe I should have found that touching — "I swear, I've never seen a man dote so much on his wife!" a nurse remarked — but it worried me. I wanted him to bond with the baby, and he was reluctant to hold her.

At first I worried it was because she didn't look like him. She had light hair, and Charlie's was dark. But I think he was afraid of hurting her — and it's no wonder; she was so small, so fragile.

He came around when his mother held her. His parents — and my parents, too, of course — were over the moon, just swooning with delight to have a grandbaby.

I stayed in the hospital for a week. When I went home, my mother and Charlie's mother and friends took turns coming over, bringing meals and helping out.

Becky had colic and cried round the clock. She had a raw, gnawing, shrieky cry that just wore on everyone's last nerve. I remember being exhausted — just beyond exhausted. Charlie was irked and impatient. I had trouble fixing dinner or keeping things tidy or being able to sit and talk with him about his day. It was a tough time.

I dedicated myself to being a good mother. I loved that baby more than life itself. I poured all the love I'd had for Joe into her. I think, on some level, Charlie sensed that, and that was the beginning of our really bad problems, although they didn't manifest until later.

I did my best to make a home for the baby and for Charlie. I wanted to give Rebecca everything she could possibly want or need.

Once the colic subsided, things improved immensely. Fatherhood seemed to give Charlie confidence. He took on a larger role at the lumberyard, and talked his father into supplying other stores in other towns. His foot healed, but he walked with a limp, and he occasionally needed to use a cane.

He grew less clingy and cloying with me, and our private married life improved. The three of us had a couple of good years. We socialized with our family and friends, and I resumed taking photographs. My favorite subject, of course, was Rebecca.

During those early years, we were probably as happy as any other young married couple. Things were looking up, for us and for the country. We were thrilled when the war ended. The whole town poured into the streets and celebrated on V-E Day, then again at the surrender of Japan. We had a bonfire and a picnic and a spontaneous parade down Main Street. Oh, it was glorious!

When Rebecca wasn't quite three years old, I got pregnant again. Charlie was delighted — just thrilled to pieces. I was happy about it, too, certain that this would put to rest any lingering jealousies or insecurities in Charlie's mind.

And then one afternoon — I remember it was a warm day in November; Becky was down for her nap, and I was putting a Thanksgiving centerpiece on the table and wearing a sleeveless yellow cotton housedress — I heard a knock on the door. I thought it was my neighbor; Eunice was always popping over for a cup of sugar or something. I opened it, then literally fell to my knees.

"Why?" Hope asked.

Hope's voice pulled me back to the present. I stopped my rocker. "It wasn't Eunice."

"Who was it?"

"Joe." I opened my eyes and looked at her. "It was Joe."

26
ADELAIDE

Hope looked at me as if she wasn't sure if I were in my right mind or not. "But I thought Joe was dead," she said.

"Yes, I thought so, too. My every decision had been based on that belief. I thought I was seeing a ghost." I closed my eyes, and his face haunted me again.

1946
Joe was almost skeletally thin — his shoulder bones jutted through his shirt in sharp points — and his face seemed like skin stretched over a skull. Just like in the movies, I started to faint dead away. Joe caught me under the arms and half carried, half dragged me through the door to the sofa. He sat down beside me, and I touched his face, trying to determine whether he was real or whether I was dreaming.

His skin was warm, and I could feel the trace of stubble on his gaunt, clean-shaven face. "You're alive," I said, staring at him, my hand moving to his close-cropped hair. "You're alive!"

He looked much older. His mouth had lines at the corners, his hair was thinner, and his eyes seemed more deep-set. He drew me into a hug, and I didn't resist. When he started to kiss me, though, I drew back.

"Are you okay?" he asked.

I realized my hand was over my lips. I dropped it and scooted back on the sofa. "I — I still feel faint."

"I'll get you a glass of water." He strode into my kitchen, rummaged in my cabinets, and returned with a tall glass. He sat beside me on the sofa as I drank it.

"Tell me everything," I ordered.

He said that the other planes in the squadron didn't see any parachutes because he and the rest of his crew had bailed at the very last second, under cloud cover. The bombardier and gunner were shot before they hit the water; the navigator, the copilot, the engineer, and Joe were picked up by a Japanese PT boat and sent to a POW camp. Conditions were horrendous; out of all of his crew, he was the only one who survived.

"You're what kept me going," he said. "I

thought about you, and I knew I had to live."

His camp hadn't been liberated until after the war had ended. He'd been so ill and malnourished that he'd spent eleven months in a military hospital. Due to a clerical error, his family wasn't notified of his whereabouts until he was on the way home. It wasn't until he arrived at his aunt's home that he'd found my unopened letters — including the one saying I was pregnant.

He'd immediately set out to track me down. He'd already been to my parents' house. Apparently my grandmother had told him where I lived.

My heart catapulted in my chest. "What — what did you tell her?"

"Just that I was looking for you — that I'd known you in New Orleans, that I'd just been released from a POW camp. She gave me your address."

I tried to explain what had happened and why I'd married Charlie. He sat there, stoic as a statue, and said he didn't blame me. His eyes misted, though, and he swallowed hard a bunch of times.

"Our child?"

Our. Oh, Lord, how can such a short word carry so much weight? "Rebecca. I named her for my great-grandmother. She's nap-

365

ping. She — she doesn't know. No one knows. Everyone thinks Charlie is the father. We can't . . ."

"Damn it, Addie. Don't tell me what we can and can't do." His blue eyes were dark, his voice a low growl. "I spent years in a hellhole, and thinking of you was all that pulled me through. When I got out and read your letter, I nearly lost my mind. I vowed that if you'd given the child up for adoption, I'd get it back, one way or the other. And I swore that I'd marry you, and . . ."

"You never wrote my father."

"I damn sure did. The night I got back from the base."

"He never . . ." Oh my God! Father *had* gotten the letter! That's why he'd pulled me aside when Charlie and I came home married, and asked if I was all right. He must not have even told my mother, because my mother could never keep a secret like that.

Oh, dear God, did my father suspect the baby's paternity? Oh, heavens to Betsy! I couldn't bear to think of it. It was a mercy he hadn't told me or my mother about the letter, wasn't it? So why did I feel so outraged and confused?

There are pauses in the rhythm of life — space between heartbeats, time between inhales and exhales. Maybe those are little deaths. Or maybe that's when life is lived most intensely. This felt like both.

"Joe." His name on my lips was like menthol on chapped skin, both sweet and stinging, a needling balm. "Joe . . . it's too late."

My hand rested on my belly, an involuntary move. His eyes followed. The words were unnecessary, but I said them anyway. "I'm having Charlie's baby."

The door opened and Becky came out, rubbing her eyes. "Mommy?"

His eyes locked on her. I ran to her and scooped her up.

"Who's dat man, Mommy?"

"He's . . ." My throat froze, like the pipe under the house last winter — a pipe not properly insulated, because hard freezes were so rare in Louisiana that no one anticipates them. I drew a breath and started again. "He's my friend."

Joe's throat worked as he swallowed.

I held her close, stroking her back. "Joe, this is Rebecca. Becky, this is Mr. Joe."

"How'd you do," she said solemnly, extending her hand.

Charlie had taught her how to do that. He'd wanted her to make a good impression when I brought her to the lumberyard, to be able to greet people respectfully.

Joe took her hand and let her guide his in three up-and-down pumps. "Very nice to meet you," he said, inclining his head in a slight bow.

"Do you work at Daddy's store?"

My eyes filled with tears. I blinked them back. "No, honey. Mr. Joe is a pilot. He flies airplanes."

"Up in de sky?"

"Yes."

"How do you get up dere?"

"The plane goes really fast, and air presses under the wings, and it makes it go up in the air."

She thought about this a moment. "If I run really fas' with my arms out, will I go up?"

"No."

"Oh." She looked at him thoughtfully. "Good."

He burst into laughter, and she smiled back at him. I found myself looking at the same rounded cheeks, the same inset dimple on both faces.

"Can you take me and Mommy flying?"

"I've already taken your mom."

"Daddy, too?"

He looked at me. Fear, cold and clammy, raced through me. "Joe hasn't met your daddy, honey," I said quickly.

"Oh." She tilted her head as she looked at Joe. "Are you somebody's daddy?"

"Yes," he said.

"A boy or a girl?"

"A girl." I could tell he was having a hard time controlling his emotions. "Just about your age."

Tension vibrated like a crystal glass about to shatter. I couldn't stand it any longer. "Let's go get a snack, shall we?" I carried Becky to the kitchen, set her down in a chair, and turned to the sink. Joe followed me, standing in the doorway. I stared out the window, needing a few moments to compose myself. I washed an apple and cut it into slices, then set it in front of her, along with a glass of water.

She looked at Joe. "Would you like something to dwink? Mommy fo'got her manners."

I had chastised her just yesterday for asking for something to drink without first offering a beverage to her visiting friend.

He threw back his head and laughed. "Your mommy's manners are just fine."

"I have a dwink, and you don't."

"Can I — can I get you something?" I asked him.

The look on his face told me exactly what I could get him. *You. Our daughter. Our life.*

"Some coffee? Or iced tea?" I prompted.

"I'll take coffee, if it's not too much trouble."

The percolator was still on, so I pulled out a mug. I remembered exactly how he took it. I heaped in three big teaspoonfuls of sugar without asking.

He flashed a white smile, showing off the dimple that exactly matched Rebecca's.

"You remembered."

"I remember everything." *The way your lips feel on mine. The way the sunlight glistens on the hair on the back of your hand.*

"Tell me again — how do planes go up?" Becky asked.

"Do you have a piece of paper?"

When Charlie walked through the kitchen door twenty minutes later, he found Rebecca sitting on Joe's lap, biting her lip in concentration as she folded a paper airplane.

Charlie froze in the door. The color drained from his face, leaving his lips looking bluish.

He'd never met Joe — never, to my knowledge, even seen a picture of him. Oh, I suppose he could have seen a photo from our weekend together if he ever went through my stuff — and later, I had reason to think that he might have, because I learned he was jealous like that — but at the time, I thought it was either something in the way I acted, or the crackling of chemistry in the air, or the similarity in the way Becky and Joe looked.

"Hi, Daddy! Joe's showin' me how to fold planes."

"Joe?" His face grew paler still.

"Charlie," I said, stepping forward, wanting to get between them. "This is Joe."

Joe slowly set Rebecca on her feet and rose.

Charlie leaned hard on his cane. "I — I thought . . ."

"He was in a POW camp," I rushed to explain.

The two men stared at each other, two bulls protecting their herd, ready to charge.

"My camp was the last to release prisoners," he said. "They kept me at a hospital in Hawaii for nearly a year. I just got home, and when my aunt gave me the things the army had forwarded, I found Addie's letters."

"Becky, you need to go see Poppy and Ammy," Charlie said harshly.

"No! I wanna make more paper airplanes with Mr. Joe."

Joe leaned over the table to look her in the eye. "I need to talk with your mom and Charlie."

371

I noticed he didn't say "your father."

I think Charlie noticed, too, because a nerve twitched in his jaw. "Why don't you take her over, Addie, while Joe and I get acquainted."

Every muscle in my body tensed. I'm not sure what I feared might happen. Maybe I thought they'd kill each other. I only know I was terrified of leaving them alone together.

"Why don't I call and see if Mother can come and get her."

"I really don't want your parents involved. Do as I say, Addie."

I'd never heard his voice like that, although I would in the future. It was an order, dark and ominous, and something in his tone told me it would be deeply dangerous to resist. I might have resisted anyway, except for the fact that I didn't want to create a scene in front of Rebecca.

I nodded and wiped my hands on my apron, then tried to take it off. It took me a while to unknot it, because my fingers were trembling.

"Come along, Becky," I said.

"It was nice meeting you." She held out her little hand to Joe again.

"Likewise." He shook it solemnly, then gave her a hug.

Charlie lifted his cane. "Run along now."

I took Becky's hand. "I'll be right back."

"I'll be here," Joe called.

My parents lived two blocks down. Mother immediately wanted to know about the gentleman caller who had stopped by her house. I mumbled some vague excuse about Joe being a friend of a friend, and asked her to watch Becky, saying she was bored with adult conversation.

"Am not!" Becky protested. "Joe an' I were makin' paper airplanes!"

I hurried back home, worried about what was going on in my absence. Joe and Charlie were still standing in the kitchen, facing off like a pair of prizefighters.

The screen door squeaked behind me. Both men turned toward me. "Let's move into the living room," I suggested.

"No need for that," Charlie said curtly. "I've already explained things to Joe, and he's just leaving."

"You explained . . . what?"

"That we're a family. That my name is on Becky's birth certificate, and that makes her legally mine. That we don't need a scandal. That you're having my baby, and everyone will be better off if he goes away and never comes back."

"But . . ."

My eyes met Charlie's. What I saw there reminded me of the time I stopped to help a dog who'd just been hit by a car. His back end had been completely crushed, and the poor creature had gazed at me with these sinkhole eyes, so filled with pain and — this is what stayed with me the most — an odd bewilderment, as if to say, *How can this be happening? How can God allow this level of pain to exist?*

My gaze shifted to Joe. He looked at me as if he'd just hiked twenty miles in the hottest desert, and I were an icy Coca-Cola. But Joe . . . well, Joe was made of tougher stuff. Joe could take it.

And he did. "He's right, Addie. I shouldn't have come here. I just had to know. And I had to let *you* know. I didn't want you to ever find out I was alive and think that . . . to think that I didn't . . ."

Love you. Want you. Need you. I heard all the unsaid words. From the quick flinch in Charlie's jaw, I knew he'd heard them, too.

"Well, I see that you have a happy life and a wonderful family. I'll leave you alone."

"That would be for the best." Charlie limped to the door and opened it, pointedly.

Joe picked up his hat. He reached into his

pocket and held out a card. "If you ever need anything, this is where you can reach me."

"She won't," Charlie said. "Keep your card."

I took it anyway.

Joe's throat worked. He nodded and put on his hat, then shook Charlie's hand. He turned to me, as if to shake my hand, too, and I flung myself into his arms, hugging him fiercely.

He hugged me back. I tried to memorize the imprint of his body against mine. I whispered, "Write me." And then he set me away from him and walked out the door.

The silence between Charlie and me was cold and thick as a marble tombstone.

Charlie's hands clenched and unclenched. "Of all the nerve," he said. "Who does he think he is, coming here?"

"Rebecca's father."

Charlie raised his hand, and for an awful moment, I thought he was going to strike me. Instead, he smote his chest. "*I* am Rebecca's father. I'm the only father she knows, and it's going to stay that way. And don't you *ever* say otherwise."

I was afraid of him just then. He had a wild light in his eye, as if something had snapped inside him.

He glared at me. "What were you doing, throwing yourself at him like that?"

"I — I wasn't. I was saying good-bye."

That dying dog look was back in his eyes. "You said good-bye to him like you've never said hello to me. Not even when I came back from the war."

I was too raw, too torn up to deal with this. "I'm going to lie down."

I went into the bedroom, put my face in the pillow, and cried.

Charlie got drunk that night. It was the first of many times. And then he came into the bedroom, and he wanted to make love. I knew that I needed to, that he needed to, that it would be a good thing, a healing thing, but I just couldn't pretend I wanted it. I didn't say no, but I just lay there, crying. Afterward, he rolled onto his side, and the way his back heaved told me he was sobbing silently into the mattress.

My heart broke for him. I reached out and put my hand on his arm. "Charlie. Charlie, it's okay."

His hand covered mine. "I don't want to lose you."

The baby kicked. I moved his hand to my belly. "You won't, Charlie. You won't. We're right here."

But a part of me was somewhere else, and nothing I could say would really convince either of us otherwise.

27
MATT

"What book would you like for your bed-time story?" I'd been gone for three nights, and I'd missed the bedtime tuck-in ritual.

Sophie looked expectantly at me, her mouth foaming with toothpaste. "Can Hope come over and tell us a story?"

"What?"

"She makes up stories. Today she tol' us about the 'ventures of Mr. Monkey."

"It was pretty funny." Zoey carefully rinsed her toothbrush and put it in the Cinderella toothbrush holder that sat between the double sinks of the girls' bathroom. "Mr. Monkey 'scaped from the zoo in the zookeeper's pocket, and everyone thought the zookeeper was a thief 'cause Mr. Monkey kept stealing things. When a policeman arrested the zookeeper, Mr. Monkey stole his hat."

Sophie giggled, spraying foam like a rabid

dog. "Yeah. An' it looked like the hat was alive!"

"Finish brushing before you talk, Sophie," Matt said.

She spit into the sink. "So can we call Hope?"

"No. We don't want to bother her this late."

"But she wouldn' mind! She likes bein' with us."

"Daddy's right. We shouldn't call her," Zoey said, primly drying her hands. "Aunt Jillian said we shouldn't get too 'ttached to Hope, 'cause she won't be around very long."

A nerve twitched in my jaw. I didn't like Jillian talking to them about Hope, but even more, I didn't like the fact she was right.

"I'll read you a story. Which one should it be?"

The girls finally agreed on a book, and I went through the rites of bedtime — a story, prayers, kisses, and tucking in. I picked up the baby monitor I still used when I went downstairs, then waited down the hall to make sure they weren't going to get up for an extra cup of water or some other sleep-postponement excuse. Ten minutes later, their whispers subsided and the house was quiet — oppressively quiet, quiet as a tomb.

Tomb made me think of Christine's, which made me realize I hadn't been thinking about her — which gave me a weird pang of something that felt like guilt.

I rubbed my head. Everyone had told me about the stages of grief, but no one had mentioned the aftereffects. I mean, I'm over the worst of it, but now that I no longer miss her so acutely, I feel kind of bad about it. I feel as if I'm abandoning her.

That first year, I thought about her all the time. The girls did, too, especially at bedtime, when they'd cry for their mommy. It tore at my gut. It was such a relief when they fell asleep — except then, I didn't have the girls as a distraction. The evenings had been our private time — the time Christine and I would watch TV together or read together or just talk. After she died, that was when I'd missed her like a phantom limb. I don't feel that anymore, and the lack of pain feels wrong.

I wandered downstairs. I glanced at the TV, but felt no urge to turn it on. There were journals on the coffee table that I should probably read and various electronic screens to scroll through, but instead, I wandered outside, the monitor in my pocket, leaving the screen door open for extra insurance.

From the back porch, I could see the bench swing next door swaying back and forth. My chest jumped. Hope.

I haven't known how to act around her ever since I kissed her — especially since that second time. I don't really know what came over me — well, I do know, and it was out of character for me to act on desire like that — and I've found myself thinking about her a lot.

There's a lot you can tell from a kiss. I don't know if it's taste or smell or texture or what, but a kiss will tell you about chemistry. I've kissed a few women since Christine, and I hadn't felt it, but with Hope . . . oh yeah, it was there, all right. It was there in spades.

Kissing her changed the way I thought about her, I have to say that. I'd found her attractive before, but now . . . well, she'd become kind of an obsession.

Which is weird, because she's not really my type — at least, the type I went for before I was married. Maybe that's why I'm attracted to her — she's a novelty, a distraction. The fact I didn't think of Christine when I kissed Hope didn't strike me as exactly a good thing. I felt bad about not feeling bad. But maybe that's good.

I stood there listening to the tree frogs

and watched her swing for a moment. I started to turn and go back inside, but just as I did, she seemed to sense me.

She turned her head, then lifted her hand in a wave. "Hello," she called.

I walked down the porch steps, away from the house so my voice wouldn't wake the girls. "Hello, yourself. Want some company?"

"Sure — if you can leave the girls."

"I'm listening to their every move on a baby monitor."

"Then come on over." I found the opening in the hedge, wedged throughout it sideways, then crossed the lawn. She moved over in the wooden swing, and I sat down beside her, setting the rhythm akimbo.

We weren't touching, but I felt her next to me. My pulse thrummed like the tree frogs' rhythmic song. "The girls' room is looking great," I said.

"Glad you like it. I've started sewing the drapes and canopies, and should have everything finished up next week."

"The girls will be thrilled." I, however, I was going to miss her being there. "How's the packing and sorting going with your grandmother?" I asked.

"Gran and I seem to be sorting through a lot more than her possessions," she said.

"And I've gotta say, I'm having a bit of a hard time processing it all."

"Oh yeah? Tell me about it."

So she did. For the next few minutes, she poured out a riveting tale. "Gran doesn't want this gossiped about, so please don't tell anyone," she cautioned.

"I'm an attorney. I'm good at keeping secrets."

She nodded. "I figured it was safe to tell you."

She trusted me. I don't know why that gave me a warm buzz in my chest, but it did. "That's an amazing story. How does it all make you feel?"

She grinned at me. "You sound like a shrink."

I was struck by a sense of déjà vu. "Actually, I sound like Christine. She used to ask me that, and I would always reply, 'You sound like a shrink.' "

She laughed. "I've got to tell you, it's kinda weird to be marital role-playing with you."

"In reverse." In the distance, a dog barked. "You know what's really weird? To be talking about her like this."

"Like how?"

"Like . . . lightly. I worry so much about the girls' and her parents' feelings, I hardly ever mention her because I don't want to make them sad."

"You don't have to worry about that with me."

And it was a relief. I nodded. "But we were talking about you and your grandmother. Are you shocked?"

She lifted her shoulders. "Not entirely — at least, not by the news about my mother's paternity. I could see it coming as the story unfolded." The swing settled into a slower rhythm. "When I saw that photo of Joe, I knew for sure. But it's made me think about things differently. It's made me realize how little you really know someone you think you know."

We rocked in silence for a moment.

"That was the situation with my ex," she said at length. "He stepped into my life right after my mother died. At the time, I felt . . . well, you know what grief's like."

I could only nod.

"It was at a time when my friends were all getting married and drifting away, and I felt so lost and alone — like I had nothing to live for."

Thank God I'd had the girls to anchor me when I lost Christine. I nodded, encouraging her to go on.

"Kurt seemed so strong and loving and

supportive — that's what I wanted to believe, anyway — and so sure that we belonged together. And the whole time . . . well, he was after my inheritance. We'd only known each other five months when we married. I think I knew pretty soon afterward that things were kind of lopsided — that I cared more about him than he cared about me. But I thought it was my fault. I thought I just wasn't good enough in some way. I thought something was lacking in me."

My chest felt tight. "You're better off without him."

"Oh, yeah. I see that now. But at the time, I couldn't — or wouldn't. But with Gran — well, she's been there my whole life, and I guess that makes you think you know everything about someone. I guess the bottom line is, people are just not completely knowable."

"Maybe not." The tree frogs hummed to the creak of the swing.

"Were there things about Christine that you only found out after she died?"

I nodded. "I found an old diary from high school. It was mainly teenage-angsty stuff. She worried that her calves were too skinny, and I didn't know that she wanted to visit every continent." Or that she'd thought the sun rose and set on somebody named Ron Kidman, and that she'd let him feel up her breasts. "Reading that diary made me wish we'd traveled more."

"I'm sure she loved the journey she was on with you. She was probably so glad to be a mom that she didn't care."

"Yeah." I didn't say that I'd found part of a more recent journal on her computer, and that I'd read there had been times she'd felt trapped and frustrated. She'd written that I wasn't always around enough and she felt overwhelmed by two kids in diapers and she missed her job. That had hurt a lot more than knowing some jerk-off jock had groped her teenage breasts.

We rocked in companionable silence for a while. "I found her college diaries, too," I found myself saying. "Before we met, it turned out she'd had a crush on a guy I thought she hated. How did I not know she liked him?"

"What matters is that she loved *you.*"

"Yeah. But I didn't want to really know about her loving — crushing on — someone else. There's a part of me that wants to be the only one she ever loved."

"That must be how my grandfather felt. I really feel sorry for him, you know? But it doesn't matter who's first. It only matters who's last."

"That's very profound."

"That's me. Deep and profound. And probably quoting Dear Abby." She grinned, but her eyes stayed pensive. "I feel sorry for everyone in my grandmother's situation." She glanced at me. "It's kind of like that with you and Jillian."

"Huh?"

"She's in love with you. Surely you know that."

"I . . ." I looked at the live oak on the far side of the lawn, a little startled. "I wouldn't call it love."

"I would. I see how she looks at you."

Egads. Was she right? "What do you suggest I do about it?"

"Start dating someone else."

I stretched my arm across the back of the swing. "Is this a sly way of getting me to ask you out?"

She grinned and rolled her eyes. "Do I look that desperate? Besides, you already asked and I told you no."

"Ouch." I put my hand on my chest as if I'd been stabbed. "You really know how to twist the knife."

"I'm sure you'll recover." She gave me a soft grin, then looked away. As she turned her head, her hair brushed my arm on the back of the swing.

The touch made my skin feel hot and electrified. All I had to do was move my arm down, and it would be around her shoulders. The urge to do so was almost overpowering. "So why did you say no?"

She lifted her shoulders, bringing them closer to my arm. "There's no point in getting anything started when I'm just going to leave."

That's what Jillian had told my girls. I felt a fresh round of annoyance. "It doesn't have to be a 'thing.' Not a thing with a capital *T* anyway," I found myself saying. "And the fact it's temporary makes it perfect. I can be your rebound, and you can be mine. The girls already know you're leaving, so they wouldn't start turning it into a big deal. And you'd be helping me out with Jillian."

"Wow, you are one romantic dude."

I grinned. "Yeah, well, once you've seen each other covered in garbage slime, the magic's gone."

She smiled back.

I used the moment to press my case. "Seriously. There's a fundraiser for the local food pantry on Friday. It's sort of a dress-up dinner with a silent auction called Fete du Printemps at the community center, and

I've bought a table. I'll pick you up at seven."

"What about your girls?"

"Peggy and Griff are babysitting."

"That's not what I mean. Zoey thinks that Jillian is going to be their new mother."

I blew out a sigh. "I've already told her that's not going to happen. Maybe this will help convince her." I stood up, figuring I ought to leave before Hope had a chance to turn me down. "See you Friday, if not before."

I strode across the lawn, turned sideways, and edged through the shrubbery. As I climbed the steps to my porch, I found myself whistling. I realized later that it was the first time I'd whistled since Christine died.

28
ADELAIDE

Time has a way of getting away from me. I can't always remember if the last meal was lunch or supper, or if it's seven at night or seven in the morning. Even worse, whole days blend together. Sometimes I can't recall if something happened yesterday or a few days ago. I might even be missing a whole week.

I woke up and heard Hope talking with an aide in the kitchen, then a few moments later, the soft pad of her bare feet sounded in the hall. The door to my room slowly opened. "Come on in, child," I called. "I'm awake."

"It's time for your medicine," Hope said.

I sat up in bed and propped my back up with pillows. She handed me two pills and a glass of water. I downed them, then glanced at the clock as I set the glass beside it on the bedside table. Four o'clock. I'm assuming that's afternoon, because Hope was up and dressed. I looked down and saw that I was dressed, as well.

Time was flitting by so quickly. I'd better get about my business. "Want to go through my closet some more?"

Hope nodded. "Absolutely."

"Where did we leave off?"

"Joe had visited," she said. "Did you ever hear from him again?"

"Yes. Oh yes." I smoothed the edge of the sheet. "He wrote to me afterward."

"Did you write back?"

"I'm afraid so." I drew a deep breath. "Look in the closet at the back on the right side. There's a red shirtwaist with a patent belt."

Hope rummaged around, then held it up by the hanger. "Is this it?"

I nodded. "Bring it here."

She crossed the room and placed it on the bed, then sank onto the mattress beside me. I fingered the hem. "I wasn't going to write him, but . . ." I closed my eyes, remembering.

1946

Charlie wasn't the same after Joe's visit. He took to drinking more, and when he drank, he'd accuse me of writing to Joe, of harboring feelings for him. Jealousy ate at him like rotgut. I was so tired as my pregnancy progressed — housework and cooking and childcare were so difficult in those days! — and then my grandmother took ill, and my mother was down in her back, and I had to care for both of them as well as Becky. Then the holidays came and went, with all the extra shopping, baking, and wrapping. Life was just so darned hard!

One day, after a particularly bitter bout with Charlie, I poured it all into a letter and before I stopped to think, I went downtown and dropped it in a mailbox by the drugstore. I immediately regretted it, but at the same time, a churning sense of hope fluttered in my chest.

I rationalized it by thinking, *Well, if Charlie thinks I'm writing Joe anyway, I might as well be doing it.*

We developed quite a torrid long-distance correspondence. This went on for a couple of months, letters flying back and forth across the country.

Until Charlie found the letters. One evening I went to a women's auxiliary meeting at church — I was wearing that red shirtwaist, only without the belt, because of my pregnancy — and came home to find my hatboxes on the floor and Joe's letters scattered on the bed.

"What's all this?" Charlie demanded, wildly waving a page. His face was the color of a bruised plum, his scowl so terrifying I could barely breathe.

I was still holding my purse, squeezing the handle so tightly it left marks on my palm. "It's — it's nothing." I set my purse on the dresser and pulled off my gloves, trying to act normal — not because I thought it would calm him, but because I didn't know what else to do.

" 'I burn for you'? That's *nothing*? '*I lie in bed at night and replay the way you felt in my arms.*' " He flung the paper on the floor and took a step toward me. I backed up until the dresser bit into my back.

"Are you writing him back?"

"No . . . I . . ."

"Liar!"

I cringed at his bellow.

"He says so right here. '*I was so glad to get your last letter.*' " He jabbed a finger on the paper as he spoke, emphasizing each word, using an ugly falsetto as he read Joe's sentence. "What the hell do you take me for?"

"You're my husband, Charlie."

"You damn sure don't seem to remember that!"

"Quiet. You're going to wake Becky."

393

"You should be worried about more than waking her! You should be worried about losing her. And the new baby, too."

To say my heart sank is like saying the *Titanic* took on a little water. "What?"

"If you think I'll ever allow you to take my children, you don't know me very well. Becky is legally *my* daughter. My parents are her grandparents, and there is no way in hell we're going to allow a floozy like you to change that. So if you have any ideas about leaving me, you need to know you'll be leaving the children, too. And if you try to carry on behind my back . . ." His face twisted into someone I didn't know — someone terrifying, someone capable of anything. His skin was red, blotched with purple, and I thought he might be having a stroke, right then and there. "I won't stand for it. I'll divorce you, and I'll keep the children."

He meant it, too. Worse, he had the means to do it. His parents had money — at least, more money than mine. They'd do whatever it took to keep their only grandchildren in town.

After that horrible night, Charlie started watching me like a hawk, and drinking more and more. He began coming home for lunch, early, before the mail was delivered. He went to the mailbox himself. He didn't say why, but he didn't need to. He started drinking at lunch.

Another letter arrived from Joe, and Charlie nigh near went berserk. Thank God he passed out from drinking too much too fast too early in the day, or else I don't know what he would have done. I called his father and told him Charlie had a bug, and that he wouldn't be in that afternoon.

"Write him back," he demanded the next morning. He'd stayed home from work, nursing his hangover.

"No. I don't want . . ."

His face took on that mottled purple-red color again. He grabbed a sheet of paper and plunked it on the kitchen table, along with a pen. "Sit down and write what I tell you."

I slowly sank into a chair.

"Dear Joe," he dictated.

My fingers shook so hard I could hardly hold the pen. It was almost as if my muscles rebelled. He stood over me and made me write that I didn't want Joe to ever contact me again — that I was a married woman, that I loved my husband, that I wanted to keep my family intact, that I'd finally come to my senses, and that I didn't know what had possessed me to ever take up with him in the first place. He forced me to write that

I didn't love him or want him in my life, that I wanted him to leave me alone. Charlie stood over my shoulder, breathing hard, telling me what to write and making sure I did it.

I cried. I cried secretly for weeks. But as Eddie's due date drew near, I started focusing on that — and then, well, once I had him, caring for a baby and Becky and helping my mother care for Grandmother took everything I had. Charlie stopped drinking after Eddie was born. He was kind and thoughtful and tender. He promised me he'd turned over a new leaf, that he intended to be the best father and husband in the world, and it was touching, watching the way he worked at it. I loved little Eddie. I loved Becky. And I loved Charlie, too. He'd been my best friend for most of my life.

Things settled back down, and for most of a year, Charlie and I eased back into what most people would call a happy marriage.

It wasn't the most physically fulfilling for me, but then, I suspect that was the case for most married women back then. I think that's why virginity was so highly prized. Men didn't want women to have anyone to compare them against.

Things would have stayed that way, too,

except that Joe refused to believe my letter. He waited until Charlie went to a national lumber trade show — there was one I'd told him about that Charlie went to every year — and then he showed up on my porch.

I'd been folding clothes when I'd heard a knock on the door. I yanked it open without even taking the kerchief off my hair. My heart dropped to my toes, then bounced to the sky when I saw Joe standing there, his hat in his hand.

"He made you write that letter, didn't he?"

I didn't even have to nod. He read it in my eyes.

"Well, I've come for you," he said. "I waited until he went to that convention."

I pulled him into the house so the neighbors wouldn't see. He tried to gather me in his arms, but I turned away. I'd learned not to trust myself where he was concerned.

"Pack your things and the kids' things and come with me," he urged. "We'll move to California."

"He'll find us. He'll take the children."

"Then we'll move to Europe."

My head swam. I shook it. "My grandmother's not well, and I help my mother take care of her. They would be devastated. And Charlie's parents . . . they're getting older." And Charlie — Charlie would be

397

shattered, broken beyond any hope of redemption. I shook my head again. "I can't sacrifice everyone else's happiness for my own."

"What about me, Addie? What about us?"

My chest felt as if a wet bag of cement were sitting on it. "There is no us."

"There's a little girl somewhere in this house who proves otherwise." His eyes darted to the hallway, as if he could see her through the walls. "Where is she?"

"Napping. Keep your voice down — I don't want to wake her."

He moved closer — close enough that I could feel the heat of his body, close enough that I could smell him, close enough that his magnetism seemed to be heedlessly pulling me in. "Addie — I love you. And I love our daughter."

My heart — what a traitorous thing is the heart! — leapt with joy, even as it broke in two. "I have a son now, too. He's just five months old."

He placed his hands on my arms. "I'll raise him as my own. You know I will."

Shivers chased up and down my skin. I drew away and folded my arms around my abdomen. Tears thickened my voice. "Joe — please don't make this worse than it is! I'm married and have a family. Find someone else. Someone free and unencumbered."

"I don't want anyone else."

"You might think that now, but you will if you let me go. Put me out of your mind."

"Like you have me?" He stepped toward me. "You never would have married Charlie if you hadn't been carrying my child."

"I can't regret that, Joe. Don't you see? I can't regret having Eddie."

"You don't regret some other man raising my child? I know I sure as hell do."

The way things were now, one of them would be raising the other man's child, unless they killed each other and I raised them alone. There was no fix for this situation, and thinking about it made my heart feel as if it were splitting in two. "Joe — please. Just go and leave us in peace."

"Is that really what you want?"

Somewhere deep inside, I found the strength to say what needed to be said. "Yes. That's what's best for my family."

"Can I at least see Rebecca?"

"No, because she'll tell Charlie."

His sigh sounded like a soul exiting a body. He stared at his feet for a long moment, and his shoulders slumped. I wondered if this was how he'd looked when he was taken into captivity, when he had to surrender. At length he looked up. "If he ever mistreats you, Addie . . . if you ever need anything — anything at all — just let me know. You can always find me here." He gave me a business card. "I'll keep that mailbox forever. You can always reach me through it."

He grabbed me by the shoulders and bent his head to kiss me. Every fiber in my being ached for that kiss — the kiss I'd imagined so many times when I was lying with Charlie — but I knew that if I kissed him once, I couldn't trust myself not to kiss him again, and again, and again. One kiss, and I might be out the door and down the road, doing everything I knew was wrong.

I turned my head aside. "Please go, Joe. Please."

He kissed my cheek and released me. I turned my back to him and folded my arms around myself. Tears flowed down my cheeks despite my tightly shut eyes.

I heard the screen door open, then close.

"Good-bye, Addie," I heard him say in a low voice. "I'll always love you."

29
MATT

"So tomorrow's the big night," Jillian said.

She'd just dropped the girls off from ballet lessons, and they were thundering up
the stairs behind me. I stood at the front
door, trying to block Jillian from coming in.
Hope was upstairs painting and I was eager
to rejoin her. I'd gotten home from work
early today, and Hope had been telling me
the latest installment of her grandmother's
tale.

"Tomorrow?" I echoed blankly, not sure
what Jillian was referring to.

She nodded. "The fete."

"Oh, yeah." I'd bought tickets from Jillian
three weeks ago — an entire table, because
it was a good cause and Jillian was on the
organizing committee. In the few days since
I'd invited Hope, I'd been looking forward
to my date with her like a teenager anticipat-
ing the prom.

"I'm afraid I'll have to meet you there,"

Jillian was saying, "because I have to go early to help with the setup. But I'm catching a ride with Annie, so you and I won't be in separate cars at the end."

"Wait." I pulled my brows together. My thoughts had been wandering upstairs, and I figured I must have missed something. "So . . . you're saying you'll need a ride home afterward?"

Her head tilted at a weird angle and she looked at me funny. "Of course, since we're going together."

I stared at her, confused.

Her forehead creased in consternation. "I invited you to be my date."

A pit opened in my stomach area. "Oh, God. You thought . . ." I ran a hand across my jaw. The hurt in her eyes made it hard to look at her. "I, uh . . . I thought you just wanted me to come and support the cause."

I could see she was trying to smile. The effort she put into tugging her mouth into that uneven, wobbly curve made me feel like the lowest kind of vermin. "Well, yes, of course. And it was generous of you to buy a whole table. But . . . I specifically invited you to be with me."

"Oh." I shifted my stance and wished I could somehow disappear. "Well, the thing is . . ." Oh, man — this was brutal. This moment belonged in the Painfully Awkward Hall of Fame. I raked both hands through my hair, shoved them in my pants pockets, and racked my mind for something not too awful to say. "The thing is, I misunderstood. You're family, so I wasn't thinking of you . . ."

. . . *that way.* I never had. Surely she could get the drift.

"There's a first time for everything," she said in what I imagined was her cheerful, elementary-school-teacher voice.

"The thing is," I continued, "I've, uh, invited Hope."

She rocked back on the heels of her flats, as if she'd taken a blow. After a horrid moment of silence, she lifted her chin. "But I asked you. When someone invites you to something, you don't just invite someone else along."

"I — I didn't realize. I'm sorry." I swallowed, looked away, then glanced back. My ears were burning, which meant they probably looked like someone had boxed them. I wished someone had; I deserved to have my ears boxed. "I misunderstood. I didn't know it was a . . ." *Aw, hell. Better not use the d-word!* ". . . a specific invitation. I thought you were just asking for me to participate and donate like you were asking everyone else." I shifted uneasily. "It's not like we're seeing each other."

"Maybe you're not ready to start dating again yet," Jillian said carefully.

For the first time since Christine's death, I was sure I was, but I didn't want to rub salt in her wounds. I lifted my shoulders. "Look, I'm really sorry. You're welcome to join us at our table. And if you need a ride home, Hope and I can give you one."

Tears gleamed in her eyes. She put up her hands, palms out. "No. No need. I'll just take my own car."

She turned and headed to her car, walking stiffly. With a heavy heart, I closed the door.

I found both girls upstairs with Hope, excitedly telling her about their day. Hope took one look at my face, gave me a worried little frown, then turned to the girls. "Zoey, Sophie — do you have any artwork from school you can show me?"

"Yes!" they both exclaimed.

"I'd love to see it."

They raced from the room. "What's up?" Hope asked as their feet pounded on the stairs.

"Jillian thought I was going to be her date tomorrow."

"Oh no!"

"Yeah. I missed that part when she asked me to buy tickets." I blew out a long breath. "She tried to play it cool, but she was pretty upset."

"I can imagine."

"What should I do? Should I call Peggy?"

Hope looked thoughtful. "No. If I were Jillian, you calling my mother would just make it worse. I think this is one of those cases where the best thing to do is nothing."

"I feel really bad," I confessed.

"It was an honest mistake. She has to know that."

I nodded, but making the mistake honestly didn't make it any less hurtful.

"There's never an easy way to learn your feelings aren't reciprocated. It's best, though, to find out sooner rather than later — before you get over-invested." Hope's smile was rueful and self-deprecating. "And I mean that in every sense of the word."

I felt a flash of anger toward her ex. What a jerk, deliberately taking advantage of her.

The girls burst back into the room, waving artwork from preschool. Hope turned her attention to them as I watched from the doorway.

Hope was so open and easy and kind and . . . *lovely.* The thought kind of startled me, because it was a girly word, not one I would usually say out loud, but it fit her.

She caught my eye over Sophie's head. I remembered kissing her, and a whomp of attraction hit me right in the solar plexus. She gave me a soft smile that left me light-headed and happy and kind of buzzed.

Unless my radar was really off — and it could be; I was admittedly out of practice — the attraction I felt for her was a two-way street. I couldn't wait to get Hope alone tomorrow and see where it led.

30
HOPE

I peered at my reflection in the highboy in Gran's bedroom as I fastened the single strand of pearls around my neck, then turned toward Gran, my arms out. "How do I look?" I asked.

Gran clapped her hands from her seat in the rocking chair, beaming like a wrinkled cherub. "Oh, you're beautiful! You look just like Audrey Hepburn!"

I moved to the cheval mirror in the corner and eyed myself. Wearing Gran's vintage black sheath with my hair in an updo, I did, indeed, look like I belonged in an old movie. "All I'm lacking are elbow-length black gloves."

"I have some, if you'd like to wear them," Gran volunteered.

I was tempted, but I didn't want to push "vintage" into "dressed for a costume party." "Thanks, but I'd better pass."

"Oh my, don't you look pretty!" said

Nadine. The aide had worked late, largely, I suspected, to see me off on my date. She turned to Gran. "I have your dinner ready."

We helped Gran up and onto her walker. She'd no sooner gotten settled in the kitchen than the doorbell rang.

I hurried to answer it. My heart skipped a beat when I saw Matt standing there, wearing a fitted dark suit, looking, as Gran would say, "handsome as all get-out."

He seemed appreciative of my efforts, as well.

"Wow!" he murmured.

I felt my face heat under his gaze. "It's Gran's dress. I didn't pack anything for a big night out when I came to town."

"You look amazing."

"Tell your young gentleman to come in here so I can see you together," Gran called.

"I feel like I'm going to prom," he murmured.

"Sorry," I whispered.

"What for?" He took my elbow and grinned. "I just wish I'd brought a corsage."

Gran clapped her hands again as we entered the kitchen. "Oh, what a fine-looking couple! I wish I could see straight so I could take a picture."

"I can take one," Nadine offered.

Matt pulled his phone out of his pocket

and handed it to her. He put his arm around my waist, and we both smiled.

"Now take one of us with Miss Addie," he said.

"Oh, I'm better off behind the camera than in front of it," Gran fussed, but she seemed pleased as we circled around the table and posed on either side of her.

"Thank you for being so sweet about all that," I said once we'd escaped the house and gotten settled in his car.

"No problem," he said, backing out of the drive. "Reminded me of my mom, insisting I bring my prom date by the house so she could see her."

"Where are your parents?"

He shifted gears and pulled the car onto the street. "They lived in Houston. That's where I grew up. Mom died of breast cancer while I was in college."

My heart went out to him. "I'm sorry. That had to be rough."

"Yeah, it was. Especially on Dad. They'd been married thirty-two years."

"How is he now?"

"Great. He remarried a few years ago and lives in Australia."

"Australia!"

Matt nodded. "My sister married an Aussie, and when Dad went to visit them, they introduced him to a widow at their church, and, well, the rest is history."

"Do you see them often?"

"Not really — once a year or so. We Skype a lot, but Dad's the quiet type. Never has much to say."

"Are you and your sister close?"

"Yeah. She's crazy about the girls. She and her husband have been trying to have kids for years, but so far, no luck. They're thinking about adopting from Russia or China. I've been looking into the legalities for her."

Matt was a real family man, I thought — the kind of guy whose roots ran deep, who knew the meaning of commitment. Too bad we were both on the rebound, headed in entirely different directions. I'd just accepted a fabulous job in Chicago, and he had a ways to go to get over his wife. If we'd met at another point in our lives, maybe . . .

He turned into the civic center parking lot, stopping my thoughts from jumping off a dangerous cliff. He parked the car, killed the engine, then drew a long breath.

"Dreading seeing Jillian?" I guessed.

He nodded.

"We could blow this off and go somewhere else," I suggested.

"I thought about that, but I invited some friends to join us at the table."

"Well, I know it doesn't feel like it, but we're doing Jillian a favor," I said softly. "I wish I'd found out right away that Kurt was more interested in my maid of honor than in me."

Matt looked at me, surprised. "Is that what happened?"

I nodded. "I caught them together."

He shook his head. "You were married to an idiot."

His indignation flattered me. "I'm the one who felt like an idiot, not seeing it sooner. It felt like a double whammy, being betrayed by my husband and my best friend."

He gazed at me for a long moment, his eyes warm. "A lot of people would just shut down after something like that."

"Oh, I did."

"You seem fine now."

I lifted my shoulders and grinned. "Appearances can be deceiving."

He grinned back and reached for my hand. "Thanks."

"For what?"

"For making me feel like less of a jerk."

"Anytime."

We climbed out of the car and headed inside. I spotted Jillian the minute we walked under a bower of silk flowers into the dimly lit hall. So did Matt.

"Oh, man. She's wearing Christine's dress," he murmured.

"Really?" It was a beige silk dress with rhinestone shoulder straps. "It looks great on her."

"Don't you think it's weird?"

I lifted my shoulders. "I'm the wrong person to consult. After all, I'm wearing my grandmother's clothes."

He laughed and my answer seemed to placate him, but, yeah, I thought it was a little odd — especially if Jillian had planned to wear that on a date with Matt.

We headed to the bar, then circulated around the room. I was delighted to see Kirsten — and even more delighted to learn Matt had invited her to join us at his table, along with Aimee and her husband. The five of us hung together as we made our rounds of the room.

When I spotted Jillian again, a tall, lanky man was earnestly talking to her.

"Who's that?" I asked Kirsten.

"Phillip Mitchell, the new senior physics teacher at the high school. Looks like he's *ver-y* interested in Jillian."

"Let's ask him to join us at the table," I suggested to Matt.

"Good idea."

Jillian polished off her drink and reached

for a glass of wine from a passing waiter as we approached.

"Hello, Jillian," I said, mustering my warmest smile. "You look beautiful."

"Love your dress," said Kirsten, not knowing its history.

"Thank you." Jillian's gaze traveled to Matt, who was making small talk with Aimee's husband and Phillip. She drained half her glass in a single swallow.

"You smell wonderful," Aimee said. "What scent are you wearing?"

"Happy by Clinique," Jillian replied.

Aimee's brow puckered. "Wasn't that Christine's perfume?"

"Last time I checked, she didn't have an exclusive on it." Jillian downed the rest of her wine, then set her empty on the tray held by the still-hovering waiter and reached for another glass. "I've always loved it."

"Yes, but smell is most closely related to memory," Aimee said earnestly. "It might be painful for family members."

"I was family, too." Tears sprang to Jillian's eyes. "Does anyone care how painful it is for me?"

Jillian was slurring her words. Oh, dear — she'd drunk too much, and it was still nearly forty minutes before dinner. I worriedly watched as she took a long pull from her fresh glass. Aimee noticed, too. "Let's go someplace private to talk." She turned and touched her husband's arm. "We're all going to the powder room."

"I've never understood why women always have to go together," he said with a good-natured grin at Matt and Phillip.

I thought maybe I should stay back, but Kirsten grabbed my arm and pulled me along.

Fortunately, the ladies' room was empty. Aimee pulled a tissue from a holder on the counter and handed it to Jillian. "I didn't mean to hurt your feelings," she said gently.

"I know. No one does it intentionally." Jillian dabbed her eyes. "It's jus' . . . well, everyone worries about Matt and the girls and Mom and Dad, and I lost a loved one, too. She was my sister and my best friend, and I loved her as much as anyone."

"We all know how close you two were," Kirsten said.

"Well, here's something you probably don't know. Do you have any idea how hard it always was, being in Christine's shadow?" Jillian wiped her nose. "She was the oldest, so she always got first choice, first dibs, first shot at everythin' — and everythin' she tried, she was great at. I didn't want to compete, so I just tried to be different, even though I liked a lot of the same things she liked." The tears were really flowing now, just pouring down her face. "My whole life has been like Opposite Day to whatever Christine did. Even now that she's dead, I can't do the things I like if she did them first."

Kirsten patted her back. "Oh, Jillian, sweetie, you can do whatever you want."

"No, I can't! Not without being compared and judged." She let out a sound that was half sob, half hiccup. "I always wanted to lighten my hair, but Christine was blond, so I didn'. When I finally did a few weeks ago, my mother said I shouldn' try to copy Christine. And I've always loved this perfume, and . . ."

She dissolved into weeping.

"I'm so sorry, Jillian," Aimee said softly.

"You know what?" Jillian said bitterly. "I wish it was me who'd died."

"Oh, Jillian, you can't mean that." Kirsten cast me a worried look over Jillian's bowed head.

"I do. I sometimes wonder if my parents — and Matt and the girls, of course — wish I'd been the sister with the aneurysm."

"You can't think like that!" Aimee said.

"I can' help it." Her voice was low and ragged. The slurring was getting worse.

"What they don' know is, I would have traded spots with Christine in a heartbeat. I would gladly trade the rest of my life to have two beautiful children and the love of a man like Matt for even a few years."

We all exchanged concerned glances. "Honey . . . I think that wine hit you hard," Aimee said.

"Have you eaten anything today?" Kirsten asked.

Jillian shook her head. "I couldn'. I was too upset. I thought Matt was going to be my date, an' then I found out he didn' even know it was an event people bring dates to."

Kirsten looked at me. Apparently Jillian either thought Matt and I were just friends, or she was in complete denial. "Why don't I go get you some crackers," I suggested, feeling like an interloper.

"Oh, I couldn' possibly eat. I don' feel so good. I'm dizzy." She put her hand on her mouth. "An' quizzy."

"Why don't I drive you home," Kirsten offered.

"But I don't want to miss . . ." Jillian cut off mid-sentence to make a staggering dash to a toilet stall.

"Go pull your car around to the kitchen entrance," Aimee told Kirsten. "We'll take her out the back door."

31
MATT

I pulled my car into my own driveway and killed the engine, then realized I was operating on automatic pilot. "I should have stopped next door to let you out at your grandmother's place."

"It's a short walk." Hope smiled at me. "Thank you for a wonderful evening."

"No — thank *you*." Conversation between us had flowed like water at the fete — easy and effortless, spreading in all directions. We'd talked about everything from work to football, from science to movies. We'd danced, and although I'm not much of a dancer and avoid it when I can, I'd loved the slow songs, because it had given me the chance to hold Hope in my arms.

The only glitch in the evening had been Jillian's sudden disappearance — and even though I felt mean admitting it, that had been a relief. Hope had explained what happened, and I was glad that Kirsten had

417

stepped up and handled it. I would have felt obligated to take Jillian home myself if I'd known about it.

As it was, everything had worked out. Kirsten had taken Jillian home, persuaded her to eat something, then made it back to the fete in time for dinner.

"Before you agreed to go with me, I'd kinda been dreading this evening," I told Hope. "But as it turns out, this was the best time I've had in a long, long while."

She smiled, her eyes warm. "Me, too."

I leaned toward her, intending to kiss her. Before our lips could make contact, though, the porch light flared on and Peggy stood in the open doorway. "I thought I heard your car," I heard her call.

Apparently, there was the downside of having your former mother-in-law as a babysitter, I thought darkly.

"Hi, Peggy." Hope opened her door and gave a little wave, not giving me a chance to round the car and open the door for her. I climbed out of the car and walked to Hope's side.

"Did you have a good time?" Peggy asked.

"Wonderful," Hope said.

"Jillian called and said she'd had to go home sick."

I wondered what else Jillian had said.

418

"Yeah. How is she?"

"She said she's better."

"Good," Hope said.

"Did the girls behave?" I asked.

"Oh, they were little angels. They went to sleep very easily."

"Great. Peggy, if you don't mind staying for just a moment, I'd like to walk Hope home."

"Oh, sure, dear."

The door closed. I walked Hope down the sidewalk, then up the steps to her grandmother's lit porch. We stood there for a moment, just looking at each other. Her eyes were soft and warm, her parted lips an invitation.

I put my hands on her waist and drew her to me. She leaned in, and my mouth met hers. *Soft* — her lips were soft and velvety, warm and exciting. Her arms wound around my back. I deepened the pressure, then felt her stiffen.

"Peggy's looking out your living room window," she whispered.

With a heavy sigh, I opened my eyes, only to see Adelaide's neighbor on the other side, Mrs. Ivy, peering out her blind. "She's not the only one watching us."

Hope laughed, opened the screen door, then turned the knob on the wooden one.

"Well, good night," she said, disappearing inside.

I blew out another heavy sigh and turned around. Across the street, Griff was peering out the window, as well. Irritated, I lifted my hand in a wave. He awkwardly waved back.

I walked to my home and opened the door. "Thanks for babysitting, Peggy," I said.

"You're welcome, dear. It's always a pleasure."

She picked up her purse, but made no move toward the door.

"I'll walk you home," I said.

"Oh, no need. I called Griff, and he's watching for me."

"Oh, so it's *you* he was watching for. Were you two exchanging hand signals?"

She had the grace to blush. "Matt, dear — Hope is a very sweet girl."

I nodded. I could tell a "but" was coming.

"You need to be careful, though, dear."

I raised my eyebrows. "I don't think she's a serial killer or anything."

"No, of course not. She's a wonderful artist — the girls' room is just looking spectacular — but she's only here for a short time. And if you get involved with her, the girls will get attached, and . . ." Peggy pulled her sweater tight around her shoulders. "Well, it would be hard for them to have another loss."

I tamped down a rush of annoyance. Why did everyone think they had the right to get all up in my business?

"And Jillian . . ." Peggy continued.

Oh, boy. Here it came.

"Well, this is none of my business, but Jillian thought the two of you were going out tonight, and the fact you brought Hope — well, frankly, it upset her."

I ran my hand across my jaw. "Yeah, I picked up on that. And I apologized. I didn't realize she thought it was a date. Because the truth is, Peggy, I just don't see her that way."

"Well, maybe in time . . ."

"No." I cut her off abruptly. "It's just not there."

She shifted her purse to her other arm and nodded. "Well, honey — all Griff and I want is for you to be happy. You deserve nothing less. But the girls want a mother, and every woman you date, well, they'll cast her in that role."

The woman the girls were currently casting was Jillian, and I *wasn't* dating her, but I didn't want to put Peggy in the middle of things.

"I would hate for them to get their little hearts broken," she said.

"As far as Hope's concerned, you're worrying about nothing, Peggy. They're well aware that Hope is just here temporarily. But quite frankly, I think they need to get used to the idea of me dating." I opened the door. "Thanks again for watching the girls."

"It was my pleasure. It always is."

"Next year, I'll hire a sitter so you and Griff can come to the fete, too."

She flicked her wrist. "Oh, there's nothing that would have dragged Griff away from the ball game on TV tonight. And I love spending time with the girls."

"They love spending time with you, too."

"I'm so glad you moved to Wedding Tree."

I nodded. "It's worked out pretty well." For everyone, I thought as I closed the door, except for Jillian. And quite possibly me.

32
ADELAIDE

The next morning, I was eating a bowl of oatmeal Nadine had prepared when Hope entered the kitchen, dressed in shorts and a T-shirt. "How was you evening, dear?" I asked.

"Lovely."

"I bet it was." I cast a pointed glance at the aide, who reluctantly left the room. She already knew what I was going to ask about, but I wanted Hope to answer freely. I waited until she was out of earshot, then leaned forward. "Eunice Ivy says Matt kissed you."

The incredulous look on Hope's face made my finger itch for a camera. She glanced at the clock over the oven. "It's not even seven o'clock, and you've already talked to Mrs. Ivy?"

I nodded. "She was waiting on the porch when the aide arrived at six. She couldn't wait to tell me. She said you saw Peggy spying on you, and that's when you came inside."

Hope turned away to pour a cup of coffee. "Was the whole town watching?"

"Just the neighbors." I gave her a wink. "In the future, it's probably best to do your canoodling someplace more private."

"We weren't . . ." Hope's face flamed. "It was just a good-night kiss, that's all."

"Oh, I don't blame you, dear. He's a very handsome man. But not much happens in this town without everyone finding out. It's always been that way."

Hope opened the refrigerator and pulled out a carton of yogurt. "That must have made things hard for you with Charlie and Joe."

She was deliberately changing the topic. I recognized the tactic, having employed it plenty of times myself, but I let her get away with it, because it was high time I told her the part I'd been dreading. "Oh, my — that's God's own truth. And there are other truths I have to tell you. What do you say we get back to my closet when we finish here?"

"Sure."

After breakfast, Nadine gave me my medicine, and I told her we didn't want to see her until lunchtime. Hope and I moved into my bedroom, where I settled hard into my rocking chair. I paused a moment, then gathered my courage. "Open the closet. On the floor on the left side, there's a box with a red lid. I want you to pull it out."

Hope found it and brought it over to me. "Open it, dear."

She set it on the blanket chest beside the rocker and lifted the lid. I reached in and picked up an infant-sized little white sailor suit. It was yellowed, but the red and blue trim was intact. I smiled. Seemed like yesterday that I was burping a baby on my shoulder.

"This was Eddie's?" Hope asked.

"Yes."

Next she lifted out a dress Mother had made for Rebecca — white eyelet, now yellowed. Hope oohed and aahed over it.

My chest tightened at what was coming. "Pull out what's under it."

She lifted out two layette sets, still in tissue, unworn and pristine. One was yellow, one was green. She lay them across my lap. I didn't realize my eyes had teared up until she handed me a tissue.

"Mom told me you had a stillborn baby," Hope said softly.

And all of a sudden, here we were — at the very part I didn't want to talk about,

425

even though we'd been heading toward it all along. "Well, dear, that's not exactly right."

"No?"

"No. That's what everyone thought, but . . ."

A cloud was settling over me — a dark cloud of stormy memories. "Sit down, dear. There's something I need to tell you."

1947–1948

Life went on for us after Joe's last visit, but I started avoiding marital relations with Charlie. Something about seeing Joe again had stirred up a streak of bitterness. Maybe it had always been hiding inside me, but I didn't fully realize it until after Joe's second visit.

The magnitude of all I was losing out on — travel, adventure, earth-stopping sex — hit me anew. I was angry. Angry at God, angry at fate, angry at Charlie — even, God help me, angry at my children and my parents and grandparents. I was angry at everyone who put daily demands on me, who kept me trapped in what felt like a life of drudgery.

Mostly, I think, I was angry at myself — and anger turned inward festers.

I couldn't stand for Charlie to touch me.

I'd feign a headache, or fatigue, or pretend to already be asleep. "It's your wifely duty," Charlie finally told me.

Well, he was right — but having him tell me I *had* to make love with him just made me all the more reluctant. I gave in, but I acted like a rag doll instead of an active participant. I resented him, and my resentment — my passive aggression, I guess you'd call it — well, it tore Charlie up on the inside. He wanted something from me that I wouldn't give, and the more he wanted it, the more stubborn I grew.

"Tell me you love me, Addie," he'd beg.

"I love you," I'd say, my voice flat as a pancake.

"Say it like you mean it."

"I am!"

But I wasn't. And God help me, but there was something about his begging, something about the naked neediness of him that made it hard as the dickens for me to give him what he wanted.

"Kiss me back when I kiss you," he'd tell me.

I'd pucker up like a fish, but keep my lips immobile.

"Open your eyes," he'd say as he made love to me. I'd gaze at the ceiling like a store mannequin.

He'd pepper me with questions. "It's Joe, isn't it? It's Joe again."

"How could it be? You made me send that letter."

"Did he come here? Did he come when I was gone?"

"Yes!" I finally told him. I was at the end of my rope, and I wanted to wound him, to make him realize all his efforts couldn't stop Joe from loving me. "Yes, he came here. He didn't believe I wrote that letter. He wanted me to go away with him. I refused and he left. End of story."

But as far as Charlie was concerned, it was just the beginning. It ate at him. He questioned me more and more. Did I sleep with Joe? Did I kiss him? How long did he stay? Did he see Becky? How many times had he visited? The more he questioned, the more perverse and angry I grew. He started drinking again. The more I withheld affection, the more he drank. And the more he drank, the more I withheld.

After a month or so, he begged my forgiveness and tried wooing me. He brought me flowers. He did the dishes. He had his parents watch the children so he could take me on a romantic weekend to a cabin by a lake near Jackson. Bless his heart, he couldn't have known that it would remind me of that blissful time with Joe. He only knew that I sobbed all weekend. Charlie cried, too. "How can I make you love me?" he asked, making me feel like a monster, but not making it any easier to show him affection.

My saving grace was that Charlie started traveling. His early efforts to convince his father to branch out and expand the hardware side of the lumber business started paying off. Instead of just running a retail store in Wedding Tree, they'd become a supplier to out-of-town five-and-tens and general stores, providing them with nails and screws and other items. There were plans to open another full lumber store in another small town. Charlie was usually gone two nights a week, and on those nights, I would breathe easier. The children and I would usually have dinner with my parents or his parents. None of our surviving grandparents were doing too well at that point, and my maternal grandmother lived with my parents.

One morning after Charlie had been on a trip — it was the Saturday before Easter, I distinctly remember that — he came home at ten in the morning. That was unusual, both because he'd been gone on a Friday night — and Good Friday at that! — and because when he traveled overnight, he was usually far enough away or had enough business to keep him busy all day, so he never returned before evening. The other thing that was unusual — for the hour, anyway — was that he reeked of alcohol. I don't know how he'd driven home in that state; perhaps he finished off a pint in the driveway. All I know is he was slurring his words when he stumbled in. He seated himself at the kitchen table, sent Rebecca outside to play, told me to put on a fresh pot of coffee, and ordered me to sit down.

"There're going to be some changes around here," he declared. "I've decided that what's good for the gander is good for the goose."

I eased myself into the chair across from him, thinking he'd drunkenly mixed up the metaphor. I was about to say something, but his eyes held a diamond-like glint that made my blood run cold. "What kind of changes?"

"It's high time you 'preciate all that I've done for you. Not every man would marry a woman pregnant with another man's child, then put up with her treating him like dirt."

"I — I do appreciate all you've done, Charlie."

"No." He thumped his hand on the table so hard the saltshaker slid off the cherry-printed tablecloth, onto the linoleum floor. "In order to 'preciate it, you need to fully 'xperience it for yourself."

By then, I felt like I had ice in my veins. "What are you talking about?"

He glared at me, all cold-eyed. His nose was red and I saw a glimpse of evil in him that I'd never seen before. It struck me as the underbelly of love; if you flipped the emotion over on its back like a turtle, the opposite side would be black and sin-soaked and gin-fumed. Anyway. He sat there, his eyes red and shining, scary as any Halloween mask. He leaned forward, his forearms on the table. "You're gonna raise my illegitimate child, and you're gonna love it as your own."

I must have half laughed, because he pounded the table again and stood up. He loomed over me, and for the first time in a long, long time, I was scared — physically afraid — of Charlie. This was a man I didn't know.

"I got a girl pregnant." He hitched up his pants, as if he was proud of this. "She's gonna have a baby, and she's gonna give it to us to raise."

I stared at him, uncomprehending.

"We're . . . going to adopt?"

"No, damn it. Aren't you listening? No adoption's needed. It's mine." He thumped his chest with his right hand.

I sat there, trying to take this in. Charlie had been unfaithful? The thought sent my mind reeling, but the matter of adultery didn't hurt at first. Oh, it did later — but I knew I was largely at fault for that. At that moment, I simply couldn't process what he was saying. "You want everyone to know you're having an illegitimate baby?" I asked.

"No. And no one ever will, because they'll think the baby's yours. You're going to start wearing padding." He leaned back against the kitchen counter, a pleased smirk on his face. "People will think you're pregnant, and when it gets close to time, we'll go to Mississippi. Dad's planning on opening a store up there anyway; I'll stall it until the timing's right. Folks'll think you had the baby there."

I felt as if I were in a nonsensical dream. "That's crazy. It'll never work."

"Why not?"

"Well, for starters, no one will believe I'm pregnant."

"They will if you look like you are."

"But it's ludicrous, Charlie. Women touch other women's pregnant bellies. Especially family. Your mother. My mother. My grand-

432

mother. Your grandmother. It will never, ever work."

"It Goddamned *better* work!" His fist thundered on the kitchen counter so hard the toaster keeled over. I don't know what was more surprising, the toaster falling or Charlie taking the Lord's name in vain. In all the years I'd known him, I'd never heard him do that.

"You'll make it work. You'll keep them from touching you."

"How?"

"That's your problem." He staggered back to the table. "I'm sure you'll think of something. You do a damn fine job of keeping *me* at a distance."

"I'd — I'd have to see Dr. Henry." He was the town doctor who'd attended me during both pregnancies.

"Nah. We'll say you're seeing someone in Mississippi since that's where the baby's going to be delivered."

My thoughts were like a goldfish in a bowl, circling round and round, making no progress. "Charlie, this is insane. I won't do it, and you can't make me."

He leaned toward me. "Can't I?"

"No."

"You want to lose your children?" His mouth curled into something that sent a

433

shiver up my spine. It was evil, pure evil. He pulled a flask out of his pocket, unscrewed it, and took a long swig. "I've kept some of your letters from Loverboy. You think any judge in this parish would think you were a fit mother if I were to pull those out?"

Eddie woke up in his crib and started to cry. I left the room to see to him. When I came back to the kitchen, Charlie was gone, and so was his car.

Charlie came back before midnight and passed out in bed beside me. The next day was Easter, so I got up, pulled my church clothes out of the closet, then slept the rest of the night on the sofa. I wasn't going to awaken him. Let him miss Easter service. Let him miss the family luncheon. I'd say he wasn't feeling well and wouldn't get out of bed; everyone could draw their own conclusions. Let the whole town talk about him, for all I cared.

But he woke up and got dressed and acted just as nice and pretty as you please, playing with the children and making them both laugh. He even helped hide the eggs for Becky's Easter egg hunt and changed Eddie's wet diaper. I thought he might have been in a blackout the day before, because he didn't mention a thing about a baby or another woman. I figured he probably just made the whole thing up to terrify me.

After church, we all gathered at his mama's house for Easter dinner. My mother and father were there, along with my grandmother, and, of course, Charlie's parents and grandmother. I took both a peach pie and a butterscotch pie. We all sat and ate ham and green bean casserole and carrot and raisin salad. Right before we served the desserts, Charlie stood up.

"I have an announcement to make."

My heart thudded hard in my chest. *Oh, no. Please, God, no.* Maybe it was something to do with his father's business. I looked at my father-in-law, but his face looked just as puzzled as I felt.

"Adelaide and I are havin' another baby."

Everyone broke into excited chatter. "When?" Mama asked.

"In September," Charlie said.

"Why, Adelaide. You're not showin' at all!"

"We wanted to keep it a secret because she's been having a bit of a hard time," Charlie said.

"Oh, my dear!" my mother exclaimed, turning toward me. "What's the problem?"

"I — uh . . ." I was literally speechless. I couldn't believe that he'd just announced such a falsehood like that, so publicly, with no warning.

"Woman troubles," Charlie said. That was code for bleeding. And no one — not even mothers and daughters — talked about that back then. Why, when I'd started my period at age thirteen, I'd thought I was dying. My grandmother on my father's side had died of colon cancer, and I thought that's what I had. My mother noticed blood on my underwear the next day when she did the laundry. She handed me a sanitary napkin, told me women had this happen every month, that it was a woman's curse, and I'd just have to wear a pad and bear it.

"What does Dr. Henry say?" Charlie's mother's face was scrunched with worry. I suddenly recalled Charlie telling me she'd miscarried several times after his birth. My own mother had had a difficult labor with me and was unable to have any more children.

"She's not seeing Dr. Henry. She saw a specialist in Mississippi when we went to the lake a few weeks ago." Charlie turned to his father. "We'll be opening the branch store in Jackson in September and I'll want to be there, so I figured we'd rent a place for a few months. I wouldn't dream of being away from her at a time like this."

My mother cocked her head and looked at me oddly. "You went to a doctor on a Saturday?"

"Yes. This doctor sees patients six days a week," Charlie said smoothly.

"You don't have to go to Mississippi, son," Charlie's dad said. "I can handle that store opening."

"No, this expansion is my responsibility. I'll go get it started, hire a manager to run it, and then after the baby is born and things are running smoothly, we'll come back here."

Charlie's father pushed back his chair. "Well, I think this calls for a toast!"

He went to the cupboard in his study, and returned with a bottle of sparkling wine. And everyone toasted and drank to my health, and I sat there, miserable, the lie lying like a boulder on my heart.

"Do you want me to come and stay with you in Mississippi?" my mother asked.

"Thank you, but no," Charlie said before I could even open my mouth. "We've talked about it, and we don't want to take you away from Grammie. What would be most helpful would be if you and Mom could take turns keeping Becky and Eddie for us once we get close to the due date."

"Of course. We'd be thrilled to do that."

Oh, he was smooth. I never knew how smooth he could be. This wasn't the same Charlie I knew, the insecure, bumbling Charlie. Evil had made him a silver-tongued devil.

I wondered if the other woman had taught him how to lie so adroitly. How many times had he lied to me when he was seeing her? I'd always thought I could see right through him. Somewhere along the line, he'd turned into a world-class deceiver. If I hadn't known he was lying now, I would have been as sucked in as my family; he was just that smooth.

"Mommy — you're havin' a baby?" Becky asked me.

I swallowed. This was the point of no return. It was one thing to lie to my parents, quite another to lie to my child.

Charlie did it for me. "Yes, honey. You're going to have another baby brother or a baby sister."

"A sister! I want a sister."

Later, as we were cleaning up, my mother looked me up and down. "My word, child — you're not showing at all. And you must be four months, give or take."

"You know, Beula was like that," said my grandmother. "She carried her second baby toward her back. The doctor said he was sitting near her spine. Guess that's what's going on with Adelaide here."

She reached out her hand to touch my stomach.

Charlie grabbed her arm, stopping her. "The doctor said people should keep their distance from Adelaide's stomach, that she and the baby might be vulnerable to, um, electrical impulses from other people. He said just patting her belly can cause a transfer of electricity that can be harmful."

"Why, I never heard of such a thing!" my mother exclaimed.

My grandmother and Charlie's mother murmured in agreement.

"Me, neither," said Charlie, "but this doctor says it's a brand-new medical theory, and since Adelaide's had problems, we want to follow his advice to the letter, no matter how odd it sounds. Can't be too careful."

"Well, I guess that's right," my mother said. "But what about the children? She's going to be holding them and picking them up."

"The doctor said that children don't have near as much of an electrical current as the hands of adults, so that should be all right."

33
ADELAIDE

"And they believed that?"

I opened my eyes to find myself in the rocker in my bedroom. I'd forgotten Hope was there. I'd forgotten I was talking aloud. It seemed so real, like was I back in the past, just living it all over again.

I nodded. "Antibiotics and X-rays and all the things you take for granted now were brand-new back then, so discoveries about electrical impulses didn't sound like too much of a stretch. But then, no one expected Charlie to lie about a thing like that." I know I sure hadn't. I hadn't known Charlie was that imaginative.

"What did you use for padding?" Hope asked.

"An old quilt. I cut it up and made a small lump, and sewed tie strings to it. I added little pieces to it as the months went by, making it bigger. Lordy, but it was hot that summer! I was careful, but Becky walked in on me one morning as I was getting dressed. I turned away, flustered, but she'd already seen.

" 'What's that?' she'd asked, pointing.

"I tried to stay calm. 'It's a bumper for the baby. To keep it from getting hurt. Because the doctor said it's sickly.'

"Becky ran to greet Charlie with the news when he got home. 'Guess what, Daddy! Mama's wearin' a pad over the baby to keep him safe.'

"Charlie grabbed her. 'Who else have you told this to?'

" 'No one,' Becky had said.

" 'Well, be sure you don't.'

" 'Why not, Daddy?'

" 'Because we don't talk about undergarments.'

"But I reckon he felt that it was unlikely she'd keep quiet, because he made me go over to my mama's house that night and casually mention I was wearing a pad to protect the baby from electrical impulses. The next day, he went to Jackson to find a rental house. He moved us there at the end of the week, and there we stayed for the next three months."

That night, I dreamed of my mother. I'd been worrying about facing her in the

441

afterlife. I didn't know what she knew about the non-pregnancy.

"Oh, I knew something was wrong," she said. In my dream, she was sitting on the back porch swing, pulling beans from a paper bag and snapping them into a red ceramic bowl. "You didn't look a bit happy."

"Why didn't you say something?"

"I couldn't, dear; it wasn't my place. That would have been meddling in your marriage, and folks just didn't do that. But I knew you two were having problems." Mother reached into the bag. "Truth is, I was afraid you'd been . . ." Her voice lowered to a whisper. ". . . raped."

"Mother!"

"Well, you'd occasionally go off by yourself to places a woman shouldn't go without an escort. There were a couple of times you asked me to watch the children, then Mildred Pilcher told me she'd seen you at the lakefront, taking photos of pelicans or geese." She snapped a bean clean in half. "I was afraid the baby wasn't Charlie's."

Truth be told, a similar worry had crossed my mind.

"How do you know the baby is even yours?" I'd asked Charlie when we'd gotten back home from that fateful Easter dinner and the kids were down for a nap.

442

"I just do."

"But if this woman slept with you, she might be sleeping with fifty other men, as well."

"I could say the same thing about you." Charlie had gone straight for the kitchen cabinet where I'd hidden the scotch, a thundercloud of a scowl darkening his face.

"You know me, Charlie. How well could you possibly know this woman?"

"How well did you know Joe? For all you know, he's actually married."

The words had shocked me. I'd stared at him for a moment. He was out of his head. When it came to Joe, he was crazy.

But in my dream, my mother calmly swung on the porch swing and pulled another bean from the bag. I reached in and took one, helping her. "It would have meant so much, Mother, if I could have talked to you about things."

"I know, dear." She carefully snapped the bean, her face a picture of peace and serenity. "But ladies didn't talk about those things back then."

I woke up covered in sweat. My mother's beatific expression, her lack of remorse or regret, her apparent complete acceptance of whatever she'd done or not done . . . How could she feel that way about her mistakes,

443

yet be so insistent I fix mine?

I guess it was because she was on the other side. I still had to struggle to get there.

I pushed down the covers and rolled over. It wouldn't be much longer — a couple of months, a year maybe — certainly no more than two or three. Death was growing inside me like a baby waiting to be born. I could feel it, getting stronger. Sometimes the hairpins in my bun vibrated with the knowledge like tuning forks.

I glanced at the alarm clock glowing on the bedside table. Three thirty. There was still a lot of night left to get through. I closed my eyes and tried to fall back asleep. I wasn't sure if I was dreaming or not, but Mother's voice seemed to come out of the air-conditioning vent. "You need to clear everything up before you join us, sweetheart. Becky is counting on it."

Becky — my beautiful, precious, brilliant Becky, taken from me far too soon. The daughter I'd loved more than life itself, yet never really had understood. I'd always thought that the secret about her real father was the reason there always seemed to be some distance, some friction, between us.

She and Charlie didn't have that problem, not until she was older and determined to be a career woman. To Charlie's credit, he

444

treated her just as well as he treated Eddie when she was little — better, actually. Becky was smart as a whip and serious and hung on Charlie's every word. Eddie, however, was easily distracted and emotional, and Charlie had been harsher with him, trying to toughen him up.

I understood Eddie. I could always read him, always empathize with his emotions. Becky and I, though, seemed to be on a different frequency. Communicating with her was like trying to listen to a radio program and getting lots of static interference. Was the secret about her conception somehow blocking us, or were we just ill-fitting personalities who couldn't really tune in to each other's hearts and minds? Was it my fault? Or did some mothers and daughters, through no fault of their own, just never seem to be tuned to the same channel?

34
MATT

I'd had a hell of a week at work, so I was glad to just chill with the girls on Saturday. Unfortunately, their idea of chilling involved having me braid their hair so they could look like Von Trapp siblings. Apparently they'd watched *The Sound of Music* with Peggy while I was at the fete.

"Ow, that hurts!" Zoey said as I finished tightening the elastic band in her hair.

"Sorry, sweetie."

Her eyes filled with dismay as she regarded herself in the hallway mirror. "It's all crooked and lumpy."

Sadly, it was true. One pigtail was lower than the other, and a clump of hair was pouching up above the other one. I took the comb and tried to smooth the lump to no avail. "Maybe we should go across the street and let your grandmother do it."

"No. I want Jillian."

"She's not here."

"She would be if you'd marry her."

I was spared from having to answer by a knock on the kitchen door. Sophie opened it.

"Snowball!" she exclaimed. "You came!"

I followed Zoey around the corner and saw Hope holding her grandmother's little dog. My heart picked up speed. "Hey there."

"Hey."

"Snowball wanted to come see me," Sophie said. "She was barkin' through the fence and Hope was in her backyard, so I asked if she could come over."

"Sophie, you shouldn't be bothering the neighbors."

"It's no bother," Hope said. "And she's exactly right. Snowball wanted to pay a visit." She set the dog on the floor and held out a small ball to Sophie. "I'm sure she'd love to play outside with you."

"Me, too!" Zoey said. Both girls ran out the back door, Von Trapps forgotten, the dog following happily behind.

"They've been begging me for a dog of their own," I said, just to have something to say. Seeing Hope scrambled my thoughts.

"You should get them one. It'd be good for them to have a pet."

I noncommittally lifted my shoulders.

Hope's eyebrows rose. "Don't you like dogs?"

"I think they're great. It's just . . . Christine wasn't a dog person."

To her credit, Hope didn't say "So?" She didn't even look at me like I was an idiot. She didn't need to. I heard how ridiculous my comment sounded as soon as I said it.

"I guess it would make me feel . . . disloyal or something," I tried to explain. "As if the girls were being raised contrary to the way she would have done it. I don't know if Peggy and Griff . . ." I stopped myself. I ran a hand down my face. "I'm realizing how lame my reasoning is as I'm talking. Guess it's time to move on, huh?"

Her gaze was like being wrapped in a blanket taken straight out of a warm clothes dryer. "There are no timelines for these things."

When was the last time I'd felt okay after sounding like a dunderhead in front of someone? I hated sounding sappy or being wrong, and yet Hope made me feel all right about it. I gave a self-conscious smile. "Yeah, well, I guess old habits die hard. I'll give it some thought."

We stood there, just looking at each other for a moment. "It's good to see you," I said.

"Good to see you, too. I hope I'm not

448

interrupting. Gran's taking a nap, and I thought I could use the chance to touch up the mural and hang the hardware for the canopies. I'm nearly finished."

"The girls will be so thrilled. But I'm going to miss having you over here so much."

"Even though you're hardly ever here when I am?"

"I like the idea of you being here," I said. "I think about you a lot."

The air around us heated. Her mouth curved in a smile. "What do you think?"

"About doing this." And just like that, I bent down and kissed her. It seemed like the most ordinary thing in the world, but the sensations it stirred in me were anything but ordinary. Her mouth was soft and succulent, and when her arms wound around my back, it felt like time and place just melted away.

The patter of small feet warned of a child's imminent arrival. We both pulled back as the back door opened.

Hope's lips were red, her cheeks rosy. "I, uh, better get to work on the mural." She turned and fled up the stairs to the girls' bedroom as Zoey walked in.

Zoey looked at me accusingly. "Why were you standing so close?"

I didn't think she'd seen us, but I didn't

dare deny it. "None of your business," I said.

"Well, I don't think that's 'propriate."

"What?"

"My teacher taught us about 'propriate and in'propriate behavior. Like how you don't yell and run around indoors, and how you don't let strangers get too close and 'vade your personal space. An' I don't think that you and Hope were being 'propriate, 'cause you were 'vading personal space."

I have to say, I was flustered. "I, um . . ."

"Besides, I want you to marry Aunt Jillian," Zoey continued.

This refrain was getting tiresome. "I've told you, sweetheart. I don't like Jillian like that."

"Maybe if you kissed her, you would," Zoey persisted.

Damn. Maybe she *had* seen us. "It just doesn't work that way." I rubbed my hand across my face. "Hey — I thought you wanted to play with Snowball. What are you doing in here?"

"I came in to get her a bowl of water in case she's thirsty."

"That's very responsible of you."

She nodded solemnly. "I'm responsible enough to take care of a dog of my own."

Zoey had the makings of an excellent attorney. In the span of less than a minute, she'd thrown me off balance and made her case. I would hate to come up against her in court. I pulled a disposable plastic bowl out of the cabinet and handed it to her.

She carried it to the sink and stood on tiptoe to fill it. "Come outside and play with us."

I thought about Hope upstairs in their bedroom and was tempted to decline — but I couldn't trust myself not to invade her personal space again. Besides, Zoey was watching me closely.

"Are you playing Von Trapp family?" I asked. "Because I refuse to wear lederhosen and sing."

"What's lederhosen?"

"Shorts with suspenders."

Her face broke into a sunshine smile. "Well, you don't have to wear that, but I bet we can make you sing."

It was not a bet I was willing to take. Because the truth was, my girls could coerce me into doing just about anything.

Anything, that is, except get involved with Jillian — or keep my distance from Hope.

35
HOPE

Kirsten poured foam onto my cappuccino the following Wednesday morning during a lull in her business. "I'm so thrilled you've agreed to do the mural here! And so is everyone else on the block. The drugstore, the hardware store, and the insurance agency have agreed to each pay you an extra two thousand dollars to include them in it."

"Wow. You might have missed your calling, Kirsten," I said. "You should be in art sales!"

"It was easy. I showed them the photo of the mural you did at Matt's house and told them it would be a permanent billboard."

I'd finished the girls' room on Monday. Matt and I had moved their furniture back that evening, and the girls had been so excited they'd insisted on sleeping in their princess gowns. Life at Matt's house pretty much had been a nonstop princess-a-thon ever since.

I'd brought a photo of the room to Kirsten yesterday, and she'd immediately taken it to the neighboring businesses.

I perched on a barstool at the coffee counter and gave Kirsten a teasing grin. "Maybe you should take my job in Chicago and I should stay here."

Kirsten put her hand on her hip. "Maybe you should forget about Chicago and stay here, period. I know a hunky neighbor of yours who would no doubt agree."

My heart somersaulted at the thought of Matt. For the last few nights, we'd been meeting in the swing in my grandmother's backyard after the girls went to bed, talking and, well, making out a little.

Just a little, though — because Mrs. Ivy could see us from her upstairs window, and we'd caught her watching on more than one occasion. As delicious as Matt's kisses were, knowing that they'd be reported to the entire neighborhood put a damper on my ardor.

So did the thought that a once-in-a-lifetime job awaited me and I was just a short-timer in Wedding Tree. "I can't just forget about Chicago," I said, taking the cappuccino she handed me.

"Well, you can at least enjoy Matt while you're here."

"That's true." I took a sip. "We're going out to dinner this Saturday."

"Ooh, another date!"

"It's not a date-date."

"In what way is it not?" Kirsten arched an eyebrow as she picked up a bar rag.

"Well, it's not like anything is going to happen."

"That's only because neither of you has a place to get down and dirty."

"Wow. I love your romantic phrasing." But she was right. Matt's house was off-limits because of his daughters, and Gran's house was out of the question.

She smiled as she wiped down the counter. "With a husband who's been gone for five months, believe me, down and dirty sounds a lot more romantic than wine and roses."

"What's he like?"

"Sam? Oh, he's wonderful. Totally worth the wait."

"How did you two meet?"

"At college. But we didn't start really dating until he finished a tour of duty with the marines. He said he didn't want to be pining for me while he was in Afghanistan." She put the rag over the sink and smiled. "But he said he pined anyway."

"Aw!" I took another sip. "So now the pining's mutual."

Kirsten nodded. "We e-mail all the time and we Skype when he's in port, but there's nothing like that physical one-on-one. He keeps promising that each trip is his last, but the money's really good, and . . ." She sighed. "The truth is, I'm not sure he'd ever really be happy settled down." I caught a glimpse of intense sadness in her eyes. Before I could think of anything to say, she turned to the sink. "Hey — do you like romance novels?"

Apparently she didn't want to talk about Sam anymore. "Yeah, I love them."

"Well, I belong to a book club, and we're reading Kristan Higgins."

"Oh, I'm crazy about her stuff!"

"Want to join us? We're meeting at my house next Tuesday."

"I'd love to. Who comes?"

"Most of the ladies you met at the tree planting and a few others — including Jillian."

"I felt so bad for her at the fete," I said. "Have you seen her since?"

"Yeah. And she asked me if something was going on between you and Matt."

I kind of held my breath. "What did you tell her?"

"That you two really liked each other and were hitting it off." She leaned across the counter and lowered her voice. "She'd heard that Matt kissed you good night."

"Oh, good grief."

"She tried to act like it didn't matter, but I could tell it bothered her. She said she'd thought Matt had invited you to the fete just to be neighborly." Kirsten poured herself glass of water. "It's kind of sad, how selective a person's vision can be."

"Tell me about it," I replied ruefully. "My husband and my best friend were having an affair right under my nose, and I was the last to know."

"I think there must be some self-protective mechanism that kicks in."

"I think you have to have a lot emotionally invested to activate it."

"Well, I think Jillian is pretty emotionally invested in Matt. She said that it's good he's showing interest in someone new, because it means he's getting over Christine and is ready to move on." Kirsten gave a wicked grin. "Then she said it's too bad that you're only in a town for a few more weeks, but she didn't look like she thought it was bad at all."

36
ADELAIDE

"You said you moved to Mississippi a few months before the baby was due," Hope prompted.

I opened my eyes. Apparently I'd dozed off, or maybe my thoughts had just meandered. Sometimes it's hard to tell the difference.

My granddaughter and I were in my bedroom. It was the next day — or maybe the day after, or the day after that. Time had become liquid, moving and spreading all around. I was sitting in my rocker, and Hope was holding three loose housedresses with sunflowers on them.

No. It was one housedress, the one I'd asked her to pull out of my closet.

She brought it over and laid it in my lap. The fabric was light, but touching it, I could almost feel the heaviness of the padding I'd worn under it that summer.

Unbidden thoughts. The phrase floated

through my head. Maybe that wasn't the word, *unbidden* — but then again, maybe it was. Unbidden, as in unexpected and unwanted and uncalled-for, leaving you all undone. One moment you're doing something perfectly ordinary, and the next, you're overrun by memories and feelings that leave you reeling and gasping.

I had a lot of those in the months that followed that Easter dinner where Charlie announced my so-called pregnancy. I closed my eyes and fell back into my story.

1948

We moved to a rental house in Jackson, a squalid little two-bedroom thing. Charlie had deliberately picked a place too small for either of our families to stay overnight.

The days ground on. Charlie was busy starting up the new store, and caring for the kids kept me hopping. He stopped drinking when we moved, and things eased between us. He finally told me a little about the other woman — about as much as I'd told him about Joe. She was someone he'd met at a roadside bar. He'd been lonely and she'd been a good listener. She'd just been dumped by someone she loved, and well, that was when he'd been eaten up with jealousy over Joe, and they'd gravitated toward each other because hurt attracts hurt. He said they hadn't meant anything to each other in any way that really mattered.

As time went on, I actually began to look forward to the baby, to having a new life to care for. Maybe Charlie and I could build a new life together, as well — his, mine, and ours. Maybe, in some weird way, this really would even the score.

The first week in September, both sets of our parents drove up and picked up the children. They would care for them in Wedding Tree until the baby was born, freeing me to rest during the last weeks of my "pregnancy."

At first I was lost without them, but then . . . well, Charlie and I fell into a new pattern when it was just the two of us. We'd play card games at night and take walks. He made me laugh with stories and impressions about the people working in the new store, and he'd ask my opinion about situations and dilemmas, and we even began to make love again.

Up until then, I'd refused to sleep with him. I'd told him if I had to pretend to be pregnant, he had to pretend so, too, and if I were having a difficult pregnancy, the doctor would forbid relations. But in those last couple of weeks, we were almost like honeymooners. Maybe it was the freedom of not having to wear the padding in the house when it was just the two of us; maybe it was the shared secret that bonded us. For whatever reason, I felt happier in my marriage than I ever had. I felt optimistic for the future.

On September 24 — I'll never forget the date; it haunts me every year — I knew something was wrong. I'd been restless all day, like a cat about to birth her kittens, then Charlie didn't come home for dinner. That, in and of itself, was unusual. He'd become solicitous and caring. He'd started bringing me flowers and dancing with me to the radio and treating me like a woman he was trying to woo.

Charlie swore he wasn't seeing the other woman, but I knew he stayed in touch somehow to see how the pregnancy was progressing. I wasn't jealous of her, which might be a little odd, but I knew he didn't love her. I felt sorry for her, actually. To have a baby, then give it up . . . My womb ached just thinking about it. I'd been faced with the choice and I hadn't been able to bring myself to do it. I worried that this woman wouldn't be able to, either, but Charlie said she absolutely didn't want a baby, that she would have aborted it if he hadn't talked her out of it.

I'd pestered him about her, wanting to know more about her, but there was a stubborn streak in Charlie — a part that wouldn't give in. I have to admit, I admired that part of him. I just wished he'd used that stubbornness in a better way.

That night, the night of September 24, it got to be nine, then ten o'clock. A thunderstorm rolled in, and the rain poured down in torrents. I grew anxious. Was the baby coming? I inventoried all the baby's things I had on hand — a bassinet, blankets, baby formula, a layette, bottles, diapers . . . I touched each item, longing to put it to use.

Was Charlie at that woman's house, waiting to bring the baby home to me? Back then, men didn't take part in delivery, but maybe he was hanging around if the baby was on the way. If that were the case, though, why didn't he call and tell me? I picked up the phone three times and asked the party line operator if it was working. I would have picked it up again, but I was too embarrassed. Instead, I paced the floor until it was a wonder I didn't wear a path in the linoleum.

As the night stretched on, another scenario formed in my mind — a scenario more likely than a baby on the way and no call from Charlie. Chances were, Charlie was just back to being his old drunken self. He was probably at a bar, leaving me stuck alone in the storm, unable to leave the house without wearing the oppressive padding because we'd led all the neighbors and townsfolk to think I was in the family way.

The more I thought about it, the more indignant I became. Why, I had half a mind to call my folks to come get me.

And say what? *Mother, Father, I was lying to you about being pregnant?* I sank onto the old floral sofa with a hard sigh, feeling the springs dig into my backside. The width and breadth of the lies I'd told made confession impossible. For a girl who couldn't lie well, I'd sure come up with some doozies. It was like being halfway across a swamp, surrounded on all sides by alligators. There was no way out but through.

I finally dozed off on that beaten-up sofa, then jerked awake to see Charlie limping through the door, looking like he'd been through a battle. I glanced at the clock in the kitchen; it was a few minutes before five in the morning.

Backlit by the porch light, his hair and clothes glistened with rain. A puddle formed on the floor around him. Good Lord, he

462

was soaked to the bone. His face was pale, and his mouth was set in a tight line.

He reeked of cheap bourbon. My heart clutched in my chest.

"It's over," he said, closing the door. A hint of light through the window kept the room from being totally black.

"What do you mean?"

"The baby. It's all done."

I pushed up on my elbows, my legs still stretched out on the sofa, my heart pounding with excitement. "It's born?"

"Yeah."

Anticipation flooded me, but stopped short of joy. Charlie didn't look like a man celebrating the birth of a child. And that whiskey smell — it always came with trouble. "Where is it?"

He wavered, like a man with a ship rolling under his feet. "Dead."

I couldn't breathe. "What?"

"Something wrong with your hearing?"

Oh, dear God. His voice was cold, dangerous, knifelike. Whoever had called it "Demon Rum" was right. When Charlie was drinking, he was like a man possessed.

I swung my feet off the sofa and turned on the lamp on the side table. That's when I saw he had blood on his shirt — lots of it. I put my hand to my throat. My pulse fluttered under my palm like hummingbird wings. "Was it stillborn?"

"Might as well have been."

"What does that mean?"

"Same as I said." He sank into a vinyl chair in the breakfast alcove, next to the living room.

A sick, sour taste filled my throat. My eyes fixed on his shirt, my mind spinning, my stomach tight with fear. Something was terribly, horribly wrong. "Did you help deliver it?"

"No."

"Then why are you all bloody?"

"Don't ask questions."

My stomach roiled. I thought I might throw up. "B-but I have to know what happened. Everyone will want to know what happened — our parents and grandparents and the children . . . everyone."

He sank his head in his hands.

Fear gripped me so hard I shook. "Was it a boy or a girl?"

"Boy."

"So . . . where . . . where is he?"

"No more questions!" he bellowed.

I stared at him, trying to make sense of the situation. *Oh, Charlie — what have you done?*

"Don' you worry about it. Just get your

464

stuff together. We're going back."

"Now?"

"Later today."

"But . . ."

"No buts." His voice had that old, ugly, mean tone. "You should be happy about this, Addie."

Happy?

"You're off the hook. You don't have to raise a bastard."

"But, Charlie . . . after all this, I wanted . . ." Hysteria was building in my chest. My gaze went to the empty bassinet in the corner of the room. "What did you do, Charlie?"

"Nothin' that concerns you."

"But it does! Of course it does! Our family . . . everyone . . . I was . . ." My gaze went to the hated padding at the end of sofa. *Expecting.* That's what I'd become in the course of wearing it. *Expecting a baby.* Wanting, longing for a baby. And over the last two weeks, when I'd finally felt happy in my marriage, I'd been wanting, longing for a new beginning with Charlie, as well.

He misread my anguish. "I'll do all the explaining. We'll say the baby was born dead last week. You've been sedated, too upset to talk about it. The doctor advised waiting until you were over the worst of it before we

465

told family, because you'd had a nervous breakdown. You'll take it easy at home for a couple of days, and in a couple of weeks, you'll carry on as if nothing happened."

"But what . . ."

"No more questions!" he thundered. "That's it."

But of course, the "no questions" rule didn't apply to family. Charlie called home later that morning and talked to his mother, who then put my mother on the phone. When we arrived home that evening, both sets of parents were waiting for us at our house, their faces gray and grim and worried.

Charlie carried me out of the car and into the bedroom, tucked me in, and sat on the edge of the bed, a physical barrier between my mother and me. "What happened?" Mother's eyes were so shadowed and sad that mine welled with tears just looking at her. "When did you know there was a problem?"

"She hadn't felt the baby move for several days," Charlie said. "We went to the doctor, and he said there was no heartbeat."

He hovered beside me, his eyes a dark warning glower.

"Why didn't you call and tell me?" Mother asked.

"I — I wanted to, but . . ." I stammered.

"She couldn't," Charlie cut in. "The doctor kept her knocked out."

God, how I wish that part was true.

"You should have called," said Charlie's mother from the doorway.

His Adam's apple bobbed. "I decided to wait until she was better. The news was bad enough without worrying you all the more about Addie."

"He's always been so sensitive about my feelings," Charlie's mother said in a low voice. She put her hand on his back. "You said on the phone it was a boy."

Charlie nodded.

Mother's hand trembled as it covered her mouth. "What did you name it?"

"We didn't."

"Well, you have to," Mother insisted. "We need to plan the funeral."

"The doctor handled it," Charlie said. "He said it was for the best, that it would help Addie get over it if she didn't have a place to go and mourn. He said the child was dead before it was born, so it was never actually alive."

"Oh, Addie!" My mother threw up her hands. "Oh, heavens. Didn't you want your child to have a Christian burial?"

My mouth felt lined with cotton. I tried

to swallow.

"She didn't have a say in the matter," Charlie cut in. "I made the decision while she was still knocked out. Addie never saw the baby." He put his arm around me. "The doctor said we need to put all this behind us and get on with our lives. I would appreciate it if you'd spread the word, because it might make her have another nervous breakdown if she has to talk about it to everyone in town."

"Yes, yes. Of course," Charlie's mother murmured.

"That goes for family, too." Charlie's tone was uncharacteristically authoritative. "The doctor said she shouldn't have to deal with a lot of questions. I'll tell you everything you need to know, so please don't pester her about it."

"And your families accepted the story?" Hope asked.

I opened my eyelids. Hope was sitting on the edge of my bed, her face sad, her eyes enormous. I nodded. "Yes. Back in her day, Charlie's mother had had several miscarriages, and she'd suffered some serious depression over it. Melancholia, they used to call it, where she couldn't get out of bed.

That helped make the story understandable."

"But you never found out what happened to the baby?"

"No." A heaviness weighed on my chest, a heaviness that had been there for decades but I'd tried to ignore. How could I have lived with it all these years? "I don't know what happened, but I know it was something awful."

"Maybe not, Gran. Maybe Granddad helped with the birth and he was traumatized because it had gone so wrong."

"No. Three things convinced me Charlie did something terrible." I held up the pointer finger on my right hand. "The revolver that he always carried in the glove box was gone. On the trip home I opened the glove box looking for a tissue, and Charlie nearly drove off the road, he was so upset."

I lifted a second finger. "Charlie wouldn't let me near the trunk of the car when we were packing up in Mississippi. He was trying to hide something — I knew him well enough to know that. So I peeked in when he went back in the house for a bag and sure enough, there was a piece of luggage I'd never seen before. It was tan with dark brown stripes, and it looked brand-new." I looked at Hope. She was watching me, her forehead furrowed. I lifted my third finger. "After we got home, that very night, Charlie went out and buried it in our backyard."

"Oh, Gran!" Her hand flew to her mouth.

"I didn't see where he buried it. That's what I need your help with."

Hope's eyes were round as full moons.

I sank back in my chair and closed my eyes. The events I'd tried so hard to forget for so many years began pressing in. I started talking, and before I knew it, I was reliving the past.

1948

That day we got home, Charlie convinced my mother that he'd take care of me and she should go back to her house for the night. I was too upset to sleep, and Charlie hadn't come to bed. I knew I'd have to stay in bed much of the next day — my parents thought I was just a week out from childbirth, remember, and that's how things were done back then — and I was restless. I got up and roamed the house and I looked out the window.

And there was Charlie, with that piece of luggage. He was holding it in one hand and coming out of the shed with a shovel in the other. And then Eddie woke up crying —

he'd apparently picked up on the sadness and tension of everyone, and it gave him a nightmare — and I went to his room to comfort him. I spent probably forty-five minutes reading to him and getting him back asleep. When I went downstairs, Charlie was washing up at the kitchen sink.

"What are you doing?" I asked him.

"Washing my hands."

Lady MacBeth came to mind. "I see that," I said. "I meant what were you doing in the backyard with that luggage?"

His face got all mottled and red. "I don't know what you're talking about."

"I saw you. You were getting a shovel out of the shed and you had that striped suitcase."

He turned off the faucet and grabbed a dish towel. "It's dark. You can't be sure of what you saw. And sometimes, Addie, what happens in the dark should stay there." He pressed the towel to his face for a moment. When he pulled it away, I saw that his hands were shaking. "Addie — I'm so, so sorry. All I wanted . . ." He looked at me. Tears rolled down his face, and for a moment, he looked like the little boy who'd been my friend in grade school. "All I ever wanted was for you to love me just a smidgeon as much as I love you."

He sank into a chair, put his head in his hands, and sobbed. I've never heard anything so sad — it was a heart-wrenching, from-the-soul sob, so loud I feared he'd wake the children. He seemed like a child himself — lost and lonely and heartbroken and scared. And . . . I felt the exact same way.

I thought, *What will happen if I learn that he did the horrible thing I fear he did?* And I could come up with no good outcome. If I knew for sure, wouldn't I have to do something? What would that be? What would it do to our children? To his parents? To my parents? To our grandmothers? The shame would destroy us all.

He was right; I didn't want to know. So I decided to let the things of the dark stay in the dark.

I opened my eyes and looked at Hope. "Whatever Charlie did, he'd done because he loved me, and I'd driven him plumb out of his mind. It was as much my fault as Charlie's. I was as guilty as he was. And I've lived with the shame and guilt of that all my life. But now . . . well, now I've got to clear it up before I meet my maker."

Hope's arms wound tight around me as she knelt beside my chair. "Oh, Gran — you

472

had so many people's lives to think about! You just did what you thought was best."

"Best isn't the same as right. I let lie pile upon lie."

"You tried to protect your children! And anyway, it doesn't make sense that Granddad would have deliberately killed the baby. Why on earth would he have done that, after you'd gone through the pregnancy ruse and were willing — eager, even — to raise it?"

I drew a deep breath. "I've thought and thought about that, all these years. And all these years, I've wondered . . ." I stopped.

"What, Gran?"

"Well, a man can never be sure that a child is really his." I drew a deep breath and voiced my most secret thought. "All these years, I've wondered if that baby was black."

37
HOPE

I waited until eight thirty that night — after Gran went to bed and I knew it was past the girls' bedtime — and I called Matt.

"My grandmother told me something I need to talk about," I whispered into the phone.

"Come on over."

He let me in the kitchen door, poured me a glass of wine, then sat with me at the breakfast room table and listened somberly as I poured out the whole sordid tale.

"Do you think your grandmother's fears are justified?"

"I don't know. Maybe her memory is playing tricks on her — or maybe she misunderstood what was going on. One thing is certain, though: she won't rest until I find that suitcase."

Matt's eyes were somber. "If you find it, and it contains what she thinks, you'll have to call the police."

Oh, dear Lord. The possibility of a murder investigation hadn't even occurred to me.

"Are you prepared to do that? And what about your uncle?"

Eddie. Poor, sweet, tenderhearted Eddie. We texted every day and he called several times a week. I'd kept him up to date on Gran's story, and so far he'd been entirely sympathetic.

"Will he be torn up to find out his father was a murderer?" Matt asked.

I considered the question. "He'll be upset, but I don't think it'll devastate him. They were never that close. My grandfather wanted him to be a man's man, and Eddie . . . well, he's into flower arranging."

Matt smiled.

"Granddad used to say things like 'don't be a sissy' and 'you're acting like a Nancy boy,' things that were really hurtful."

"It's a big leap to go from knowing your dad was antigay to learning he might be a murderer."

"True. But when I told Eddie about Joe, his first question was, 'Is Joe my father, too?' He seemed disappointed that he wasn't."

Matt was silent for a moment. "You know, there's another option here, Hope. You can write all this off as the ramblings of an elderly woman who had a head injury and let it go. She might not remember telling you about it in the morning."

"Oh, she'll remember." I took a sip of wine. "Everything she's told me up until now has been leading to this. She said she has to take care of this so she can die in peace."

"And you said you'd help her." It wasn't a question, but a statement.

He knew me pretty well. I nodded.

Matt took a thoughtful sip of wine. "Does she have any idea where to look?"

I shook my head. "Just the backyard."

"Well, suitcases have metal hinges and locks. I know someone who has a professional metal detector. I'll see if I can borrow it."

My heart warmed. I put my hand over his. "Thank you so much, Matt."

"Hold your thanks until we see if we get anywhere." He squeezed my fingers and looked into my eyes, his expression grim. "You may not thank me if we find what your grandmother fears."

38
HOPE

Kirsten lived in a loft above the coffee shop. A separate doorway led to the staircase, and when she opened the second-story door, I felt like I'd been transported to London or New York. It had high ceilings, an industrial feel, and a vibe like a loft in Soho or Tribeca.

"This is amazing," I said, looking at the wall of windows out the back, the modern decor, the industrial look of the high ceilings. "I'd never have guessed there was anything this cool and urban-looking in Wedding Tree."

"There wasn't until Kirsten," said Aimee.

"Oh, yeah?"

"Absolutely," said a rotund woman wearing a strawberry-printed shirt. Kirsten introduced her as Linda and told me she was a strawberry farmer.

"Kirsten raised the taste level for all of us," Linda said. "Came back from college on the East Coast with all kinds of highfalu-tin ideas."

"Linda, you think cappuccino is highfalu-tin," Freret teased laughingly.

"Well, it is! Don't know why you need to go to all that trouble for a cup of coffee."

The women all laughed good-naturedly.

"I think you know almost everyone," Kirsten said.

I looked around and saw all of the women from the Friends of the Forest outing, plus a few new faces. I shook hands with Lauren, a real estate agent who had met with Eddie about listing the house while Gran was in the hospital.

"How're things going?" she asked.

"Slowly," I confessed.

She smiled. "That's to be expected. I think it's so great that you're helping your grandmother out this way."

Kirsten introduced me to two women on the side of the room. "Rose is the produce manager at the grocery store, and Sarah is a piano teacher. And of course you know Jillian."

"Of course." I greeted the two new women and started to give Jillian a hug, but she held herself in a rigid way that made me opt for a handshake.

"Come and get a mojito," said Kirsten.

I sauntered over to the kitchen bar, then

fell into a conversation with Jen the librarian about possibilities for a mural in the children's section. I told her I wouldn't be in town long enough to paint it myself, then found myself regretting it as we discussed ideas.

Kirsten dinged a spoon on her glass. "All right, ladies — time to actually discuss the book." I followed the other women to the center of the room, where two curved white sectionals floated over a bright African-style rug like commas.

"So what did you think of *In Your Dreams?*" Kirsten asked when we were all settled.

"I thought it was wonderful," said Linda. "I just loved the characters and the way they interacted."

"Yeah. They had such witty conversations!"

"I wish my husband were half as interesting as the hero," said Marie.

"Fictional men are so much sexier than the real thing," sighed Rose.

"What did the heroine think was essential in a relationship?" Kirsten said.

"I didn't have to time to read the book, but personally, I'd say the most essential thing is someone who puts me first," Clarabel declared.

"I want a man who understands the work-life balance," Freret said.

"I'd be happy with a man who understands the golf-life balance," sighed Aimee.

Everyone laughed. I remembered from the dinner conversation at the fete that Aimee's husband was an avid golfer.

"Someone who meets his responsibilities," said Linda.

Everyone nodded. "Someone who listens," said Sarah.

"Someone who loves with his whole heart," I chimed in.

"Ooh, that's a good one," Kirsten said.

Everyone nodded — except Jillian. She looked right at me. "If you feel that way, you shouldn't date Matt."

The room fell silent, except for a side conversation the grocer and strawberry farmer were having in the corner. Apparently I wasn't the only one too stunned to speak.

Marie leaned forward, her forehead scrunched. "Wait — Hope's dating Matt?"

"Not *dating* dating," I muttered weakly.

"They kissed. Mrs. Ivy saw them," Lauren announced.

"The thing is, Matt will never love anyone the way he loved Christine." Jillian's face was earnest, her voice somber. "Any other woman will be always second best."

"Oh, that's really sad!" said Jen.

"Yeah, Jillian. And maybe that's not the case," Marie said.

"Oh, it's the case, all right. Christine was his first love and she'll always have part of his heart. Some women would be okay with it, but a woman who wants to be loved with a man's whole heart . . . well, Matt just doesn't have a whole heart to give."

Once again, awkward silence enveloped the room.

"Bummer," said Jen.

"I think the key is knowing what you're getting into from the start," said Linda, who'd just finished talking with the produce buyer and apparently had missed the fact that Jillian's comments were aimed at me.

Kirsten sent me a sympathetic glance. "Well, let's get back to the book. How would you summarize the theme?"

The conversation moved on, but my mind never moved much beyond Jillian's remark.

After the book discussion, Kirsten brought out coffee and a decadent chocolate tart. "We have one more matter to discuss," she announced. "Miss Addie is leaving next month, and I think it would be wonderful if the whole town gave her a surprise send-off party."

"Ooh yes!" the group murmured.

"I'll host it in the coffee shop," Kirsten said. "It'll be the unveiling of Hope's mural and the shop's extra room."

"Perfect!" said Lauren. "How can we help?"

"Spread the word, but emphasize it's to be kept secret from Miss Addie. And get everyone to gather up photos she took for them. I want to have an exhibition of her work along the walls."

The women all chattered excitedly about ideas for the party.

It was after eleven before I headed home. The sting of Jillian's words was largely washed away in the excitement of planning Gran's party, but an underlying sadness remained.

It didn't really matter if Jillian was right or wrong about Matt, I realized as I climbed Gran's porch, because I, too, was leaving Wedding Tree in a month. There was no point in thinking about the long term when our relationship was destined to end in a few short weeks.

And therein lay my problem: How could I keep that knowledge from ruining the little time I had left with him? And even more importantly, how did I keep from falling in love with him?

Love? I stopped short and stared at his house — at his window, where he was sleeping. No. I wasn't — I refused to be — falling in love with Matt. I liked him, I found him wildly attractive, but I couldn't be — I wouldn't allow myself to be — falling in love with a man I'd never see after a few more weeks.

Gran was upset when I first told her Matt was going to help us try to find the buried suitcase on Saturday.

"You told him?" She'd clutched her chest and stopped rocking in her bedroom chair. "Oh, dear. What on earth did you say? What must he think?"

I hadn't realized how terrifying it would be to learn that the secret she'd hidden for more than sixty years was suddenly out in the open, known by a virtual stranger.

I patted her hand. "I just said that you thought Granddad had buried something and that you don't know what it is, but you'd always felt the need to find out."

Gran drew in a ragged breath, then slowly exhaled. After a moment, she nodded. "Well, it'll all be a matter of public record when everything is said and done. Guess I might as well get used to the idea."

"When do you want me to tell Eddie your

suspicions?" I asked her gently. I'd told him everything else she'd told me, but I'd held off mentioning the buried suitcase.

"Later. After we see if we find anything."

I leaned toward her from my perch on her bed. "You know, Gran, it's entirely possible there never was a baby. Maybe Granddad was just trying to jolt you into understanding how hard it was on him, knowing that you loved someone else."

"Oh, child — I thought that, too, when he first insisted on the whole crazy scheme. But then I found a book on baby care hidden among his work papers. It had dog-eared pages about what to do when a mother rejects a baby and how to make an adopted baby feel like your own. Mind you, this was a man who didn't read a single book when either your mother or Eddie were born." She set the rocker back in motion. "That, more than anything, convinced me things were just as he said. He was worried I wouldn't accept this baby."

I swallowed hard.

Her hand turned under mine so that we were palm to palm. She squeezed my fingers. "Thank you for helping me with this. You have no idea how much this means to me."

Matt showed up bright and early Saturday morning, carrying a large metal detector and a complicated set of instructions. He fiddled with the settings, then set the instructions on the garden table. "I think we're ready to give it a go. Do we have any idea where to start looking?"

"Maybe Gran has some photos of what the yard looked like in 1948."

We traipsed inside and asked her. Sure enough, she did — and amazingly, she knew just where to find them. "That last attic box in the dining room — the one with the red tape. It's full of albums. The dates are on the outside."

Matt hauled it out and we gathered around, opening albums on the dining room table. It was a virtual treasure trove — so fascinating that I all but forgot why we were looking through it. There were photos of my mom and Uncle Eddie as children on a metal swing set. There were close-ups of flowers, wide shots of the backyard, and several photos of a tall, lean man in a fedora by the shed, his face shaded by the brim of his hat.

Gran's finger lingered on the photo.

"That's Charlie."

I'd seen dozens of similar photos, but for the first time, it occurred to me that in all the pictures where Eddie was a toddler or older, Gran almost always had photographed my grandfather so that his expression was unreadable. She always captured the essence of her subjects; she'd chosen to photograph her own husband as unknowable.

"Did you notice anything unusual about the backyard?" Matt's voice pulled my rambling thoughts back to the present. "Anything moved around, any ground disturbed?"

Gran shook her head. "I made a point of not looking."

"It was fall, so there would have been leaves on the ground," Matt mused.

Gran nodded. "That made it easier to turn a blind eye."

Matt shuffled through the photos. He held up one of Mom and Uncle Eddie hunting Easter eggs in the backyard. "You had a vegetable garden in the back?"

"Yes."

"That's a likely place, because the ground would have been softer," Matt mused.

Gran nodded. "Charlie tilled it every spring."

486

"Did he till it the following spring?"

"Yes."

"So if he buried it there, it's probably at least three feet down. We'll set the detector for that depth, then."

We went outside, and Matt fiddled with the metal detector. Holding the handle, he waved the round coils of the machine parallel to the ground over the dirt beside the patio. The detector pinged.

"There's something here!" I said.

Matt looked at the dial. "It says it's brass or steel. That's positive; that's what the hinges and locks were most likely made of."

Excited, we both manned shovels. To our disappointment, we uncovered a pair of pliers.

Each ding led to an equally lackluster find. After two hours, our collection included nine bottle caps, eight nails, two garden trowels and thirty-eight cents.

Sophie's and Zoey's heads appeared over the fence.

"Whatcha doin'?" asked Sophie.

Matt glanced up. "Looking for something."

"Is it buried treasure?" Zoey came through the shrubbery.

"Sort of," I replied.

"Wow! Can we help?" Sophie followed her sister into Gran's lawn.

"No," Matt said.

"Why not?" Zoey asked.

"Because this is grown-up work."

I hated that Matt was giving up valuable time with his daughters to help me. I moved closer and whispered, "There's no reason they can't join us. If we find something, we can take a break and pull it out later."

We were interrupted by Jillian emerging through the shrubbery opening. She was wearing a top cut low enough to show cleavage and fitted jeans, and her hair had been straightened. She looked lovely. My chest tensed.

"Hello," she said.

I smiled. "Hi."

Matt lowered the metal detector. "I thought Peggy and Griff were watching the girls at their house."

"They were. But Sophie wanted to get her paints, and since I was visiting Mom and Dad, I offered to bring them over."

"Well, thanks." Matt wiped his brow with his forearm. "I, uh, think the girls are going to stay and help us out for a while."

"Looking for anything in particular?"

"It's buried treasure!" Zoey informed her.

"Wow. Sounds intriguing."

Neither Matt nor I bit at the bid for information.

"Need an extra hand?" Jillian asked.

"No, thanks." Matt's tone was just short of being curt.

"Okay. Is meatloaf all right for dinner?"

"I, uh, won't be home for dinner. Peggy and Griff are watching the girls."

"Oh?" Jillian arched her brow inquisitively.

Matt straightened. "I'm taking Hope out tonight."

"You mean on a date?" Zoey scowled.

I felt my face color.

"Yeah," Matt said.

Jillian's cheeks blotched red. "I — I see."

"Thanks for asking, though. About the meatloaf." Matt turned on the metal detector again.

"No problem." She headed back to the house, her back stiff.

A wave of pity swept through me. I felt like I should say something, but nothing appropriate came to mind.

"Well, that was awkward," Matt said.

It still was, I thought, as Zoey glared at me. I smiled at her. "Want to help us dig? I think there are extra shovels in the shed."

"We're gonna hunt for buried treasure!" Sophie said, hopping up and down.

I could tell the lure of treasure was vying

489

with loyalty to Jillian as far as Zoey was concerned. Apparently the treasure hunt won out, because she was still there when I came out of the shed, and immediately started arguing with Sophie about who got the bigger shovel.

39
MATT

We were seated on the wooden deck of a restaurant overlooking the Tchefuncte River in Madisonville. The sun had just set, the fireflies were out, and a boat slowly drifted by. Across the table from me, Hope smiled. She was wearing a white sundress, and it made her skin look like apricots. It was a setting ripe for romance.

Except for one thing. Two things, actually.

"Can I have another dinner roll?" Sophie asked, squirming in her chair.

"No. You won't have room for your dinner," Zoey said authoritatively.

The girls had happily dug in Miss Addie's backyard the rest of the day, then Hope had suggested we invite them to join us for dinner.

"Saturday is one of the few days you and the girls get to be together," she'd said.

"But I want to spend time with you."

"I'll be there."

"I meant alone."

"I don't want the girls to think I'm taking you away from them."

"This isn't at all what I'd planned," I grumbled.

She'd grinned. "Maybe you need to work on becoming more flexible."

Flexible. Huh. I'd been plenty flexible all day, trying not to peer down Hope's shirt or stare at her shapely tush as she bent over to dig. I felt like a perv, lusting after her in full view of two kids, a dog, and an elderly lady.

The fact was, I'd expected things to move in a new direction tonight — a direction involving lots of skin-on-skin contact, although the logistics were vague. In the back of my mind, I thought that if things got hot and heavy, we might head to the Hampton Inn in Covington for a few hours. Instead, here we were, chastely separated by two sharp-eyed chaperones.

"You have very nice manners, girls," Hope said. "I'm impressed with the way you're sitting up straight and remembering to keep your arms off the table."

I was impressed, too — at the way Hope had managed to find what was probably the first moment all evening that both girls had their arms off the table. I liked the way she caught them behaving well and encouraged it.

Both small spines immediately straightened. "My mother always said good manners were important," Zoey announced.

My heart gave a little wrench. Zoey hadn't been old enough to remember anything Christine had said — had she? She'd probably gotten that information from Peggy or Jillian.

"You'd make a nice mommy," Sophie told Hope.

"Thank you, sweetheart," Hope said with a smile.

"So why aren't you one?" Zoey asked.

"Well, for starters, I'm not married."

"But you were. Aunt Jillian said you were married, and then you got divorced." She said the word in almost a whisper, as if it were naughty.

Hope took a sip of water. "Yes. Yes, I was."

"Divorce is bad," Zoey said.

"Well — it's nothing anyone ever wants to happen," Hope said, before I could even frame a response. "And it's certainly sad."

"What's divorce?" Sophie asked.

"It's when people break their wedding promise," Zoey told her.

"It's more complicated than that," I said irritably.

"Jillian said people divorce when they quit loving each other," Zoey said.

Sophie's blue eyes grew round and wet. "Can daddies divorce their children?"

My heart felt tight and hard as a basketball. "No. Never."

"But if grown-ups divorce . . ."

"Honey." I scooted back my chair and pulled Sophie onto my lap. "I could never, ever stop loving you or Zoey."

"So why aren't you a mommy?" Sophie said to Hope. "You were married, and married people are supposed to have kids."

"Not all married people are fortunate enough to have kids," I said.

"They do unless they don't want them," Zoey said. "Aunt Jillian said."

Thanks a lot, Jillian. I forced myself to unclench my teeth and made a mental note to tell Jillian that my kids could do without her version of birth control information.

"Sometimes it just doesn't happen," Hope said.

"Did you want to be a mommy?" Zoey asked.

"I would love to have children," she said.

"Maybe you could be our mommy," Sophie said.

My mouth went dry. Hope's eyes met mine.

"Don't be a nimwit," Zoey said. "Daddy wouldn't marry someone who divorces husbands, 'cause then she might divorce him."

"Zoey, don't call your sister names," I said, grabbing onto the part of the conversation I could form a coherent thought around.

The waiter appeared at our table just then, juggling plates of salad. Sophie launched into a tale about snails eating the lettuce in her grandmother's garden, and the conversation, thank God, veered onto more manageable topics.

But Hope seemed subdued the rest of the evening, and after we'd left the restaurant, gone home, and tucked the girls into bed, we walked downstairs in silence.

"I'm not sure this evening was the best idea," she said on the landing.

"Because of what Zoey said? Don't put any stock in that."

"It's not that. I'm worried we're confusing them. They don't understand casual dating."

I didn't understand it, either. "The person who's confusing them is Jillian. She's been overly informative on topics she has no business discussing."

"We don't know the context of that conversation."

"True. But I can imagine."

We'd reached the living room. We both stood at the back of the sofa.

"What did you mean by 'casual dating'?" I asked.

"Short-term. Nonphysical."

"Does it have to be both?" I stepped closer, close enough that I could feel the heat of her skin. "I don't want to be nonphysical."

Her breath caught. Our gazes locked, and her face tipped up. I leaned down and kissed her. Her arms wound around me as the kiss sweetened and deepened.

Oh, dear God — she tasted like honey and salt, delicious and intoxicating. Her breasts were warm and soft against my chest. I sifted her hair through my fingers and held her head, and she gave a little moan against my mouth.

"I need to go," she whispered at length.

"Not just yet." I kissed her neck, then reclaimed her mouth.

Many long, languid, torturously sweet moments later, she pulled away. "Matt, we're playing with fire. The girls could come downstairs at any moment."

She was right, but I felt drugged with lust.

"We need to get up early and begin the search again tomorrow." She moved out of my reach, toward the door.

"What if we strike out again?" I asked. "I have to return the metal detector on Monday."

"I asked Gran that, and she said her mother told her we would."

"Her mother?"

Hope sheepishly lifted her shoulders. "Apparently they still have conversations."

"What if her mother's wrong?"

Hope smiled. "Gran said if we do our best, she'll be satisfied."

"And you?" I asked, drawing a finger along her cheek. "Will you be satisfied?"

The way her eyes darkened sent a shot of heat right to my groin. "That's an unfair question."

"I was hoping it would be." I stepped closer. "What would satisfy you, Hope?"

She drew a shaky breath. Her eyes held an answer that made my blood race. She put a hand on my chest — then gently pushed me away. "You could let me leave."

"No satisfaction in that at all."

"Yes, there is." She put her hand on the doorknob. "You'll have the satisfaction of knowing you're a wonderful father."

"Not the kind of satisfaction I had in mind."

She smiled. "It's true, though."

"You think?" I regretted the question the moment I asked it. What kind of loser blatantly fished for a compliment that way? But it was the most important role of my life, and her opinion mattered.

"Absolutely. You're a wonderful dad. They're two very lucky little girls." Her hand drifted to my jaw, warm and soft. I took it, turned it, and kissed her palm.

And with that, she slipped out of my arms and out the door.

40
HOPE

Those kisses burned on my lips, even after I'd showered and put on my pajamas and applied ChapStick. They burned as I crawled into bed, and as I lay first on my right side, then on my left, then on my back, staring at the ceiling.

It occurred to me that kissing Matt was like getting bitten by a mosquito carrying dengue fever or West Nile virus — it had left me hot and weak and slightly out of my mind.

Unlike a mosquito bite, though, kissing Matt was pleasurable — intensely pleasurable, pleasurable almost beyond description, the kind of pleasurable that barreled into the future, creating thoughts of other things that would feel just as good or even better. His hands roaming over my body, for instance, or his mouth . . .

I rolled over, tossing the sheet off me, letting the breeze from the overhead fan cool my skin. It wasn't as simple as whether or not Matt and I got involved with each other. There were two little girls to think about — two little girls longing for a mother. And while I adored those girls, I knew nothing about children or mothering.

Which was a non-issue, I reminded myself, because I was going back to Chicago. I wasn't one of those people who could leave their hearts out of lovemaking, so there was no point in getting anything started.

Besides, even if I weren't going back to Chicago — which I was; the job was a once-in-a-lifetime opportunity, and I'd be an idiot to pass it up — what were the chances we'd actually end up together? The odds of marrying any one person you dated were slim — very slim. I'd seen enough friends date guy after guy after guy, sometimes for months or even years, only to watch them eventually break up. And those were two free, unencumbered couples, not people recovering from a divorce or — even worse — the death of a spouse.

And Matt wasn't recovering from the death of just any spouse. From everything I'd ever heard, Christine was the equivalent of Superwoman. How could anyone ever live up to the legacy of a woman who was, by all accounts, brilliant, beautiful, tasteful, athletic, the perfect hostess, and a model mom? Who would even want to try to fill those stilettos?

No, a future with Matt wasn't something I could even consider. He hadn't given any indication it was something he was interested in anyway; he'd talked about a temporary relationship. A fling, basically. And I wasn't a fling kind of girl.

But maybe I should be, just this once. Maybe Kirsten was right. Maybe a little hot stuff was just what I needed — and just what Matt needed, as well. The memory of that kiss made me hot and flushed all over again.

Even if I decided to go for it — which I probably wouldn't, because deep down, I'm a big chicken — where and when would we make love? Not at his house. Not at Gran's, certainly. And no matter how desperate I was, I didn't want to resort to motel rooms in the next town.

No. It was a bad idea, for many, many reasons.

But it was such a danged appealing bad idea that I couldn't get it out of my head.

I dozed off around midnight. Something abruptly awakened me I thought it was a voice, then decided I must have been dreaming. The alarm clock on the nightstand said ten minutes after three a.m. Thunder rumbled in the distance. I rolled over, figuring that I'd confused thunder for a voice, then worried that I might have heard Gran.

I'd better check, I decided. I crept downstairs without turning on any lights and followed the sound of snoring down the hall. By the glow of a nightlight, I saw Gran sound asleep in her bed — the night nurse snoring on the cot beside her.

Thunder cracked again. I started back toward the stairs, then froze. Another sound — one that sounded like the clink of metal on metal — clanked in the backyard. I veered toward the dark kitchen and headed to the window. Oh, dear — lights were moving around in the back of the garden!

My heart galloped. My hand shook as I reached for the phone. My first thought was to call the police, but then lightning lit the sky — sheet lightning, the kind that doesn't streak, but just illuminates the clouds like an overhead flashbulb — and in that instance, I saw the distinct outline of three men, digging.

A stream of cold ran straight to my core. It didn't make sense, but I was sure this was somehow related to Matt's and my efforts to find the suitcase. If I called the police, I'd have to explain it all to them, and Gran's secret could come spilling out, and . . .

Without thinking further, my fingers punched in the speed-dial number for Matt.

He answered on the first ring, his voice thick with sleep.

"Some men are digging in the backyard," I whispered.

I heard the rustle of fabric, and imagined him climbing out of bed and going to his own window. He muttered a low oath. "How many?"

"I think I saw three. I started to call the police," I whispered, "but . . ."

"I'll be right over."

"I'll meet you outside."

"No. Stay indoors." The words were an order. "They might be armed."

I ran back upstairs, pulled off my pj's, and scrambled into a T-shirt and shorts, not bothering with undergarments. No way was I going to cower indoors if Matt was going out there. I headed back downstairs and, on impulse, grabbed a poker from the fireplace tool set in the parlor. I watched the hedge — Sophie's secret gate — and when another flash of lightning lit the sky, I saw Matt emerge from the shrubbery.

I stepped out the kitchen door, closing it

quietly behind me. Clutching the poker, I ran to the large oak and hid behind it, watching Matt advance on the men.

"We're gonna get electrocuted out here," I heard one of them say.

"Nah. That storm's still a long ways off," said another.

"Freeze or I'll shoot!" yelled Matt.

All of a sudden, a bright light illuminated the men. Only they weren't men at all; they were teenagers, probably fifteen or sixteen years old. I realized that Matt was holding some kind of large spotlight, the kind you might find at a roadside construction site.

They all threw their hands up in the air and squinted toward him.

"What the hell do you think you're doing?" Matt demanded.

"N-nothing," said one of them.

"You can tell me, or you can tell your parents down at the police station." Matt's voice was hard. "Your choice."

"We — we heard there was treasure," said a tall, gangly boy with buzz-cut hair.

"Where the hell did you hear that?" Matt demanded.

"Mike's girlfriend works at the snow cone stand, and . . ."

"Don't use names!" blurted a shorter boy with dark, Johnny Depp–style hair — ap-

504

parently named Mike.

"Sorry. Anyway, she overheard two little kids talkin' about how they were helping their neighbor lady find some treasure in her backyard, and we, uh, thought we'd help out."

"That's what you're doing, huh? Helping out?" Sarcasm dripped from Matt's words.

"Well, yeah. We weren't gonna keep it or nothin'."

"Right. Just helping the elderly from the goodness of your heart."

"Please," pleaded the third boy, who had blond hair and big, scared eyes. "Don't turn us in."

"Yeah," said the smaller one. "I'm up for a scholarship, and this would ruin everything."

"Let them go, Matt." I stepped forward.

Matt's head whipped toward me, then back at the boys. It was too dark to see his expression. "For all we know, they're out every night, robbing old people blind, taking things they think they'll never miss."

Matt's light illuminated the blond boy's chagrined expression. "We wouldn't do that. We'd never do that. Please. We didn't mean any harm. We just wanted to find the treasure."

"Yeah," Mike mumbled. "Nothin' exciting

505

ever happens in this town."

Matt paused as if he was thinking it over.

"Gran would want them to have a second chance," I prompted.

Matt sighed. "This appears to be your lucky day, boys. Get on out of here — and keep your mouths shut. I won't be so lenient if I find another group of kids digging here tomorrow."

The boys scrambled for the fence.

"Wait! Don't forget your shovels!" I called.

"She means your parents' shovels," Matt said.

Only one boy — the one who said he needed a scholarship — came back. "We're really sorry. Thank you."

Grabbing the shovels, he tossed them over the fence and scrambled after them. His shorts ripped on a ragged board.

The sound of pounding footsteps receded into the distance. "Thanks," I said to Matt.

"No problem." He strode toward me, his light pointed at the ground. "Why didn't you stay in the house like I asked?"

"I thought I could help."

"With that?"

I followed his gaze to the poker in my hand. I grinned sheepishly. "It was all I could think of. I didn't know you'd be armed."

"I'm not."

"But you said stop or you'd shoot — and you had your hand on something in your pocket."

He pulled a cell phone out of his pocket along with a baby monitor. "I couldn't just go off and leave the girls unattended."

Adrenaline was coursing through my veins. It was short step from fear to outrage. "You let those boys think you had a gun?"

He lifted his shoulders. "I didn't know who I was dealing with when I said that."

"Exactly." The danger he could have been in made me furious. "So if they'd been armed, they might have shot you."

"All the more reason you should have stayed in the house."

"That is not the point!"

"So what is?"

"That you took a huge risk, and you won't even acknowledge it was dangerous and stupid."

"Hey, I'm not the one running around with a fireplace poker."

"You are the most unreasonable, pigheaded, stupidly macho . . ."

He set the work lamp on the ground, closed the distance between us, and clamped his mouth on mine. His lips were soft and luscious, and the minute they touched mine, I forgot why I was mad and what I'd been about to say. The anger morphed into something else, something hotter and more irrational. His five-o'clock shadow rasped my skin. I dropped the fireplace poker, and wound my hands around his back. His hands sifted through my hair as he angled his face to kiss me more deeply.

My fingers moved under the back of his T-shirt. His skin was warm, his muscles hard. I felt his erection press against my belly.

The rain that had been threatening started to sprinkle down.

"This isn't wise," I murmured.

"Why not?"

"Because I won't want to stop."

"Who says we have to?" His lips slid down my neck, creating goose bumps up and down my spine.

"Do you have protection?"

"No. But there are things we can do without it. Is the shed locked?"

His lips were close to my ear. The erotic tickle of his breath made a shiver chase through me. "I know where the key's hidden." His lips found mine again.

I couldn't bear to break the kiss, so I walked backward on tiptoe toward the garden shed — and then he picked me up. I wound my legs around his hips and let him carry me, still kissing me, to the shed. I reached up and pulled the key from the top of the left shutter.

He set me down, took the key, and unlocked the door, then pulled out his cell phone and used it as a flashlight.

"There's an old picnic blanket on the middle shelf," I said.

He grabbed the blanket and shook it out, then spread it on the floor. He opened the window, closed the door, then knelt on the blanket and reached for my hand.

I sank down beside him. And then we were kissing again, kissing and touching, touching and kissing. Outside, the sprinkles became a torrent, pounding on the roof. He pulled my shirt off over my head and took my nipple in his mouth. When he sucked, an arrow of heat ran right down my middle, right to my very core.

He moved over me with his hands and mouth until I was ablaze, melting and molten, throbbing for relief from the relentless, aching heat. His mouth traced a path down my stomach. He dipped his tongue into my belly button, his fingers working their way up my thighs.

He paused to pull my shorts down and

off. "Going commando, I see."

"Well, it was a commando operation," I replied.

His laughed against my belly, and finding humor in such heat . . . well, it only made it hotter. Righter. Realer. More intimate.

"I appreciate how you managed to dress for the occasion on such short notice." He kissed me some more. "Or did you plan this out? Did you pay those boys to give you an excuse to call me?"

"I thought *you* paid them."

He laughed again, and pleasure, just as intense as the physical pleasure, but more deeply centered, located in the part of me that was more than just a body, pulsed through me. He made me feel . . . amazing. Treasured. Appreciated. Swept away, yes, but swept right into the moment. We were both right here, right now, fully present, traveling together on a rotating planet revolving around a burning star. The heat of his breath moving upward on my thigh sent me into a delicious spiral of pure, burgeoning desire. The pressure of his fingers, the indescribably tender, firm urging of his mouth created an irresistible vortex of need and pleasure. My legs quaked and my body stiffened and all at once, I was teetering on the ledge — a ledge where in the past I often used to think, *This is it. I'm nearly there,* and that thought, that brief step back from the moment to observe it, would make it impossible to fall into the abyss of abandon. But Matt disallowed that option. He simply, masterfully, lifted me off and over — and I found myself flying and crying, all at the same time.

At length, he kissed his way back up my belly, up my chest, up my neck, to my mouth. "You are so beautiful, so wonderful, so delicious," he said. "That was such a turn-on."

I could feel his erection pressed against my belly. "Your turn," I murmured, unbuttoning his jeans. His manhood jutted out as I freed it from the zipper.

I pushed up his shirt. His pecs were firm mounds, topped with flat brown nipples, dusted with dark hair. His abs were flat and hard, banded with muscle. I kissed my way down a trail of dark hair below his belly button.

I touched his erection, and it jerked toward my hand. "I think he likes me."

"Oh, Hope," he groaned. "That feels . . ."

Words failed him. I loved that, loved making him speechless with pleasure. When I pushed him over the edge, I felt like Arch Woman of the Universe.

He pulled me into his arms afterward so that I lay on top of him, skin to skin. "Hope," he whispered. He put his hands in my hair and turned my face so that his lips could reach mine. "You're . . ."

Something on the floor beside us crackled. I froze, thinking it was a mouse — and then, suddenly, over the rain thrumming on the roof, I heard a babbling sound, like a voice. Terror shot through me. "What's that?" I whispered.

"The baby monitor. Sophie sometimes talks in her sleep."

"Oh." I blew out a relieved sigh, then abruptly rolled off him. "That monitor — does it just work one way?" I asked.

"You mean, can they hear us?"

I nodded.

He grinned. "I know leaving the house and having sex in a neighbor's shed probably won't earn me the Father of the Year award, but trust me, I stopped short of broadcasting our little interlude into my daughters' room."

Of course he had. Of course he'd thought of his girls. And then his actual words hit me. "Was that what it was? A 'little interlude'?"

"Well, it wasn't a full concert, that's for sure. You had me so turned on that if we'd had protection, I'd be embarrassed at my lack of self-control."

"That's not what I meant, and you know it." I swallowed and looked down, feeling curiously close to tears. " 'Interlude' just sound so . . ." Small. Transient. Insignificant. I struggled to find a less needy-sounding word. ". . . seedy."

His lip quirked in a grin. "Well, this *is* a potting shed."

I elbowed him, but his humor had lightened my mood.

He cupped my face. "Hope, that's the best thing that's happened to me in a long, long time. I'm crazy about you."

"Me, too."

Emotion hummed between us, then Sophie murmured again through the monitor. I reached for my shorts and scrambled into them. "You'd better get back home before your girls wake up."

"Yeah." He kissed me on the nose, then pulled on his clothes and folded the blanket. I closed the window while he put the blanket back on the shelf, then he ran out and retrieved the fireplace poker from the lawn. He handed it to me, ushered me out, then locked the door and put the key back on top of the shutter. "I'll wait until you're safely inside."

I ran through the rain, aware of him watching me, and turned to wave once I opened the kitchen door. Lightning lit the sky, and I saw him move through the hedge.

I hurried upstairs, still clutching the poker. I didn't trust my hand to be steady enough to return it to the hearthside tool rack without waking Gran or the aide, and I didn't want to have to explain myself or my actions. How could I explain something I didn't really understand myself? Besides, all I wanted to do was get into bed and relive every thrilling moment.

41
ADELAIDE

I opened my eyes see a pair of overly cheerful morning aides standing by my bed.

"Top of the mornin' to you, dearie!"

"Good morning." I rubbed my eyes, which temporarily reduced the number of aides by half.

"Do you need something? I thought I heard you talking."

"Must have been talking in my sleep." Seems easier to tell her that than to admit the truth: I see dead people.

Oh, I know that's not original — I know it's a line from a recent movie — although Hope would laugh if she heard me call it recent, because it's probably a dozen or more years old now.

The thing is, I saw Charlie. I think it was a dream, but it seemed as real as my encounters with Mother. It jarred me, because it never occurred to me that I'd have to deal with him again once I'm dead. I guess I hadn't figured we'd end up in the same place.

But then, it's also just recently occurring to me that I might have underestimated the mercy of God. That's a very scary concept, that. If God is as merciful and gracious as the dream suggested, he might have higher standards than my level of forgiveness.

I like to think that I forgave Charlie, but maybe I haven't, not entirely. If I haven't, I'd better get to work on that, because it's going to be harder if Hope unearths what I fear she will.

But then, it might be even worse if she doesn't. How am I supposed to forgive Charlie — fully and completely, the way I know I need to — if he's buried something so deeply that I can't fix my part in it?

Holy Moses, but this is a mess.

In my dream last night, he was dressed in a blue suit — bluer and brighter than men normally wear — but it looked wonderful on him. He was able to walk without even a trace of a limp, and he escorted me to a beautiful ornate door — one with carvings and leaded glass that shot rainbow-colored prisms like firecrackers when the light hit it. He held it open for me. I was about to walk inside, but all of a sudden, I realized I was just wearing a housecoat, and this looked like a grand hotel. I was afraid of embarrassing him. He just smiled and urged me in.

I walked through the door, and saw a giant white grand piano. It dawned on me that this was a performance hall, and I was at the edge of the stage. A large audience of fancy-dressed people filled the vast auditorium.

Well, I don't play piano, beyond a few simple hymns I can play one-handed, and half of "America the Beautiful," which was a song I had to memorize for a recital when I was eight. I'm certainly no virtuoso. I realized I was about to be humiliated. Even worse, I was going to disappoint Charlie, who just stood there, beaming.

"I can't do this," I whispered.

"Sure you can." Charlie put his hand in the small of my back and urged me forward.

The crowd burst into applause. I skulked to the piano, my head down, and sat on the bench. The audience hushed to an expectant rustling.

I closed my eyes and tentatively began "Onward, Christian Soldiers" with my right hand. I knew only two chords to add with my left, but then, all of a sudden, I felt a surge of energy gather in my chest. It's as if the notes were floating in the air, and I inhaled them, and they were rushing through my veins, and my fingers were flying across the keys. Out of nowhere, I was able to effortlessly play beautiful, magnificent, heavenly music — every tune I've ever heard, and other songs too beautiful to imagine, so beautiful that the roof floated off the auditorium. It was glorious and thrilling and freeing — like when I knew a photo was right, and my finger was just clicking away at the shutter, and I lost all sense of time. I was playing like that, just reveling in the music and the moment, so filled with joy that I was lighter than air.

Charlie smiled, his face just radiant, and said, "I'm so glad you're letting all that music out. I knew it was in you all the time."

And then I thought, *How is this possible? I can't play piano,* and suddenly, I couldn't. The music stopped. I was back to pecking out a melody with my right hand, and I couldn't do even that. I hit sharps and flats. I felt so awful, so humiliated and embarrassed, like I'd let everyone down and made a total fool of myself. I ran off the stage and woke up in a sweat.

Well. It was so real. So real. So *real!*

"Mornin', Miss Addie! Let's start this beautiful day off with a dose of fiber," said the aide, who disappeared into my bathroom

518

and returned with a handful of pills and a glass of water. I think her name is Hazel — no, Hannah. I don't much care for her. She fills in on Nadine's days off, and she's too cheerful, too bossy, too hail-fellow-well-met and jolly, like a department store salesman who reeks slightly of gin. Not that Hazel or Hannah smells of gin. Might do her good to have a nip or two, though. Maybe then she wouldn't be so intensely smile-faced. But there's something about her, something that tells me she's not nearly as smugly cheerful as she seems. She's got a secret life. If not gin, then maybe sherry or a little sweet wine. Or maybe cigarettes. Or gambling. Or men.

That thought makes me smile, because she's got one of those no-fuss, short haircuts that does absolutely nothing for her appearance. No, not men. A woman doesn't wear her hair like that if she wants to be an object of desire.

One of the hidden joys of being old and having people think I'm half-addled is that I can say whatever I want and just wait and see what happens. "Have you ever had a grand romance, Hannah?"

"A what?"

"Have you ever been passionately, madly, swept-off-your-feet in love?"

"Why — why — why on earth would you-alls ask such a thing?"

"Just curious. There are so many things no one ever discusses. And I don't know why not, since those things are often the most interesting."

She turned away. "I don' know what you're talking about."

I waved my hand dismissively. "That's what I figured."

She turned back around, her chin lifted, her mouth in a tight, miffed line. "Well, it so happens I *does* know a thing or two about romance."

"Oh?"

"Yes. I done been married thirty-two years."

"Marriage and romance aren't necessarily the same thing."

"Well, course they are!" she exclaimed.

"Really?" Her certainty intrigued me. "How did you meet your husband?"

"I had a friend who fixed me up with her older brother. He had a stutter, an' he was too shy to ask me out himself, so she set it up for us to meet at the movie theater."

"How interesting! What happened?"

"The very next day, I married him."

"The next day!"

"He had a good job, and a place to live.

And I couldn' take the beatings no more."

My heart flopped like a fish. "The beatings?"

"Yes. My mama used to beat me for growing such large breasts." She whispered the last word.

"Oh, dear Lord. How awful! That wasn't your fault."

"I know, but it made my stepfather look at me."

"Oh, my." Oh, my, indeed. "Oh, you poor dear!" Well. That certainly made me see her in a new light. Isn't that always true, how a little fresh information can make everything seem different?

"Upsy daisy with your glass, ma'am. You need to drink all your water with that fiber."

I drained the glass and handed it back to her. "Are you and your husband happy?"

"Oh, yes," she said. "We suit each other just fine."

Suit. Such a sweet, old-fashioned term. Lovely, really — although lacking in passion.

Or maybe not. For all I know, she means they're well suited between the sheets.

For her sake, I hoped so.

But then, if he were her one and only, maybe she wouldn't know the difference. Not for the first time, I thought that was

why women used to be so carefully chaper-
oned — to protect men from comparisons.
If I'd never kissed Joe, would I have been
ecstatically happy with Charlie?

No, I decided. Even as a virginal youth,
I'd known there was something more.

42
HOPE

I awoke to sunlight pouring through the window. I stretched like a cat, feeling warm and content, as if the sunshine were flowing through my veins. I'd had the most wonderful, vivid dream . . .

I opened my eyes and saw a heap of wet clothes on the floor. My heart quickened. Oh, dear Lord — it hadn't been simply a dream. I *had* made love with Matt!

Well, sort of. We stopped shy of doing the actual deed, but it had been lovemaking all the same.

I sat up and ran my hand through my hair. I didn't know how to feel about it. Part of me was thrilled and happy. Part of me feared I'd made a terrible mistake.

Okay. Calm down. Why would it be a terrible mistake?

The answer was less than reassuring: *because I* was *so darned thrilled and happy.* I'd been very clear about not wanting to get emotionally entwined only to leave town. Besides, what if Matt started behaving all avoidant and awkward, the way some guys do when they regret sleeping with a woman? Regardless of what Matt had said last night, he might feel differently this morning.

Well. As Gran always said, you couldn't uncrack an egg. What was done was done.

I hurried through the shower, threw on fresh shorts, and ran downstairs, where Gran was finishing her breakfast.

"How are you this morning?" I asked.

"A little tired," she said. "I wonder sometimes if sleep isn't more exhausting than being awake."

"You must have a lively dream life."

"Oh, my dear, you have no idea." She took a sip of tea. "Today's the day you and Matt will find that suitcase."

"I hope so, Gran. We'll do our best." I debated whether to tell her anything about the visitors last night, then decided against it. It would serve no good purpose and was sure to upset her.

"I have a good feeling about it," she said.

I heard a noise in the backyard, and saw Matt coming through the shrubbery opening, carrying the metal detector. He waved and strode toward the back porch. I opened the door, feeling anxious and self-conscious, not sure how to greet him.

He gave me a hug — one that was tighter, longer, and warmer than the standard-issue hello hug — then came into the kitchen and bent down to plant a peck on Gran's cheek.

My heart danced. "Can I get you some coffee?"

"Sounds great." His smile let me know he was definitely not having any regrets.

He turned to Gran, then angled his thumb toward the dining room. "Okay if I look at the dining room mural for a moment?"

"Of course," Gran said. "Hope does beautiful work, doesn't she?"

"Sure does," Matt said from the other room.

He came back into the kitchen a moment later and sat down across from Gran. I placed a cup of coffee in front of him and sat down beside him.

"I have a question, Miss Addie."

"Certainly. Ask away."

"Well, you have a partially rotten stump in the backyard next to the shed. I think it's the pecan tree that's pictured in Hope's mural in your dining room. When did you cut it down?"

"After Hurricane Katrina. More than half of the branches had broken off and it was leaning."

"Was it planted after the suitcase was buried?"

Gran gazed thoughtfully out the window. "It might have been. One spring Charlie got a deal on a truckload of pecan trees. The store sold them. It was the first time they'd sold trees, and Charlie's dad was miffed — said they were a lumberyard and hardware store, not a nursery. Anyway, Charlie planted three of them here, as well as three at both of our parents' houses." Gran looked at Matt, her eyes bright and excited. "If someone wanted to make sure something remained buried, the best way to do it would be to plant a tree right on top of it, wouldn't it?"

Matt nodded. "Would it bother you if we dug up the tree trunk?"

Gran's hand covered her chest.

"Are you okay?" I asked, immediately worried about her heart.

"Yes, honey. I'm just feeling . . . Oh, I'm so sure you're right, Matt. And the fact Charlie planted trees on everyone's property — well, that would have kept me from being suspicious."

"If it's okay with you, then, that's where we'll look." He turned to me. "I'll be back in an hour or so. I'm going to rent a stump grinder and a saw, and we'll get to work."

"Where are the girls?" I asked.

"At Sunday school. After church, Peggy, Griff, and Jillian are taking them to the zoo in New Orleans." He briefly placed his hand on my back as he rose.

The simple touch warmed me to the core. I watched him pull his cell phone from his pocket as he walked out the back door, then turned to my grandmother. "Gran, are you sure you're ready to deal with the consequences if we find that suitcase?"

"Yes, dear."

"You know you'll have to tell Eddie."

"Oh, I know, honey."

"We'll have to call the police, as well. You could be in some kind of trouble for not reporting your suspicions."

Gran's chin tilted up. "I'd rather face the consequences here in this world than in the next."

I swallowed.

"Ready for your bath, Miss Addie?" The aide stood in the doorway, a towel over her arm.

Gran turned and smiled. "Absolutely, Hannah. Wash me white as snow."

We'd been at it for about two and half hours — alternately using the stump grinder, shovels, a pickax, and the metal detector, working on the trunk itself and digging a trench around it, then stopping to see if we got any metallic readings. The sun was hot, my shirt was sticking to my skin, and my stomach was growling. I was about to suggest I go make sandwiches, when Matt stopped the grinder for about the zillionth time.

"Did you hear that?"

It was hard to hear anything over the roar and whine of the engine.

"Not really."

"I think we hit metal."

He lifted the metal detector and turned it on. Sure enough, it pinged.

Excited, we both climbed into the trench and looked. All I could see was dirt, sawdust, and tree root. "I'll take the pickax to it," Matt said.

He swung it like a miner. Amazing, how hard pecan wood can be. I wondered how long it took for wood to petrify. After picking and chipping for what seemed like an eternity, the corner of a something distinctly non-treelike emerged. It looked like the metal corner of a trunk.

My pulse raced. "Wow."

Matt nodded, his mouth tight. "Let's work this sucker free."

It took another hour and two broken

handsaw blades, but he managed to cut away the stump to reveal a suitcase. It was metal, with tattered remnants of dirty cloth still stuck to it in spots.

I went in to tell Gran. She was seated at the kitchen table as the relentlessly cheerful aide made lunch. "I need to talk to my grandmother alone for a moment."

"I'm in the middle of making tuna salad."

"That's okay. I'll take over."

"Well — okey dokey."

We waited until she left the room. I suspected she was listening at the door. This aide had been full of questions about what we were doing in the backyard.

"You found it?" Gran asked eagerly.

I nodded.

"Oh my goodness." Gran's face was pale, her voice breathless. "I knew you would. Is it — is it still closed?"

"Yes."

She closed her eyes for a moment. When she opened them, she personified the term Steel Magnolia. "I want to be the one to open it. Tell Hannah to go on home."

I went into the other room and delivered the news.

"Oh no — I can't leave! I'll be fired by the agency."

"Well, then, we need you to go to the

store. Gran needs . . ." I searched my mind for something difficult to find. ". . . powder toothpaste. The whitening kind for sensitive teeth."

"I've never heard of such a thing!"

"Well, try to find it. And get her some hand lotion, too. The kind that's scented like cucumbers and lime."

"Where on earth will I find that?"

"They sell it at the bath shop at the mall in Hammond."

"But that's thirty miles away!"

"Take Gran's car."

I handed her the keys, walked to the front the door, and held it open.

She lifted her head and sniffed. "I know you're just tryin' to get rid of me."

"I'm just asking you to do your job."

She shot me a dirty look but gathered up her purse and left. I stood on the porch and watched until she pulled out of the driveway. "All clear," I said, striding back into the kitchen.

As I helped Gran into a chair on the patio, Matt spread newspapers on the outdoor table. He carried over the rusted suitcase and set it down.

We all stared at it, as if it were a genie's bottle. Gran slowly reached out her hand.

"It's locked," Matt gently said.

Her hand froze in midair, then fell into her lap. "Can you force it open?"

Matt pulled a screwdriver from his toolbox, wedged the flat edge against the lock with his left hand, then picked up a hammer. With a single loud bang, the lock gave way.

I watched Gran's lips firm. "I want to be the one to lift the lid."

"I'll go get you some gloves," I volunteered. I ran to the shed and grabbed a pair of cotton flowered gardening gloves. Gran's hands shook as she pulled them on.

"It's rusted," Matt said. "I'll need to pry it loose." He worked with a crowbar until the suitcase lid creaked and started to give.

"All right, Miss Addie," he said. "Put your hands beside mine, and we'll open it together."

Her face was pale, her skin so thin and translucent I could see the blue veins underneath. Her eyes held a combination of fear and determination that I can only call courage. Her lips disappeared as she pressed them tightly together.

Matt's leather gloves pushed upward on the suitcase lid, Gran's frail, flower-gloved hands pushing beside them. With a squawk that sounded like something from a horror movie, the lid abruptly swung upward.

Gran peered inside.

"Oh my God," she whispered.

43
ADELAIDE

I stared inside the suitcase, then pressed the back of my cotton glove against my mouth.

"What?" Hope asked, her voice quavering. "What is it?"

I couldn't speak.

"Something covered by a blanket." Matt moved aside so Hope could step up beside me. I continued to stare at the partially rotted pink-and-blue blanket, stained and dirty. A baby blanket — one I'd never seen before. My stomach and heart felt as if they'd swapped places.

"Do you want me to lift it?" Matt asked.

No. Truth was, I didn't want to see what was underneath. I wanted to slam the lid and pretend we'd never found the damned thing. But I couldn't do that. I'd done that for all too long.

"I'll do it." My hand shook. Covered in that flowered cotton glove, it didn't even look like it was attached to my arm as I peeled back that blanket.

Inside, something was wrapped in what looked like it had once been newspaper, but now resembled papier-mâché.

I tugged on it. It came off in big chunks. And underneath . . .

Bones.

I recoiled. "Oh dear Lord." Hope's arm circled my shoulders. *Oh, Charlie — how could you?* A sob escaped my mouth.

"Wait." Matt leaned in. "This isn't human."

"What?"

He moved the newspaper. "The head shape is all wrong, and so are the teeth."

Teeth? Babies don't have teeth!

"It looks like the remains of a dog," Matt said.

"A dog?" Hope and I breathed the words at the same time.

"Yeah." Matt held back the paper and Hope peered in. "See the jaw? And there's some fur."

"It's definitely not a baby," Hope said.

Not a baby. *Not a baby!* My own bones went limp.

"There's something else in here." Matt unwrapped something from the paper. As I watched, he pulled out an Old Crow whiskey bottle.

"Oh my. That's what Charlie drank." I felt my legs go weak. Hope grabbed my arms and helped me to a chair.

"Did you have a dog?" Hope asked me.

"No," Gran said. "Charlie always said they were too much trouble." Actually, his mother had said that, and Charlie had just accepted it, like he accepted most pronouncements from his parents.

"Did you know anyone who did?"

"Well, sure. But not in Mississippi. We didn't really know our neighbors. We stayed to ourselves because of the false pregnancy."

"This is the suitcase that was in the trunk of the car?"

"Oh, yes. I'm sure of it. I'd never seen a suitcase like that before."

Matt continued to paw through the paper. "Look — here's a dog collar and a tag!"

He lifted a cracked leather collar and read the tin tag. "Sonny. Fourteen Belmont Street, Cratchatee, Mississippi."

"Where's Cratchatee?" Hope asked.

"It's a small town east of Jackson." I sank back in the chair and pulled off my gloves. Tears filled my eyes.

"Are you okay, Gran?"

I nodded, but my mind was reeling. "I don't understand. Why would Charlie bury a dog? What happened to the baby?" Tears

535

flowed down my cheeks. I tossed the gloves aside and wiped my face on my sleeve, my gut churning. "I was supposed to straighten out this whole mess. How am I going to do that now?"

"I thought the important thing was to find the suitcase and alleviate your fears," Hope said.

"But this doesn't alleviate them!" I clasped and unclasped my hands in my lap, rocking back and forth in a chair that wasn't a rocker. "I still don't know what happened to the baby!"

"Are you sure there was one?" Matt asked softly.

"Yes. Positively. And now . . . well, now I guess I'll go to my grave not knowing."

"Are you sure you *want* to know?"

I actually hadn't been sure before, but I was now. "Yes."

Matt closed the lid on the trunk. "Well, then, I can track down this address and find out who was living there at the time."

My chest fluttered with hope. "Oh, could you?"

Matt looked at Hope, and she nodded. He grinned at me, and he was so handsome, so confident, that for a moment it was like looking at Joe. "Sure thing, Miss Addie," he said. "Sure thing."

44
MATT

Before we found the suitcase, I'd thought that all of Miss Addie's tales about dead babies and B-24 flights might be nothing more than the imaginings of a partially senile woman with head trauma. But as she filled me in on some of the details of what had happened sixty-something years earlier, I couldn't help but think what a reliable witness she'd make in the courtroom. She was coherent and exact. She told the story consistently from her own perspective, as an observer and participant. These were memories, not wild permutations of an injured mind.

Preliminary research online to find the address was nonproductive. The town map didn't even list a Belmont Street. A call to the tax assessor's office in Cratchatee County on Monday revealed that no property records prior to 1995 were available digitally, but were open to the public in files at the courthouse.

I called Hope. "Are you up for a road trip? I can take Friday off."

So that's how we ended up headed to Cratchatee, Mississippi, the following week. We left at seven in the morning because it was a three-hour drive, but the time just flew. Hope and I talked about all kinds of things — movies and music, religion and politics, current events, and even our marriages. When I told her about Christine's sudden passing, her eyes filled with tears. She reached out her hand, and I took it, and I drove like that the rest of the way, holding her hand.

I told her about growing up in Texas, and she told me about her childhood. I learned that her parents had married late in life, that her dad had been eighteen years older than her mother, and that her mom had been forty-two when Hope was born. Losing her mom had been a huge blow to her, and had left her so sad and lonely it had been easy for her opportunistic ex to take advantage of her.

Hearing how this jag-off had moved in on her when she was at her lowest point made me furious. I'm not a violent person, but I wanted to smack him in the face.

Our conversation flowed easily, covering

both deep and shallow terrain, with a strong undercurrent of sexual tension. I was not only attracted to Hope; I also genuinely liked and respected her. She was smart, fair-minded, funny, and empathetic. Hanging out with Hope felt like hanging out with a friend I'd known for years.

My father had told me many years ago that the true test of a relationship was a road trip. All I can say is, Hope and I passed with flying colors.

The tax assessor's office was at the court-house, which was located in the center of town. A helpful clerk told me that Belmont Street probably had been located outside of the actual town limits. Many dirt roads had existed in the forties and fifties that were no longer there or had been renamed.

A search of old records on microfiche showed that the street had been located about eight miles west of town and that 14 Belmont had been owned by an Edsel Wortner. Apparently the house had been torn down to make way for a new housing development in the sixties. No current listings for Wortners were listed in the Cratchatee records or any online search sites.

"You need to find some old-timers," the assessor's clerk told us.

"Where should we look?" Hope asked.

"Well, there's the nursing home on Elm Street."

"Most of the folks in there have dementia," said a woman wearing a Realtor's name tag who was doing a title search. She'd been listening unapologetically to our conversation. "If I were you, I'd start with the downtown diner."

So that's what we did.

A cowbell jangled over the door as we walked in. Sure enough, a couple of elderly men — one with an oxygen tube in his nose, chewing on an unlit cigar, and the other dipping snuff — sat in the back booth, sipping coffee.

A waitress with long blond hair had her back to us as she cleared the plates from a table. "Sit anywhere you like," she called. When she turned around, I was shocked to see that her face was creased and wizened, her upper lip long and pleated like corrugated tin. Her monkey-ish face was about fifty years older than the lush mane of hair. The disconnect threw me. I stared for a moment before it hit me: she was a senior citizen wearing a Blake Lively wig.

Hope spoke up while I was still gathering my wits. "We're looking for some information. We found a dog tag with an address among my grandmother's things, and we were wondering if anyone here could tell us where the property is."

"What's the address?"

I told her. She pulled her mouth to one side as she raked food off the plates into a trash can. "Never heard of that one." She turned and hollered to the men in the back. "Buster, Willard — y'all ever hear of Belmont Street?"

"Hotchkiss Road used to be called that," the one with the oxygen said. "My uncle used to live there."

We headed to the back of the diner and introduced ourselves. The men returned the favor. The one with the oxygen was Buster.

"Can we sit down and buy you a cup of coffee?" I asked.

"We'd be delighted." Willard scooted over in his booth and smiled at Hope. His large size left about six inches of clearance for Hope. "Our coffee is always on the house, but I wouldn't mind a piece of that pecan pie."

"Gertie'll skin you alive if you eat that," Buster said.

"What she don't know won't hurt her," Willard replied.

"You think anything happens in this town that Gertie don't find out about?"

"Pshaw."

I pulled up a chair for Hope, then sat down beside Buster.

Willard raised his hand. "Myrtle, darlin', would you bring me a piece of that pie? And don' you go lecturin' me or lettin' on to Gertie."

"I won't play no part in you killin' yourself. I've got some nonfat yogurt in the back if you want somethin' sweet."

"Hell," he grumbled. "Can't get away with nothin'. My wife has spies all over town."

After the waitress brought the yogurt, a Danish for Buster (who apparently had no wife watching his diet), and coffee for Hope and me, I started in again. "Were you all around during the late forties?"

"Hell, we've been here all our lives." Buster took a swig of coffee. "Both of us have."

"Any idea who Edsel Wortner was?"

Both men nodded. "He was a older German guy," Willard said. "Some folks thought he was a spy during the war. Rumor had it he was sent to an internment camp."

"What happened to his house?" I asked. "The records at the courthouse show he still owned it in 1948."

"His daughter rented it out," Willard said. "It was always rundown and trashy-looking."

"Do you remember who lived there in September of 1948?"

"Ha! I can't even remember where *I* lived in September 1948." Buster laughed loudly at his own joke.

"Why do you want to know?" asked Willard. He spit a mouthful of tobacco into a coffee can sitting on the table, wiped his mouth with the back of his red-splotched hand, then spooned a huge scoop of yogurt into his mouth.

"My great-uncle had a job that involved a lot of travel, and he had a lady friend here," Hope said. We'd discussed this on the trip from the courthouse; I'd advised Hope that older folks in Mississippi were so intrinsically polite they might be reluctant to talk about the scandalous behavior of a young woman's direct ancestor, so she might get better results framing the story around a more distant relative. She pulled out a picture of her grandfather — one of the few she'd found that fully showed his face. It showed a young man gazing at the camera with a tender expression — no doubt because he was in love with the photographer. "He was a drinker and a rounder. The lady ended up having his baby."

"My, my, my — a real soap opera of a situation," Willard said.

Hope nodded. "We're trying to find out what happened to the baby. The problem is, we don't know the mother's name. When we found the dog tag with the address, well, we thought it might be a clue."

Buster squinted at the photo. "I don't recognize him."

Willard took the photo, looked at it, and shook his head. "I'll tell you who might — Darlene Lynch. She's in the nursing home on Elm Street."

"Yeah." Buster nodded. "Darlene might know."

"She was the hostess at the Red Lantern honky-tonk out on the highway," Willard said.

"What's the connection to the Wortner place?" I asked.

"It was kind of a flop house within walking distance of the bar," Buster explained. "When customers were too drunk to go home or needed a private place to hoochy-cooch . . ." He cast Hope an apologetic look. "Pardon my French, ma'am. Anyway, the Red Lantern put 'em up there. For a fee, of course."

"Is Darlene still in her right mind?" I asked.

"Don't rightly know. Probably as right as it ever was." Willard looked at Buster, who let out a loud guffaw. "Just know she'll be easy to spot. She's always had a tower of flame-red hair."

Hope's face lit up. "Thank you. Thank you very much!"

It worried me, how optimistic Hope looked. She seemed to think this was all going to work out.

I had a bad feeling that even if we got the information we wanted, She would end up disappointed or heartbroken.

A separate, self-protective part of my brain sent up a warning flare. Maybe I should be worrying about just how much I was worrying about Hope.

The nursing home smelled like canned peas, urine, and floral air freshener. We were told that Darlene was in the middle of playing spades in the activity room. An aide went to ask her if she wanted to see visitors, and came back with word that we were to wait until the game was over. Hope and I cooled our heels in the lobby for twenty minutes.

Finally an aide wheeled in an elderly woman with a heavily sprayed beehive of bright red hair. She wore a boldly flowered, muumuu-looking thing that showed a disconcerting amount of crepey décolletage.

I introduced Hope and myself. "How do you do," she said, extending her hand to me with the palm down, as if she expected me to kiss it. Not sure what to do, I took it and bent over it. Hope extended her hand, too, but Darlene ignored it.

"We were wondering if you knew this man." Hope handed her the photo of her grandfather.

She looked at it for a long moment, like a poker player regarding her cards. "Who is this to you?"

"He's my great-uncle," Hope said. "We understand he got a girl pregnant, and we were wondering what happened to the baby."

"Ah." She handed the photo back to her. "And why do you want to know?"

Hope briefly explained, substituting "great-aunt" for "grandmother" and leaving out the part about the suitcase. "So . . . can you help us?"

"With what, dear?"

Hope glanced at me, her optimism visibly dimmed. "With what really happened to the baby."

She cut her eyes away in a cagey manner. "Well, now, I don't want to betray any confidences."

I leaned forward. "Please, Miss Darlene.

546

It would mean a great deal to her aunt. She's very elderly, and she says she can't die in peace until she knows what happened to her late husband's baby."

She cocked her head to the side. A loose piece of skin under her chin wagged like a turkey's wattle. "Elderly, huh? I've always had a soft spot in my heart for the elderly."

I suppressed a smile. She was probably in her late eighties, but apparently didn't think she herself fell into the category.

She narrowed her already narrow eyes. "You say your uncle is dead?"

Hope nodded.

"Well, in that case, I suppose I might be persuaded to tell you what I know." She gave me a long look, the kind that had subtext. "Let's go outside so I can have a smoke."

It took a few moments to get an aide to punch in the code that allowed us to exit. I pushed Miss Darlene's wheelchair out to an ash can beside a concrete bench by the parking lot. She drew a Virginia Slim out of a jeweled cigarette case hidden in a pocket of her muumuu. I took the lighter from her and lit her cigarette.

"Thank you," she said, batting her eyes at me and drawing a deep drag.

"Can you tell us about the woman and

the baby?" Hope prompted.

"I'm not sure I can exactly remember." Miss Darlene cast me another sidelong glance.

I pulled out my wallet and took out two twenties. "Perhaps this will jog your memory."

She gave me a sly smile. "It might be starting to come back to me."

I peeled off another bill. Miss Darlene took all three, snaked them into her wrinkled décolletage, and blew out a mouthful of smoke. "First of all, the baby wasn't his."

Hope's eyes flew wide.

"Are you sure?" I asked.

"Oh, yeah. Real sure. Joan was pregnant before she ever met the man in your photo."

"Joan — that's the name of the mother?"

She nodded. "Joan Johnson. She was a waitress at the Red Lantern. She'd had an affair with a smooth-talking huckster a month earlier. He said he sold oil field equipment, and he scammed Tommy Joe Harmon out of nearly four thousand dollars — which was a lot of money back then, let me tell you — and then he up and left town." She took another drag from her cigarette. "A month later, Joan finds out she's in a motherly way."

She shook her head and blew out a smoke

ring. "That Joan — 'bout as gullible a girl as you could find. That shyster promised to take her to Paris. Paris! Can you imagine fallin' for a line like that? She'd even asked me if I'd watch her dog while she was gone. She had this scraggly little mutt she loved more than life itself."

She shook her head. "Anyway, Joan was in a mell of a hess, as we used to say, when she found out she was pregnant. She didn't have people."

Hope's forehead wrinkled. "People?"

"Family. Her people had all moved away or died off. She was a sweet girl — she had a real soft heart. Little soft in the head, too, I think. If you saw the way she carried on about her mutt, you'd know for sure she was a mite pixilated." She pointed to her head.

"Anyway. This man — name was Charlie; I called him Charlie Horse, because he always wore such a long face — starts comin' to the bar pretty regular, every couple of weeks or so. He's a woebegone-lookin' fella. Don't know as I ever saw such a hangdog face in my life."

I pictured the man in the photo with his heart in his eyes. I could just imagine how he'd look if that heart had been broken.

"You remembered his name," Hope said,

her voice barely above a whisper.

"Honey, I remember everything that happened. He and Joan had one of the strangest stories you ever heard." She took another pull on her cigarette.

"Anyway, Joan hated to see folks lookin' sad. We all did. Customers down in the dumps never left good tips, and they have a way of dragging down the mood of the whole place. But that wasn't why Joan chatted him up. Like I said, she had a soft heart. It was her downfall, really, being that soft. She said he seemed lonely. So they started talking, and before you know it, she's told him her situation.

"Well, Charlie offered to help her out. He said he'd take care of her when she started to show and couldn't work — that he'd pay her rent and buy her groceries and pay for the doctor."

"So they had an affair?" I asked.

"No. That's the weird part. He just wanted the baby. Said he was gonna tell his wife he'd had an affair and gotten a girl pregnant, and he wanted to bring the baby home and have his wife raise it as some kind of punishment or payback or some such. He had this wild scheme about his wife padding her stomach and tricking everyone into thinking she was pregnant herself."

A mellow musical gong sounded, like the recorded dinner announcement on a cruise ship.

"That's lunch," Miss Darlene said. "I've gotta go in if I don't want to miss out."

"We won't keep you but another moment," I said. "So what finally happened?"

"Well, Joan worked at the bar until the beginning of the sixth month, and then Hank — he was the owner; kind of a gorilla, but not as bad as some I've known — told her she had to quit. Said she was bad for business, too much a reminder of the wages of sin. The boardinghouse she lived in kicked her out, too. Life was hard on unmarried pregnant girls back then." She took another toke of her Virginia Slim.

"Hank had this dive of a house he rented for special customers to use, if you get my drift, and Charlie sublet it for Joan."

"He treated her well?" Hope asked.

"Oh yeah. He was real good to her — paid for her food, maternity clothes, and everything else. Took her dog to the vet and bought it a collar with her new address on the tag because that mutt was always gettin' lost. He even bought her a new set of luggage so she could move somewhere else after everything was all over. Toward the end of her pregnancy, he even paid a woman to cook and clean and take care of her after she had the baby. Beulah was her name."

Darlene paused as a woman in blue scrubs came out the door. "Charlie would visit Joan every Friday. He'd drink and caterwaul about how his wife was cold and mean to him. Joan realized he didn't really want the baby. He only wanted to make his wife jealous, and the wife wasn't actin' jealous; she just acted as if she despised him. He'd talk about his wife and cry. He was a weepy drunk."

She took another pull off her cigarette. "Well, as Joan's belly got bigger and bigger, the baby started to seem more an' more real. Joan started thinkin' about the poor little thing, an' she decided she didn't want a sad-sack crazy man and a woman who didn't want his baby to be raisin' it. But she needed financing, to make it through the pregnancy, so she led Charlie on — and on the side, she started makin' adoption arrangements with a local doctor. He found a couple in Alabama willing to pay good money for the baby. She'd get a lump sum and the doctor would get a nice fat finder's fee."

Darlene inhaled a deep lungful of smoke. "By then, Charlie had moved to Jackson with his wife, and he was comin' by every

Tuesday and Thursday evening. Joan delivered the baby at home on a Wednesday night, and the doctor whisked the baby out of state. Joan didn't call Charlie like she'd promised she would when the baby came. Instead, the next night when he was due to visit, she made sure she had another waitress, Sarah, and her husband, Ben, with her, as well as Beulah. She was worried what Charlie would do when he found out the baby was gone."

"Oh, wow," Hope whispered.

"It's a good thing she had people with her, because when Joan broke the news, well, Charlie went crazy. Not violent crazy, just crazy crazy. They say he let out a loud yowl, fell to his knees, and rolled around on the floor, then got up and paced and cried, cried and paced. Sarah's husband poured him glass after glass of bourbon until Charlie was in a stupor.

"Finally, around three in the morning, he left the house. He wasn't drivin' too good. Sarah and Ben left shortly thereafter. They found Charlie standin' on the side of the road, a pistol in his hand."

"Oh no!" Hope murmured.

"Apparently he'd accidentally run over Joan's dog. The poor thing wasn't dead, but he was in bad shape, so Charlie had gotten his pistol out of the car and shot it to put it out of its misery. Ben grabbed the gun and put it in his own car. He said he was afraid Charlie might try to kill himself.

"Sarah and Ben drove on home, but Charlie wrapped that dog in a baby blanket — apparently he had one in the trunk for takin' the baby home — then turned around an' carried it up to Joan's front door. Well, Joan was hysterical. She thought he'd killed her dog out of spite, to get even with her. She was scared he'd come back to kill her. Charlie tried to explain that he was sorry as sorry could be, an' that he'd come back just to apologize, an' he figured she'd want to bury her dog, but he was drunk an' not makin' all that much sense, an' Joan was terrified.

"To make him go away, Beulah hauled out one of the brand-new suitcases Charlie had bought for Joan. She gave it to him an' said, 'Bury the dog in this.' Charlie left, an' Joan hightailed it out of state the next mornin', despite just birthin' a baby two days afore. Never saw nor heard of either one again."

The musical gong sounded again.

"That's last call." Darlene pulled her cigarette from the holder, snuffed it out in the sand on the concrete ash can, then put the holder in a pocket hidden in the side of her muumuu. "I gotta go on in or I'll miss a meal. The food's not that great, but I won' be cheated out of anything I'm due."

I had a feeling she'd had a life of being cheated — and the person who'd probably cheated her the most was herself.

"Thank you for talking to us." I pulled out another twenty and handed it to her.

"My pleasure. Thank you kindly." She took the bill and stuffed it in her bosom. "My goodness, it's been a while since I've been around a real gentleman!" She gave me a coquettish little wink, and for half a second, I could see her as she must have been back in the day — all womanly wiles and compliments and southern charm, parting men from their money easy as a comb parts hair.

45
ADELAIDE

I sat there, my hands limp in my lap, as
Matt and Hope finished telling me all that
they'd learned in Mississippi. Relief flowed
through me like some kind of intravenous
painkiller. Charlie hadn't killed that baby
after all! He'd never even seen it. It wasn't
even his! And that blood on his clothes — it
had belonged to the woman's dog. And the
pistol was missing because that man Ben
had taken it.

I'd no sooner tasted the sweetness of relief
than regret shoved its ugly snout in my face.
Oh, heavens. I'd been so unfair to Charlie.
So hideously, horribly unfair!

Charlie had tried to tell me, hadn't he?
He'd tried to tell me afterward, but I was
too angry — angry and disgusted and
revolted. I'd just turned away.

Oh, I should have known he couldn't do
such a thing! I should have been more sensitive! But I'd been too wrapped up in my

own heartache to think about his. I must have spoken out loud, because Hope tried to console me, but the memories were crowding in, and I couldn't hear anything except my own thoughts.

1948

I'd hated lying and pretending to be pregnant, but by the time the baby was due, I felt like I *was* having a baby. I was looking forward to having a new little life to nurture. I'd been hopeful that it could be a new beginning for Charlie and me.

But when there was no baby, it all boiled up inside me again, worse than ever. All that Charlie had put me through, forcing me to deceive my friends and family like that! I felt like such a wretchful fraud.

Of course, he must have felt that way, too, when he married me and pretended Becky was his — but that had been a good thing, a happy thing. He'd gained a child.

I had no one to talk to about it but Charlie — and I hated him. I deplore having to admit it — hate is the worst sin, isn't it? — but I did. It churned in my belly like battery acid. And I'm so sorry for it! But for months there, I just hated him.

The most shameful thing about my behavior is that I was furious he picked that particular time to turn over a new leaf. He stopped drinking, he was an attentive father, he read the Bible. He was good with the children, considerate toward me, and did chores around the house without me even asking. The nicer, the more godly, the kindlier, the more thoughtful he was, the angrier I got. I was so, so angry — white-hot, blue-flame angry.

Everyone thought I was cantankerous because I was grieving the baby. Mother insisted that Dr. Henry come see me. I was mortified. All the lies about why I hadn't seen him — his questions about my problems with the baby — why, I didn't know what to say. He thought I was having another nervous breakdown.

And maybe I was, because that's when I wrote to Joe. I couldn't keep all the secrets inside anymore. They were just eating me up, just gnawing at me day and night.

I wanted to telephone, but I couldn't. Long-distance calls went through a local operator, and the whole town would know my business. Same thing with sending a telegram. So one day, while Charlie was at work and the kids were playing at my friend Marie's house, I sat down and wrote a letter. I told him how I couldn't bear for Charlie to touch me, how just looking at him made me sick. How I dreamed about just not waking up, but I didn't want to leave my children motherless.

I begged him to please come and get me before I lost my mind.

Well, the phone rang before I finished. It was my neighbor Marie — Becky had fallen and cut her head, and it looked like she might need stitches. Well, I dashed out the door without another thought. I just dashed.

And it ended up that, yes, she needed stitches. And by the time I got her to the doctor's office, and we'd been seen, and all the stitching and instructions and everything were taken care of, it was supper time. I panicked, because I remembered I'd left the letter out. I hurried home, but it was too late. Charlie had already seen it.

I knew, because the letter was gone. So was the bottle of scotch hidden in the back of the kitchen cabinet — and the cabinet was open. There was no sign of Charlie, which meant he must be out drinking.

I thought about what I had written — the cruel things I'd said, the vile way I'd portrayed him, the revulsion I'd expressed — and, well, I just felt heartsick. Ashamed. Horrified. Horrible. The truth is, Charlie's biggest flaw was loving me, and I'd turned him into a monster. I was literally nauseous at the thought of how much that letter must have had hurt him.

But on another level, I felt something else: relieved.

He'd have to agree to a divorce now. He couldn't want to live with a wife who felt the way I did. He just couldn't. I sagged into my chair. I was tired, so tired of hiding my feelings. So tired of running away. It was time to confront this thing, head-on.

I put the children to bed — I had to cut Becky's shirt off her little body, because it pulled on over her head, and there was another round of tears because it was her favorite shirt. This last crying spell left me completely exhausted, but I was too upset to go to bed. Charlie was out drinking, and there was no telling what he would do when he got home.

I heard a knock on the door. I saw police lights outside. My first thought was, *They're bringing Charlie home because he passed out drunk.*

But it was John Carter, an officer who was a couple of years behind me in school, and he was alone. He pulled off his cap and twisted it in his hands in a way that made my stomach pull back against my spine. "Mrs. McCauley, I hate to tell you this, but Charlie's been in an accident."

The breath whooshed out of my lungs. Every scrap of air seemed to leave the cells of my body.

"He's at the parish hospital."

"Is he . . ."

My heart was in my throat, gagging me with terror.

"He's alive, but it's bad, ma'am. He ran into the bridge culvert."

"Was anyone else . . ."

He misinterpreted what I was going to ask. Apparently he'd had other experiences with drinking men, men who'd been found in situations hard to explain to their wives. "Oh, he was all by himself, ma'am. Completely alone. But . . . he'd been drinking."

"I — I see." That certainly wasn't news. I put my hand to my throat. "Was any other car involved?"

"Not that we know of. Someone might have run him off the road, or maybe he swerved to avoid an animal. Or maybe he just lost control of the car." He looked down at it his boots. "He smelled awful strong of whiskey."

Oh, dear Lord — did he do it on purpose? The thought made my legs turn to rubber. I clutched the doorframe.

"You okay, ma'am?"

"I think maybe I should sit down."

He came into the room and helped me get settled in a chair. I ran my hand over my face. He brought me a damp towel from the kitchen, which I put over my eyes for a moment.

"Is there someone you want me to call?" he asked.

His mother. And my mother. They both needed to be called. I pulled off the towel and shook my head. "I'll do it."

I moved as if in a stupor. I'm not sure if I thanked him. I called — oh, thank God for family! — my mother first. She called Charlie's parents, then came over to stay with the kids, and my father drove me to the hospital.

The whole time, I was making bargains with God. *Please, God. Let him live. I'll do anything. I'll be good. I'll be a faithful, loving wife till death do us part. I will. I swear I will.*

Charlie was in surgery when I got there. The doctors told me he'd broken both legs and his back, and he had chest injuries and head injuries. If he made it through surgery and the long recovery period that was to follow, he might be paralyzed from the waist down. They warned that he might not remember the events of the accident or even a day or two before. I prayed he wouldn't remember the letter.

But he did. They allowed me to be with him in the recovery room. As soon as he came to, he opened his eyes, looked at me, and closed them again. "I'm sorry," he murmured.

"For what?"

"For not getting out of your way."

Well, guilt just opened its enormous jaws and swallowed me whole. Let me tell you a thing or two about guilt. It's a monstrous glutton with shark teeth, rows and rows of teeth that cut and cut and just keep on cutting. There's no smooth esophagus you eventually slide down — just cuts and more cuts, and then you're in the belly of the beast, all hacked up and bathed in acid. And just when you think it might be easing up, that ugly monster spits you out, then bites down and starts chewing on you all over again.

I vowed to turn over a new leaf. I would become a better person. An upright person. A person of total integrity. I would do what the boys in the war had done: I would put one foot in front of the other and keep on marching, keep on slogging. The only way out is through. I realized now, when it was maybe too late, that the key to life was just that simple. Wherever you are, whatever situation you're in, the only way out is through.

I stayed at the hospital the next few days, while Charlie's life hung in the balance. He didn't speak again, and I began to hope I'd misunderstood him or misinterpreted his words. Maybe he wouldn't remember the letter after all.

But when I finally went home to sleep at the insistence of Mother, I found the letter and a note from Charlie tucked under my pillow.

Can't live without you.

Funny, I thought. Because I was finding it nigh near impossible to live with myself.

46
MATT

I had to leave Friday just as Miss Addie was ending her story — the children came home, then I had to take them to a friend's birthday party at a skating rink in Hammond. On Saturday morning I had to go to my office in Baton Rouge for a deposition, so I didn't get a chance to see Hope again until the next afternoon.

I called her on the way back to Wedding Tree, and she met me at her grandmother's backyard swing while Miss Addie took a nap.

"Where are the girls?" she asked, handing me a glass of iced tea.

"Jillian took them to the Global Wildlife Preserve." I put my arm around her shoulders and set the swing in motion. "So I've been dying to know — what happened with your grandfather after the accident?"

"He could never walk again. My mother and Uncle Eddie grew up with a father in a

565

wheelchair."

"Wow. That had to be pretty limiting back then."

"It was, but Gran built a ramp on the back of the house and added the downstairs bedroom. The lumberyard built a ramp, too, and as soon as he was able, Granddad went to the store every day."

"What about the store in Mississippi?"

"It was sold before it even opened." Hope took a sip of tea. "When Mom and Uncle Eddie started school, Gran began taking photographs professionally. She started with a friend's wedding, then her reputation spread. Without really trying, she had more business than she could handle."

"What about their marriage?" I was wondering if they still had sex. After the accident, could Charlie even get it up? And even if he physically could, would he want to, after finding out she secretly despised him? But those were guy questions, too crass to ask — and none of them were my business anyway. Which didn't keep me from being curious as hell.

"Mom said they had separate bedrooms." Hope tucked a strand of hair behind her ear. "She said a woman from the next town came in to give Granddad a massage once or twice a week. Mom once said she always suspected something more was going on between Charlie and the masseuse."

"Oh, wow."

"Yeah." The swing creaked in silence for a moment. "Here's the weird part: Gran hired her."

"No kidding?"

"That's what Mom told me. It was someone they'd known in high school."

I rubbed her arm and pondered that. It was a little shocking, but at the same time, it was actually very kind and compassionate. Loving, even, under the circumstances.

A strand of Hope's hair blew across my cheek, and the memory of her hair on my face when we were lying in the garden shed hit me straight in the groin.

"How 'bout I give *you* a massage?"

"Now?"

"Jillian texted five minutes ago and they're still at Global Wildlife. No one will be at my house for at least an hour."

"And Gran's sound asleep." Hope put her feet on the ground, stopping the swing, and gave me a sexy smile. "What are we waiting for?"

47
HOPE

I had an idea where we were going, but it wasn't until we hit the top of the stairs and he turned left that I knew for sure. "Are you sure it's okay for me to be in here?" I asked as he pulled me into his bedroom, where soft afternoon light filtered through the windows. "There's that spare room down the hall, or . . ."

"This is fine," he said, closing the door and locking it before drawing me into an embrace.

"You were pretty upset the first time I was in here."

"I overreacted."

"To what, exactly?" I'd been thinking and thinking about it, and I'd wondered if he'd been upset that I'd somehow defiled Christine's memory. He headed to the bed and pulled down the comforter. Was this the bed that he'd shared with Christine? The thought creeped me out a little.

"To the fact I was attracted to you."

My heart lifted like a butterfly. "You were?"

"From the moment I saw you." He sat down on the white sheets. "But I have to say, I thought you were a little . . . odd."

"Is that a polite term for cray-cray?"

"Well, you *were* wearing a fairy costume."

"It was my grandmother's nightgown."

He lifted a teasing eyebrow. "Like that's completely normal?"

I laughed and sat down beside him.

He lifted a strand of my hair. "I just thought you were, as Zoey would say, in'propriate. And when the girls came home, I had a mental image of them telling their preschool teacher that they'd seen the pretty neighbor lady in Daddy's bedroom, and having it turn into this whole small-town gossip thing." He pulled me down until we were lying side by side. "And the thing is, I wanted it to be true."

"You did?"

"Yeah. But I didn't want to want you."

"But you couldn't help yourself, because I'm so amazingly irresistible . . . even though you thought I was deranged."

"That's it, exactly." His eyes were tender and amused.

"I have to ask . . . is this the bed where

you and Christine . . . ?"

He closed his eyes. "Conceived Zoey and Sophie? No. I got a new bed after she died in that one."

"Oh!" My heart lurched. "Oh, I'm so sorry! Oh, wow . . ." I put my hands over my face. What was wrong with me, asking a question like that? "Oh, Matt — I feel terrible. That was completely tactless and thoughtless. I don't know what I was thinking! I wasn't thinking, that's the problem, and now I've gone and spoiled the moment, and you probably wish . . . I bet you want me to just leave." I started to stand up.

He grabbed my hand and pulled me back on the bed. "What I want, Hope, is for you to shut up and kiss me." He grinned at me. "Did I mention you're a bit odd?"

The terrible tightness in my gut unfurled. I grinned back and let him pull me down, and suddenly his lips were covering mine, and my motormouthitis came to an abrupt halt, because I was too busy getting thoroughly kissed.

The kiss moved to my neck, then Matt pulled off my shirt, and then my bra.

His finger traced a circle around one nipple, then his mouth followed. Heat shot right to my groin.

"I want to see you naked," he whispered

close to my ear.

"Me, too. I mean, I want to see *you* that way — not myself. I see myself naked all the time," I babbled.

He smiled. "Lucky you."

He stood up, stripped off his shirt, kicked off his shoes, then pulled off his pants and underwear in a single move. My breath hitched. I'd felt his six-pack the night in the shed, but seeing it was a whole other thing. It was hard to keep my eyes above his waist, though, because he was massively aroused.

The mattress dipped beneath me as he sank down on it, pulled off my skirt, then wrangled my panties down my legs.

"Oh, man — you're so beautiful."

I started to protest that no, my breasts were too small and I hadn't gone to a gym in ages, but those thoughts were cut off by the smoky heat in his eyes. He obviously liked what he was seeing — and I was so turned on by everything about him that my lady parts felt like they were melting.

He stretched over me and kissed me. I was so aroused I nearly forgot to breathe, but breathing didn't seem like a necessity. All that seemed absolutely essential was the continued touch of his hands on my body, the feel of his naked skin against mine, the heat of his erection pressing hard against my belly. He kissed a trail down my stomach, lower and lower until he reached the part of me that throbbed for his touch. His fingers and his tongue worked magic.

"Now," I gasped at length. "I need you *now.*"

He raised up and pulled a foil packet out of the bedside drawer. A moment later, he hovered over me, taking his time, the thick tip of him easing in, then pulling out until I ached with wanting, with longing, with raw needy need.

And then he drove home, filling me completely. I came on that first thrust, I was so ready — and then it started to build all over again, that delicious pulsating desire, spiraling higher and higher. This time he came with me.

When I finally regained the ability to think, I realized I was crying.

He brushed my cheek with his thumb. "Hey — are you okay?"

"Yeah. Just relieved. Or maybe I mean released. Or both."

"Me, too." He grinned down at me. "In fact, I probably should be bawling like a baby."

I smiled up. "Please don't."

"Okay," he said, and kissed me instead.

48
MATT

The girls burst through the front door a little after five o'clock. "Daddy! Daddy! We had the bestest day ever!"

Hope had left just ten minutes earlier. The day rated pretty high on my great-day scale, too. I came out of the kitchen, where I had just grabbed a beer.

"I got to feed the animals!" Zoey said.

"Me, too," said Sophie, not about to be outdone.

I knelt, scooped them both up in my arms, and carried them to the sofa. They were getting to be more than an armful, I thought wistfully.

The girls fought for space on my lap. Jillian stood in the doorway, smiling.

"So what did you do?" I asked.

"Well, first, we drove and drove and drove," Zoey related. She had a habit of giving factual timeline narratives. "And then we got out, and there were all these ducks."

"And geese," Sophie added.

"And other birds. And we bought some food, and fed them."

"And one of the geese tried to bite me!"

"And then we all got into a covered wagon with an engine with some other families, and we went on a ride."

"A safari!"

"Yeah. There were all kinds of animals."

"An' some of them are dangerous."

Zoey looked down her nose at her little sister. "You mean endangered. They weren't dangerous."

" 'Cept for the zebras. They're mean, so you can't feed them or ride them," Sophie announced.

"They had camels, and a baby giraffe who ate right out of my bucket!" Sophie said. "I got to pet his head! He has the softest lips."

"Yeah." Zoey nodded. "Like Mommy's used to be."

A dagger went right through my heart. Could she even remember her mother? I wondered.

"And like Aunt Jillian's," Zoey quickly added. "She's just like Mommy, 'cause they have the same genes."

I avoided looking at Jillian.

"But she doesn't wear them," Sophie said. " 'Cause Mommy was skinnier."

Jillian's face turned scarlet.

"Not those kind of jeans, dumbo," Zoey said.

"Don't call your sister names," I said. "When you were her age, you didn't know one type of jean from the other, either."

"Zoey, can you explain the difference?" Jillian asked.

"Well, one kind is what you wear, and the other is something inside you, like blood."

Sophie screwed up her face. "How does it get inside you?"

"Every living thing has a set of instructions for what it's going to look like, and these instructions are called genes," Jillian explained. "But they're spelled differently from the pant kind."

The answer seemed to satisfy Sophie, and the conversation returned to the animals. The girls ran upstairs to get their stuffed animals and reenact the Global Wildlife experience.

I felt strangely awkward alone with Jillian. "Sounds like you had a great time. I hope they weren't too much of a handful."

"Not at all. You know I love spending time with the girls." She paused. "It's a shame you couldn't go with us."

"Yeah, well . . . I had to catch up on some work from taking yesterday off."

575

"I heard you helped Miss Adelaide find some information she needed."

"Yes."

She cocked her head and looked at me, apparently expecting me to give her more information. When I didn't, she gave a forced-looking smile. "Well, it was nice of you to help out."

"And it was good of you to take the girls to Global Wildlife." This conversation was weirdly formal. I'd felt increasingly uncomfortable around her lately.

"The girls asked if I'd make dinner for them tonight," Jillian said. "They wanted carrot salad and broccoli — probably the result of watching the animals eat. It's rare when they're willing to eat such healthy food, so I told them I'd fix it."

Ah, hell. I'd planned to just order a pizza and chill with the girls — Hope was going to work on the mural at the coffee shop tonight — but now it seemed I was stuck with Jillian.

I looked at her, and she skittishly cut her eyes away in a way that made me think of a domestic abuse victim. It made me feel horrible.

"Great," I forced myself to say.

A smile bloomed on her face. For just a second she resembled Christine, and then the similarity was gone. "Well, then, I guess I'll get started. We picked up groceries on the way home."

"Okay. Thanks." I should offer to help. I'm sure that's what she wanted, but I just couldn't bring myself to do it. "I, uh, want to spend some time with the girls, so I'm going upstairs."

"Sure." She smiled brightly. I noticed she was wearing freshly applied lipstick. "I'll call you when it's ready."

The girls invited Jillian to stay for dinner, and I saw no way out of it without being flat-out rude. I focused on the girls and talked almost exclusively to them throughout the meal. Jillian sat at the end of the table, where Christine used to sit. I don't know if it was because of Hope or what, but I felt even more awkward than usual and couldn't wait for her to leave.

After dinner, I pushed back my chair. "I'll handle cleanup," I told Jillian. "You've pulled more than enough aunt duty today."

Just then Zoey sidled up, holding her stomach. "I want go to bed," she said in a thin voice. "Can you tuck me in, Aunt Jillian?"

Jillian felt her forehead. "Oh, dear — I hope you're not coming down with something. There's a terrible stomach bug going

577

around."

"Can you stay the night?" Zoey asked.

My stomach suddenly wasn't feeling so hot, either, but it wasn't because of a bug.

"I'd be happy to, but . . ." Jillian darted a glance at me. "It's up to your father."

"Pleeease, Daddy," Zoey pleaded. Her eyes filled with tears. "I miss my mommy, and I'd feel better if Aunt Jillian were here."

Boy, she really knew where to hit me. "I can take care of you, honey."

"I know, but you're not a lady. When I'm sick, I like soft hands like Mommy's."

Hell. I hated to have Jillian stay, but I couldn't find a way of denying the request that didn't leave me feeling like a monster.

"Well, if Jillian doesn't mind — okay."

"I don't mind," Jillian said. "I don't mind a bit."

49
MATT

Hope was wearing that thing I first saw her in, that sheer floaty gown from the 1940s, and we were in the diner in Mississippi, dancing like Fred and Ginger. We were doing all these wonderful, graceful, spontaneous moves — twists and dips and swings and what all. As the music slowed, I stretched her on a table — but then the lighting changed and the room kind of twirled and the table became a bed. The bed rotated and somehow so did we, so that she was behind me, spooning. She was warm and soft, and her arm was draped across my chest.

Something jarred me a little, pulling me up from the depths of sleep into shallower dream waters. I sighed and tried to fall back into the dream, imagining Hope was snuggled against me, and her hand was moving down my chest . . . down my belly . . . down to my cock, which immediately hardened.

My eyes jerked open. This was no dream. My sweatpants were loosened and a hand was closed around my penis, stroking up and down. Pleasure poured through me. Hope must have sneaked back into the house and into bed with me.

"This is quite a pleasant surp . . ." I rolled toward her, and the moonlight slanting through the window hosed my dream — and my erection — like cold water.

The face on the pillow wasn't Hope's; it was Jillian's.

"What — what the hell are you doing?" I gasped.

"Let me love you, Matt." She rose on an elbow, still reaching for my crotch.

I gripped her wrist and twisted away.

"It's okay," she purred. "It won't take away from your love for Christine. It can be so wonderful if you'll just let it happen."

"Stop it!" I scooted to the edge of the bed and switched on the light.

"You're upset."

I could barely bring myself to look at her. When I did, I wished I hadn't. She was wearing some low-cut nightgown that looked like it came from Frederick's of Hollywood. "Hell yes, I'm upset!"

"Matt, I can make you love me. I can love you enough for both of us until you do. I love the girls, and they need a mother. I'll be good for you. I can make you feel everything you felt with her, I swear it."

"Jillian, I don't want . . ." What the hell was I supposed to say? I ran a hand down my face and searched for the right words. "Look — I don't feel that way about you."

"You could if you'd give me a chance. You wanted me a moment ago. You were hard in my hand." She slid off the bed and onto her knees before me. Holy Moses — was she trying to go down on me? "Jesus, Jillian! Stop it!" I moved across the room to my dresser.

"Daddy?" I heard the door rattle. Apparently Jillian had locked it. Thank God for that. But still — Sophie was standing outside!

I adjusted my sweatpants and tried for a normal fatherly tone. "Are you feeling okay, honey?"

"Yes. But I heard voices. Is Aunt Jillian in there with you?"

Christ. What the hell was I supposed to do? If I lied to her, she could just walk down the hall and find Jillian's bed empty. She might have done that already. I opened my dresser, grabbed a T-shirt and pulled it on while Jillian wrapped herself in the bathrobe she'd apparently worn to my room. I strode

581

to the door and opened it. Sophie stood there, sucking her thumb. She peered around me and waved at Jillian.

Great, just great. She'd tell her grandparents, and everything would turn into a big ugly mess. "Jillian came in just a moment ago because, uh, she was, uh, feeling bad."

"Oh," Sophie's eyes unexpectedly filled with tears. She looked at Jillian. "Is it 'cause Zoey lied?"

"What?" I asked.

"She acted sick when she wasn't. My friend Savannah said that if you pretend to be sick when you're not, someone you love will get sick for real."

"Oh, no, honey." Jillian moved to the girl and took her in her arms. "That's not right. It's not Zoey's fault. I'm fine."

"But Daddy said you were sick."

Anger, cold and fierce as an arctic blizzard, blew through me.

"I had a bad dream that made me feel bad, but now I'm okay," Jillian said. "And Savannah's wrong. It doesn't work that way."

"Hold on a minute, Sophie," I said. "Zoey pretended to be sick this evening?"

She nodded, her eyes downcast. "We wanted Jillian to stay the night so she'd fix

582

blueberry pancakes in the morning."

I looked at Jillian. The stricken look on her face confirmed all my suspicions.

Sophie's eyes filled with tears. "I didn't mean to get Zoey in trouble."

It took all of my control to keep my voice calm. "Nobody's going to get in trouble, but I'm going to talk to Zoey. And neither of you should ever do this again, understand? Not because it'll make other people sick, but because it's not honest."

She nodded.

"Come on, sport. I'll tuck you back into bed."

I came out of the girls' bedroom a few minutes later to find Jillian sitting on the side of the bed in the guest room.

I couldn't bring myself to look directly at her. "Get dressed, get your things, and come downstairs," I ordered.

I changed out of my sweatpants and into a pair of jeans, then went to the kitchen, reached in the cabinet, and poured a stiff drink of bourbon. I couldn't remember the last time I'd felt so angry.

Jillian came into the kitchen a few minutes later, looking pale and shaken. "Matt, I didn't mean to upset you. I just wanted . . ."

I took a gulp of bourbon. It burned all the way down my throat. "It's pretty clear what you wanted."

Tears spilled down her face. "I can't help it, Matt. I love you. We would be so perfect together. I thought that if I could break through your defenses, then you'd see that."

The bourbon's warmth spread to my brain. Maybe the bourbon had been a bad idea. I certainly didn't feel any calmer. "So you told my daughter to lie to me?"

"I made sure she didn't say anything untruthful. She just said she was ready to go to bed."

"You coerced her into deliberately misleading me."

She looked at the floor. "That was wrong. I admit that. But, Matt — I can tell I'm running out of time. I've researched when a man is most likely to fall in love after the death of a spouse, and most widowers with small children are either in a serious relationship or married by now. You're ripe for the picking, and you're getting more and more attached to Hope, and she's going to leave, and then you and the girls will just be sad again. I thought if I could reach you before you and she . . ." Her voice broke off in a sob. She put her hands to her face. ". . . before you went too far with her."

Too late. But where the hell did she get the idea things worked like that?

She took a step toward me. "I know that you miss Christine. And I know that I'm not her. But I can make you happy. I know I can."

I held up both my hands, palms out. "Jillian . . . look. I just don't think of you that way."

"I know, I know, and that's the problem! You've got the sense of taboo because I was your sister-in-law, but that's just *ridiculous.*" She spit the word out as if it were rotten fruit. "You and I — we're not blood kin. And anyway, in the Old Testament, men are supposed to marry their widowed sisters-in-law, so this is the same thing."

I stared at her. *She convinced my daughter to lie to me, she woke me from a sound sleep with a hand job, she's saying the Bible says I'm supposed to marry her — and* I'm *ridiculous?* I took another swig of bourbon. Had she always been crazy, or was this a new development?

She took a step toward me, her eyes pleading. "There's nothing wrong with us being a couple — nothing wrong, and everything right. I thought that if I could get you to lower your inhibitions and see how wonderful things could be, well, then your feelings about me would change."

I held up my hands again. "Stop right

there. Don't come any closer. Listen to me, Jillian, because I only want to say this once: If I had never met your sister, and if I'd never met Hope, I still would not be romantically interested in you. There's nothing wrong with you — you're a terrific woman, Jillian — but the chemistry's just not there."

"But . . ."

"There are no buts to this. For me, there is no chemistry. None. Nothing. Nada. *Rien.* You need to accept it and move on. All of this . . ." I waved my glass, trying to encompass the whole scenario. ". . . well, it's just embarrassing."

She put her face in her hands and sobbed. I pulled a paper towel off the roll and handed it to her. The crying went on and on. I kept my physical distance.

"You okay?" I finally asked.

"I've never felt so humiliated in all my life," she sputtered.

"Yeah, well, I'm not so comfortable right now, either." I tried to lighten the mood. "I think we just raised the word 'awkward' to a whole new level."

She didn't smile as I'd hoped she would. She dabbed at the tears running down her face.

"Look," I said. "Let's just put this behind us. Go home and get some sleep."

"You won't tell . . ."

Who? Her parents? "God, no. This is just between us. We both need to put this out of our minds."

"I don't think I can ever face you again. And the girls . . ." Fresh tears filled her eyes.

"It'll be okay. We'll just act normal, and after a while, it'll go back to feeling that way." I picked up her purse and handed it to her. "You okay to drive?"

She nodded again.

"All right. Take it easy. And look — as far as I'm concerned, this never happened. I've already forgotten about it."

I watched until she climbed into her car and pulled out of the drive, then closed the door and leaned against it. Some things were easier said than done, and I was afraid that forgetting about this was one of them.

50
HOPE

Over the next week, I threw myself into clearing Gran's house, working on the coffee shop mural, and helping plan Gran's secret send-off party. Matt was working long hours in Baton Rouge, preparing for a trial. When I had a spare moment, I scoured the Internet, tracking down Joe Madisons in the Sacramento area.

Problem was, there must be about a million of them. I didn't know if I was searching in the right city or even the right state — after all, Gran's last information about him was sixty-something years old. I didn't even know if he was still alive.

I'd phoned every airline listed as operating in the United States, asking if they'd had a pilot named Joe Madison who'd worked for them thirty years ago (I figured that the more recent the records, the better the odds that airlines might still have them), and every one of them told me they couldn't access files that old and that even if they could, they wouldn't release that information. I'd sent e-mails and even a snail-mail letter to each airline, asking them to please forward it to any Joe Madison pilots who might have worked for them.

"I can't find a single lead," I told Matt when he showed up in the backyard Thursday evening, the first week in May.

He pushed the swing with his feet. "I talked to someone I know, who put me in touch with a private detective."

"I can't afford a private detective."

"I can."

My heart turned over. I couldn't believe he would offer something like that. It was the kind of thing you'd do for family, or your oldest, closest friend. Not someone who was leaving in a few weeks and would be out of your life forever.

"That's really sweet, Matt, but I don't want you to do that."

"Why not? I want to help."

"Well, as Zoey would say, 'it's not 'propriate.' "

"According to who?"

"Me."

I thought the subject was closed. Matt and I continued to meet in the evenings after the girls and Gran were in bed — we'd usually talk in the swing, and then end up rendezvousing in the shed — but Tuesday the following week, he showed up at Gran's front door shortly after dinner, accompanied by a elegant elderly woman with high cheekbones and white hair styled in a French twist. She wore a simple navy dress and red lipstick. "I hope it's not too late to be paying a call on your grandmother," Matt said.

"Not at all. She and I were just going through some old albums."

"Good. Because I have someone here I think she'll want to meet."

Matt looked me in the eye, and I knew this woman was somehow connected with Joe. My heart started pounding in my chest.

"Who is it, dear?" Gran called from the living room.

"Matt. And a . . . a visitor."

"Well, invite them on in."

I must have opened the door and stepped out of the way, although I don't really remember doing it, then led them into the living room. "Miss Addie," Matt said, "this is Viola Madison."

The woman stepped forward. Gran rose from her chair and extended a hand, and the woman took it in both of hers. "Adelaide? It's such a delight to finally meet you.

I've heard so many wonderful things about you."

"Who on earth from, dear?"

"Why . . . from Joe."

"Joe?" Gran put her hand on her chest. "Joe Madison?"

"Yes, dear. I'm his widow."

"Oh. Oh my."

I ran to Gran's side, alarmed, and helped ease her into her chair. "Are you okay?"

She sat there, her hand still on her chest. "Yes. Yes, dear." Her eyes were fixed on the woman's face. "Joe's gone?"

"Yes. He died six years ago. A heart attack."

"But the flowers —" Gran suddenly broke off. She bit her lip, as if she realized she'd said something she maybe shouldn't have said.

"What flowers?" I asked.

"Oh, nothing." Gran's hand flapped the question away.

"It's okay. I know all about them," Viola said gently. "Joe's attorney sends them."

"What flowers?" I repeated.

"Tulip bulbs." Gran's voice was thin and breathy. "Every spring they'd come. Charlie thought I ordered them, but . . ."

An image flashed in my mind — tulips

591

flaming in the front yard every March, then disappearing, leaves and all, to await another spring.

As luck would have it, Hannah was the aide on duty. She looked at Gran and Viola, then back again. "I think you-alls need a drink." She scurried into the kitchen.

"Joe arranged for you to receive the bulbs every spring for the rest of your life," Viola said.

"Oh, my. And you — you knew?"

"Yes." Viola's eyes creased as she smiled. "You were the reason he married me."

The conversation was interrupted by Hannah returning with a bottle of wine and a mismatched assortment of juice glasses. She poured all of us a glass, then took one for herself and sat down on a cane chair in the corner, actively listening. This time, no one bothered to shoo her away.

"I don't understand," Gran said. "How . . . ? When . . . ?"

"I was a stewardess. I was crazy about him — we all were. He was so dashing and handsome and charming. I was thoroughly in love with him, but he wouldn't settle down. Claimed there was only one woman he would ever marry." She took a sip from her juice glass. "I was with him right after you told him he should marry someone else and start a family of his own — and, well, I scooped him up on the rebound. We were married within two months."

"Oh my." Gran sat back, her eyes wide. "Did you have a good marriage?"

"In our own way." Her lips curved in a small, wry smile. "We loved each other, and we were willing to overlook each other's . . . flaws, I guess you'd call them."

Gran stared at her, her mouth open. She abruptly closed it, then opened it, but no words came out.

"Joe was a wonderful man in many ways," Viola continued, "but he had an insatiable craving for novelty and excitement."

"He did like an adventure," Gran mused.

"He always wanted what he couldn't have." Viola took a long draught of wine. "He had a roving eye, you know. Pardon me for saying this, but . . ."

"But what?" Adelaide urged.

"Well, it's not my place."

"Please." Gran leaned forward. "Tell me whatever you can."

"Well, through the years, I've often wondered if he could have been faithful to you, if he'd married you. Forgive me for saying it, but I have my doubts."

Gran sat perfectly still, unmoving as a rock, for several long moments.

593

I leaned forward, about to ask if she was all right. Matt put a reassuring hand on my arm.

"You know," Gran said at length, "that very same thought crossed my mind. I never really allowed myself to ponder it much; I didn't want to, because I didn't want to spoil the notion of a grand romance. But deep down, I think I had the same doubts."

I sat there for a moment, stunned. I'd been so caught up in the tragedy of the thwarted lovers that it never had occurred to me it might not have worked out.

But Gran was right. The character traits that made Joe so exciting as a young beau would not necessarily have made him a good husband. How could one woman hold the interest of a man who was always in search of the next conquest, the next adventure?

Gran leaned forward. "Did Joe . . . Did you two have children?"

Viola's lovely face, so composed until now, fell. She shook her head. "Lord knows we wanted them. That's why Joe married me — to start a family. But it turns out Joe had the mumps when he was overseas, and it left him sterile." She polished off her wine. "But . . . he had Becky."

"It's a such shame he didn't know her."

"Oh, but he did."

The color drained from Gran's face. "What?"

"He followed her progress through school and college, and when she got a job, he became a client."

"He . . . met her?" Her voice was a raspy whisper. "When she was grown?"

"Yes. Oh, she never knew he was her father, of course. But she was his investment advisor. He would go to Chicago and take her to lunch."

Gran's hand flew to her chest again.

"You see, Joe did quite well for himself. He took all of his back pay from the service for the years he was a POW and invested it in IBM and Xerox when they first started. He made quite a fortune. He had a real knack for wheeling and dealing."

"I knew he had a sharp mind," Gran said. "Becky took after him that way."

"He was very proud of Becky. Loved to say she's the one who really made his fortune. He always gave her a generous Christmas 'bonus.' She refused to take it, so he started sending it to her anonymously." She grinned. "Much like he sent you the tulip bulbs."

"Oh my." My grandmother's hands fell to her lap.

"As for Becky, I believe she always gave her gift to charity."

Gran nodded. "That sounds like Becky. She wouldn't do anything that wasn't on the up-and-up."

"Well, that brings me to the topic I really came here to discuss." Viola set down her juice glass.

"Good heavens — what more could there be?"

"Joe made provisions for Becky or her heirs in his will. He didn't want to cause problems or scandal for you, Adelaide, so it specifies that the funds could only be dispersed after your death — or in the event that Becky learned of her true parentage. Since Becky is gone and Hope knows the truth, well, the criteria is met. So I've brought her a copy of the part of the will that pertains to her."

She reached into her bag — I think it was Prada, although I'm not as knowledgeable of expensive bags as my ex was; he said you could identify clients with the means to purchase serious art by the handbags they carried, although I've had friends who've gone into hock to buy a bag, so to me, an expensive one just means a person's shelled out a lot for one item — or maybe even bought a fake. I had a friend who used to buy fakes.

But that had nothing to do with what was going on here. My ADHD flibbertigibbet mind was off on a tangent, because I was having a hard time processing what Viola was saying. I forced myself to focus as she pulled out a manila envelope and held it out to me.

"My attorney wants you to call him after you've had a chance to read through this."

I gingerly took the envelope. I almost didn't expect it to feel solid, the moment seemed so surreal. "I — uh — this isn't necessary," I stuttered.

"Nonsense. Joe wanted you to have it. For what it's worth, Hope, Joe kept tabs on you, too. We have one of your sketches hanging in our living room."

Now I really felt as if I were having an out-of-body experience. "But . . . how? My art was never really for sale." My ex-husband had refused to carry any of it in the gallery. He said it cheapened our collection.

"From a college exhibition your senior year."

He'd bought my college art? "He — he knew where I went to college?"

"Oh, yes, honey. He flew in to see that exhibit."

My heart felt strangely warm. A grandfather I'd never known had been watching out for me?

"It's the pen-and-ink of a little wren in an azalea bush. I think it's marvelous."

I'd always loved drawing birds. I felt my face heat. "Thanks," I mumbled.

Gran and Viola talked some more, but I had trouble following the conversation. Hannah's evening replacement arrived and she resisted leaving, but I wasn't really jarred out of my dazed state until Viola stood, took both of Gran's hands, and promised to stay in touch. She kissed me on the cheek and told me the same. I walked with her to the foyer.

"Just one thing before you go." Gran had risen and was scooting her walker forward. "However did you handle it? Weren't you jealous?"

Viola paused. "Oh, I admit, it bothered me sometimes — especially when we learned Joe couldn't father any more children. But I knew what I was getting into when I married him. I made a conscious decision that I'd rather have as much of Joe as I could than have none of him at all." She smiled. "You were the one woman he couldn't have, so of course you were the one he always wanted." She walked out the

598

door, toward a large town car waiting at the curb.

Matt went with her. A uniformed driver got out and opened the door, and Matt helped her in. I waved as the car pulled away from the curb.

Matt returned to the house, and we both went back in the parlor.

"Open the envelope, Hope!" Gran urged.

I realized I still held it in my hand. I walked over and passed it to her. "It belongs to you."

"Oh heavens, no, dear! I promised Charlie I wouldn't take a dime from Joe, and I'm not going to start now. Besides, what does an old woman like me have to spend it on?" She thrust the envelope at me. "That's yours. Joe intended it for Becky and her heirs — and that's you, dear. I won't hear another word about it."

Matt sat beside me on the sofa. My hands shook. I pulled at the flap, then extracted a document. I scanned it. When I got to the part about what he bequeathed to Rebecca Elizabeth McCauley, the figure mentioned had more zeroes than I'd ever seen in one place. I showed it to Matt. "Is this for real?"

Matt look it over. "Looks about as real as it gets."

"What did he leave you?" Gran asked

eagerly. I passed the document to her. Gran's eyes widened. "Oh, my gracious!"

"I could buy a home!" I said, stunned.

"You could buy two houses and still have money left over to invest!" Gran clapped her hands together. "Oh, honey — I'm so happy for you!"

"Thanks." I grinned, but the expression felt forced. Truth was, I didn't feel happy so much as numb. I could buy a condo in Chicago. I could buy a gallery of my own. I could . . .

The evening aide came into the room. "Time for your evening medicines, Miss Adelaide."

Gran nodded. "I think it's time for bed, period. It's been a long day. But you two young people should go out and celebrate." She turned to Matt. "Matt, dear, I don't know how you found Viola, but thank you. Thank you, from the bottom of my heart."

"My pleasure, Miss Addie." He kissed her cheek. I did the same, and we wished her good night.

"Want to go out for a drink?" Matt asked when we were alone in the room. "Peggy's watching the girls."

"I think I'd rather just go out on the porch."

Matt refilled our juice glasses, and we

moved to the front porch swing. The day had cooled and a pleasant breeze lifted my hair off my neck. "So how *did* you find Mrs. Madison?"

"Through a private detective."

My feet dragged on the porch, stopping the swing. A hard, hot knot formed in my stomach. "I asked you not to hire one."

"I know, I know. But I already had."

"And you didn't tell me?"

Matt rested his juice glass on his thigh. "After I learned how you felt about it, I called to pull him off the case. It turned out he'd already found Mrs. Madison and learned you had an inheritance coming. He said Mrs. Madison insisted on meeting you and Addie and telling you in person. She wanted it to be a surprise. So I decided to just let things play out."

I knew it was petty of me; I knew I should feel grateful, but the thought that I *should* feel grateful for him going against my wishes made the knot in my stomach smolder like a coal. "So you just kept me in the dark, because you figured you knew what was best."

"No. I didn't say anything because I didn't want to blow a potential bonanza for you."

The knot tightened and burned. "There's no excuse for not telling me."

Matt looked at me. "Whoa — what is this?"

"I want to make my own decisions about my life, that's what this is."

"I thought I was doing you a favor. I hope you'd do the same for me if anyone ever shows up out of the blue wanting to give me nearly a million dollars."

"You should have told me," I said stubbornly.

"So you could do what? Contact her on your own? I was afraid that if Mrs. Madison didn't get to handle it the way she wanted, she might decide to wait until Adelaide was dead to give you the money. It would have been entirely within her rights. I was trying to look out for your best interests."

His logic was sound, but my feelings weren't responding to logic. "You have no right to presume that you know my best interests better than I do."

He held up his hand. "Wait a minute. You're actually mad at me for bringing in a woman who just handed you an enormous check?"

"No. I'm mad at the way you did it." He was just like my ex — making high-handed decisions about my future without consulting me, acting as if I were somehow incompetent.

It punched my buttons — and not just because of my ex, I realized. It was how I'd often felt around my incredibly accomplished, brilliant, glass-ceiling-crashing mother.

"Know what, Hope? 'My way or the highway' isn't usually the best strategy. Sometimes things work out best when you trust other people."

"I tried that once, and it didn't work out so well."

He looked at me, a look that lasered right through me. "So that's what's really going on here, huh? You're done with trust because of your ex? You've got such big control issues that you can't deal with any deviation from a plan?"

"Of course not."

"You sure? Because that's how it looks from here." He set his glass down on the porch railing with a final-sounding thump. "Well, I promise you this: the next time someone wants to give you a bank vault of money, I'll keep in mind that you don't want my 'interference.' " He rose. "I think I should say good night."

The thud of his footsteps on the porch echoed in a hollow part of my chest. I knew I was being unreasonable. I knew I should admit it, that I should apologize, that I

603

should thank him, but some stubborn, unreasonable, angry part of me resisted.

We were going to be over in just a couple of weeks anyway. All that would happen in two more weeks was that I would grow to love him more, and it would hurt that much more when I left.

Love. Oh God. Was that what I felt for him? Despite my best intentions, had I fallen in love with Matt?

I knew the answer even as my mind formed the question. I loved him, and here he was walking away from me. I put a hand to my mouth, but it didn't stop the word from coming out. "Wait!"

He stopped, but didn't turn around.

"I — I know I'm being unreasonable."

He slowly turned toward me.

"I'm sorry." I rushed down the steps and into his arms. The solidness of his chest, the strength of his arms around me — it felt so good, so comforting, so terribly, awfully . . . *temporary.* Tears welled in my eyes.

His hand tangled in my hair. "It's okay."

I nodded against his chest.

He pulled back and looked down at me. "You're crying. Are you still angry at me?"

"I don't know what I am," I confessed. "Confused, I guess. This is a lot to process."

He smoothed my hair back from my face.

"Yeah, it must be."

"Part of me wants to stay mad at you."

"Why?"

"It'll make it easier to leave."

"So don't."

Fresh frustration welled up in me. "Matt, art majors wait their entire lives for something like this to open up. This inheritance is a lot of money, yes, but it's not enough to live on the rest of my life."

He blew out a sigh. "Yeah, I know."

"Besides, you and me — this is just temporary. Our way of getting over the hump and back into dating."

"I kind of thought we'd moved beyond that."

My heart gave an irrational jump of joy, only to feel like it had plunged off a cliff. "Matt — we both know a long-distance relationship isn't going to work. Your schedule is so packed you can barely carve out a full evening for a date, much less weekends away. And my new job is going to be really time intensive."

A nerve worked in his jaw. "Let's talk about this later. I don't want to spoil the time we have left."

I didn't, either. I reached up, looped my arms around his neck, and pulled him down for a kiss, only to see a figure standing behind an open curtain next door.

"We're being watched," I whispered.

He turned and waved to Mrs. Ivy. The curtain immediately dropped back into place.

Our laughter broke the tension. He kept his arm around me. "Listen — Peggy and Griff want to take the girls to the beach as a beginning-of-summer treat. They're planning on leaving the morning after Miss Addie's going-away party."

Leaving. Going away. Each phrase cut me like a razor. "Sounds nice."

"So I was wondering if you'd go away with me for a long weekend in New Orleans."

"That's the weekend I'm leaving."

He lifted his shoulders. "It can be a send-off celebration. We'll get a room in the French Quarter and spend Thursday, Friday, and Saturday night."

Three days of bliss in his arms. "Oh, that sounds wonderful!" I murmured before I had a chance to censor myself.

"Okay, then. We have something to look forward to."

I immediately had second thoughts. Oh, God, what was I doing? A weekend of splendor, and then what? I'd be more in love with him than ever. It would make the inevitable good-bye all the harder. Tears

606

trembled on the edge of my lashes.

"Hey — are you still crying?"

"No." It was a ridiculous thing to lie about, since my cheeks were wet and my vision was fuzzy. "Not *sad* crying anyway. This is emotional, overwhelmed crying." I looked up at him in the deepening twilight. "Know what would help?"

"What?"

"A visit to the potting shed."

"You shameless hussy."

"You've turned me into one."

"Is that so?" His arm tightened around me, and he angled down a sexy grin. "In that case, I'd better check out just how good of a job I did."

51
HOPE

I was adding shadows to the mural in the back room of the coffee shop when the black plastic drape covering the doorway moved aside and a female voice squealed, "Oh my gosh — this is *amazing!*"

I looked up to see Freret standing in the doorway separating the main coffee shop from the new addition, bouncing on her ballet flats.

"Shhh," Kirsten said. She was standing on a ladder, hanging photos on the opposite wall. "What are you doing back here anyway? You're not supposed to see it until the surprise party."

"It's not *my* surprise party. It's Miss Addie's," Freret said, walking into the room and staring at the mural. "Which I'm not sure is a good idea anyway, given her age. A surprise like this might kill her."

I'd worried about the same thing. "I checked with her doctor, and he said she

608

should be perfectly fine," I said. "Besides, he'll be here."

"I want the unveiling to be a surprise for the whole town," Kirsten said.

"News flash: since the whole town is donating pictures, they already know. Here are mine, by the way." Freret handed Kirsten a stack of photos and stared at the mural. "Hope, you've done an incredible job!"

"Thanks." I still had some spots to fix, but I was pretty proud of the way it had turned out.

"Hope is astounding. Look at the pen-and-ink of her grandmother's house she did as a going-away present for Miss Addie." Kirsten held up a five-by-seven I'd sketched from one of Gran's photos.

"Oh, that is so gorgeous! I'd love to have one of my parents' house to give them for their fiftieth wedding anniversary. Could you do that?"

"Sure," I said. "Just give me a photo of it."

"Really?" Her face brightened. "You know, I can think of about a dozen people that would pay top dollar for house sketches. You could make a whole career out of doing this. Are you sure you don't want to change your mind and stay in Wedding Tree?"

"Actually, I'd love to." The answer surprised me as I heard it come out of my mouth. "I love it here. But this job — well, another one like it is unlikely to come around."

"Excuse me for saying so, but men like Matt don't come around every day, either," Freret said.

The mention of Matt made my heart flutter. "Things aren't like that between us."

"I've heard reports from Mrs. Ivy that say otherwise," Freret said.

Kirsten snickered.

"You know what I mean," I said.

"No," Kirsten said. "We don't."

"It's a short-term thing. It's not forever after."

"If you hung around, it might be," Freret said.

"Well, I can't blow off one of the best jobs in the art world for something that may or may not happen with a man who may or may not be over his late wife."

Freret's eyebrows rose. "So Christine's the issue?"

"Not *the* issue, but I guess she's *an* issue," I said. "The biggest issue is that I have a great new job in Chicago."

The bell over the front door rang. Kirsten stepped down from the ladder. "Well, my issue right now is tending to the customer who just walked in."

"And I need to get back to the bank," Freret said.

"Thanks for dropping off those photos," Kirsten said.

I drew a breath of relief when they left. But the mention of a future — or was it the lack of one? — with Matt left me restless and unsettled.

52
HOPE

The next ten days passed in a frenzy of activity. Eddie and Ralph flew in and set to work making the house look like an HGTV makeover. They put the furniture I wanted into storage, shipped the furnishings they and Gran had selected to California, and filled in the gaps with rented modern pieces and paintings, which gave the place a hip, eclectic look.

"This place looks absolutely stunning!" Lauren said when we took her on a tour of Gran's home so she could photograph the place for the real estate listing.

"You can thank Hope for handling all the decluttering, packing up, and repairs," Eddie said.

I swept my hand toward Eddie and Ralph. "And these two are the maestros of design."

"There's only one little thing you might want to fix." Squinting, she held her thumb and index finger about a half inch apart.

"What is it?" Eddie asked.

"Well, there's a missing section in the fence between your yard and the neighbors'. It's hidden behind the shrubbery and I don't think it'll make or break a deal, but it's a little . . . odd."

Eddie looked at Hope. "It wasn't there when I was growing up."

"I don't remember it from my childhood, either, but it was there when I arrived this spring," I said. "The neighbor's daughters use it to visit Gran."

That night at dinner, Eddie asked Gran about it.

"Oh, that." Gran laughed. "It's so the good-looking man next door could come over and visit without the neighbors seeing."

"You built that for Matt?" Ralph asked.

"Heavens, no, dear! Although I'm sure it's come in handy for him and Hope."

I felt my face turn fifty shades of red. How on earth did Gran know?

"They've been dating?" Ralph looked at me with raised eyebrows.

"That explains the candle I found in the potting shed," Eddie whispered to me. "Or should I call it the love shack?"

"Stop it!" I roughly elbowed him.

"You have me intrigued, Miss Addie,"

Ralph said. "Who took out the fence?"

"There was a gentleman who lived there in the seventies, whose wife had Alzheimer's." She turned to Eddie. "Do you remember him?"

"Vaguely," Eddie said. "Glen something, wasn't it?"

Gran nodded. "Glen Adams."

I put down my fork and stared at Gran. Eddie and Ralph did the same, then we all exchanged a look. Was she saying what we thought she was saying? "So you and Glen . . ."

"We became very close friends during some hard years. Charlie, of course, was paralyzed, and then he died. And poor Glen's wife didn't even know who he was. He cared for her at home as long as he could — longer than he should have, actually; she roamed the house at all hours and kept running away. He finally had to put her in the nursing home. And then he was out there every day for most of the day, even though half the time she thought he was trying to harm her."

"Oh, Gran."

"After she died, he moved to Dallas to be near his daughter. We met up several times a year. He went with me on some of my trips abroad."

"You loved him?"

"Oh, yes, honey."

"So why didn't you marry him?" Eddie asked.

"Oh, we talked about it. But his kids were very sensitive — they hated the idea of their mother being replaced, and he didn't want them to know that we'd seen each other when she was alive — although I don't think that you can cheat on someone who has already mentally gone. Besides, we didn't consummate our relationship until she'd passed. It was a line neither one of us wanted to cross."

"Well, there's a lot two people can do besides actual consummation," Ralph said.

His words echoed Matt's the night we'd caught the kids digging in the yard. My already warm face grew hotter.

"Hey!" Eddie put his hands over his ears. "This is my mother we're talking about!"

"Glen should have stood up to his children and the gossips and married you," I said.

"Oh, I never wanted to marry again." Gran buttered a roll, as if we were discussing something as mundane as the weather. "I liked having my own space and being able to come and go as I pleased without having to answer to anyone. Plus I wanted to travel more than he did. For a long while

615

there, though, we gave each other a lot of comfort."

"So you had another romance in your life," Ralph said.

"Oh, more than one, dear. You know all those years I traveled?"

We all nodded our heads. Throughout my childhood, Gran had taken lots of exotic trips.

"Well, there a French man who'd meet up with me. He was single, too, and the kind of person who didn't want to be tied down. Oh, we had the best times! I think one reason it was so wonderful was because we only saw each other often enough to not get sick of each other."

"I had no idea!" Eddie put his napkin on the table, clearly flummoxed.

"And later, there was a man in New York who had the most delightful sense of humor. We visited Hong Kong and Australia and Tahiti together." Gran speared a dainty bite of salad. "There were other little flirtations here and there along the way, but those were the main ones."

"Wow!" said Ralph, clearly impressed.

It took Eddie a moment to close to his gaping jaw. "I'm gobsmacked."

Gran laughed. "Most people don't really know what goes on in another person's private life." She primly took a sip of iced tea. "Most of us keep secrets because we're afraid of being judged. Funny thing is, the person who judges us the most harshly is usually ourselves, so our guilt and regret and shame just fester in the dark."

"So the answer is complete disclosure?"

"Oh, no, not necessarily," Gran said. "The answer is forgiveness. Of others, of course, but most especially of ourselves."

Eddie put down his fork. "How, exactly, do you do that?"

"Yeah," Ralph asked, leaning forward.

"It's taken me ninety-one years to figure it out, but after Hope and Matt found out the truth about that baby, I had to find a way to forgive myself or else die of remorse. I know this will sound strange to you, but Mother gave me the key."

"Is she still on the ceiling?" Ralph asked, clearly intrigued.

"I honestly don't know," Gran said. "I don't see her, but she talks to me sometimes. And I distinctly heard her say, 'Pack your burdens in a suitcase and give it to God.' "

Eddie, Ralph, and I looked at each other. Maybe Gran was further gone mentally than we'd realized.

"That's when it hit me: forgiveness is not

so much something you do as something you *don't* do. You stop carrying your guilt and anger and resentment around. So I pictured it as a big old heavy suitcase I've been lugging around everywhere. I imagined carrying it onto a train and hoisting it into the luggage compartment. Then I climbed off and watched the train leave the station, going faster and faster and getting smaller and smaller until it disappeared down the track. And then I walked away, feeling light and free."

My throat felt strangely tight. I think Eddie's did, too, because his eyes were glistening.

"And that worked?" Ralph asked.

"Yes, dear. You might have to picture it a couple of times, but then when an old regret comes up, you just remind yourself, 'I got rid of that baggage.' "

The doorbell rang. "Oh, that'll be the Weldon sisters," Gran said. "They said they'd come over for a visit tonight."

I helped Gran up and onto her walker while Eddie got the door. And later that night, I dreamed about helping Gran load her steamer trunk onto a train, then watching the train levitate off the track and into the sky, where it soared away like an old warplane.

53
ADELAIDE

I should have suspected something two days later, when Hope took me and Eddie and Ralph to the coffee shop to see her mural at five in the afternoon. Not because she was taking me to see her work — I'd been asking to see it, and she'd kept telling me it wasn't finished yet — but because it was the afternoon before I left town for good. I was such a jumble of mixed-up emotions about leaving Wedding Tree for the last time, though, that it slipped right past me — plus it made sense, since Eddie said he wanted to take us all out to dinner.

My first clue should have been Eddie's red cheeks. That boy has always gotten flushed when he's excited about something. My second clue should have been Hope's attention to her appearance. She wore a fitted pink sundress that made her skin glow, and she seemed as high-strung as a cat on a tightrope. I chalked it up to nervousness at showing us her work.

My third clue should have been that there was a parking spot right in front of the coffee shop. And if that weren't enough, I should have known something was up when there wasn't a soul in sight. "Looks like someone rolled up the sidewalks," I said.

"Everyone quits work early on Mondays," Ralph said.

"When did that start?" I asked. "No wonder the economy is in trouble."

Hope got my walker out of the trunk, unfolded it, and helped me to the door of the Daily Grind.

It looked dark and vacant. "Are you sure this is open? It looks like the lights are off."

"It just looks that way because the windows are tinted," Eddie said.

Hope put her arm around me and opened the door — and sure enough, it was dark inside. I was about to say something, but suddenly the lights came on and a huge crowd yelled, "Surprise!" Well, it was good thing Hope had a hold of me, because I darn near passed out.

The place was packed. Practically everybody in town was there — including most of the residents of the nursing home.

Kirsten appeared at my elbow. "You didn't think we could let you go without throwing the biggest party this town has ever seen, did you, Miss Addie?"

Well, I gotta say — I was flabbergasted. I put my hand on my chest.

"You all right, Miss Addie?" my doctor asked.

"Yes. Yes, indeed."

Eddie and Ralph ushered me further into the room. After a moment of breathlessness, I felt buoyed and light and floaty as a kite. "My goodness, my goodness," I muttered, over and over. The high school band started playing "Stand Up and Get Crunk," the official song of the New Orleans Saints, and the local dance team did some high kicks on the coffee bar.

Person after person came up to me. It was only when the band stopped playing that I could understand what they were saying.

"Miss Addie, I want to thank you for how much you've meant to my family," said Rachel Reed, who worked at the pharmacy and knew everything about everybody. "You've photographed all of my big life events. My high school graduation. My wedding. My baby's christening. Her first birthday. Her high school graduation. You've been a big part of the best moments in my life."

"Miss Addie, your photo of my mother is the one thing I took with me when we

621

evacuated during Hurricane Katrina," said the middle Boudreaux boy — who wasn't a boy at all anymore, considering his graying temples.

"The pictures you took of my grandmother are the only ones I have," said a teenaged girl I couldn't place.

"I love the photo you took of our house," said Bitsy Mangus.

"The picture you took the day my shop opened has been by the front door for forty years now," said Wendall Preaux, who ran the local shoe repair place.

On and on it went. At length I turned to Hope. "This is all incredible, but I wanted to see your mural."

"And see it you shall," said Kirsten. She cleared a path, and Hope, Eddie, and Ralph escorted me through a door into the back of the building.

"Oh my!" I gasped. It was just like being in the middle of the street outdoors, only in miniature. There was the barbershop, the cleaners, the coffee shop, the real estate agency — all painted along the wall — and through each painted window, I saw someone I recognized. There was Charlie in the hardware store, and my mother at the cleaners, and — oh heavens! The man in the barber's chair was a handsome young airman who made my heart flutter. On the sidewalk — oh my — there was a picture of me! I looked to be in my late twenties, and I was taking a photo of Eddie and Becky as children in front of the bakery. A lump the size of an egg formed in my throat. "Hope, honey, you don't have one ounce of an inkling of how talented you really are."

"Nor do you. Look." She turned me around to face the opposite wall. It was entirely covered with photos. I looked closer. They were photos I'd taken — photos that went back decades. The back of the room held two partitions, which were also covered with photos.

"Oh my," I muttered.

"Gran, the New Orleans Museum of Art wants to do a special show of your photography," Hope said.

"You're kidding!"

"No. I'm not. And some of your prints . . . Well, Eddie has a gallery that wants to sell them in California."

"That's right, Mom." Eddie was at my elbow, his round face beaming. "Hope sent me some of your work from the sixties and I've had copies made, and we've got buyers already lined up."

"Well, goodness gracious!" This was all too amazing to take in — and in the midst of it, people kept coming up and telling me how much they treasured photos I'd taken of them or their loved ones.

Among the display of townspeople was one that didn't belong there — one that I had hidden in the bottom of my closet: the photo of a young airman in uniform, smiling just a bit. But the one that made my heart turn over and nearly overflow with emotion was a photo of Charlie on the porch of our house, my favorite photo of him.

"Oh my," I murmured.

The mayor clanged a spoon against his beer mug, and the roar of the crowd shushed to a murmur. He tapped it again, and the room fell silent. "Ladies and gentlemen, if I could have your attention, please. As you know, we've gathered here to show Miss Addie our love and appreciation, and to give her a big send-off to California. Her son, Eddie, wants to say a few words."

Eddie edged his way to the coffee bar. "Mother always wanted to be a photojournalist." He looked straight at me. "She worked as one during the war, and dreamed of traveling the world and capturing all of the important news of the day. She thought she'd put those dreams away when she had my sister and me. She thought she gave them up to raise her family and care for my father, and his parents, and her parents." His gaze lingered on my face, full of love. We'd sat up late for five nights, talking, since he and Ralph had come to town, and I was eager to spend more time with them in California. "She might not have known it at the time, but she *did* capture all the important news of the day. She captured the highlights in the lives of everyone in this town."

"Darn tootin'!" Harvey Angus yelled. "And we sure do thank you for it!"

The crowd laughed and burst into applause.

"That's right, Miss Addie," said the mayor. "And we want you to know how very much you mean to all of us, and how much we appreciate all that you've contributed to our lives."

My eyes swam. Eddie was right — I *had* covered stories that were big and important and far-reaching, and I hadn't even realized it.

But it wasn't my photography that was my major achievement. No, sir; my greatest achievement was my family. I looked at Eddie, his eyes shining with pride. My little Eddie, so teased in school, was happy and thriving, loved and loving, caring for the dental health of hundreds of patients. I thought of my brilliant Becky, so bright that men who made millions turned to her for advice on how to invest it. I thought of Charlie and his father, how they'd provided the supplies that had helped build and repair most of the homes in this town. I thought of my father, who'd talked many people out of foolish lawsuits they would have later regretted, lawsuits that would have ruined other people's lives.

I looked at Hope, my lovely, gifted granddaughter, talented beyond what she dared even dream for herself.

Oh my goodness — what if we all are? What if everyone held so much potential that the world could barely contain it?

Over the din of the crowd, I heard Mother's voice. "See there, Addie? I told you that you needed to find out the truth. And the truth is . . . we are all so much more important than we know. We don't have a clue how wide our ripples ride out on the waters of the world."

"You were right, Mother," I whispered.

"But so were you, child," Mother replied. "So were you."

54
HOPE

"What a wonderful party," Peggy said as Eddie and Ralph led an exhausted Gran out the door. "I enjoyed it every bit as much as Miss Addie!"

"Me, too," said Aimee, picking up an empty glass.

"Me, three," said Kirsten, rolling up the white butcher paper that had served as tablecloths.

"Thank you so much for putting this together." I looked at Kirsten and the other women, affection forming a knot in my throat. "Gran was so moved."

"It was our pleasure." Lauren smiled at me. "And speaking of moved, you've done wonders, getting her home shipshape in such a short time. It ought to sell quickly. I just learned that a major communications company is moving its headquarters here, so about a hundred new people will be relocating to Wedding Tree."

Lucky them. I added another cake-smeared paper plate to the stack in my left hand.

"Speaking of moving, Jillian called this afternoon and told me she'd accepted a teaching job in Atlanta," Peggy said.

Everyone murmured at once.

"No!"

"Really?"

"Why?"

Peggy lifted her shoulders. "She said she wanted a fresh start."

"She's going to join us at the beach tomorrow!" Zoey said.

I knelt down. "It sounds like a wonderful time."

"Yeah," Sophie said, "But she's movin' away. An' you're moving, too." Her eyes filled with tears. "Why does everyone have to go away?"

The lump in my throat grew bigger. "So new people can come. Maybe you'll get new neighbors with children you can play with."

"But they won't give us painting lessons."

"Or tell stories about Mr. Monkey!"

Tears tracked down both girls' faces. My eyes were getting pretty watery, too.

"I love you, Mizz Hope," Sophie said solemnly.

"Yeah." Zoey nodded.

"Oh, I love you, too!" I gave them both a big hug, touched by the easy way they said the words I didn't dare voice to their father. Their warm little bodies smelled like outdoors and cake and banana-scented sunblock, and I thought my heart might crack. I kissed their cheeks. "Have a wonderful summer."

"Can we come see you in 'cago?"

I blinked back my tears. How was I supposed to answer that? "I'd love it if you did."

Thank God Griff came to the rescue. "Hey, girls — who wants a piggyback ride to the car?"

"I do!"

"Me, too!"

Moods instantly elevated, both girls tried to climb on his back.

"Hey, Matt, come over and saddle up, too," Griff called.

Matt dropped the paper plates he was gathering into the trash and came over. Sophie jumped on his back. "I'll take them to the car, then come right back," he said.

"You should go on home and tuck them in," I told him. "This is the last night before their beach trip."

He nodded. "Come over when you get through here," he murmured to me.

629

Sophie hugged his neck. "Bye!" she called to me.

"Bye." Zoey waved.

I forced a smile and waved back. My throat felt as if I'd swallowed a goose egg as I watched them head out the door.

It was after eleven when I stepped onto Matt's back deck.

He was waiting for me. "Quite a party," he said, handing me a glass of wine as I settled beside him on the glider.

"Yeah. Gran was still excited when I got home."

He put his arm around me. It felt so right and warm. I just wanted to stay there forever. My heart constricted in my chest. "What time does your big trial start?"

"At nine in the morning. But I have a staff breakfast at six thirty."

"You better get to bed, then."

His hand moved to the back of my neck. "I can think of something that could help me relax."

My pulse started a familiar tattoo, but my heart was breaking. Tears threatened my eyes. "I'm really tired. And with Gran still awake, and Eddie and Ralph all in the house . . ."

"I understand." He stroked my hair. "I'm

really looking forward to this weekend."

I nodded, but my heart felt like a mass of coal. The weekend in New Orleans was a prelude to my move to Chicago. Our time together in Wedding Tree was practically over.

"I can't wait to get you all alone." He moved my hair and kissed my neck.

Oh God. How could I go away for a weekend with him? I would only fall more deeply in love, and leaving would be all the harder.

He angled in for a kiss. I found myself holding back — and he must have felt it, too, because he pulled away and caressed my chin. "Are you okay?"

"Yeah," I murmured. "Just really drained."

"Go and get some sleep, then." His finger flitted over my cheek. "I'm staying in Baton Rouge the next two nights, but I'll be in touch, and I'll see you Thursday afternoon. This is going to be the best weekend ever."

I gave my best imitation of a smile, then slipped off the porch and through the hedge, just as the tears I'd been holding back began to fall.

55
HOPE

TWO DAYS LATER

Chicago was hot, but it was a drier heat than in Louisiana. The wind blew my hair in my face as my friend Courtney and I walked into a coffee shop in Hyde Park.

Courtney had left her husband in charge of her two toddlers and driven in from the suburbs to help me look at condos. "That last place was perfect," she declared as we waited for the barista to complete our orders. "It had a great view, a balcony, a powder room as well as a full bath, and it was completely renovated. And those wide-planked hardwoods were to die for!"

"Yeah. It was pretty nice."

"Nice?" Courtney's eyes widened. "It was perfect!"

And it was. The problem was, I couldn't get up a head of steam about it.

"The agent said you need to move fast," Courtney reminded me. "There are five other interested buyers looking at it just today."

"Yeah, I know."

"So what are you waiting for?" Courtney demanded. "The place is fabulous, and it's just a block from your work. There's no way you're going to find anything better."

She was probably right. The condo had plaster crown molding, vintage light fixtures, and many of the charming old-fashioned touches I loved, as well as all the modern updates I wanted. But it didn't have a garden out back with azalea bushes. It didn't have a swing in the backyard or the front porch. The sounds out of that bay window were of traffic and sirens, not wind rustling through the oaks. There was no screen door that neighbors could yoo-hoo through. The door opened into an overly lit narrow hallway that smelled vaguely of Chinese food.

"Tell me one thing that's wrong with it," Courtney said.

"It's in Chicago."

She scrunched her forehead into a confused frown. "You want a place in the suburbs?"

Being surrounded by children and families would only make me feel more lonely. I shook my head.

"Oh, I get it. You're pining for that guy in Louisiana."

I blew out a sigh and watched a woman cross the coffee shop, holding the hand of a little girl about Sophie's age. "I think I'm pining for Louisiana, period."

"It's just a matter of getting re-acclimated." The barista put our drinks on the counter, and we headed for a table recently vacated by a guy working on a tablet. Courtney licked a bit of foam off the rim of her cup. "Look, you may not want to hear this, but as your friend, I feel the need to tell you anyway. Through no discernible effort of your own, you've landed one of the most sought-after jobs in the art world — a job that not only pays well but offers the opportunity to travel and meet fascinating people and influence what kind of art gets seen by thousands of people. That is power. That is a fabulous opportunity. And thanks to your newly discovered late grandfather, you can afford an incredible place to live. Frankly, I'm green with jealousy. Seems to me you've got the world by the tail. So what's with the Debbie Downer attitude?"

She was right. I was behaving like an ungrateful wretch. I put down my iced tea and leaned forward. "Here's the thing — I rediscovered what I love about art. It's not looking at it and assessing it and evaluating it as an investment prospect. I like making art, not making money for other people from it."

She lifted her shoulders. "So do both. Paint in your free time."

"I won't have much free time."

"Well, that's good. It'll keep your mind off your Louisiana heartthrob. And you're in the perfect situation for a job like this. It's not like you're tied down with a husband and kids."

Funny how this pep talk was doing just the opposite of what it was meant to do. My purse buzzed with the "Matt's calling" ring.

"Isn't that your phone?"

"Yes."

"You're not going to even look at it?"

I didn't need to.

"Ah. How long are you going to keep avoiding him?"

I lifted my shoulders. My throat felt too tight to reply.

After seeing Gran off with Eddie and Ralph yesterday, I'd grabbed the first plane to Chicago. I hadn't trusted my resolve, so I'd waited to text Matt until after I'd landed.

A weekend together would just make good-byes all the harder. Decided to spare us both and head back to Chicago early. Loved every minute with you.

He'd immediately called me. I considered not answering, but I couldn't do that to him.

"You're standing me up, and just leaving a text?" he'd demanded.

"I don't have anything else to say, other than what I wrote you." Tears had pooled in my eyes as I waited for the baggage carousel to start. "I couldn't enjoy the weekend, knowing it was just a long good-bye. I didn't see the point in dragging things out."

"Who says it has to be good-bye? Last I heard, planes fly back and forth all the time."

My voice sounded choked and raw. "Matt, we both know a long-distance relationship won't work. You struggle to make time for your kids as it is, and my new job will involve lots of weekend functions and travel."

"I thought we'd talk about all that this weekend."

"There's nothing to talk about. I — I have to hang up now. I see my bag."

"Wait — you're already in Chicago?"

"Yeah. Sorry — gotta go."

He'd called right back. I hadn't answered. He'd texted.

This is a pretty one-sided decision.

Please don't make it harder than it needs to be.

"That small town wouldn't be the same without your grandmother there," Courtney said, pulling me back to the moment.

"I know," I sighed.

"And chances are, things wouldn't have worked out with this guy. The fact you both knew it was going to be temporary might have been part of the appeal. That's what makes a spring fling so romantic."

Was that all Matt and I had had together? A spring fling?

No. There had been a lot more to it than that — on my end anyway. But falling for him wasn't a good enough reason to give up the biggest career opportunity ever likely to come my way. If my experience with Kurt had taught me anything, it was that career decisions needed to be made solely by me, based on facts and sound reasoning, not emotion or persuasive arguments. I would be a fool to pass up this job.

But some part of me — some wistful, old-fashioned, sentimental part, the same part that loved negligees and peignoirs and honeymoon words — would probably always secretly wonder otherwise.

ONE MONTH LATER

"I need you to go to an art festival in Miami next week."

I was sitting in my boss's office, gazing at a massive Wintrope on her wall. I knew the painting was appraised at $750,000. I knew it was entitled *Energy*. All the same, I couldn't help but think that the artist was running a scam, because it was nothing but a blob of orange on solid red. I could have painted it in five minutes flat.

"We'll have several clients there," Ms. McAbbee continued.

I nodded.

"And be sure and pack some evening clothes." She looked at me in a way that meant she was trying to convey something she didn't want to come right out and say. "I realize you're new, but schmoozing is a very important part of what we do."

So she'd noticed I'd ducked out early and kept to myself at the last few events. After discussing a few other matters with her, I headed back to my office — I had an office to myself, a real office with a window! — and gazed out at the view.

In the past month, I'd technically done everything I was supposed to do. I'd moved into a new apartment. I'd decided to take a short-term lease so I could look around and find something to buy that excited me as much as Gran was excited about her new city. (Gran and Snowball were happily settled in an assisted living apartment in San Francisco, two blocks from Eddie and Ralph. Ralph had set her up a Facebook account, convinced her to give digital cameras a try, and now she was regularly posting photos.)

I'd bought new clothes. I'd gotten my hair trimmed. I'd even gotten a makeup makeover. I spent the day on the computer, looking at art, researching statistics, and finding comparables, and in the evenings, I was expected to go to gallery openings, galas, and other places collectors frequented. I was busy all the time, but I didn't feel like I was accomplishing anything. I felt like a stand-in for someone else's life.

My phone rang. I recognized Gran's number and quickly answered. "Hey — how are you doing?"

"Just dandy. But I need to ask you to do a favor. I need you to go to Wedding Tree for the closing on the house."

Gran's house had sold for full list price to an investment consortium the first week it was on the market.

"Eddie can't get away, and the closing company says they need someone from the

639

family to be present to sign the papers."

"Can't the attorney do it?"

"Afraid not, dear."

"When is it?"

"Next Friday."

I checked my calendar. I'd have to miss a black-tie affair. My boss wouldn't be pleased, but I was delighted to get out of the obligation. When I'd taken the job, it had been with the condition that I could take a few days off within the first few months if I needed to take care of family business. "Okay."

After we hung up, I contacted the title company in Wedding Tree, then went online and made arrangements for a fast swoop into town and a fast swoop out. I called Kirsten.

"You'll stay with me, of course," she said.

"That's really sweet, but I'm not staying the night. I hoped I could meet you someplace private for lunch."

"You're wanting to avoid Matt?"

She knew me too well. "How is he?"

"I haven't seen much of him. Peggy says he was grim when you left, like after Christine died, but Freret saw him at the bank yesterday and said he was laughing and cracking jokes."

My heart sank. Hadn't taken him long to

640

get over me, apparently.

"You've seen Peggy? How are the girls?"

"Adorable. She brought them in last week. They were wearing the costumes from their ballet recital. And Zoey lost another tooth."

"Really?"

"Yeah. They're growing up so fast."

And I was missing it. I was as crazy about those girls as I was about their father. The empty spot that had ached in my chest ever since I'd left felt like a fresh wound.

"Jillian came back for a long weekend," Kirsten continued. "And guess what — she's met someone in Atlanta."

"Really?"

"Yeah. Apparently it's pretty hot and heavy. She sold her house, and he's coming with her to the closing next month to meet Peggy and Griff and the girls."

"Wow." Jillian was in a relationship — and she, too, was selling a house. "Sounds like a real estate boom in Wedding Tree."

"It is. That new software business has started moving here. Apparently the founder lived here for a few years when he was a teenager, and he's decided to move back."

"I remember Lauren said about a hundred employees would be moving to town."

"Yeah. It's not huge, but it's big for a town the size of Wedding Tree."

We talked some more, and then I hung up. Something inside, some gnarly little weed of emotion that I thought was dead and gone, oozed some bitter juice. It took me a moment to identify the taste. When I did, a zing of shame shot through me.

Jealousy. I was jealous.

Of Jillian?

No. Not Jillian. I was actually happy for her. It was about time she got beyond the shadow of her sister.

So who, then?

All the new people moving to Wedding Tree, I realized. I was jealous that they got to live there, while I had to live here.

"Whoa, girl," I muttered to myself. "What's going on?" A coworker walked by and gazed in curiously. I fiddled with my phone, pretending I was talking into it. I was losing it, talking aloud to myself. I gathered up my things, headed to my apartment, and phoned Gran.

"I just realized I'm jealous of the people moving to Wedding Tree while I'm stuck in Chicago," I blurted.

"Who said you're stuck in Chicago?" she asked.

"This is a wonderful opportunity that will never come my way again."

"Sounds like you're reciting a line from a

script. How can it be wonderful if you don't really want it?"

That made me pause. "But I *should* want it."

"*Should* is the most useless word in the English language. What would you rather be doing?"

"Painting murals and living in Wedding Tree."

"Well, then, there's your answer."

"But . . . Matt asked me to stay, and I'm afraid that's influencing why I want to be there. And I don't want to build my life around a man."

"Seems to me you already did," Gran said mildly.

"What?"

"Well, if you're not doing what you really want to do because you're avoiding Matt, you *have* built your life around him."

"That's ridiculous."

"Yes, it is. But that's exactly what you're doing, isn't it?"

I stared out the window. Was it true? In trying to avoid the very thing I swore I'd never do again — compromise my career for a man — had I gone and done it?

Oh, fudgeruckers. I had! For an entirely different reason, to be sure, but it still had the same result.

Even worse, I'd made a career decision based on the opinions of others. I'd taken a job I didn't really want because everyone said it was too good to turn down — but who the heck was everyone? Courtney? My old friends from college? People I didn't know or really like in the art world? People like my ex?

Was I still trying to prove I was somehow good enough?

My eyes filled with tears. A moment later, my chest filled with a sense of giddy optimism. So . . . if I didn't really want the job, and I didn't really want to live in Chicago, and I *did* want to live in Wedding Tree, well, then, what the hell was I doing here?

"Listen to your heart, honey," Gran said.

I clutched the phone tightly against my ear. "How do I know it's my heart talking, Gran, and not fear or insecurity or neediness?"

"It'll tug at you. It'll pull and pull like a fishing line when the bobber goes under. But you've got to get rid of the deadweight that's got you snagged — all that guilt and anger and fear — before you can fully feel it. You've got to forgive everyone who's ever hurt you, and most of all, you have to forgive yourself. Pack it in a suitcase and send it on its way."

I hung up the phone with Gran and paced around my apartment. I needed to forgive my ex — and I needed to forgive myself. I needed to let the past go.

And all of a sudden, it hit me: I could. I'd been feeling like a victim and a loser. I'd been feeling so guilty for having the bad judgment of marrying my ex and losing Mom's inheritance that I'd lost all faith in myself.

I'd made a mistake, yes, but I'd corrected it, and I'd made lots of good decisions since then. Going to Wedding Tree, helping Gran, making new friends — even falling for a stand-up, good-hearted, grounded man like Matt. All of those things were good decisions, decisions that more truly reflected who I really was.

I *could* forgive myself. And as for my ex — well, he was the one who'd ultimately lost. Yes, he'd used me and run through my money, but it hadn't made him rich, and it sure hadn't made him happy. The rumor mill had it that he was courting a wealthy woman nearly twice his age. When it came to the things that really counted in life, he was dirt-poor. He was to be pitied.

And so was I, if I stayed here in a life I didn't want.

Right then and there, I felt as if I'd put

down a backpack full of rocks. The room felt brighter. "Thank you," I whispered, although I wasn't sure if I was talking to God, or Gran, or maybe myself.

No. I *was* sure.

I was talking to all three.

56
HOPE

"Are you sure you don't want to stop the sale of the house?" Kirsten asked for the umpteenth time on the drive from New Orleans to Wedding Tree. She'd insisted on picking me up at the airport so we could spend more time together since I was only in town for the day.

"I told you, Kirsten — I don't want to see Matt every time I go outside."

The thought of seeing him at all was, quite frankly, killing me. I'd treated him terribly. I'd run out on him, avoided his calls, and ignored his texts and e-mails. After a week, he'd given up trying to contact me. He was probably furious at me — and I couldn't blame him. I'd behaved dreadfully.

All the same, I was planning on moving back. I was going to follow my dream of painting and living in a small Louisiana town.

"I think I might want to look at places

twenty minutes or so away — in Madisonville or Covington, maybe. That way I won't
see Matt and the girls every time I go to the
grocery store."

I especially didn't want to watch him meet
and date someone else. If our temporary arrangement to help each other over the hump
had worked for him, well, I didn't want to
have to witness the results.

Kirsten gave me a sympathetic smile.
"Poor darling. You've got it bad."

I did. And I knew I'd have to address it
soon, but I just wasn't up for it today.

Today, I was selling Gran's home to a
faceless investment consortium, then flying
back to Chicago to pack up my belongings.
As Gran liked to quote from the Bible, "Suf-
ficient unto the day is the evil thereof." In
other words, each day has enough trouble
of its own without borrowing trouble from
tomorrow.

57
MATT

I checked my silenced phone for the umpteenth time, not because I was expecting a text or call, but just for something to do. I was in the conference room at the title company, the door closed, pacing. I'd asked the real estate agent to schedule the meeting earlier than necessary, so that I would have time to talk to Hope privately.

The room was cool, but I was sweating. Maybe I'd made a colossal mistake. The more I thought about it, the more certain I grew that Hope would be furious. She would see this as another example of me trying to tell her what to do, to control her, to run her life.

I wasn't sure exactly what I was going to say, and every time I tried to prepare something — me, an attorney who always had the right words, who practiced and prepared briefs all the time! — I drew a blank. Everything sounded ridiculous.

Because she'd be right. I *was* trying to persuade her to my way of thinking. My life depended on making her see things the way I saw them.

The door abruptly opened, and there she was. She wore a gray tailored dress and heels, and her hair was different — a little shorter and straighter and more tamed down — but she was just as beautiful as I remembered, and seeing her again took my breath away.

For a second, I dared to hope I was having the same effect on her, because she froze in the door, her hand on the handle, and stared at me. "What are *you* doing here?"

My hopes were dashed, but not demolished. "Hope, we need to talk."

She took a step backward, her eyes round with alarm. "I — I have a closing."

"I asked them to postpone it for half an hour."

Her chin tilted up a bit. "That was a little high-handed, don't you think?"

"Yeah. But since you've refused to talk to me or answer my texts, it was all I could think of."

For a moment I feared she was going to turn on her heel, but then her posture slumped. She sighed, closed the door, and slowly walked into the room. "I owe you an apology for that."

I didn't want an apology, damn it. "I'll settle for a conversation."

She nodded, not meeting my eyes.

"It's great to see you."

"Likewise."

I gave her a quick hug and a kiss on the cheek. She smelled like Hope — soft and warm and fresh, like grass and sunshine and flowers — but she held her body aloof and leaned away from me. My heart broke a little. "You look great. Different, but still beautiful."

She looked down at her dress, then a ghost of a grin flitted across her face. "Yeah, well, shorts and flip-flops aren't part of the Chicago dress code."

I smiled.

Our eyes met, and that old connection flared between us. She grinned back, a full-fledged, Hope-like grin. "How are the girls?"

"They're good. They're at an equestrian day camp this week."

"Oh, how fun for them!"

"They're enjoying it." I stood there like an idiot, just smiling at her. I could have done that all day. When I finally gestured for her to take a seat at the table, her smile faded. She slowly lowered herself into a conference chair.

Now what? I didn't want to sit across the table from her, but if I wanted to look in her face, I had no other option. Maybe asking her to sit had been a mistake.

She looked up at me. "Look — I'm sorry I ran out on you like that. I was just . . . well, I didn't want to drag things out. I knew I was leaving, and it was ending, and I thought . . . well, let's just get it over as quickly and painlessly as possible."

Wait — she thought I'd come here to tell her off? Nothing could be further from the truth, but if it made her willing to listen to me, I'd play along for a while. I tried to match her somber expression. "Like ripping off a Band-Aid?"

She nodded. "I know it was rude and inconsiderate. I just . . . well, I guess I kind of panicked. And every time the phone rang and I saw your number, my heart would go into overdrive, and I didn't know what to say, so I just didn't answer. I'm really sorry I handled it that way. I — I just thought it was for the best for both us. I didn't mean to treat you badly. I mean, it was bad for me, too. In retrospect, I realize I should have called you before I left, or maybe told you in person, but . . . well, I just couldn't bring myself to do it. It was just too painful."

Painful was good. Painful meant she

cared. And apparently she still cared, because she was doing that rambling thing she always does when she's nervous. I rubbed my jaw, trying hard to hide the delight rising in my chest.

"I don't blame you for being angry," she continued. "You have every right. It was selfish of me to just avoid you like that. You deserve to tell me off. You'll feel better after you vent, so go ahead. Get it all off your chest."

I stifled a laugh.

"Seriously." She tucked a strand of hair behind her ear. Her expression was so earnest that it made me want to grin, even though my chest felt like it was being squeezed in a vise. "Let's get it over with. I don't think you can say anything that I haven't already said to myself, but you deserve the chance to say it, so let me have it. The buyer will be here soon."

"He's already here."

"Oh, he is?" She turned toward the closed conference room door, then looked back at me.

"Not out there. Right here." I pointed at myself.

"What?"

"*I'm* buying your grandmother's house."

"*You're* Property Investments, Inc.?" She

stared at me, hard.

"Yes."

"But what . . . Why . . . why didn't you . . ."

I moved around the conference table and sat beside her. "Hope, don't take this the wrong way. I'm not trying to control you or manipulate you or anything. Or maybe I am, but not in a bad way. It's just that, well, I thought that if I bought the house, you'd have a place to stay when you visit Wedding Tree. And if not, well, it's a good investment, with all the new people moving to town, so . . ." I drew a deep breath and decided to just lay it out there. "The truth is, I needed a reason to make you come back, sit down, and talk to me."

She stared at me, her lips parted. I couldn't tell if she was angry or incredulous or what. "You bought my grandmother's house to make me come back here and talk to you?"

I hurried on. "There are some things I wanted to tell you during our weekend in New Orleans, but you skipped out before I got the chance."

She held up her hands in a "stop" motion. "Is Gran in on this?"

"She, um . . . yes."

Her wide eyes grew even more enormous.

"Here's the deal, Hope. If you're really happy in Chicago, the girls and I can move up there. I can find a law practice easily enough. Jobs and places aren't home. People are. And you . . . you feel like home to me."

Her arms dropped, and so did her jaw. "What . . . what are you saying?"

"What I wanted to tell you in New Orleans, damn it! I love you, Hope. I want a life with you." It took my entire air supply to say that — and then I couldn't breathe until she answered.

She took so long my vision started to grow fuzzy.

"Matt, I know you'll always love Christine," she said. "And don't get me wrong — that's beautiful, and you should. But . . . the thing is, I don't want to be second best."

Was that her only objection? Relief flooded my veins. "You aren't. You never have been. You never could be."

"But . . ."

"No buts about it. Yes, I loved Christine. But loving her doesn't mean I can't love you just as much — or maybe even more."

Uncertainty clouded her eyes.

I leaned forward. "I loved Zoey to death when she was born. I couldn't imagine ever loving another child as much as I loved her, but then we had Sophie, and I fell head over heels all over again. And any children you and I have together — well, it would be just like that. Love isn't something you run out of. It's not a finite resource. The more you give, the more you have to give. I've had more experience loving now than I did when I married Christine. And when you project it out over the course of our lifetimes, that means I'm going to love you more."

She looked at me, and I could tell that now she was the one holding her breath. I took her hands. "Look — I know you might need some time to absorb this. It might seem like I'm kind of springing this on you. But here's the bottom line: I'm willing to make whatever changes you want so that you and I and the girls can be together from here on out."

58
HOPE

I stared at him across the table, trying to keep my heart from bursting out of my chest. Did I dare believe what I wanted to believe?

I knew all about denial and self-deception, about not seeing things you don't want to see or deal with. God knows I'd done that with Kurt.

But was it possible that self-deception could work the other way, as well? Was it possible to keep yourself from believing that the thing you wanted the very most in the world, you already had? Was it possible that I was getting — *that I already had* — my heart's desire?

His gaze poured into mine. "So . . . what do you think?"

I think that my heart has never felt so full. I think I'm more blessed than anyone ever had any reason to be. I think that God is generous and kind beyond all comprehension. I think that it's going to be so much fun to tell you that I already quit my job and plan to move back. I think that I can't wait to see Zoey's next lost tooth and hear Sophie's next breathless tale.

Matt looked kind of blurry through my damp eyes, but I'm sure I was grinning like a loon. "You love me?" I asked, my voice kind of raw and raspy.

"With all my heart."

"Oh, Matt — I love you, too! That's why I couldn't stand to spend any more time with you!"

The corners of his eyes crinkled as he smiled. "Do you realize how insane that sounds?"

"Only as I heard myself say it. It didn't sound that messed up in my head."

We both laughed. He reached out and stroked my cheek, and I think he would have kissed me, but I couldn't stop talking. "I have so much to tell you . . . like how I already quit my job and I'm moving back to Louisiana, but now, thank God, I don't have to move to Covington or Madisonville in order to avoid you."

He pulled back. "Wait — you're already planning to move back? But you were planning to avoid me?"

"Yes, because I love you so, and . . . and

now I'm rambling. I always ramble when I'm excited."

"I've noticed." His eyes sparkled like sunshine on the lake. "Want me to help you stop?"

I nodded, then wrapped my arms around him as he gathered me close and kissed me. My heart felt like it would jump out of my chest, but my thoughts settled in to one single, solitary thought:

Home. I was finally, really home.

59

ADELAIDE

THE FOLLOWING APRIL

The airplane's microphone crackled to life. "Ladies and gentlemen, we should be on the ground in approximately fifteen minutes. It's raining in New Orleans, so we're going to hit some bumpy weather on our descent. Flight attendants, please take your seats."

"We're almost there, Mom," Eddie said. "Time to fasten your seat belt."

Oh, fiddle. I hated restraints of any kind — almost as much as I hated being treated like a child. Truth was, I knew my short-term memory was faulty and my hearing was bad and I couldn't always remember the names of things, but I was still me, inside, and I hated being told what to do. I'd mostly recovered from my fall — I no longer had rib pain, my headaches were less frequent, and most of the time I didn't see double — but there was no recovery from old age. Time marches on.

I bit my tongue and let Eddie click the metal contraption around my lap. No point in telling him that I wasn't going to die today in a plane crash or a bumpy landing; Mother had hinted I was going to get to hold a great-grandbaby or two before I left this earth. What mattered, I'd learned, wasn't being right or having all the answers, but loving and being loved. Both Eddie and I felt that way when I let him watch out for me.

"I sure hope this rain stops before Saturday," Ralph worried.

We were returning to Louisiana for Hope and Matt's wedding. They were holding it in the nature preserve, under the Wedding Tree — which struck me as the loveliest, most ideal location imaginable.

Ralph and Eddie, who'd been acting as unofficial long-distance wedding planners and fretting like mothers of the bride, were worried that it might be cold or rain, but I'd convinced Hope it wouldn't. I hadn't exactly said that Mother promised it would be a beautiful day — truth was, Mother had quit talking to me as soon as I'd moved to California nine months ago — but I'd told Hope that she shouldn't worry, that the weather would be perfect. I'd spoken as if I had some special knowledge.

And I did. I knew that a little rain wouldn't ruin the wedding; they could simply hold the ceremony under the tent that would be set up nearby for the reception if they needed to. I also knew that it was the things that didn't go as planned that you talked about and laughed about years later. I knew that whatever happened would be absolutely wonderful.

And I had another bit of special knowledge that I'd imparted to Hope: don't let fear dictate your decisions. When things don't go as you think they should, it's because God has something better for you down the road.

Take Charlie's accident, for example. I've never told anyone this because it just doesn't sound right, but those were some of the most contented years of my life. Charlie and I got along just fine as companions — we were easy and comfortable with each other, able to make each other laugh, and we loved each other's families. We might not have had the right chemistry as lovers, but when all that man-woman stuff was removed from the equation, well, we were as contented as most long-married couples I've known. Truth is, Charlie was basically a homebody at heart, and I was a people person, better suited for a career. When we more or less switched roles, married life got a whole heck of a lot easier.

When Charlie had opened his bruised eyes in the hospital after that awful attempt to take his own life, I finally saw his bruised soul. I realized then that he was broken, and he'd been broken for a long time. Part of that was my fault, I know, but mostly, it was his parents'. They'd never allowed him to think beyond the narrow script they'd written for his life, and he'd always viewed any deviation as a miserable failure. More than anything, Charlie didn't want to let them down.

I'd leaned close to his ear. "I promise I'll never leave you," I whispered, "but don't you dare ever try to leave me like that again. From this moment forward, we'll put every-thing behind us and never speak about the past again."

He'd smiled a faint smile and given a nod that must have pained him something ter-rible.

And we never did. We never discussed Joe or the baby or the suitcase he'd buried. Truth is, I was always afraid that bringing it up would make him try to take his life again. We lived life one day at a time. We raised our children. We cared for, then buried, our grandmothers and our parents.

Through it all, I helped Charlie with basic living tasks and acted as if there was nothing unusual about it. Truth be told, it gave me a sense of purpose I'd never had.

The only real bone of contention between us was Charlie's way with the children. Becky and Eddie both felt that Charlie was awfully critical of them. I tried to make up for his gruffness with tenderness and unconditional acceptance. Charlie was definitely stuck in his ways, unwilling and unable to see the way the world was shifting, stubbornly insistent that women should be soft and pretty and men should be tough and unemotional. Funny how both Becky and Eddie ended up standing those roles on their ear.

Our plane dove under the clouds, and all of a sudden, I could see the giant curve of the Mississippi River that gives New Orleans its nickname "the Crescent City." I remembered the first time I'd seen that from the air, nearly seventy years ago.

Parts of that river were hundreds of feet deep. Sunken boats and people and trees and God-only-knew-what all lay at the bottom. Jagged, horrible, ghastly things — all covered with water.

Love was like that, I thought. Soft enough to dive headfirst into, yet mighty enough to move the earth. Essential to all life, and in some ways, alive itself. Love and water were both always moving — pouring, pooling, changing form, flooding, flowing, wearing down the hardest substances on earth with time and sheer persistence. Both were there even when you thought they weren't — flowing in underground aquifers, moving through pipes, wafting in molecules of air, pumping through hearts. What was that word from the Bible? Omnipresent. Yes, both love and water were like that.

And love, like water, was a great leveler. No matter how jagged and ragged and deep the valleys and scars, love, like water, covered it all, making it beautiful and even and shiny.

Love was like water in another way, too. When it spills into your life, it always splashes into unexpected areas. I grinned as I remembered water tumbling from a vase of tulips onto a certain officer's jacket.

Eddie took my hand. "Why are you thinking about, Mom?"

We were lower now, approaching the runway. I could see puddles of water on the ground, reflecting like mirrors.

"How love is like water," I said.

"Very romantic sentiment," Ralph said, "but I still hope it doesn't rain on Hope's wedding day."

"Actually, I kind of hope it does," I said.

Both Eddie and Ralph gaped at me. "Why on earth would you hope a thing like that?" Eddie asked.

"Because," I said with an air of mystery — an air I could only now carry off, and only because everyone thought I might be half senile, "life's not about being perfect. It's about getting wet."

I closed my eyes as the engine grew louder and the wheels bumped the runway, and remembered the way I'd feared another plane, seventy years ago, had been about to run into the lake — how I'd worried that I'd gone flying only to end up drowning.

As it turns out, I actually had.

■ ■ ■ ■

READERS GUIDE
THE WEDDING TREE

BY ROBIN WELLS

■ ■ ■ ■

DISCUSSION QUESTIONS

The Wedding Tree addresses several different themes. Here are some questions to consider as you discuss the book:

Family Values / Societal Mores

1. We're all shaped by family beliefs and the "rules" of society. The culturally acceptable behavior of women in particular was very limited in the 1940s and '50s. How did Adelaide, Charlie, Joe, Hope, and Hope's mother, Rebecca, react to their family's expectations and the societal rules of the day?

2. What were the different expectations that Hope's mother and grandmother had of her?

3. What messages did you receive from your family? Have you accepted them or rejected them?

Loss and Letting Go

4. All of the characters lost or had to let go of something — objects, people, habits, emotions, plans, secrets, etc. Name some of the things Adelaide, Charlie, Joe, Hope, and Matt gave up (voluntarily or involuntarily) and how it affected them. Was the loss ultimately a good thing or bad thing?

5. What are some of the things you've let go of in life? Is there anything you need to release in order to move forward?

Growth and Change

6. How did Adelaide, Charlie, Hope, Matt, and Jillian grow and change over the course of the book?

7. Do you believe people can genuinely change? Why or why not?

Avoidance, Procrastination, and Fear

8. People often try to avoid confronting truths or situations that are potentially painful. What things did Adelaide want to avoid facing? What was Hope trying to avoid? Have you ever avoided a painful situation? What finally made you decide to address it?

Forgiveness and Acceptance

9. Each character needed to forgive someone and/or accept an unchangeable situation. Who or what did Adelaide need to forgive or accept?

10. Who benefits most from forgiveness? Is there a person or situation in your life that you need to make peace with?

ABOUT THE AUTHOR

Robin Wells is a national bestselling author who's won the RWA olden Heart Award, two National Readers' Choice Awards, the Holt Medallion, and CRW's Award of Excellence. She lives in Texas.